The Price of Land in Shelby

HARDSCRABBLE BOOKS—Fiction of New England

Laurie Alberts, *The Price of Land in Shelby*
Thomas Bailey Aldrich, *The Story of a Bad Boy*
Anne Bernays, *Professor Romeo*
Chris Bohjalian, *Water Witches*
Sean Connolly, *A Great Place to Die*
Dorothy Canfield Fisher (Mark J. Madigan, ed.),
Seasoned Timber
Joseph Freda, *Suburban Guerrillas*
Castle Freeman, Jr., *Judgment Hill*
Ernest Hebert, *The Dogs of March*
Ernest Hebert, *Live Free or Die*
Sarah Orne Jewett (Sarah Way Sherman, ed.),
The Country of the Pointed Firs and Other Stories
Kit Reed, *J. Eden*
Rowland E. Robinson (David Budbill, ed.),
Danvis Tales: Selected Stories
Roxana Robinson, *Summer Light*
Rebecca Rule, *The Best Revenge: Short Stories*
Theodore Weesner, *Novemberfest*
W. D. Wetherell, *The Wisest Man in America*
Edith Wharton (Barbara A. White, ed.),
Wharton's New England: Seven Stories and Ethan Frome
Thomas Williams, *The Hair of Harold Roux*

OTHER BOOKS BY LAURIE ALBERTS

Goodnight Silky Sullivan, stories

Tempting Fate, a novel

The Price of Land in Shelby

A NOVEL BY

Laurie Alberts

UNIVERSITY PRESS OF NEW ENGLAND   HANOVER AND LONDON

UNIVERSITY PRESS OF NEW ENGLAND
publishes books under its own imprint and is the publisher for
Brandeis University Press, Dartmouth College, Middlebury College Press,
University of New Hampshire, Tufts University, and Wesleyan University Press.

University Press of New England, Hanover, NH 03755
Printed in the United States of America 5 4 3 2
First paperback edition 1997

The following chapters were previously published, in somewhat different
form, in the following: "Void" in *Explorations 1995;* "Dealing" in *Goodnight
Silky Sullivan,* University of Missouri Press, 1995; "Gateau" in the *Onion
River Review,* Summer 1996.

Library of Congress Cataloging-in-Publication Data
Alberts, Laurie.
    The price of land in Shelby : a novel / by Laurie
Alberts.
        p.   cm. — (Hardscrabble books)
    ISBN 0-87451-782-6. — ISBN 0-87451-844-x (pbk.)
    I. Title. II. Series.
    PS3551.L364P7   1996
    813'.54—dc20   96-24556
    ∞

To Tommy, the source;
Michael, the inspiration;
and in memory of
beautiful Barbara McGrath, 1961–1995

The author wishes to thank Alice Martell as ever, Joe David Bellamy for his faith and suggestions, and Minrose Gwin for encouragement when it was sorely needed.

Contents

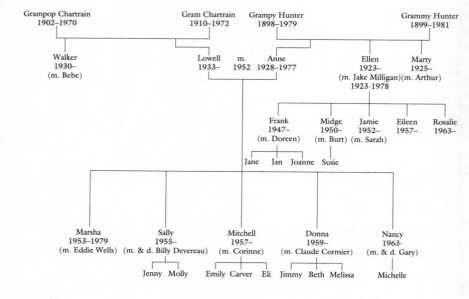

The Chartrains and Milligans family tree

The Price of Land in Shelby

PROLOGUE

[Masonville, 1965]

DAD PUT ON his camouflage vest and went up into the woods with his shotgun. "Can I come?" Mitchell asked. "Geddouta here," Dad said. Mitchell followed behind him, but far enough back so Dad couldn't see. Dad's angry steps made twigs snap. Mitchell didn't know what Dad thought he'd shoot making noise like that. He always told Mitchell to be quiet in the woods. He got too far ahead, so Mitchell came back.

It wasn't even hunting season yet. A man from Fish & Game came to Mitchell's third grade class and talked about that. How you should only hunt in season, and you shouldn't jacklight deer, and you should keep your dogs chained so they don't run them. Nothing sadder than a deer hamstrung by dogs, the Fish & Game man said. He showed them a picture. Dad said nobody's going to tell him how to feed his family.

Mitchell stopped at the mossy room where he and his sisters played mossy games sometimes. It was a shady place under a bunch of maple trees where the ground was as soft and green as a fuzzy rug. On one side was a stone wall topped by a strand of rusty barbed wire. A maple had grown almost all the way over the wire, so it resembled a mouth holding barbed wire in its lips. Mitchell knew trees didn't feel anything; still, it looked like it would hurt.

He stayed there a while, knocking pine cones off the wall with acorns, pretending he was shooting six-point bucks. Blam, blam, blam.

When Mitchell got back to the mill yard, his middle sisters, Sally and Donna, were playing in the shavings by the pine slash. "We're making nests," Donna said. She sat in a pile of shavings and drew it around her, piling the wood chips high over her waist. Sally had her own little pile. "Cheep, cheep, cheep. We're waiting for the mama bird to come feed us," they cried. "Cheep. Cheep."

Mitchell dug up a worm from under the broken cement blocks by the water tap and held it over Donna's face. "Here's your breakfast," he said, dangling. It squirmed, both ends moving away from his fingers as if they didn't know they were attached to each other.

"Geddoutahere!" Donna shrieked. "Mom! Mitchie's putting worms on us!"

"Then I'll eat it," Mitchell said, and popped it in his mouth. It tasted like metal. He spit it out, only it landed in Donna's hair by accident.

"Mo-om! Mo-om!" Donna jumped up, sending shavings flying.

Mom opened the door. "Can't you kids play nice?" she begged. "Please?" Her face was all blotchy like she'd been crying again.

Yesterday, when Mitchell and the girls went next door to see the kittens, Aunt Bebe said, "I guess your mother ought to be happy now you're moving to her folks'." She was wearing Uncle Walker's pajamas under her robe and drinking coffee, even though it was almost time for lunch. They could hear the baby screaming in the back room.

Mitchell thought of what Mom had told them: Grampop was going to sell the sawmill because Dad and Uncle Walker couldn't stop fighting. Nobody was gonna get nothing, Grampop said.

The kittens were crawling around in a cardboard box on top of an old yellow nightgown. There were four kittens, all grey calicos.

Calico cats were always girls. They had milky blue eyes that didn't seem to be looking at anything. Mitchell put his finger in one's mouth and it tried to suck. The room smelled like kitty poop and bacon grease.

"Your momma thinks she's better than the rest of us," Aunt Bebe said. "But she ain't. She might a been the teacher but she weren't such a lady when she had to have him, if you know what I mean. And him barely out of school. A real scandal."

"We got to go home now," Mitchell's oldest sister Marsha said, putting her kitten back into the cardboard box.

"Can we keep one?" Sally begged.

"You better ask your mother," Aunt Bebe said. "I don't know what those fancy grandparents of yours over in Shelby are gonna think about that."

When Mitchell went to put a kitten back in the box, it set its claws into his hand. He squeezed it hard, in its middle, just for a second, and it made a pathetic little squeak. He could feel its tiny ribs, so skinny they felt like the springs of a Slinky. He could crush them easy if he wanted to. He wanted to. But he put it back in the box.

"What's a scandal?" Mitchell asked when they got out the door.

"You shut up," Marsha said.

Now Marsha came out onto the steps, sticking her elbows out like some kind of big shot. "Quit throwing worms, Mitchell Chartrain, or I'll tell Dad on you."

"Birdies!" cheeped baby Nancy, dragging her doll by its hair across the yard. "Birdies!"

"Feed me!" Sally called. "I'm in my nest."

Mitchell kicked shavings and they flew through the air like the snow in Grammy Chartrain's glass ball. The girls got shavings in their hair, but he didn't mean to.

Then Marsha got them going, singing that song that made him mad: "Mitch, Pitch, fell in a ditch, going to marry a dirty old witch, Mitch, Pitch, fell in a ditch, going to marry a dirty old . . ."

Mitchell ran up and hit Marsha in the belly. She scratched his face, and they rolled in the shavings. Nancy the baby was crying. Stupid crybaby. That's when Dad came back. He didn't even care who started it. He just grabbed Mitchell by the back of his shirt, lifted him into the air, and set him down hard on his behind. The girls were already sneaking away. Only Sally looked sorry for him.

"Go get my belt," Dad ordered.

Mitchell sang his own song: I hate them. I hate them. I hate them.

CHICKEN

[Donna, 1973]

ON EARLY APRIL evenings when the world was shaking loose of its frozen cover, ice receding on the ponds and ditches, peepers shrieking out their need for one another, and the earth was turning to sun itself briefly on its axis, Donna began playing "Chicken" on the highway.

With her best friend Therese, an eighth grade classmate at Shelby Middle School, Donna walked down to the interstate after supper, smoking cigarettes stolen from her father's pack of Luckies. They made an odd Mutt and Jeff pair. Donna was short and compact, her dark curly hair bouncing about her shoulders, while Therese was lanky and pale, towering over Donna as their heads bent close for secrets.

Sometimes boys who drove by slowed down and tried to talk to them or ask for dates, the engines of their cars and pickups rumbling. When Donna and Therese turned up their noses and refused to speak, the boys would gun away, yelling obscenities, peeling rubber. Then Donna, the brash one, would scream insults after the retreating cars—"What's the matter, can't you find girls your own age? Why don't you go play with yourself!"—while Therese giggled and shushed her. They walked on, pleased and frightened by the attention they were still too young to receive.

When it got dark enough, they cut through a hole in the chain link fence that ran along the highway. They took turns stretching themselves out, face up, in the right hand lane of northbound Interstate 91. Traffic was intermittent that time of night, and they could hear the engines of the big semis winding up the hill from Putney a long way off. The passenger cars came quicker, a slice of headlights approaching, a whir of air displaced by speeding metal.

You couldn't sit up to look—that was the rule. They counted: one, two, three, four, five . . . until the car was almost on the one lying there, and she'd panic and roll away and up, scrambling onto the breakdown lane and into the ditch.

Sometimes the cars would honk and swerve, and once someone must have reported them, because a state trooper came looking. He rolled along, lights flashing, directing a spotlight into the roadside brush. They hid, terrified, faces averted from the searching beam, until the trooper drove away. Then they shrieked with nervous laughter about how their parents would kill them if they got caught. They decided to call it quits. But within a couple of days, they were out on the highway again, stretched and waiting.

They never really spoke about what they were doing after the first time, when Donna dared Therese to try it, and then did it herself to prove it was no big deal. What Donna felt, lying there, arms stretched out on pavement still faintly warm from the spring sun, under an arc of emerging stars, was too shameful to admit. It wasn't just about being brave and bold and wild—there was another secret part of her that wanted to lie there and not move when the lights came down at her, as frozen as a jacklit deer. She wanted to taste that moment of destruction; she craved it in a part of her she didn't recognize, and sometimes she felt a coward for rolling away from it, saving herself from certain knowledge.

Mostly, though, it was just being fourteen, too young to drive, with nothing happening and nowhere to go. Donna had to get out of the house, where her mother slid around like a ghost, head bald from the chemo, covered with a phony-looking wig. She had to get away from Dad, muttering to himself at the table while he salted his beers and cursed his children, his life.

All the time now, there was something Donna wanted, but she couldn't name it. Something that kept her hopping in itchy waves of frustration, as though her growing bones were going to pop right through her skin. Some strange energy kept her walking dark dirt roads at night while buds swelled and leaves unfurled around her, claiming a life she was afraid she'd somehow miss.

She only felt relief when lying on the dark pavement waiting for that sweep of lights approaching, or galloping her horse no-handed, arms held out shoulder high, the reins flapping loose, the rhythm of hoofbeats filling her head.

They rode after school, Donna, her next oldest sister Sally, and her baby sister Nancy. Three girls on horses bought cheap: Sally's buckskin Dusty, traded for wages their father hadn't received on a milking job; Donna's stiff-jointed old Chief, saved from the knacker; and Nancy's black pony Devil Dog, who kept a fuzzy winter coat year-round and tried to bite anyone who came near.

Once the frost went out of the roads and the mud-season ruts had dried and flattened, they rode the good mixture of dirt and clay that makes Vermont roads so springy under hooves. On Clavell Brook Road at dusk the girls careened around bends, spread out in their usual formation: Sally first on Dusty, followed by Donna on lumbering Chief, and the pony Devil Dog falling behind, while Nancy, yellow braids flopping, kicked his fat sides and hollered, "Wait up! You guys, wait!"

They were late returning from a 4-H meeting on Exley Hill and pushing hard to make it home. Chief, who had a case of the heaves, panted as he galloped. His flanks puffed like a bellows under Donna's legs. In fading light she smelled lilacs, and spun her head to admire the dim outline of a neat brick colonial house with black shutters and a fan louver over the front door—wondering what it would be like to live in a place that nice, instead of the tar-papered ranch house her dad would probably never finish building—and then, without warning, she went down.

She was thrown clear, to land with a hard thwack on her hip in the road. She got up and swiveled around to spot Chief, who was scrambling to his feet. The pony caught up and stopped in his tracks, nearly unseating Nancy.

"What happened?" Nancy asked, settling back in the saddle. "How come you fell?"

"I don't know," Donna said, shaking her head. That's the way it always was with a fall—you were galloping, and then you were on the ground, and you felt nothing but surprise. "He must've stumbled or something." She limped over to Chief.

The old horse stood with his head hanging. When Donna picked up the reins, Chief leaned against her, pressing his big face into her shoulder, nearly knocking her down. His whole body trembled.

Up ahead, Sally had figured out that no one was following her. She pulled Dusty up short and spun around, trotted back to join them. "You guys okay?" she called.

"I'm not sure," Donna answered. She pulled the reins gently and Chief attempted a halting step. He squealed, and his skin shivered as though tormented by flies.

Sally vaulted off Dusty and came over, squatting by Chief's feet. Donna watched her sister's hand, pale in the near dusk, run down Chief's left foreleg, then stop. When she saw it, Donna sucked in her breath. Below the old horse's knee, the top of his cannon bone no longer fit the lower half. It jutted crookedly, as if someone had bumped a stack of bricks.

"We better get a vet," Donna whispered. Panic had stolen her voice.

"It's broke, Donna," Sally said, her own voice shaking. "He's gonna have to be put out of his misery."

"You don't know," Donna protested. "It might not be broke."

Nancy started crying.

"I'm going over to that house and ask for help." Sally gestured toward the brick colonial behind the lilac hedge. "Nancy, you keep Dusty and Devil Dog walking until they cool off."

"Wait!" Donna cried out, but Sally hurried across the street.

Sniffling, Nancy led Dusty and Devil a little way up the road, then circled back.

Donna, 1973 [9]

"Keep them moving," Donna hissed, because anger at her little sister was the easiest feeling she could muster. Nancy opened her mouth to complain, then led the horses in another loop up the road.

Chief's neck and shoulders were already lathered from the run, and now from fear. He tossed his head, spraying Donna with flecks of foam. She ought to cool him too, she thought, then realized that with his broken leg it didn't matter. "I'm sorry," she whispered. "Poor Chiefy, I'm sorry."

A car swung around, its headlights illuminating the sweat on Chief's flanks, catching the rolling white of his terrified eyes. The car braked, sliding on gravel.

"What's going on?" a man's voice called out. A fat guy in an undershirt climbed out of a low-slung station wagon with taped windows and peered through the darkness.

"Our horse got hurt," Nancy sobbed.

"Jeez. You want me to call the cops?"

"What are you girls doing out riding in the dark anyway?" a peevish female voice joined in. "We might've hit you."

"Will you can it?" the man turned on his wife.

Donna hid her head in Chief's lathered neck. Go away, she begged silently.

Sally reappeared, breathless with her mission. "Dad wasn't home. I called Gram. She went up to the cabin to get Mitchell and Jamie. They should be here soon."

Mitchell and Jamie—Donna's older brother and cousin. They'd know what to do. A waver of improbable hope coursed through her.

Another face peered over Sally's shoulder, an elderly man with spectacles, the owner of the brick house, Donna guessed. Instantly she resented the crease of concern on his face, his expensive forest green chamois shirt and red suspenders. If she hadn't been looking at his fancy house, this might not have happened. Probably some rich retired guy who'd just moved here from Boston.

"Must be a stress fracture," the man said, shaking his head. "What a shame. I guess the horse was just too old for it."

"He was fine!" Donna snapped. She knew what the man was saying: it was her fault.

More cars braked to a stop. A ring of white faces formed, garish in the glow of headlights. There was nothing to do but wait while the old horse trembled and shivered in shock. All three girls were weeping by the time Mitchell and Jamie arrived in Gramp's jeep.

The boys got out of the jeep slowly and blinked in the glare of the onlookers' headlights. "What's happening?" Mitchell asked stupidly. He pushed his blond hair out of his eyes. Jamie gazed about in amazement. His fingers tapped a jittery rhythm against his long shanks. They both looked vague and confused, as if they didn't know what they were doing there.

"Didn't you bring a rifle?" Sally demanded.

"Gram didn't say to." Mitchell opened his palms.

"I've got a shotgun," the owner of the brick house announced curtly. "I'll go get it." He disappeared into the dark.

"You guys are stoned or tripping or something, aren't you?" Sally accused.

Jamie grinned weakly and Mitchell shrugged.

They were stoned. Donna hated them for that.

New cars appeared, people got out to stare. Donna heard a baby crying, a mother shouting at her kids to get back in the car. She didn't want to be there. She wanted to be home in her bed, under the covers, listening to Nancy's asthmatic snores across the room. Instead there were sweaty reins in her hand, an animal in pain. She turned to undo the girth, and eased the saddle off Chief's swayed back. The familiar odor of horse sweat rose from the saddle blanket.

"That's a good idea," one of the spectators commented. "Once he's put down they won't be able to . . ."

"Shut up!" Donna screamed, spinning around to face them. "Shut up all of you!" She dropped the saddle at her feet where it lay in a heap like a leathery road kill.

Sally put a hand on her shoulder.

Donna yanked away. "I want to take his bridle off. He shouldn't die with a hunk of metal in his mouth. It's not like he's going to run away." She slid the leather straps over Chief's ears, eased the bit out so it wouldn't clank against his teeth. His eyes rolled white in their sockets but he held his head still, submissive even in pain.

The man with the shotgun returned. "Maybe you ought to move the animal off the road so he won't block cars," he suggested.

"He can't move," Donna cried, wrapping her arms around Chief's soaked neck. "Don't try to make him."

"Okay, okay, you girls better go on inside now and let these boys handle it," the old man said, holding out the shotgun.

Nobody moved.

"Shit, I can't do it," Mitchell said. "I'm too fucked up."

"Hey, don't look at me." Jamie backed away. "I don't want to shoot a horse."

"You girls go on inside the house," the old man ordered. He sounded angry. "Go on, all of you. I'll take care of it."

Sally put her arm around Donna and started to lead her off. Chief raised his head and whinnied after them—a piercing, desolate cry.

"No! Don't!" Donna screamed.

"He's in pain," Sally said, pinching Donna's shoulder. "We've got to." She turned to the old man. "Hurry up, just do it, please!"

Donna turned to look, but Sally jerked her around. Then the shotgun blasted through her. Donna recognized it: the same crash she would have felt on the highway, the thing she had wanted to know. In the dark, she could make out Chief splayed on the damp dirt road, head thrown forward, legs bent under. Donna still knew nothing.

That night her father put down his can of Schlitz to breathe smoky sour beer breath at her from a strangely gentled, puffy face. "I'm awful sorry, baby. He was an old horse. We'll get you another."

Donna stared at him blankly. Whose father was this, suddenly solicitous? Not hers. She ran and hid her head in her mother's lap, let her mother's fingers run through her hair while she cried. Her mother's knees, newly bony, protruded through her plaid wool skirt. Donna gripped them. She wanted her mother not to be sick anymore. She didn't want another horse, ever. She wanted Chief. More than that, she wanted it not to be her fault.

In September, Donna called Claude. Something you weren't ever supposed to do. Marsha, her oldest sister, had said so. You didn't call boys, Marsha instructed in that know-it-all tone of hers, standing with hands on hips, wavy red hair flying around her head, a diminutive boss no bigger than ten-year-old Nancy. You waited for boys to call you, Marsha explained impatiently, and then when they did you let the phone ring at least four times before answering, and if they asked you out, you pretended you weren't sure if you were free. Donna listened to her oldest sister's rules of dating etiquette, and then she called Claude anyway.

It wasn't that she had such a big interest in Claude or anything; now that she was in ninth grade and riding the bus up to the Union High School, she liked lots of boys and lots of boys liked her. Calling Claude was impulse, mostly. She'd seen him driving his dad's tractor that afternoon. The four o'clock bus she'd taken home after cheerleading tryouts veered out into the road to pass him. Claude stared straight ahead, embarrassed to be caught hauling a load of manure in a spreader from one of his family's many fields to another, his back wide through his sweatshirt, his hair catching the gold of afternoon autumn light. Donna thought, why not?

She looked his number up in the book and dialed. It rang twice, and one of Claude's hulking older brothers answered dully, "Yeah, he's here." The receiver clattered down, and she could hear the brother call out in a nasty falsetto, "Claude, some little pussy wants you." Donna almost hung up. The brother's guffaws muffled Claude's annoyed, "Cut the crap," and then he was there, breathing shyly into the phone.

"Yeah? Who's this?"

"Hi. This is Donna Chartrain." There was a long pause. She

pictured Claude racking his brain to place her, and again thought of hanging up.

"Donna . . . Donna Chartrain . . . You Mitch's little sister?"

"Yeah."

"Oh. Hey. I've seen you at school."

Donna felt heartened—even though he was in eleventh grade, he'd seen her and remembered. "I saw you today, when I was coming home from school. On a tractor."

"Oh jeez. That."

"I just thought . . ." Donna trailed off, unsure what to say— she just thought he looked cute? She had a thing for guys pulling loads of manure? She giggled nervously.

"Hey." Claude brightened, finally figuring out the gist of her call. "You want to get together or something?"

"Sure."

"So, uh, you free now?"

"Yeah." Another one of Marsha's rules broke with a satisfying snap.

As soon as they'd arranged a place to meet and hung up, Donna hurriedly dialed Therese—to gloat, to beg moral support—but her friend wasn't home. She made Therese's mother promise to have her call that night. "Tell her it's important!" Donna urged.

After ten minutes of trying on clothes and examining herself from all angles in the mirror, Donna ran out of the house wearing exactly what she had on when she started: jeans, a white turtleneck with little green hearts printed on it, a jean jacket. Her mother was resting in the bedroom with the shades drawn and the door half closed, so Donna didn't stop to invent a lie.

They met outside the playground of the Boys' Home, halfway for both of them. Claude was already there, leaning against the slide. His hair was wet from the shower he must have taken as soon as they got off the phone. Donna was pleased, figuring he wanted to impress her.

"Hey," Claude said.

"Hey," Donna replied. Up close, he looked big, farmboy big,

with a jutting Adam's apple, a wide rack of shoulders, and broad, dangling hands. His face was smooth, square, unremarkable, cutting that fine line between good-looking and bland.

"So how's it going?" he asked.

"Okay." She waited for Claude to take charge of the conversation. She figured she'd done her part in calling him.

"So, uh, how you like being in high school?" he ventured.

"It's cool. But my math teacher, Mr. Witt? He's really mean."

"Yeah, Witt-less can be pretty bad." Claude worked his shoulders nervously, as if talking to a girl was giving him a stiff neck.

The silence stretched between them.

"I tried out for JV cheerleading today," Donna announced. "Want to see?" She stepped back and performed a couple of leaps and lunges from the routine Marsha had helped her memorize. Her jeans were tight in the crotch so she didn't do the final split. "It's kinda hard without shorts," she said, pushing her hair off her face, breathing hard.

Claude grinned. "That's pretty good. Think you'll make it?"

"I don't know." Donna tossed her head. She could feel herself imitating Marsha's flirtatious gestures without intending to. "I don't really care. Some of those cheerleaders are pretty snotty. You going to the practice game Saturday?"

"Can't. Got to seed winter rye."

"They make you work hard, huh."

Claude shrugged. "I guess."

To avoid the next silence, Donna abruptly walked toward the swing set. Without turning, she could feel Claude following, and took pleasure in knowing he would. She chose a rubber-treaded seat and pushed off. Claude took the swing beside hers, and they rose and fell in opposite rhythms. It was easier, not so awkward, staying in motion.

Leaning back, Donna caught sight of the tops of maples, still green, with only an early touch of red on a leaf here and there, set against a sky gathering dusk. For a moment, she just wanted to be a kid on a swing instead of a girl on a sort-of date. The tops of the white clapboard Boys' Home buildings flashed by. She thought of the kids who lived there; for years she'd seen them splashing in their pool in the summer, lining up in twos to be loaded onto buses for field trips, noticed lights on in some of the dorm windows during holidays—kids who had nowhere to go. She'd always pitied them with that funny near-satisfaction that comes from knowing it wasn't her. But if her mother died from the cancer, she'd almost be an orphan too. Dizziness from leaning back melded with choking fear. Donna dragged her toes in the dirt, stopping her swing, and forced the thoughts away. Her stomach gently flip-flopped back into place.

"I heard what your brother called me on the phone," she said.

Claude quit swinging, grimaced. "I'm not like him."

Donna cocked her head. "What are you like?" It gave her a tiny rush of pleasure to know she was making him uncomfortable. She had some power over him she couldn't yet decipher.

"I don't intend to end up on the farm, that's for sure," Claude said, scuffing dirt with his heel.

"Why not?"

"I got too many older brothers, for one thing. There's not enough to share. Dad don't want to chop it all up. But anyway, I want to run my own business. I got plans."

"Like what?"

Claude stared across the playground toward the slope where the pastures from the Boys' Home farm ran down to the Connecticut River. "Earth moving. You know, haul gravel, dig foundations and such. I'm going to buy a dump truck soon as I can."

Donna looked at him again, appraising. His eyes were grey, the lashes thick and black. She hadn't noticed them before. She didn't know any kids who talked like that, so serious. She wasn't sure if that made him deep, or simply a dink. Her brother Mitchell had lots of plans—like becoming a sea captain or building a boat—but they were dreams, and they changed from week to week.

"You want to see it?" Claude asked.

"See what?"

He blushed. "Our farm."

"Sure." When Donna got up the seat of the swing caught her

hard behind the knees. It hurt, but she didn't let on. They walked the mile, taking a path in the woods through a clearing where big kids drank sometimes. Marsha's boyfriend Eddie hung out there. Marsha, the priss who didn't drink or smoke dope wouldn't admit it, but everyone knew.

It would have been pretty without the trash. In the cool darkness of the woods, ferns caught sprinklings of late sun. The center of the hangout was an old cellar hole. Donna imagined the colonial house that must have stood on top of the tumbling, mossy rocks, its apple trees and lilacs overgrown with hemlock and birch. Now the hole held moldy mattresses, a broken lawn chair. Beer cans and cigarette butts littered the ground.

"Do you ever hang out in here?" Donna asked, kicking a broken Miller bottle out of the way.

"Nah. My brothers do sometimes."

"But you aren't like them."

"Right." Claude smiled. He reached for her hand, fumbled for a second, latched on.

Donna's hand felt hot, awkward. A little thrill traveled from her fingers up her arm. She was being led someplace she was willing to go.

When they came out on the road again, Donna dropped Claude's hand in fear that someone from her family might drive by. It was turning dusk already, and she hoped that she wouldn't be recognizable. They reached the edge of the Cormier cornfields.

"C'mon," Claude said, stepping in between the rows of rattling stalks. The dirt was soft underfoot. Donna's sneakers sent up puffs of dust. For a moment she lost sight of Claude, and all she could hear was his breathing and the rustling of the dry husks. As soon as they stepped out of the cornfield she smelled silage. Long red cow barns stretched away, and behind them towered red tile silos.

The Cormier Dairy was the biggest farm in Shelby, maybe in Windsor County. Claude's parents were French Canadians who'd come down from Quebec and done well. Donna couldn't remember if her father had milked for them, since he never stayed at any job very long. She hoped not.

Beyond the barns, the farmhouse was lit with a pale yellow glow from a downstairs window. The kitchen probably. She pictured Claude's mother making dinner: a big woman, she figured—she'd have to be to give rise to all those big Cormier boys—with big farmwife arms sticking out of a short-sleeve dress. She thought of her own mother at home, getting up from the afternoon naps that never left her rested, shuffling around the kitchen sighing. It was Donna's turn to wash dishes tonight, Sally's to help cook. Probably they were already sitting down to supper. The image of Dad hunched over his beer, glowering at them all, made the back of her neck shiver. She ought to be heading home now, but she didn't want to.

Claude led her past a row of sheds hardly bigger than dog houses, where spindly calves lay on beds of straw. "These are the veal pens," he informed her. The calves seemed dazed, lifeless.

"The pens are awful small."

"You can't let them walk around at all or the meat gets red."

"It's cruel," Donna said, turning away.

Claude shrugged. "Maybe. They're just bull calves. They're no use on a dairy farm. You eat meat, don't you?"

"Not veal." She didn't say that the only meat she got at home was venison when Dad shot a deer. He always got his store-bought steaks and burgers, while Mom scrimped by feeding the kids macaroni.

Claude brought her to the doorway of one of the milking parlors. Bare high bulbs illuminated fly-specked walls. Bony-hipped black and white Holsteins munched hay at their stanchions, while automatic milkers pumped away at their teats. All that rhythmic sucking embarrassed Donna. Although her father did this work for other farmers, she'd never been around it much.

Sometimes, to bug her mother, her father said they would've done better to live in a tenant house on some farm; at least no farmer would hold what he owed over him. Donna didn't really know if her mother's father held things over Dad or not. It had started out good: Dad helped Gramp Hunter in the plumbing business, and Gramp gave them the three acres to build on. But nothing had turned out right. She considered what it would be like to live in a tenant house on Claude's farm. She thought of his older brothers and decided she wouldn't like it.

One of the cows raised its tail to release a stream of green liquid shit into the cement gutter. The odor hung over everything, but Claude probably didn't even notice it anymore. When a man moved past the door, Donna ducked back.

Claude whispered, "Jerry. My oldest brother. He's the one that'll get the farm."

He led her round to a pen behind the cow barn. "Our bull Pete's in there," Claude said. Donna didn't think they even kept bulls around anymore; she thought it was all a matter of artificial insemination, some goop in a tank of liquid nitrogen or something. It was half-dark now, and she heard Pete before she saw him. He was standing against the back wall of the twelve-by-sixteen pen, a pale hulk breathing in low, explosive gusts. He was big. His horns hooked upward above a neck wrinkled with muscle, a fleshy hump rode his shoulders, and his balls hung nearly to the ground between his back legs, big pink pendulums that swung as he shifted his weight.

Donna turned and saw Claude half-smiling as though he was proud of the bull, but not just normal proud, the way you'd be proud of a car or something. Maybe he thought having a bull like that somehow reflected back on him, and it was his big pink balls hanging to the ground. Or that, even more than the cows and their teats being sucked, the bull was another dirty joke he and his brothers shared.

Annoyed, she asked, "You ever go in there?"

"Shit, no," Claude said. "Are you kidding? He got loose once and it took four guys to catch him, and they were chasing him around on tractors and such. You'd have to be crazy to get in there with him."

"I'm not afraid," Donna challenged.

"Yeah, right." Then he laughed, a short derisive bark.

That's what got her, that laugh. He might as well have been his brother calling her a pussy on the phone. Or her dad, with that nasty sneer he reserved for when any of them admitted to caring about something. "You don't believe me, do you?" she demanded.

"Okay, okay, you aren't afraid. Forget it," Claude said. "C'mon, I'll show you the rest."

Donna eyed Pete. The bull ran his tongue over the flat pink plate of his nose, licking the snot out of his nostrils. How could you be afraid of something that licked its own snot? Taking a deep breath, Donna pulled herself up the six-foot-high wooden planks of the pen. She straddled the top board, dangling a sneakered foot. When Claude glanced around, his bland face shifting to alarm, she smiled a taunt and popped over. Hitting the mucky dirt, she skidded and almost fell but caught herself and was up again, heart pounding. The bull uttered a bellow of surprise. Donna took two big strides across the corner of the pen and hit the other fence.

"Donna!" Claude shouted.

Pete was in motion, pawing and snorting, but Donna was already clambering up the other side of the pen. She flipped over the top slat and landed on safe ground just as the bull smashed into the stout boards with his curved horns. He stepped back and rushed the fence again for good measure.

"Jesus Christ, Donna, you crazy?" Claude's voice was high and strained. "You could've got killed."

"I would've done a cartwheel in there but I didn't want to get shit all over my hands," Donna bluffed. Her heart still pumped at a sickening rate and she could taste adrenalin, that metallic rush, on the back of her tongue.

Claude grabbed her then. "You really are crazy! I almost shit when you started to fall . . ."

Donna tried to laugh, but she choked and it ended up a strangled cough. For some stupid reason she was crying.

"Why you want to go do something like that?" Claude asked, pressing her against his chest, holding her hard to still her shaking. She could feel his heartbeat right through his shirt, a rapid throb. Something inside her softened: she wanted to be held like this, a child against her mother, forever. Claude kissed her, half-missing her mouth, smearing her lips across her teeth when, startled, she turned her head. He seemed almost as surprised as she was. Holding her hard above the elbows, he pushed her back to look at her, his grey eyes widening. Then he pulled her toward him and kissed her again. This time their mouths met dead on. All Donna could think of was that his lips were a lot softer than she would've expected, and there was a shaving nick she hadn't noticed before on his chin.

She'd kissed boys before, plenty. Even back in sixth grade, hanging out behind the middle school, ducking behind the dumpster on a dare. And after dances at the Shelby Youth Center, with Paulie Abbott, the principal's kid, who begged to walk her home. They'd stop to kiss at every street corner, dry little pecks so his braces wouldn't hurt her mouth. At the Youth Center she danced with lots of boys, even slow dances, letting them press close with their urgent bulges, their grinding hips, knowing that there was something they wanted. It wasn't all that much different from the ping pong games in the Center basement, the skits organized by the minister's wife. It was just play. Practice for something to come later.

"Let's get out of here and let Pete settle down before someone comes to see what's wrong," Claude whispered huskily. They passed silos, tractors, a junked pickup, and then they were standing in front of the tenant house. Its white clapboard siding glowed dully, and the dark green front door hung half open.

"It's empty," Claude said. "You want to go in?"

Donna hesitated. Was this what Claude had in mind from the moment she called him, some plot cooked up with his brothers to lead her to a dark, empty house? She glanced up at Claude's grey eyes, read their uncertainty, and didn't believe it. In any case, she didn't care.

"No one's lived here since my brothers got big enough to work," Claude said, pushing through the door. "When we were little we had a hired man who lived here with his family. After they left, we kinda used it as a clubhouse."

In the dimness, Donna detected a low ceiling, bare hanging bulbs with dangling strings, a wall with a hole punched through the plaster above the dark wainscoting. She wondered who had done it: Claude's brothers fighting, or the hired man, who came in from milking as mean as her father, as angry not to be living on his own land?

She followed Claude into a room full of sagging, metal-framed beds. He reached down to brush mouse turds off a mattress, then pulled an army blanket from a dresser and spread it over the ticking. A whiff of mothballs filled the air. Claude sat down. Donna stood before him, wavering. What was she doing here? But when he reached up from the bed, placing his hands on her shoulders, and pulled her close between his legs, she knew. She was here for this, because touch was everything. At the feel of his hands her will went right out of her; touch spoke a language she didn't know she knew, something real familiar.

They kissed again. Then they were lying face to face on the bed, staring at each other while Claude's hands, big rough farmboy hands, moved gently on her back. She didn't know where she should put her own hands. She didn't want to do something wrong to make him think she was just a dumb ninth grader, so she followed his lead, running her fingers along the slabbing muscles of his back. Claude's hands slid around to her front, up her rib cage to run over her breasts. She was amazed that her small breasts could feel so much: the rush of heat running from her nipples straight between her legs made her gasp. Encouraged, Claude pushed up her jersey and reached around to struggle with the hook on her bra. She felt her nipples tighten with the shock of cool air.

Claude paused. "You aren't built like your sister, are you?" She figured he meant Sally. Marsha was a tiny thing and anyway, she'd already graduated two years ago. Sally, a year ahead of Claude in school, was stacked.

"You disappointed?" Donna challenged.

"No! I like you this way. Just right. I used to see you last summer jumping off the ledges at the quarry. You were the only girl who would jump from the high one. You didn't have these yet." He ran his fingers lightly over her breasts, as if to assure her of their significance. "You always looked like so much fun," Claude continued. "I said to myself, wonder who she'll be in a few years."

"You didn't know me when I called," Donna pouted.

"I didn't know your name. But I knew you."

Then his shirt was off too, and their chests pressed against each other. Something else new: the electric rub of skin on skin, as if flesh was transformed just for this occasion. She saw that her body had only been hers in a certain way until this—muscles did what she asked, carried her, let her leap in a cheerleading routine or jump off a cliff into water—and now it was as though she'd been granted another sense, her skin made new with heat and shivers and pulse and breath and lips and fingertips.

She heard the sliding buzz of a zipper far away. And he was asking, Can I? Can I? He was tugging on her jeans, sliding them. And then under her hand his thing felt funny. Bony and hard and soft all at once. But big. She didn't see how something like that could fit inside her and then he was pushing and she was pushing too and it just pushed right in.

It didn't even hurt. People said you could do that to yourself from horseback riding. But it was supposed to hurt and it didn't. He'd think she wasn't a virgin. She didn't care. Didn't care. Didn't care.

Claude, eyes shut, face clenched in concentration, drove into her and Donna tried to match his beat. Push and breathe, push and breathe until it caught her. She was amazed by the wave of red that filled her, like looking through your eyelids on a sunny day. And the cry that broke from her throat as though some animal inhabited her, a voice that wasn't hers, or hadn't been until now.

Claude groaned and went still. Donna stared up at the cracked ceiling plaster. Her blood ticked in her veins. Now what? They hardly knew each other. Claude's weight, something she hadn't noticed before, grew heavy as a sack of grain. She struggled beneath him and he rolled off.

"God, I'm sorry. I didn't mean to go so far," Claude said.

"It's okay."

"I thought you'd say stop."

"I didn't want to."

"Me neither." Claude smiled, kissed her. "You're really something. I can't believe you're a ninth grader."

Donna laughed, it sounded so foolish.

"I never did that before," Claude admitted.

"Me neither."

"We didn't even use anything."

"Don't worry. I think it'll be okay." The Russian roulette aspect of it excited her; there had to be a price, or it wouldn't mean anything.

Claude got up to look out the window. His back was still dark from a summer tan while his buttocks shone white, but when he moved from the window and came toward her he became just a dark shape. Something flitted across the backs of her eyes, something internal, a shape that recurred in her dreams or what she thought were dreams, the vision of a man standing over her while she slept, a threatening shape leaning down. Fear caught in her throat, followed by a wave of nausea.

"How you doing?" Claude said. At the sound of his voice, the shadow picture vanished.

"I've got to go now," Donna said. "What time is it? I'm really late. I'm supposed to be home for supper." She scrambled for her clothes and hurriedly pulled them on, searching through dustballs under the bed for her bra.

Claude reached for his jeans. "Let me get one of the trucks, I'll drive you."

"No. I got to go now." She rushed out the door, feet thumping on hard-packed dirt, past still-lit cow barns. An evening fog floated over the fields as the air cooled. Heart big in her chest, she rustled through the cornstalks, fumbling in the moonless dark. Then she heard Claude's breath as loud as when he was on top of her. A roaring filled her ears when he grabbed her and pulled her down.

"Hey, hey. Just wait a minute," Claude demanded. He pressed her beneath him in the dust, held her. "Don't run off, Donna. I'm going to drive you. You'll get home faster that way."

Donna lay still.

"I want to drive you," Claude insisted. "You just wait here, okay?"

She sat up and nodded, an obedient child. She wasn't even certain why she'd bolted like that. Listening to the frogs belching in a nearby swamp, the cows lowing, the breathing of the world she'd finally entered, she felt her restlessness drain away.

Claude came thumping around in a pickup, no lights, the rumble of the engine loud. She climbed in and he flicked the lights on as they swung away from the barns, cut through a tractor road around the back of the cornfield, and out onto the asphalt. They passed Therese's house. Donna knew she wouldn't call her friend, wouldn't tell her. Therese would never do what she had done.

When Donna shut her eyes she saw her own house against her lids. Mitchell's window would be black—he was probably out smoking dope with Jamie. In the living room, the blue glow was her mother watching the tube. She pictured her father's slumped hulk in the kitchen, passed out with his head on his hands. In the big girls' room, Sally would be doing homework, Marsha reading *Mademoiselle*, maybe taking one of those stupid personality tests. In the younger girls' room, Nancy would be snuggled up with her stuffed animals. Donna could see their room as clearly as if she were there: her collection of china horses gathering dust on a shelf, her dolls moved over to Nancy's side, the ruffled vanity she'd begged for two Christmases ago as starched and prim as ever.

But it wasn't her house any longer. It was more like a stranger's house glimpsed from the highway, a geometry of light, and then something forgotten in the rush of wheels on pavement.

ZOO RAISED

[Mitchell, 1974]

"TWO BUCKS, CHARTRAIN. I'll give you two bucks to take my turn tonight." Billy Barrow patted his dirty jeans pocket and gestured toward the camel pen where Ahmoud, looking loftily down his nose, grunted and spat.

Mitchell took one look at those weird camel legs with their calloused knees and horny, banana-shaped toes, legs that could kick in any direction, and said, "Right. And miss the sight of you running for your life?"

"Eat camel shit and die, Chartrain."

"Probably will, but not today." No way Barrow was going to buy him off for two bucks. Every time Mitchell didn't have to feed that vicious camel was like a death row reprieve.

Mitchell had one last trip to make on the kiddie train. He tipped his dopey engineer's cap at Barrow, who slumped away as though Mitchell had just sold him into slavery, and then Mitchell made his way through the line of tourists: little kids gripping bags of popcorn, flatlander mommies in skimpy halter tops, and their dink husbands wearing Bermuda shorts and crew-cuts, as if they'd never heard of Steppenwolf or the Stones.

He climbed into the engineer's seat, knees to his chin, blew the steam whistle, and shouted "All aboooooooooooard!" feeling like the biggest dink of all.

When everyone was fastened in, Mitchell released the brake, threw the clutch, and let the old 283 rumble forward, going slow down the dip that ran past the fake iceberg in the duck pond, through a forest of ten-foot-tall candy canes in need of paint, chugging past Teddy Rogers in front of the Elf Cottage. As usual, Rogers was half-cocked on the peppermint schnapps that he hid in his coffee mug, but who could blame him? If Mitchell was forty years old and had to go to work every day wearing green tights and curled up shoes, he'd shoot himself. He swung the train past Mrs. Claus's Kitchen, where inside, tourists slopped up pancakes at four in the afternoon thinking they were getting Real Vermont Syrup, when Mitchell knew for a fact it was just Log Cabin poured into tins decorated with pictures of horses hauling sap sleds. *They'd* never had horses to run their buckets, just him and Gramp Hunter and Dad and Jamie, busting their balls and their backs, until Gramp finally broke down and bought tubing. When the stored tubing got chewed up by mice this winter, Dad gloated, pleased with his father-in-law's loss. Dad could sure boil syrup, though. Even Gramp admitted that, probably the only good thing he ever said about him.

The train huffed, pulling its load up a small rise. Jeez, it was hot out here. Humidity hung over everything as though the maples breathed it out of their heavy leaves, and the plume of steam felt like a sauna blowing back in his face. You had to wonder why these flatlander geeks from Massachusetts and Connecticut wanted to play Christmas in July. Nothing else to look at, Mitchell supposed, just hayfields and hills.

He peeked at his watch, let her pick up a bit too much speed on the downgrade that circled the petting zoo. Anything to break the monotony of ten trips a day and cleaning up after dribbled ice cream and baby barf.

Mitchell slid into his usual fantasy: he was chugging through a miniaturized landscape, the hills made of plaster of paris, the trees of moss glued to twigs, like in the model train magazine he'd seen.

Which always left the question of what giant was standing over him with his hand on the controls, directing his circumscribed journey, the tiny, repetitive loop. It was the kind of conjecture that could really put you into the Twilight Zone if you let it. Fortunately, he couldn't run too far with it, because the worst turn was coming up and Mitchell had to ease on the brakes.

Last week he had derailed, going too fast around this corner, trying to give the kiddies a thrill. Oh, it was beautiful—six gaily painted train cars stuck in the mud, tourist mommies and daddies hauling their kids by the armpits while they tiptoed through duck shit and cow plops, Chessworth passing out complimentary tickets, scared to death of being sued—but there was no sense getting fired with five weeks left before school started. Maybe Mitchell didn't ease up on the brakes quite enough, because he heard squawking behind him. Tip of the engineer's hat. Screw 'em.

Back in the station, the kids begged to sit in Mitchell's seat. He put one up there, a freckled little redhead in a Yankees cap, the plump mommy in stretch shorts all goofy with her camera, wanting Mitchell in the picture, even with his sweaty too-long hair plastered to his forehead. He could just imagine the photo: his gummy smile dominating a snapshot in a stranger's album.

When he got the train swabbed down he headed for the petting zoo to feed the animals and clean cages. For obvious reasons, Chessworth made them shovel shit after the last train ride.

The white-tail deer looked dazed in their pen, wilting in the heat. They came over like puppies, noses snuffling. There were a couple of spotted fawns, and outside the wire mesh kids were calling "Here, deer-deer."

He couldn't help it, the fawns always made him think of that scene in *Bambi* after the mother dies, when Bambi wanders around calling "Mother? Mother?" in this pitiful voice. They shouldn't be allowed to show that kind of shit to little kids. It could traumatize them for life. It had traumatized Mitchell for months, anyway, when he was six, and it was probably the reason he was such a wuss about deer hunting, one more reason for Dad to be pissed.

Mitchell tossed ears of wormy corn to the raccoons hiding in their barrel. He felt sorry for them, caged when they ought to be free to risk their lives crossing the highway at dusk. Then it was time for the slop bucket, full of leftover lettuce and squashy bananas from the A&P for Charley the Chimp.

Charley was Santa's Workshop's problem animal, although Hugo the Clown loved Charley's hairless butt. Hugo was okay. A big old guy with a sagging gut and a soft face, Hugo started out as a Shriner entertaining kids down at the burn hospital in Boston, and when he retired from DB Pipe Fitting he took on the clown job. He picked up Charley when the Franklin Park Zoo went defunct.

Every morning Hugo made Mitchell and Billy Barrow go through this ritual, shaking Charley's hand while he held the chimp on his chain and smoked his last cigar of the day until the tourists went home. Chessworth wouldn't let Hugo smoke in costume. Mitchell had nothing against Hugo, or Charley either. It was just that he knew where that monkey's hand had been.

Charley had a problem with the solitary vice, only it wasn't so solitary, because he spent half his time jerking himself off in the corner of his cage, using any piece of trash he could get his hands on. It was pretty funny watching the parents yank their kids away, the kids whining, "Mommy, what's he doing?" Mitchell guessed if he was locked in a cage like Charley he might want to fuck an old soda cup, too. At least Charley didn't have a mother who yelled through the bathroom door when she thought he was taking too long a shower. But sometimes Mitchell looked into those bright, beady eyes and felt sorry for the poor ape. Too smart to live caged up like that, dying of boredom. He wondered if Charley dreamed of escape. Maybe he fantasized jungles, or a pretty chimp babe. He'd probably never seen either, though, having been zoo raised.

"How ya doing, boys, how ya doing?" Hugo came over to bid goodnight to his chimp like there was no difference between Charley and Mitchell and Billy, and maybe there wasn't. Billy had black hair and long arms that hung nearly to his knees, and a back so hairy he had to squeegee the water off himself after a dip in the quarry. Even on the hottest days Chessworth wouldn't let Billy take off his shirt when he was riding the mower. Mitchell was blond and smooth-bodied, but he figured his ape-ness was a personality thing, a matter of style.

To Chessworth and the tourists, he was just a dumb hick kid who shoveled shit and drove a kiddie train for a living, a kid who would probably flunk eleventh grade. Not because he was stupid, Mitchell knew, but because he couldn't be bothered with those boring-ass assignments. And when he did get interested, he went on too long, like that twenty-seven-page book report he wrote on *Captains Courageous* that his teacher marked "excessive." It wasn't his fault if nobody could see what a great book it was.

When they were done bucking hay into the pens, Billy and Mitchell hunkered behind the antelope barn, sharing one joint to get them home.

"That fucking camel nearly nailed me," Billy complained. "I'm going to turn him loose opening day of hunting season."

Mitchell laughed. "Some New Yorker would probably shoot him before noon and think he was a moose. What we ought to do is put some weed in his feed. Mellow him out. Hey Ahmoud, want to get high?"

"Ought to sneak in here with a shotgun," Billy muttered.

Billy could never see the humor in a situation. Of course it wasn't quite as funny when it was Mitchell's turn to feed the fucker, but why worry about that now?

Billy headed south toward Putney, so Mitchell had to hitch the six miles north up Route 5 to Shelby. Nobody wanted him today, but he didn't really care. He walked slowly along the highway shoulder, listening to the whir of insects in the high grass, the suck of hot tires on pavement, meditating on a couple of girls zipping past in a blue Camaro. Massachusetts plates, naturally. He finally got picked up by his former eighth grade social studies teacher, Mr. Edwards, who had a square head that was too big for his skinny neck and mean little eyes. Edwards was a Vermont chauvinist, like those male chauvinists the women's libbers were always yelling about on TV. While Edwards jammed Marlboro butts into his ashtray and raved about all the things the flatlanders were doing—raising land prices and making higher taxes and thinking they had a right to stand up and squawk about trailer zoning at Town Meeting—Mitchell savored his buzz and the shivery cold of Edwards' air conditioning. Outside the window of Edwards' Buick, hayfields were scalped into stubble and sweaty crews bucked bales.

If Mitchell squinted his eyes enough to block out the tractors and the hay crews, the smooth rolling green fields almost looked like the ocean, and he could picture it: standing on the bow of a double-masted schooner, the waves spraying up, nothing but three thousand miles of ocean beckoning . . .

"You stay in school now," Edwards advised as he pulled over at the bottom of Gramp's road to let Mitchell out.

Yeah, yeah.

"You hear me?" Edwards demanded. "We got to keep what's ours, and we aren't going to if kids like you turn into no account bums." He spun gravel under his back tires and rolled away.

Mitchell wondered if Edwards was making some backhanded stab at Dad. Dad wasn't out of work *that* much.

Walking in the door, his peaceful mood gave way and his chest closed up like it always did when he saw Dad glowering at the table with a beer. It was amazing how many hours Dad could spend resenting his father-in-law. Gramp's neat clapboard house across the road, with its slate roof and canopied berry bushes and pruned apple trees, might as well have been a personal affront. Mitchell slid past, trying to avoid Dad's ugly.

Marsha stuck her nose out of the big girls' room. She had her wavy red hair wrapped up on orange juice cans, trying to get it to lie flat like Cher's, but she looked like a space goon. "Ugh," Marsha said, getting a whiff of zoo.

"Up yours," Mitchell mouthed, and Marsha slammed her door.

In the shower, Mitchell ran hot water to get the grime off, then stood under a blast of cool. He couldn't help admiring the way his body was bulking up, shoulders and biceps thickening. He was already as tall as Dad, although Dad actually wasn't that tall—a short, round-faced pug of a man, Lowell Chartrain only loomed large in the eyes of his family.

In clean tee-shirt and shorts, Mitchell lay down on his bed and opened his envelope of boat pictures. He studied the plans he'd written away for, the classic seventeen-foot Whitehall sailing skiff he would build some day. Elegance was the word that came to mind when he ran his fingers over the drawings. The language alone entranced him: steam-bent stems, carvel strakes, futtocks. He shut his eyes and smelled a whiff of salt spray, heard the snap of a mainsheet in the wind. He'd only seen the ocean twice, when Sally drove him over to the coast of New Hampshire for a day at the beach. But ever since he read *Captains Courageous*, he'd been in love with the idea of the ocean and the boats that sailed across it.

"Dinner," Donna announced, poking her dark curly head through the door.

Mitchell shoved his plans back into the manila envelope as though caught looking at dirty pictures.

Even though the door was open, the kitchen was stuffy. Untaped sheetrock, marred by handprints and grease splatters, covered the walls. The plywood subfloor awaited linoleum. Dad would probably never finish building the house, he was so mad at Mom for making them move back to her parents'. Still, it was better than the years when they had all lived downstairs in the capped foundation, rooms marked off by hanging sheets.

There were two kinds of dinners in their house, neither of them a pleasure: the kind when Dad ate with them, which was generally miserable, and the worse kind when dad wouldn't eat, but sat at the table all evening, smoking Luckies and salting his beers. Then around nine o'clock, when the kids were hiding in their rooms, he'd get out his bucket of lard and start frying chicken or potatoes. On those nights acrid smoke, a staticky burned emanation, filled the house. Mitchell could already tell what kind of supper this would be.

Mom set the steaming dish of baked spaghetti casserole in the center of the table. "I got a nice pork chop for you, Lowell," she cajoled. "You sure you won't . . ."

"Leave it be, will you Anne? I told you I ain't hungry."

Marsha and Donna exchanged glances. The kids scooped over-cooked tomatoey casserole onto their plates, poured out glass-fuls of the thin, swirling reconstituted dried milk that had replaced the real stuff, ever since Dad got in an argument with Vinton Carlisle and was no longer milking at the dairy. Mitchell pictured his cousin Jamie eating across the road with Gram and Gramp Hunter, pouring big glasses of chilled whole milk, shoving Gram's homemade cookies into his mouth, stacking them up beside his plate on the polished plank table in Gram's spotless kitchen. Mitchell wondered what they'd had for supper. Gram always served three different kinds of homemade bread, cookies, rhubarb sauce with ice cream, and she always had Royal Lunch crackers around.

Mom, stiff-backed, hustled pans at the stove, and Mitchell and his sisters sat silently, faces close to their plates, eating rapidly to get out of there as fast as possible.

"Jesus Christ," Dad said, turning on Mitchell, "you want me to get you a shovel?"

Mitchell felt the forkful of casserole turn to mush in his mouth.

"Gram said she's gonna help me make an A-line dress for school," Donna ventured. "She's gonna take me to Newberry's to pick out a pattern."

"Sure," Dad said bitterly, hoisting his beer can. "Everything's great across the street. You like it so much why don't you move on over there like your freeloading cousin?"

Donna opened and closed her mouth like a landed fish.

Sally looked up from her plate. "Jamie doesn't freeload. He helps Gramp," she said softly.

Mitchell was surprised. Usually Sally was so lost in her own world she didn't seem to be there.

"Go ahead and stick up for the hippie sonovabitch," Dad said, voice rising. "I know what's going on between you two."

"Lowell," Mom warned.

"Nothing's going on," Sally protested. "We're friends."

"I know what's going on up there in that shack, goddammit, and I'm going to put a stop to it."

"Lowell, that's enough." Mom tilted her head in the direction of eleven-year-old Nancy.

"I know he's screwing my daughter and it's gonna stop!"

"Lowell!"

"He's half out of his mind on pot and marijuana and whatever else they take, and he's after you too. He's a menace."

Mitchell couldn't help himself: he laughed. The thought of Jamie chasing after Mom was too much.

"What's so funny?" Dad demanded.

"Nothing." Mitchell took a big swig of the bluish milk. He could feel it start to rise through his nostrils. Donna smirked and he kicked her under the table.

But Dad was just building up steam. "I don't want him back in this house and that's it. And none of you should hang around him anymore. I don't know why they took him in."

Mom slouched against the stove, her wig tilting, shoulders slumped in defeat. "Life is short, Lowell," she wailed. "Do we have to fight like this?"

Marsha leaped from the table and put her arm around Mom, glaring at all of them as if only she cared.

"Somebody ought to turn in that draft-dodging bum," Dad mumbled. He got up and hunted in the fridge for another beer.

Jamie wasn't a draft dodger. He'd gotten a high number in the lottery. But Dad acted like he wished the war had lasted long enough so that Mitchell could get drafted.

Dad sat back down, popped his beer can, and looked them over coldly as though he'd been short-changed. Nancy, with her braids unraveling and her too-big, hand-me-down clothes, sat still as a scared rabbit. Donna wiped a forkful of baked spaghetti around and around on her plate. Sally had already retreated back into her dream world. She hummed softly.

"Cut that out," Dad barked.

"Jesus," Mitchell said.

Dad reached across the table and back-handed him, fast as a striking snake.

Burning tears filled Mitchell's eyes. "What? I didn't do anything."

"Don't you cuss me. Don't you forget who's who in this house. And if you want the belt you just keep asking."

Mitchell snapped from his seat, plate clattering, and shot out the door. He nearly stumbled on the cement block that served for a step. Behind him, Dad shouted "Get back here," but Mitchell kept moving. His heart pumped hard in his chest. He hated him.

Mitchell walked fast by the pen where his sisters' horses worked on piles of hay, then broke into a jog up the rutted dirt road. He ran between tumbling stone walls half hidden by ferns, through pine forest and hemlock groves. He circled the clearing past Jamie's cabin and ran on, veering onto one of the old logging roads that ran up to Rocky Ridge. He slowed to a walk as the trail tilted up. His ragged breathing eased enough that he noticed the hemlocks and birches giving way to a stand of pale grey beech, and heard the light splash of Vesey Brook off to his left. It was a good two miles to the ridge, and mosquitoes clouded around him, but then a breeze at the top, where it was open ledge, drove the bugs away.

Mitchell looked down through the power line, past the heavy leaves rustling in the light wind, to the distant rooftops of West Shelby, where the rich hippies lived. Tofu Flats. There were communes and rumors of orgies. He'd seen them working in their yards, braless, long-haired girls bending over gardens, and bearded guys working on old Saabs and Volkswagens. Why they wanted to live like Dad's folks, with goats and garbage in their yards, was beyond him. At least they made the swimming holes more interesting.

The wind died and the bugs returned, so Mitchell headed back down the logging trail. Dusk was coming on. A kerosene light burned in Gramp's old sugarhouse, which served as Jamie's cabin. It always darkened early, hidden as it was under a canopy of huge rock maples scarred by sugaring taps.

Mitchell peeked through the window. Inside, Jamie lay stretched out on his bed, smoking a joint underneath the mounted six-pound bass he was so proud of. Mitchell pressed his nose against the glass, making a face, waiting to see how long it would take Jamie to sense that someone was watching. Jamie scratched his thigh, stared up at the exposed insulation in the ceiling, content-edly sucked on his joint. When Mitchell mimicked a screech owl, Jamie sat up with a start. He glanced around, spotted Mitchell, and gave him the finger.

"Gotcha," Mitchell said, yanking the door open.

"Yeah, but wait for the payback. Now I got a reason to live." Jamie extended the roach. Mitchell paced the cabin, smoking, until the roach burned his fingers, then he flopped on Gram's old maroon plastic couch. It was upholstered in some kind of forerun-ner of naugahyde and it had old-fashioned carved wooden arm rests. Gram bought it because the salesman told her it would wear better than leather, but he hadn't told her that it would tear and split at the seams. It was comfortable, though, and big enough to sleep on. Mitchell picked up Jamie's guitar and started strumming softly. He wanted to learn to flat-pick like Doc Watson. He won-dered if you had to be blind to play music so good.

"What's up?" Jamie asked.

Mitchell quit strumming. "Blow-ell says you're screwing Sally, and you're after Mom too." He grinned at the thought.

Jamie shook his head. "I'm a busy guy."

Mitchell was almost certain that Jamie hadn't screwed anybody. He was shy around girls. That was one thing Mitchell had over Jamie: last spring, he'd gotten Amy Mercier to go down by the tracks with him, neither of them thinking about poison ivy.

"You think he'll do something to Sally?" Jamie asked.

"Nah." Mitchell was the only one who got beatings from his father—part of the privilege of being the only son, like having a room to himself while the girls had to share. "But you better watch out. Ever since he quit Carlisle's he's been on a tear. He's got it in for you. Not that I blame him."

Jamie shrugged and rolled up another joint, carefully picking through seeds and stems in a baggie.

Mitchell put the guitar down. "I'm gonna get out of here. I'm not going back to school this fall."

Jamie nodded approvingly. He'd gotten kicked out of school himself down in Massachusetts a few years back.

"I'm gonna join the Merchant Marine or the Coast Guard," Mitchell added.

"You're too young."

"I'll be a stowaway."

"You can work on a farm, get room and board 'til you're of age."

That's probably what he'd end up doing if he stuck around. Milking, like Dad had been doing off and on ever since he quit working for Gramp's plumbing business.

"I got an idea," Mitchell said, the plan rushing into his head full-blown and perfect. "Let's get out of here. Just you and me. We'll hitch up to Maine, get jobs on boats, be fishermen or something. Maybe keep going, up to Newfoundland or Prince Edward Island. We can camp on the beach. I got a paycheck coming tomorrow. We'll cash it and be out of here." He could see it all: the dark spruce along the shore, their canvas pup tents glowing in the dusk, smoke rising from their campfire.

"Sounds good," Jamie said. "Only Gramp and I got a furnace to put into Shattucks and about fifteen of Gramp's old ladies to take care of."

Mitchell deflated. All Jamie wanted to do was help Gramp. He worshiped the old bastard. Mitchell leaned back against the couch and shut his eyes. The campfire sputtered out, his pup tent collapsed in the cold Newfoundland wind. "What'd you do today?" he finally asked, although he didn't really care what Jamie did as much as he wanted his company. But there were rules, a social contract, like the principal said every time Mitchell got called to his office, and he knew he had to pretend interest.

"Unplugged a kitchen sink for one of Grampy's widows, then went down to Bratt to fix a bathroom in a dorm at the International School."

Mitchell pictured them, bouncing along in Gramp's jeep headed for Brattleboro, sharing a bag of Gram's sweet rolls, laughing, and he felt a stab of jealousy.

"Yeah," Jamie said, "it was pretty funny. Gramp and I were down there in Bratt working in one of the dorm bathrooms, got the toilet all torn up. And this Indian girl comes in holding a toothbrush. She's pretty dark and foreign looking, dressed up in this sari-thing, and she gets all flustered when she sees us. 'Beg your pah-don,' she says, in this perfect British accent, 'so sorry.' Gramp looks her over and says to me real loud, 'Jamie boy, tell her we only speak English.'"

Mitchell barked with laughter. "Ha! Perfect Grampy. Deaf as a post. The old bugger."

"He's a beaut," Jamie said.

Mitchell glanced over at Jamie and saw the look of affection on his cousin's face. Jamie would always love Gramp more than anyone; Gramp would always prefer Jamie. A mean desire to disrupt that happy picture rose in his gut. He said, "Jeez, that old bastard burns me. Looking down his nose at us all the time. I can't wait 'til he kicks off."

Jamie shook his head disgustedly. "Gramp never did anything to you but buy you poles and take you fishing."

Mitchell's cheeks flushed. He couldn't talk to Jamie about Gramp. He couldn't make him see that it was Gramp's fault that Dad couldn't keep a job or finish building their house. And now Gramp had driven a wedge between him and Jamie.

Mitchell escaped outside to piss. There were fireflies in the clearing, looping around the tall grass, crazy love-struck things, blinking off and on searching for each other. Watching them, he felt so lonely he wanted to put his head down and bawl.

"You can sleep here tonight," Jamie offered when Mitchell came back in. He wasn't one to hold a grudge.

"Nah." Mitchell figured he'd already ruined everything, and anyway, he could see Jamie yawning. In minutes he'd be dead asleep. Jamie was a great sleeper.

Mitchell felt his way back down the road in the dark. All the lights were off in both houses, Gramp's and theirs. Behind him in the pen, Sally's buckskin stamped and snorted softly. Mitchell considered flinging a rock across the street at Gramp's house to disturb its perfect exterior. Because even though it was Dad he hated, it was Dad he loved, and somehow the skinny old man had conspired with Mom to reduce him.

No. It had to be all Gramp's fault. Mom was too sick to blame.

Mitchell stopped at the sight of Gramp's jeep sitting there in the driveway next to Gram's Ford. He checked—keys in the ignition. He opened the door slowly, trying to keep it from creaking, then got in, eased off the parking brake, and let in the clutch so it rolled silently back down the hill.

At the bottom he cranked her up and slid into first, hit the gas, and took off, thundering through the dark of the hollow, past the ghostly shapes of the Holstein herd that belonged to the Boys' Home. The gas gauge read ¼ tank. Bouncing over the washboards on the dirt road, something eased up in his chest. He turned onto Route 5 and pushed her up to fifty, about as fast as the old rust bucket would go. Summer air whipped by the windows. He wished he had a tape deck, or even a radio, instead of the deafening bounce of pipe wrenches in the back. He hummed, and imagined accompanying himself with flashing glissades on the guitar, the strings biting into his fingers.

If he practiced he could be really good. He had perfect pitch. Mom had tested him when he was eight. He imagined himself sitting in a spotlight on a club stage. Girls in the audience would want his phone number, and Dad, leaning back in his chair with a beer, would announce proudly, "That's my son." Music was the one thing Dad still loved. He used to sing all the time back in Masonville, while Mom played the piano. But now that they lived in Shelby, Mom only played after school, before Dad got home. And since she'd gotten sick she hardly played at all.

Mitchell turned onto Interstate 91 and started north. He saluted when a trooper passed him. Nerves of steel. Ha! Good thing the taillights worked.

He exited at Windsor, and cruised the back roads where Gram's folks had lived before they lost their farm. A moon had risen. The white clapboard houses sailed the hillsides like ships, visible in glimpses between the fenceline maples. Most of them weren't farms anymore; they were summer houses for rich people from New York and Boston.

Something about the dark night and the moon reminded him of car rides as a kid when they went back to visit Dad's folks in Masonville. Marsha always positioned herself up front between Mom and Dad; Sally, Donna, and Nancy shared the back seat, and Mitchell stretched out in the wayback, pretending he was riding a motorcycle beside the car, jumping culverts and ditches. When it rained, he staged races between the raindrops on the window. On clear nights, he could never figure out how the moon knew enough to follow them wherever they went, no matter how many turns they took. When they passed houses in the night he was awed by the mystery of their lit windows: people having their own arguments over dinner, other kids hiding in their rooms. It was unimaginable that so many people would never know him. An incomprehensible riddle, like trying to conceive of infinity, or trying to picture what was beyond the edge of the universe.

Mitchell pulled back onto the highway and headed south down 91. He could hook over into New Hampshire and head on up to Maine, stand on a coast and feel nothing but openness spread before him. He'd get a job in a boat yard, on a boat. But when he looked down the gas gauge was dipping and he didn't have a penny in his pocket, so he had to turn around.

Mitchell parked the jeep, the gas tank empty, in Gramp's driveway, not even caring if anyone heard. It was already light out, and Mitchell was beat. He walked down Route 5 headed for work, which wouldn't start for another three hours. No cars passed. He finally sneaked into a barn and slept stretched out on some scratchy hay bales. He woke fast, thinking he was already late from the sound of the cars going by. He had a sudden urge to do something mean and low, like lighting the hay barn, but he didn't have any matches.

He got picked up by a guy in a business suit headed for Brattle-boro, who wanted to know if Mitchell had any grass to sell. After Mitchell said no, they rode in silence.

When he arrived, it was time to feed the animals at Santa's Workshop. Hugo was there already, holding Charley on his chain, taking him for his morning constitutional. Hugo beckoned Mitchell over to shake the chimp's hand.

"Got into something didn't you?" Hugo said.

Mitchell looked at him, puzzled, and then reached up to touch the sore spot on his cheek where Dad had struck him. It must have left a mark.

"Girlfriend got me with her elbow while I was going down on her," he said, full of shit. He'd never gone down on anybody, and didn't want to. But it was fun to see Hugo look pained. Hugo didn't like rough language. He was smoking a cigar while wearing his clown suit, but Chessworth wasn't there yet so it didn't matter. Hugo cut a ridiculous figure—his patchwork overalls ballooning, crazy red hair around his head, a white greasepaint face, and an orange smile with a stogie sticking out of it.

Charley, his glossy black fur reflecting the morning light, reached out his palm solemnly. Mitchell grasped it. The chimp sniffed at him and squeezed hard, too hard. Alarmed, Mitchell pulled his hand back, but the chimp hung on. A crazy tug of war ensued, with Mitchell's hand yanked between them.

"C'mon, Charley," Hugo said. "Let go. He's got a crush on you Mitch," the clown added, trying to make a joke.

Then something happened to Charley's face. The rubbery globe of his upper lip lifted into a grimace, yellow teeth bared, stinking chimp breath billowing. He screeched and began pounding on Mitchell, hitting him hard, in the face, in the ribs, with his powerful arms. Mitchell couldn't even fight back, he was so shocked. He just tried to roll into a ball so that the blows would land on his back.

Hugo screamed, "Charley, No! No! Charley!" hauling him back by the chain, and Mitchell rolled away. Hugo looped the chain around a water spigot and everyone—Mitchell, Hugo, the chimp—just stood there breathing hard.

"God Mitch, I'm sorry," Hugo kept saying, gasping for breath. "He's never done anything like that." Mitchell was scared for the fat old clown, afraid he was going to have a heart attack right there. He just nodded, backing away until he was around the corner of the hay barn. He sat on a bale with his head between his knees, feeling the ache in his ribs, imagining the rising black bags under his eyes.

He couldn't figure it out. How come Charley had gone after him when he hadn't done anything but bring him bananas and slop? It wasn't fair. None of it was fair. But of course fairness didn't matter. It had nothing to do with what you'd done; you just got your beating.

Hunched over, guarding his soreness, Mitchell started shaping the story for Jamie. It was a beauty. How many guys could say they'd been beat up by an ape? He'd been monkey-mangled. Chimp-handled. Jamie would bust a gut. A fucking monkey. Queasy laughter spurted out of Mitchell's mouth like a belch.

He looked up. He saw Billy Barrow approaching, ready to razz him about it being his turn to face the camel, unaware of what had just happened. Mitchell decided he wasn't going to go into that camel pen and risk himself again, not today or any other day. He stood, still laughing, still shaky, and headed down the driveway, ignoring Billy Barrow's open mouth.

The first tourists were pulling into the parking lot, unloading strollers and warning their kids about what they'd get if they didn't behave. Mitchell kept walking, head down, hunched over his aching ribs. Out of the corner of his eye he saw Chessworth climbing out of his green Lincoln, patting long strands of hair over his bald patch. Chessworth spotted him, called out in annoyance, "Hey, Mitchell! Mitch, where do you think you're going?"

Mitchell kept walking. He heard Chessworth's car door slam. When he got to Route 5, Mitchell stopped. The day's heat was already building. Crickets chirped in the tall grass. He crossed the street, stood there. Home pulled at him like a comforting sickness, like lying in bed under the covers with the flu. When he shook his head to break free, little tracers of pain streaked his vision. The road stretched north and south, its possibilities endless. Too bad—Jamie wouldn't get to hear about this one after all. Mitchell stuck his thumb out, headed for Maine.

VOID

[Donna, 1974]

CLAUDE WOULDN'T DANCE. He shuffled self-consciously, swaying vaguely to the music, leaning heavily on Donna during a slow song. When someone put on Peter Frampton, Claude retreated to the torn vinyl couch to sit with a beer between his big knees. It didn't matter, because Donna knew he was watching her. She loved being watched: it made her feel more real.

In Sally's rented trailer, on a hot August evening, Donna whirled and shimmied. She raised her shirt, tucking it under her bra so the fan would blow cool air on her wet belly. She could feel the eyes of the boys on her. Dopey Rusty Eberhardt (called Ever-hard because of his hopeless passion for Sally) swiveled his hips to match Donna's gyrations and shouted "Take it off!" Eddie, Marsha's short, muscular boyfriend, raised his umpteenth beer and hooted. Once again, Eddie had snuck away from disapproving Marsha to join them in the party trailer.

The party trailer was a rusting turquoise mobile home down by the tracks on the Shelby/Bellows Falls line. After graduating in June, Sally and her friend Lisa had moved in and split the $90 rent. Sally waitressed at the Saxton's River Inn, going for the big tips, while Lisa cooked at the Boys' Home and brought home stolen food from the kitchen. The trailer, heaped with empties and greasy pizza boxes, and furnished with castoffs from the dump, was always hopping. Best of all, Sally's tiny back bedroom was available for Donna and Claude.

In a break between songs, Donna stood panting, wiping the sweat from her forehead. Plump, sunburned Lisa was trying to snuggle up close to Rusty on the couch. Sally and their cousin Jamie hunkered over the record player. They were all drunk or stoned, all of them except for Donna. She didn't need to be drunk to feel loose. She didn't even care that much for the taste of beer. It was enough to be dancing, to know what would come later when she and Claude slipped into the bedroom. For ten months they'd been doing it in the tenant house at his parents' farm, or up at the beaver ponds, or in the truck. The party trailer made everything easier, almost safe.

The music started up again. Donna threw her hands over her head, tossed her damp hair, wriggled her bare belly, wiggled her butt. Across the room, half-embarrassed, half-proud, Claude leaned back against the couch, watching. She knew he was aroused.

"Take it off!" Rusty shouted.

Donna ran her hands over her body, pantomiming a strip-tease. She'd do it for real if she felt like it—lift her shirt over her head and give them a thrill. It gratified her to know she could pull Rusty Eberhardt away from his passion for Sally, away from Lisa's doughy, desperate hands. She could force away the eyes of her shy cousin Jamie, fill him with shame. She could even steal Marsha's Eddie. She was sure of her power; it ran through her like a pulsating current, her own bright force. She was fifteen and she could make any boy want her, but she wouldn't go out with any of them, because there would never be anyone else for her but Claude.

When the music stopped, Donna flopped on Claude's lap, pressing her wet forehead to his cheek, relishing his soft groan as he clasped her close.

From inside Sally's minuscule bedroom the music sounded muffled. Out in the living room, voices rose in argument, then broke to laughter. Claude moved above her in the tiny, stale room. Outside the open window fireflies swooped. The humidity pressed like a weight on her chest, as close as the sweat on her skin, as close as Claude. Donna thought she might meld with it all and be the sound of crickets, the dull windup of trucks on Interstate 91, the evening Amtrak heading for Montreal. She felt a strange vertigo, a fear that the pieces of her might split apart and fly through the screen out the open window, to be sucked into the hot August night. "Claude," she whispered, "Claude," begging him to keep her from disappearing.

Claude pressed his lips on hers, mistaking her urgency for passion. Donna wrapped her arms around his back, clinging hard, willing to let fear and passion be confused. Eventually it didn't matter, nothing mattered but the blurring between her and Claude and then the opening, the hot red surge.

Donna hurried up Gramp's road in the dark with the feel of Claude's hands on her skin like an echo, reverberating. She knew Claude was waiting at the bottom of the road, unwilling to leave while he could still hear her footsteps hurrying away from him. She shivered with pleasure at the memory of him suspended above her. She never used to understand her father's drinking, or Mitchell and Jamie with their dope, but now she knew what it meant to need something over and over again.

She was in front of the house and it was time to be careful and quiet. The lights were off across the street at Gram and Gramp's, and only a dim bedroom light issued from the back of her own house. Donna opened the screen door by infinite increments, willing it not to squeak, then turned the knob on the wooden door slowly, slowly. The cats meowed and rubbed against her. Donna pressed the door shut and breathed relief.

"Donna? Is that you?"

She froze at her mother's whisper.

"Yeah," she whispered back, attempting to judge the anger there. But Mom's low voice only meant she didn't want to wake

Dad, didn't want trouble. Although Donna's eyes were adjusted to the dark, she didn't see her mother at first. Then she picked her out seated at the piano, hands spread over the closed cover.

"What are you doing out so late?" her mother began.

"What are you doing up, Mom? You don't have to worry about me."

"How can I sleep knowing you're out God knows where?"

"You never stayed up for Mitchell." They both knew it was a weak argument—her mother hadn't stayed up for Mitchell, and it had been almost a month since he'd disappeared. Only Sally had received a postcard featuring a lobster, with no return address. It was a sore subject, one she shouldn't have raised. Guilt swelled in Donna's chest. Her mother was ill. She had only finished her latest chemotherapy two months ago. "I was just over at Sally's." Donna forced a casual tone.

Mom sighed. "Was Claude there?"

"Yeah. So?" Donna's voice rose. "Lots of people were there."

"Shhh. You'll wake your father," Mom warned.

Donna went to the refrigerator, studied its contents in the small interior light. She reached for an apple. Dreamy again at the memory of Claude's lips on her belly, she raised the fruit to her mouth and bit into it with a sharp crunch.

"Those aren't washed yet," her mother hissed. "There's poison on them. Rinse it off."

Donna shrugged and ran the water for her mother's benefit. Mom always worried about everything, and more so since the cancer. "Go to bed, Mom," Donna counseled, nibbling on her apple.

Her mother got up from the piano and walked into the kitchen, leaning her bony frame against the refrigerator. "I'm serious, Donna. Your father and I are very concerned about how much time you spend with Claude."

Donna put her hands over her ears. "I don't want to hear this," she said.

"Please," Mom begged. "Listen to me. I was young once too."

Donna blocked her mother's words, her own growing dread. Her mother had never been young.

"I just don't want you to ruin your life," Mom said.

Donna had to bite her tongue to keep from saying: You mean like you did? At least she loved Claude. She couldn't imagine anyone ever loving her father.

Mom sucked in breath, released it. "We've decided to limit how much you can see him."

Donna threw her half-eaten apple on the floor. "You can't stop me! You're just jealous. You don't even know what love is!"

Her mother's slap whooshed the air out of Donna's lungs.

Donna raised her hand to her cheek, glared. Her mother had never hit her before. "I hate you," Donna said.

From the bedroom her father mumbled, "What the hell . . . ?"

Donna leaned close to her mother's pale, shadowed face, coldly observed the tears forming there. "You can't stop me," she challenged. "Claude's the only thing I care about. I'll kill myself if you try to stop me." She whirled and ran down the hall. In front of the bathroom—she must have been standing there listening—Marsha grabbed Donna and yanked her inside, closing the door. She turned the faucets, ran the water loud.

"Leave me alone." Donna jerked away from her sister's grasp.

"You're killing her," Marsha spat, all her fury at their mother's illness concentrated in her need to blame. "Don't you know that? You're killing her!"

"Mind your own business. What do you know? You don't even know where your boyfriend is right now, do you? But *I* do."

"You little bitch," Marsha said.

"Fuck you." Donna peered into the mirror where her mother's handprint marked her cheek.

"It's back," Marsha said, crossing her arms on her chest. "Not that it matters to you."

"What?" Donna splashed her burning face in the sink.

"The cancer, you selfish brat. It's in her uterus now."

For an instant the terrible words formed in Donna's mind: I

don't care. If she won't let me see Claude, I hope she dies. Immediately, the shameful thought was replaced by the enormity of her sister's statement, but the damage was done.

Punishment was swift. Donna knew but she didn't want to know. She knew but she couldn't admit it. Her period was late. That didn't have to mean anything, she wasn't really all that regular. But then there was the nausea in the morning, the faint ache in her lower spine that she couldn't ignore. What clinched it was when she threw up in the toilet at the Shelby Motel where, under-age, she chambermaided illegally four mornings a week. It was too stupid. She was just out of ninth grade and pregnant.

"We'll get married," Claude offered when she told him.

They were sitting in his pickup down by the Shelby bridge. Donna noticed a mother mallard piloting her ducklings along the riverbank. The duck must have given her offspring some special danger signal, for the lot of them suddenly revved up into high gear, paddling madly, tiny wakes streaming behind. Donna didn't know ducks could move that fast.

"We were planning to anyway," Claude continued. "So what if it's a little sooner?"

For a moment it actually seemed possible. What was the difference? They would get married eventually. Claude was making money already with the bashed-in old dump truck he'd bought, carrying loads of peastone and gravel for Cabot Construction. If they got married no one could keep them apart.

But it was only a dream. She couldn't let her mother find out she was pregnant. Her father would probably shoot Claude, and her mother would die of the shame. It would kill her—Marsha's words echoed in her head.

"It probably isn't even legal," Donna countered. "I'm only fifteen."

"Well, what should we do?" Claude laid a work-calloused hand on her neck. It felt irritatingly scratchy. "We got to figure *something* out," he said.

"We?" Donna turned on him, suddenly and unreasonably angry. "I don't think this part's about 'we' anymore."

In the end it was Marsha who made all the arrangements. She knew a girl who knew somebody who'd done it—went down to some doctor in Massachusetts and was home the same day.

They drove to Springfield in Marsha's Dodge, telling Mom they were going to shop at the Bay State Mall. Claude offered to come and Donna wanted him to, but Sally and Marsha shut him out. "You'll be glad in the end," Marsha insisted. "You don't want him to think of you like that." So Donna agreed. Everything was out of her hands now as her sisters closed ranks.

Headed south on the interstate into Massachusetts, seated between Marsha and Sally, Donna felt herself sliding away into the perfection of the landscape. The geometric precision of the long, sharp-angled tobacco barns and the broad green plains of the Connecticut River valley stretched out under big puffy white clouds. Nothing looked real. She didn't recognize her life anymore.

"It wasn't like you said," Marsha announced abruptly to Donna, talking loudly over her Dodge's bad muffler.

"What?" Donna blinked herself back into the rumbling car.

"They *did* marry for love. Mom told me all about it. She lost her job at the school in Masonville to be with him."

"Why're you talking about that now?" Sally demanded. She put a protective arm around Donna's shoulder. "She doesn't need to hear about that now."

"Well I just . . ." Marsha pursed her lips, banged the horn at a driver who cut too close.

Married for love. Donna couldn't take it in. It was always Marsha who knew everything; Marsha was Mom's favorite, her confidante. Before she got sick, Mom used to roll on the floor with

Marsha, tickling, giggling like a girl. Donna shut her eyes. Oddly, a snapshot of her father as a slim young man in army uniform rose behind her closed lids. When she opened them again, they were passing the Tri-County Fairgrounds in Northampton.

In a three-story frame building on the outskirts of Springfield, the receptionist took their cash. It looked like any ordinary waiting room, similar to the clinic in Bellows Falls where they went for their vaccinations. The same boxy couches and chairs, the same vague green landscapes on the wall. Only there were no magazines, Donna noticed. No *Highlights for Children* or *Woman's Day*.

"We'll be right here," Marsha said as the nurse led Donna through a swinging door.

"Can't you come?" Donna pleaded.

"Don't worry," the nurse said. "I'll be there with you and it'll be over in a flash." Donna wasn't reassured. The woman didn't seem very nurse-like. She was a busty bottle blonde in a too-tight dress, not even a uniform, with an ugly boil on the back of one hand and a gold chain flashing on her ankle.

The examination room was cold. When the nurse left, Donna changed into her johnny gown and then hopped up on the papered table as instructed. She could hear someone crying in another room. The door opened and the doctor came in. He was tall and tanned and bald.

"Assume the position. It's one you ought to be familiar with." He winked conspiratorially.

Donna didn't know what he meant. She'd never been to a gynecologist before.

"Put your feet up," the doctor ordered impatiently, jamming her bare feet into the metal stirrups. Donna's stomach clenched. Over her head someone had tacked a poster of a cat clinging to a branch: Hang In There! it said. The nurse with the boil came back into the room.

The doctor took a metal clamp from a tray and thrust it inside her. Donna nearly shot off the table.

"It's just a speculum," he said. "Lie back down."

When she was clamped open, a phone rang. The doctor rolled his chair away and answered.

"Yeah. Yeah. Okay. Sell them, I told you Morty, get rid of them fast." The doctor slammed down the receiver, rolled back.

Donna stared up at the stupid poster. Her breath came in quick gasps. He'd touched the phone with his gloved hands. The nurse with the boil had probably touched it too. Now he was putting his dirty gloves inside her.

"This'll sting but it'll make you go numb," the doctor intoned.

Donna squeezed her eyes shut against the needle. Claude, she thought, please, Claude.

"You'll feel a little discomfort now," the doctor said.

It wasn't discomfort, it was horrible cramping pain. The nurse gave Donna her hand but Donna didn't want to touch her. Instead she dug her fingers into her palms, trying not to scream. A machine clicked on, whirring. A vacuum cleaner inside her, sucking it all away. The whirring stopped. Almost as soon as it began it was over.

"Can I see it?" Donna asked, propping herself on her elbows, straining to see the tray the nurse whisked away.

The doctor snapped off his rubber gloves. "There's nothing to see. It's just a clot of blood."

Claude's baby. Just a clot of blood. Claude's baby. Just a clot of blood. Claude. Clot. The words jangled in her head.

"It's all taken care of," the doctor said over his shoulder. "Lie there a few minutes and we'll get you out of here. No funny business with your boyfriend for two weeks. Vicky, get her a pad."

The nurse swished out of the room. Donna lay still, her bare knees in the air, her feet still in the stirrups. It was over. She'd thought being pregnant was her punishment, but now she knew that her punishment was not just the baby's intrusion, but its loss. A clot of blood. What had it looked like? She tried to picture her baby, but instead an image rose of her mother's body, its severed parts: they'd taken one breast, then another, and soon the very insides that made her a woman were to be sucked out, just as Donna's insides had been.

In the baby's place, an emptiness now bloomed inside her—an enormous, echoing void. Slowly, Donna lowered her feet from the stirrups, rolled on her side, and curled into a ball. The cramping had started again, a sickening throb that she believed would last forever.

AN ENCYCLOPEDIA
OF THE NATURAL
WORLD

[Jamie, 1969–1976]

WHEN JAMIE WAS expelled from high school for putting his history teacher in a headlock, Ma cried and Pop entered him into the apprentice steelworker program. The union pay was absurdly high. Jamie walked the beams amid the hiss of the ingots and the flare of blue gas jets. He would be the third Milligan steelworker, the only one of the kids to make Pop proud. He walked the bridge, and the water swirling below made him dizzy. It wasn't that he was afraid. He loved heights—all that training on the trestle playing hooky, walking backward on the rails. But he didn't want to be a steelworker, didn't want his life laid out in beams, shaped by harsh geometry, enclosed.

Jamie drove his father to and from work. No matter what Pop drank the night before, he was always sober on the job. The days weren't bad. Jamie admired Pop's control with the welding torch, his insistence on doing a job right. For the first time they chatted, Pop going on about his high school days back in North Walpole, when he'd been head of the drama club, or his own father's bar-room exploits. He told how as a young man Grampy Milligan dove off a bridge through a hole in the ice, trying to save a water boy who'd slipped.

Jamie was happy enough to let Pop talk. But as soon as work was done and they stopped at the package store to buy Pop's nightly six-pack and pint of whiskey, the day turned sour. Holding aloft the bottle in the car, Pop said, "I know this is my drug just like you got your drugs. It's the same thing." He slammed his beers and whiskey so hard he was sloppy drunk before they made it home. Teary-eyed, Pop said he'd never be the man his father was, he wasn't fit to lick Grampa Milligan's brawling Irish boots.

Jamie squinted at the BMW in front of their bumper, its chrome dazzling. He didn't have words anymore. All the words choked off inside him, blurred into mumbling lights. A glaze at the side of his eyes. He could see it as clear as though it was happening: a slip on the bridge. His own free fall through the air. The next job was going to be a nuclear power plant in Connecticut. He didn't want to do it even if Pop was proud. His hands shook in the morning like some old wino, although he never drank. At night he lay in bed trembling. He'd have to go out into the woods then, to breathe.

At home, smelling of beer and whiskey, Pop stood behind Jamie and massaged his shoulders. Jamie shrank from his touch. It made him uneasy the way Pop always bragged on him, as though the rest of the kids didn't count.

"You're a good-looking boy, Jamie. You got a beautiful body. God made you beautiful in his image. I look at you and it makes me proud that you're my son. Now let me give you some advice. Don't let any of the girls get you doing stuff you'd be ashamed of. Now I saw you fooling around with that Miller girl . . ."

"I wasn't fooling around," Jamie cut in. "We were just talking."

"It starts with talking. Now first off, that girl's too young. And all she's got going for her is that round little behind, but she isn't a girl for you Jamie. She isn't a nice girl. A clean girl. You don't want to mess around with that."

"Jesus Dad, will you forget it?"

"Now don't go taking the Lord's name."

"Sheesh."

Pop's hands moved on Jamie's shoulders again, then down to caress his chest. "Now look at that chest of yours, son. A beautiful body."

Jamie got up, pushing his father's hands away in shame.

In the kitchen, Ma beat cake batter in a bowl with a wooden spoon. Pop leaned into the refrigerator for another beer.

"What are you doing to him, Jake?" Ma asked.

Jamie paused at the bottom of the staircase. It wasn't like Ma to interfere.

Pop snapped the top on his beer. "What are you talking about?"

"He's got to grow up, you know. Sometimes it seems you'd rather have a priest than a boy."

Pop slammed the counter. "Oh, so that's it, is it? When we got married you agreed to raise the kids in the Church. And now I see you've held it against me all along."

"You know that's not true, Jake. It's not about the Church."

"The hell it isn't. Just like your high and mighty father. Didn't want you to marry an Irish Catholic bum!"

"Jake!" Jamie's mother exclaimed, and then she was crying. "You promised. You promised you'd never tell."

Pop made the refrigerator door rattle as he grabbed another beer and slammed out of the kitchen.

"Gramp doesn't like us 'cause we're Cath-licks." Eileen sneered between the railings of the stairs. Jamie cracked her in the face and her nose popped bright with blood. "Mo-om," she screamed. "Mo-om!"

Late at night, Jamie lay awake listening as Pop stumbled up the stairs and into Eileen's bedroom. "Who is it? Who is it?" Eileen mumbled in her sleep. Jamie lay in his bunk beneath Frank, heart pounding, listening to the muffled sound of his father's voice, and Eileen's frightened, "I'm sleeping, Pop. Go to bed." He only breathed again when he heard Pop stumble back into the hall.

Down on the trestle they smoked joints and threw the stubby roaches into the water. It made Jamie paranoid, the giggles riding just above a train of hysteria, like the rumbling on the rails before the freight appeared. He preferred acid, the glittering and pulsating patterns it gave everyday objects. A serving of spaghetti coiling on his plate at supper like a nest of pale snakes. The kaleidoscope in his mother's eyeglasses.

At night they slid up to darkened houses in Eddie Bickell's Firebird with the crunched fender, Eddie light on the gas to keep the muffler from rattling. The first time Jamie just sat in the car, and then he was in there with them, going through people's things. Once they even did it with the old couple snoring away in the bedroom. There was a breathing thrill to a darkened house, to taping the window pane with wide grey duct tape, knocking it out with a quick thump, reaching in to unlock it. Then the feel of what didn't belong to him under his fingers: silverware, jewelry, women's clothes. Jamie didn't want any of the stuff, but he brought it home: a service automatic, coins, religious medals, decorative swords.

"Where'd you get this stuff?" Pop asked, fingering the collection on Jamie's bookshelf.

"Nowhere. I'm just borrowing it from a friend."

Pop shrugged and left the room.

Jamie stole a car in broad daylight from a convenience store lot and drove it twenty miles before abandoning it on the side of the road. He drove into Springfield to buy heroin for Cory Sipio's brother. Joey Sipio had been to Nam; Jamie wanted him to like him. He bought the smack, according to directions, from a skinny whore with a cockeyed black wig who worked near the old train station. "Anything else you want, baby?" she asked. "Anything else?" Her laughter mocking as he backed away.

Joey Sipio sat on a sagging cot. "Hold my arm, Jamie, hold my arm," Joey said, making Jamie's hands squeeze on his biceps to push up the vein when he stuck in the needle.

They broke into an abandoned house that looked as though the owners had been abducted by aliens. Dirty plates and silverware still lay on the dining room table. When they found nothing of value, Cory and Eddie began to trash the house, breaking chairs, toppling bureaus. Cory came downstairs with a long braid of silvery hair tied with a ribbon—someone's memento. When Eddie poured catsup over it, Jamie went outside to heave. He knew he was done with something.

He woke in the middle of the night sweaty, his heart pounding. He took out the stolen objects, the coins, the gun, hid them in the back of his closet, then took them out again. He dressed and went outside, buried them behind the house. Then he went into the woods and cut down the dope he'd been growing. Back in the house he listened to his parents breathing. His father snoring downstairs on the couch. His mother in bed. His own room closing in, closing in. He was suffocating. Jamie grabbed a blanket and went out and slept in the woods by the trestle. He didn't know where he was going, only that when the car he hitched a ride in slid past the familiar Shelby exit, he had to get out. He arrived at Ma's parents' house before seven. Gram Hunter was serving breakfast: sausage, eggs, fried potatoes, and gravy. The odors made Jamie swoon.

"Well look who's here! Look who's here!" Gramp shouted, deafer than ever. A clown's smile pulled up the droopy lines of his lean face. He burped loud: "B-o-wwwww."

"Horace!" Gram exclaimed.

"Eleanor, you got some breakfast for the boy?"

Jamie rolled his head from side to side to ease the crimp in his shoulders. "I was wondering if I could stay here for a while."

"That'd be fine! That'd be fine!" Gramp yelled. " 'Course you'll need to go buy yourself a fishing license."

"I hardly slept at all last night," Gram complained, filling a plate for Jamie. "Horace kept bumping me with his elbow."

"What makes you think it was my elbow?" Gramp leered. He got up and stumped across the room. He had a crooked leg, twisted out from the knee, the result of jumping over barrels in a competition as a boy, and a glass eye too; he'd lost the real one in a boiler explosion. He always had a scab on his forehead from banging his head on pipes. Gramp was a plumber, a town boy from Bellows Falls who had dreamed of farming, while the farmers dreamed of selling out. Gramp had bought the hundred acres in Shelby in the forties. When the Hectorville train depot went out of service, he bought that too, dismantled it, and reassembled it on his hill, slate roof and all. First it served as his hunting camp, then as home for Gramp, Gram, Ma, and her sisters Anne and Marty. Now it was just the two of them: Gramp sugared the maples and planted a garden so big that Gram spent half the season canning.

Gram was a farm girl born near Windsor. She was as thick in the hips and legs as Gramp was wiry and thin. Jamie had seen where she grew up: a big green clapboard house with three chimneys standing on a slim triangle of bottomland cut off by Interstate 91. The only story she told about her girlhood was of the day the hired man came in to report that her father had hung himself in the barn.

When Gramp left on a plumbing job and Gram was washing the breakfast dishes, Jamie headed for the woods. Across the street Uncle Lowell's family lived in the capped foundation of an unfinished house. Mitchell and the girls were at school already. Jamie walked up the dirt road that separated Uncle Lowell's and Gramp's houses. An eighth of a mile uphill the road gave way to a rough logging track lined with brush. Where the maples had been thinned to improve the sugarbush, a thick carpet of ferns covered the earth. Light filtered through the canopy in splashes. Jamie squinted and kept walking, although his breath rasped in his throat and his muscles felt weak. He passed the sugarhouse. Pop would already be at work. Jamie shook his shaggy curls to force the thought of Pop's disappointment from his head.

He kept walking, over crumbling stone walls, scrambling up steep ledge, mossy and damp with rivulets, then through pine with the hot smell of needles baking, and into the sun beyond Gramp's land. Blackberry brambles scraped his wrists as he climbed a ditch and entered the orderliness of apple trees in their rows. Out in the full sun a terrible lethargy pulled him down. He curled up under the split trunk of an apple tree and slept.

Waking, Jamie knew immediately he was being watched: two whitetail does stood just beyond him, sniffing his sneakered feet. Jamie held his breath. The does lingered, their gentle eyes showing nothing more than mild curiosity as they whuffled leathery black noses, absorbing his scent. When they wandered off, stiff-legged, unalarmed, Jamie could have cried in gratitude. He took it as a blessing.

When Gramp got home, the jeep rattling into the driveway, Jamie couldn't help listening carefully to how he parked. His father always hit the accelerator before turning off the ignition; he said a little gas in the carburetor made the car easier to start in the morning. If he wasn't too far gone he only revved it once. When he was really drunk, though, he banged into the scarred maple by the corner of the garage and revved the engine wildly, over and over, a futile roar that made Jamie cringe. But Gramp just shut off the engine.

That afternoon Jamie drove Gramp into the woods in the rusty jeep, driving up old logging paths so steep they nearly tipped over. "Whoa, Nellie Bell," Gramp said, slapping the Jeep's door with pleasure. Gramp pointed out the trees he would tap and those he was giving a rest; he lectured on the merits of thinning the sugarbush. Jamie felt his eyes refusing to focus, a whir in his head. Gramp didn't say anything when Jamie stopped the rumbling jeep, backed around, and headed down toward the house.

Behind Gramp's house lay an enormous pile of butt logs that needed splitting for the sugaring arch. Many of them were knotty and as big as three feet across. Gramp lifted the splitting maul as if in slow motion, over his head and down. The log cracked. Gramp set a wedge, lifted again, so slowly it seemed to Jamie that the maul suspended over Gramp's head just might fall backward. Smiling at Gramp's pace, Jamie lifted high and snapped his maul down hard. The thick blade bounced off the stump. He lifted again; this time the log split halfway, exposing pale heartwood. Two hours later Gramp was still going, slow and sure, the pile of split logs scattered about him, and Jamie hurt in every muscle.

Gram set out seven different kinds of homemade jam with supper. Jamie ate fifteen oatmeal raisin cookies and several glasses of milk. He watched "Sanford and Son" on TV with Gramp. Gramp threw his head back, roared at Redd Foxx. It was his favorite program.

"I don't know how you can enjoy that nasty show about that dirty old man," Gram fussed as she fitted Gramp's shirt over the point of the ironing board. Gramp just snickered.

Jamie climbed the stairs to the big open room over the garage that housed Gramp's bell collection. Gramp kept the glass bells downstairs on a shelf by the fireplace, but the kids were always allowed to ring any of the bells upstairs. Alone in the room, Jamie fingered the dust on farm bells, railroad bells, elephant bells, camel bells, cowbells, a church bell with a missing clapper, school bells, even a jade bell from Thailand. "I've traveled the world with them," Gramp said of his bells, and when he was little Jamie imagined his grandfather coursing waves on a steamer ship and galumphing across deserts on a camel. Ma said the furthest Gramp had ever been was down to Boston with Gram to see the opera.

On a trunk in the bell room, Jamie found the *Encyclopedia of the Natural World* that he and Gramp had pored over when Jamie was nine, studying raccoons, and a book of pressed leaves that Gramp and his mother had made when Ma was little. Each leaf was labeled in a child's hand: alder, red maple, sugar maple, birch, poplar, oak. He turned the pages gently, careful not to break the crumbling leaves. That night he dreamed of Gramp and Ma walking through woods knee-deep in crisp leaves, Gramp—old as he was now, although Ma was only a little girl in the dream—pointing up toward the trees. A heron flew up and the trees overhead turned into a river.

Jamie slept fifteen hours and nobody woke him. He lay in bed in midday light, remembering a fishing trip when he was ten: At dusk they had drifted down the Connecticut River. Gramp sat in the stern of the rowboat. Jamie shared a seat in the middle with his cousin Mitchell, whose sturdy knees were twice as thick as Jamie's bony knobs. All three lines trailed behind the boat. Occasionally, Mitchell whipped his line over Jamie's head and grinned when Jamie ducked to miss the hook.

Jamie trailed a finger in the warm river; water gliders sped away on their skinny pontoons. He imagined setting up camp along the riverbank, where the silt gathered in a smooth trackless mud. He could sneak in under overhanging branches, watch the water sliding past, hide from everyone, and in the morning swim when the mist was still on the river. He'd live like Daniel Boone in the TV show, trapping muskrats and squirrels. All he needed was his pocketknife and fishing rod, his Cub Scout sleeping bag.

"See that?" Gramp asked, pointing his pole downriver.

A great blue heron flapped up from the opposite shore trailing long, hinged legs. Silently, they watched its low flight until it merged with the dusk.

"He's going home to bed, boys. Guess we ought to call it a night."

"But we haven't caught anything," Mitchell protested.

Jamie didn't believe there was much to catch in the Connecticut River. It was enough for him, drifting in a boat with Gramp.

When they tried to reel in, they discovered that all three lines had become twisted together.

"You're gonna have to cut them," Mitchell said, gleeful at any kind of destruction.

"Now don't be so hasty," Gramp advised. "Row us over into that eddy there." Jamie and Mitchell, an oar apiece, pulled the boat into the quiet circular current behind a fallen river maple. Gramp hauled the balled-up lines into his lap and set about slowly untangling them. Starlings twittered noisily as they settled in the branches. Dusk gave way to near-dark. Unseen animals rustled in the undergrowth along the banks. Jamie and Mitchell slapped at mosquitoes. Gramp didn't seem to notice the horde of bugs spotting his bald head as he bent to his task.

"Hey!" Mitchell said. "D'you see that?"

"What?" But then Jamie heard the splash and saw the ripples. And again. A big bass leapt to the surface, fell back into the water. Another rose, then another. The water was alive with feeding fish. Something was hatching, scattering feed across the river. All around them fish rose to the surface, jaws agape, splashing and slapping. Jamie and Mitchell sat open-mouthed, hushed, in the midst of the roiling frenzy, while Gramp's slow fingers carefully eased the knots.

"We got work to do," Gramp said every morning.

Jamie called him The Man of a Thousand Projects. He was seventy-one and still working as a plumber, but there was always other work to be done. Rototilling. Cutting pine slash and butt logs for the sugarhouse. Maple, oak, and cherry for the wood-stove. Window sashes to paint, windows to reglaze. Brush to clear in the woods, apple trees to prune to attract deer. Jamie bent his back to the work.

They drove over country roads with the deafening clatter of Gramp's tools in the back of the jeep. On the job with Gramp he sweated joints, first shining the corrosion off the copper pipes before brushing on the acid flux, then heating the pipes with a propane torch to draw the solder into the joints. There was relief in the simple, demanding task, a miniaturized version of the hiss and flash of his father's steel bridges.

They drove up to Chester to work on a stone house with a clogged bathroom sink. Like most of Gramp's lady clients, this one was well past middle age, a rounded woman with neatly set curls, rouged cheeks, and a matching grey wool sweater and skirt. Large pearls edged the top of her apron. Jamie and Gramp fol-lowed her into the kitchen, where the table had been set with floral placemats, two plates, two cups, and a sugar-glazed pecan coffee cake. Out in the truck their paper lunch sack held a pile of Gram's sweet rolls.

"This is my grandson, Jamie," Gramp said. "Jamie, this is Mrs. Bates."

Widow Bates, he'd called her, on the drive up.

Mrs. Bates fluttered after a third cup and plate from the cup-board and added them to her tableau. She stood against the counter, smoothing her apron over her big breasts.

"Looks dandy. We'll do our work first, Muriel," Gramp said.

Jamie went out to the jeep for the tools. In the bathroom

Gramp kneeled down creakily, his bad leg swung out at an angle. He carefully set a piece of glass behind the opened pipe, so that when the acid went through it wouldn't splash the wainscoting. He covered the linoleum with a tarp. "No sense in making a mess," he said. When the job was done, and Gramp had drunk his coffee and nibbled his cake, Mrs. Bates asked Gramp if he'd mind fixing a shutter that was flapping in the wind. She'd do it herself, she said, only her vertigo made her scared.

"I'll do it," Jamie offered.

"Horace is a very capable man," Mrs. Bates said curtly, as though Jamie had doubted Gramp's prowess.

He sat at the kitchen table eating a second, then a third piece of coffee cake; he chased a stray pecan around his icing-glazed plate. Through the window Mrs. Bates stood at the bottom of the ladder, as if to hold it steady. When Gramp came down Jamie saw, or thought he saw, Mrs. Bates reach up to touch Gramp's cheek. Gramp paused for a moment, and then he was lifting the ladder and Mrs. Bates was turning away. In the silence of the kitchen, a cuckoo clock creaked its chains and sent forth its silly message.

Gramp whistled as they drove South on route 103, back to Shelby.

"You know, Jamie, I never wanted to be a plumber. I always wanted to be an agronomist, but there was no money to send me to school. My sisters were already down at Smith College. Dad's business was going under and I had to help. You be sure you do whatever it is you want."

When Jamie went home to Holyoke to visit, Pop opened the door and slapped his face. "Why didn't you tell me you didn't want to be a steelworker?" Pop demanded. "All you had to do was tell me. You didn't have to run off like that."

Jamie stood silently in the doorway, the touch of Pop's hand imprinted on his cheek.

Gramp and Jamie spent a morning torching frozen pipes and replacing busted ones in the basement of a brick colonial in Putney while the owner's daughter practiced piano scales over their heads. The repetitious drone made Jamie sleepy. It was cold outside, bitter, with a crust on the snow and the sunlight dazzling against the brittle tree trunks. The basement was warm and Jamie sweated in his padded overalls.

Through the floorboards, a classical radio station turned up loud broke through while the pianist rested. Gramp hummed along. Then the piano student began following an intricate piece. Hesitant and soft at first, she grew louder, more certain, no longer following the radio but merging with it, matching each swoop and dash, rising with the eerie, discordant wail of violins. Gramp stopped twisting a Stilson wrench and gazed upward, spellbound. When it was over, his applause echoed in the basement. "Scriabin," he said, wielding his wrench again. "You don't know how hard that was, what she just did."

Gramp collected old pitcher pumps from junkyards and farms. Jamie helped him recondition them for the International School in Brattleboro, one of his plumbing clients. That fall, when the pumps were shipped to a project in Honduras, Gramp decided to go along. He drove a VW bug all the way from Brattleboro to Central America with two other old men, the founders of the International School, although they wouldn't let him drive too much because of his one eye. In Honduras they went from village to village, setting up wells and pumps. Gramp sent letters all along the way, describing the palm trees, the sweep of the ocean, the villagers who were still carrying water by bucket from streams. On the back of a picture postcard of Mexico City, he celebrated the beauties of Tegucigalpa. "Whoops," Gramp wrote at the bottom. "Wrong card."

The day Gramp came home, Gram bustled about the house cleaning and baking, all her enthusiasm for Gramp's return transferred to the wooden rolling pin and the dough she spread beneath it. When Gramp came through the unlocked door Gram rose from her chair, leaning forward as though to move toward him, but then only stood there.

"Eleanor, hello," Gramp said as simply as though he'd been gone three days instead of three months. "Well, well, well, look who's still here!" he exclaimed, spotting Jamie.

Jamie waited for their embrace, but Gram stood awkwardly, hands stiff at her sides, frozen in a shyness as deep as Ma's. Gramp hung his hat on its hook and reached for the pile of mail on the hall table.

"Well, Horace," said Gram. "I suppose you're hungry." She moved toward the kitchen, released from her spell.

"Supper'd be fine," Gramp said.

Uncle Lowell finished the house across the street from Gramp's and they lived upstairs now instead of in the foundation, Mitchell with his own room, and the four girls paired off by age. Marsha was his oldest cousin, the same age as Jamie. The year she graduated, the year he would have graduated, she gave him a wallet-size photo of herself—red hair ironed straight, blue eyes determined— with an inscription on the back: "I know you're a very screwed up person and I hope you get yourself together someday." Marsha hung out with Gram all the time or with Grampy's old maid sisters, while the rest of them partied up in the old sugar house in the woods.

Mitchell was growing up husky and tough, with a thatch of thick blond hair, a broad nose, and a way about him, mysterious to Jamie, that made the girls disappear into back bedrooms with him at parties. When Jamie accompanied Mitchell, he always ended up leaning against a wall, stoned, watching the swirl of bodies.

In the summers Jamie and Mitchell jumped thirty feet from the ledges into the rocky pools of the Cold River. Winters, they skied the ridge behind Gramp's land on old wooden downhill clunkers wired to their rubber boots. They packed snow for jumps and hurtled over drifted stone walls, each stunt faster and more dangerous, both unwilling to admit they were scared.

In March and April they gathered buckets of sap from Gramp's taps on snowshoe. They stayed up all night boiling, taking turns throwing pine slash and hardwood into the roaring arch. Heads ghostly in the sweet spume of steam, they laughed and scratched, made cups of tea using weak hot sap dipped from the evaporator trays, until it seemed even their pores were permeated with maple, a musky dark sweetness that rolled over and over on Jamie's tongue and filled his nose.

Sally was Jamie's favorite girl cousin. She was sweet-natured, muscular, and busty, the one with whom he took long walks, sat in the sugarhouse, and confessed his wacked-out theories: that he could hook into her dreams through his own dreams; that upstairs at Gramp's he slept on the floor in the doorway because he was living on a threshold.

"You're deep," Sally laughed. Her dream was to go away to an equestrian school in Virginia, so she was saving her money from waitressing. The girls kept horses behind the house. Jamie stood on Gramp's porch and watched Sally gallop her buckskin up the dirt road bareback, taking the corner at breakneck speed, the horse stretched low, Sally elbows out and whooping.

At night he couldn't shake the image of her breasts swelling under a torn sweater speckled with hay. His own cousin. He punished himself with hundreds of sit-ups and push-ups, straining to diminish sin with exhaustion. He used to do them at home, too. In school the girls had made him dizzy. Under his bed he'd hidden pictures ripped from magazines. He winced at the memory of the furious passion, the fear of being found out, the damp in his sheets, on his shorts. He'd thrown away his shorts rather than let his mother find them. Girls were a matter for shame: the wet mess on his leg at the first and only dance. The confusion of his sisters' whirling underwear. The breasts that filled his closed eyes. There was shame to every fluid. Shame in the thoughts he had at night in bed. Shame in the priest's stale smell through the screen at confession.

Jamie and Sally dropped acid in the sugarhouse. They sat on broken armchairs, in a room littered with mouse nests, and looked out at the falling snow. The black and white edges of everything vibrated faintly, and when Jamie gazed at Sally he thought he might get lost in the blackness of her eyes, French Canadian eyes as dark as Uncle Lowell's. They gripped each other's hands. When

Sally got up to stamp her frozen feet, Jamie hugged her. Or maybe it was she who wrapped her arms around him. He could feel his beard tickle her nose and chin. His hand slipped inside her jacket just for a moment, before he pulled away. Sally said she felt like walking. Through the sugarhouse window Jamie watched her red plaid hunting jacket slide between the blackness of the maples—a flashing pattern that repeated itself over and over on his retinas—and then just the snow falling, falling, before he got up and walked home.

He woke in the snugness of his blanket to shouting voices below: Uncle Lowell's drunken growl and Gramp's high-pitched anger. "He's screwing my daughter," Lowell ranted. "Don't tell me he ain't!"

"The boy's upstairs asleep," Gramp insisted.

"Sure, go on and protect that no-good hippie piece of shit. But I ain't gonna stand for it."

"Lowell, damn you, put that thing away. And don't you ever set foot in my house again."

The screen door slammed. Boots stomped on the porch.

"What is it?" Gram's frightened voice rang out. "Horace, what is it?"

"Trash," Gramp said. A chair scraped and then Gramp thumped back upstairs, his bad leg dragging.

Jamie hoisted himself up to the window. In weak moonlight, Lowell stumbled back across the road, boots squeaking on dry snow. A shotgun dangled over his arm. Jamie wondered where Sally was, but he knew it wouldn't matter. As always, it would be Mitchell who got the beating.

Jamie began to divide his nights between Gramp's and the sugarhouse.

"I don't know why you want to sleep in a dirty old shack," Gram complained. "You might as well stay here."

"Let him be," Gramp chided. "The boy's got to find his own way."

Jamie took the cupola off the sugarhouse, when winter came.

He was fixing the roof and didn't want to deal with leaks, so it no longer looked like a sugarhouse, but merely a cabin of rough barn boards with the tar paper still exposed on the side that backed up into ledge. He added an enormous many-paned window he bought off a lawn for fifteen bucks, an aluminum screen door, a load of insulation covered up by pine sheathing, some painted plywood overhead. He mounted the six-pound small-mouth bass he caught one lucky summer over his bed—a single bed, seven feet long, jerry rigged so that his long legs wouldn't be forever sticking over the edge. There was a big enameled kitchen sink that drained right outside, but no running water.

Jamie dipped from an open spring thirty yards from his door. A woodstove and a Coleman two-burner provided for cooking and heat. There was no electricity; kerosene dimly lit the cabin. The outhouse stood over a hole that no one ever bothered to dig very deep, since the sugar house was only meant to be used in season.

On one wall hung a blown-up photograph of Gramp pointing a skinny arm into an ocean sunset; it was taken in Honduras, the one time Gramp ventured away from home. Jamie hung two of his own drawings—cross-hatched, intricately shaded—one of a pitching pirate ship, the other a scene in which a swooping tree with writhing snake-like roots loomed in a mountainous land- scape over a buckskinned mountain man. Every branch of every pine tree on the hillsides had been drawn in. There were three old rocking chairs and a surprisingly fine Oriental rug Gram had pulled down from her attic.

When Jamie lay in his extra-long bed staring upward, the mounted bass's pink bunghole hung right over his face like a comment: he'd never have a woman, never be worthy of one.

Goofing with Mitchell in Gram's kitchen, Jamie wolfed down half a carton of ice cream straight from the box. Mitchell, who liked to eat slowly, filled a soup bowl and went in to sit down with Gram and Gramp in front of the TV.

Gram's eyes bulged at the size of Mitchell's bowl. "P-I-G Hog, that's what you are."

"But Jamie already ate . . ."

"P-I-G Hog!" Gram repeated.

Jamie hooted from the kitchen.

"You bastard." Mitchell laughed. "You get away with everything."

Mitchell stole Gramp's jeep one night and brought it back with the gas gauge on empty. Gramp stood in the yard shaking his head. "I can count on you, Jamie," he said. "You're the only one." That was the night Mitchell disappeared. He showed up two months later with a tale about a married woman who seduced him in the tacky motel room he was being paid to clean, but because it was a Mitchell story, he admitted to being so nervous he came on her leg. Mitchell moved into the sugarhouse instead of back home with Lowell, and Jamie couldn't blame him.

On a late September day, when only corn stubble remained in the fields and the clouds shifted shadows over the hills along the Connecticut River, Gramp found Jamie's crop of marijuana plants rising six feet tall in a clearing hacked out of brush. As grim as the Reaper, Gramp wielded a scythe and poured kerosene over the fallen plants. He didn't light a match, in case the smoke incriminated him or addled his mind, but even without burning they were ruined.

When Jamie discovered the destruction he ran all the way down to the house, heart pumping with outrage. He found Gramp splitting apple logs behind the barn.

"You've got no right, boy," Gramp chided, reading his face. "I don't want to ever see you grow that stuff on my land again."

An old rage rose up in Jamie's throat. In helpless fury, he picked up Gramp's axe and threw it down into the logs and shavings. It clattered against a stone. "You can't tell me what to do," he screamed.

Gramp's face mottled. "I can tell you not to abuse my damn tools."

"I'll do whatever I want, old man."

They stood facing one another, fists clenched, shoulders tensed. Then Gramp slumped, shrank. Carefully he set the axe down against the chopping block and turned toward the house.

A few days later, when Jamie was eating at the house again, although in silence, Gramp came running out of the bathroom naked, his surprisingly long penis whipping about, his hands on his throat, choking. Jamie grabbed him by the shoulders, slapped him hard on the back. White pills popped out of Gramp's throat and spewed across the hall.

"Jesus, Jamie. You saved my life boy. I tried to swallow four aspirin at once, for my arthritis, and they got stuck. You saved my life." Then Gramp looked down at his swinging nakedness and started to laugh.

A waitress friend of Sally's, Tina Overbrook, began hanging around. She was twenty-two, a year younger than Jamie, and divorced, with a three-year-old daughter Rosie. It amazed him that Tina could have amassed such a history already, when he hadn't even asked a girl out on a date.

Tina and Rosie lived in Bellows Falls, in a two-room apartment with peeling linoleum and water-stained ceilings. Jamie began to drop by her house regularly, his hands hanging at his long shanks in shyness. Each time he brought something—a boxed pizza, a chunk of quartz he'd found in the woods, or one of his drawings. He brought a sketch pad, pencils, charcoal, and a gum eraser, and sat on Tina's couch, working on intricate sketches of mountains and trees and snaking rivers, where he'd live someday.

Tina liked to talk, mostly about her ex, who'd run off with a waitress while Tina was pregnant, or about her last boyfriend, Carl, who used to drink himself into a stupor every night. Jamie just listened, intimidated by her experience in matters of love.

Tina started leaving Rosie with Jamie when she went out with

Sally. He gave the little girl a bath, marveling at how accepting she was, a tiny child offering up each arm to be scrubbed. It broke his heart that she trusted him so completely, when it would be so easy to do her damage.

Once, after he and Tina had shared a bottle of wine, he followed her into the kitchen. Tina leaned over a sink of dishes. Jamie put his arms around her, hunched over because she was so much shorter, and pressed his nose into her neck. They just stood there like that until Tina finally twisted around and kissed his lips. "You're different," she said.

The next night a storm rattled the windows and coated the roads with glare ice. When it was time for Jamie to hitch back to Gramp's, Tina said he might as well stay. She led him to her bed and they spent the night just holding each other. Jamie lay taut and erect for hours, but satisfied, amazed that he had his arms around a woman at last.

He wanted to give her everything, his life, but he had no idea how to do anything more than hang on. They were a family— Tina, Rosie, himself. It was enough for him, and for Tina too, it seemed. But when the weeks went by and Jamie still hadn't made a move, she pushed him away.

"You're a virgin, aren't you?" Tina blurted, sitting up to light a cigarette.

Jamie was silent.

"Twenty-three and a virgin." She shook her head. "I can't handle *that*."

"I can learn. I want to learn," Jamie promised, fervent.

"This is too weird." Tina stubbed out her cigarette and pulled the quilt around her as though to define their separation. When Jamie touched her, Tina shuddered. He spent the night lying on his back, sleepless, cursing himself.

"Well, I guess I'll just have to rape you," Tina offered in the morning, rising to make Rosie's oatmeal.

"That's probably what it would take," Jamie said quietly. He meant it as a plea, though afterward he wondered if Tina might have misunderstood.

In the afternoons he worked in Gramp's shop, finishing his Christmas present for Tina, a coffee table fashioned from a polished pine burl.

"I'd have to guess you like that girl," Gramp remarked, coming out to watch.

Jamie borrowed Gramp's jeep to deliver his gift. Another truck sat parked in front of Tina's house. Tina blushed when she introduced Carl, her old boyfriend. A six-pack of Bud, mostly empties, littered the kitchen table. Carl, thick-shouldered, grinning, with a beer in his fist, put a hand on Tina's neck.

Jamie sat on the living room couch, helpless, raging, while Tina and Carl went into the bedroom "to talk." Rosie climbed up on his lap, but sensing his mood, jumped down again. Eventually the little girl fell asleep on a bean bag pillow on the floor.

An hour later, Tina and Carl were still in the bedroom. Jamie got up and drove the coffee table back to Gramp's. Out in the woodshed he split it to smithereens, letting the ax fall over and over until it was kindling.

Gramp came out in his bathrobe, stood silently watching. "That's enough now, son," he said.

Jamie went back to spending his evenings at Gramp's. He decided to read Gram's books. She belonged to a club and had all the classics: *War and Peace, Dubliners, The Great Gatsby.* It took him two months to get through the first one, *For Whom the Bell Tolls.* He'd always been the slowest reader. In elementary school the letters twisted and reversed themselves, and while reading aloud in class one day he'd said "clean underwear" instead of "clear water" and all the kids had laughed.

"I got admiration for you, boy," Gramp said the day Jamie finished that first book and went to the shelf for another. "That's like one of those wheelchair athletes finishing a marathon."

Every evening the three of them sat in the living room, Gramp at his desk on one side of the chimney doing his paperwork; Gram on the other side of the chimney, reading or mending; Jamie, with his long skinny legs hooked over a chair by the window, face close to the page, struggling with the fixity of words in rows that opened into distant steppes and forests, alps and pubs.

Sometimes Jamie thought it was the little girl he missed most, her upturned petal face, her peacefulness as he swirled the wash-cloth dreamily over her delicate skin.

While target shooting in the pasture, Gramp's rifle jammed. Jamie saw the shell in the chamber, but Gramp kept working the piece, trying to unjam it. When the rifle went off the bullet grazed Mitchell, who'd gone down to adjust the target.

"Christ, Gramp," Jamie yelled.

"It felt like ten bees," Mitchell said, rubbing his arm.

Gramp put the rifle down, shaking. "I'm an old fool. I'm never going to shoot again."

Gramp was seventy-seven and slowing down. He was still plumb-ing, but only four days a week, and he never took on any new clients, just serviced his regular collection of old ladies, many of whom never paid their bills. His hands shook and tremors rippled his wrinkled cheeks. His vision blurred and occasionally his mind wandered. Up at the Dartmouth hospital in Hanover, they diag-nosed Parkinson's.

At home, Pop was sick with stomach cancer. He couldn't drink anymore, could barely eat. He kneeled in bed, the only position in which he could find a bit of comfort, and cursed the God that had betrayed him. He seemed to think that because he gave up drink-ing every year for Lent he was due some special dispensation. "After I spent a lifetime being a good Catholic," Pop railed. "This is what I get. I never should've believed a word of that hocus-pocus. Not a word."

Gramp started worrying about money. He rented out the taps on the sugarbush, although Jamie reminded him of his own words—that overuse could weaken and even kill the big old rock maples.

Then Gramp had twenty acres logged for stumpage, despite Jamie's pleas. The noise of chain saws and skidders blasted the forest; downed tops and stumps littered the woods. The old dirt road to the sugarhouse grew soupy with skidder ruts. Jamie walked through the wreckage, sickened.

Gramp sold off fifty acres to a developer over the hill. The price he got was barely worth it, but Gramp worried he couldn't make his taxes on a hundred acres and the house. The appraisal had gone way up since the regional high school was built in Bellows Falls. Gramp feared if he didn't sell off, he'd lose everything.

"Don't worry," he promised. "When I die the rest will be yours. Gram will keep the house but you'll have the land."

"What about the rest of them?" Jamie asked anxiously. "Don't you want to divide it up even?"

"I'm giving it all to you," Gramp insisted. "You're the only one who deserves it, the only one I trust."

Jamie didn't want to bear the weight of his brother's, his cousin's resentment, or the weight of Gramp's bad judgment. It was time to strike out on his own. He needed a wilderness bigger than fifty acres cut off by a highway and marred with logging cuts. He'd already lived with Gram and Gramp for six years—he could hardly believe it—and it was time to find something for himself, a place where no one would know him, a place where he could make his own way. He had a plan: when spring came, he would take his backpack and hitch across Canada to the Northwest Territories or the Yukon and be a homesteader. At night he studied maps by kerosene light in the sugarhouse, entranced by town names: Moose Jaw. Yellowknife.

Gramp was leaning on him more and more. When Jamie wanted to hitch down to Holyoke to visit Pop in his sickbed, Gramp invented work that had to be done first, and then when Jamie insisted on leaving, he got hurt and huffy.

"I need you here, boy," Gramp implored.

Jamie's stomach began to ache again from the pressure, the way it had when he was in school and couldn't keep up with the reading.

Pop offered the money for a ticket on the train across Canada. "I can't take it with me," he said. "You might as well try your dreams."

"Don't go," Gramp begged.

Jamie set his departure date for March. He had to leave before everything they'd had together was ruined. He wanted to remember the Gramp who said "Do whatever it is you want," not this clinging, frightened, suspicious old man.

Gramp refused to say goodbye or wish him well.

Jamie hitched to Montreal to catch the train in the midst of a March thaw. Snowbanks melted into rivulets running on the side of the highway; buds on the red maples were swollen mauve. In Montreal he was scared by the enormity of the city with its skyscrapers, the startling fact that people indeed spoke French. He sat for three days upright in a seat on the Canadian Pacific. The train rocked on, stopping in every tiny native village for one or two passengers, its whole heaving length shuddering into stations that were merely platforms, as Ontario spruce gave way to Saskatchewan and Alberta plains flooded with snowmelt, all of it sealed behind the train's glass windows.

Jamie longed for a chance to smell the earth he was passing over, a chance to stretch his legs. When he learned they would travel through the Canadian Rockies in darkness, that he wouldn't even see, let alone walk through, mountains larger than any he'd ever known, he decided he'd ridden far enough. He got off late at night near Jasper and made camp in an empty lot behind a church.

Jamie woke at dawn to ice on his beard, the sides of his tent sagging with the weight of new snow, and hastily broke camp before he was discovered. The air was thin and sharp. The only food he had was rice. He cooked up a potful on his camping stove while waiting for a ride, and then had to toss it on the roadside when a car pulled over to pick him up. His first ride, a self-professed heroin addict on his way to Vancouver to live off the bounty of a welfare province, bought Jamie eggs in a roadside cafe in Kamloops. He offered to take him all the way to Vancouver but Jamie declined, turning off at the road north to Prince George.

He slept on round smooth river rocks the size of dinner plates on a tributary of the Fraser River, amid big stumps and whole trees stranded on the banks as though tossed.

Businessmen, truckers, and hippies picked him up and dropped him off. Jamie ate their proferred meals, or boiled pots of rice. Sometimes he held handfuls of raw rice in his mouth until they softened and could be swallowed. The rides grew shorter and his waits grew longer as villages stretched further apart. Cars slid off the road in sudden ice storms. Moose ducked into woods, or simply stood and watched as he passed.

A young woman with lank blond hair, a battered face, and a five-year-old son picked him up in a rusty Fairlane. All day long they shared their stories — Marie was escaping a husband who beat her and their son. She was headed now for a friend's goat farm, where she would stay until she figured out her next move. Jamie guzzled tea from Marie's thermos, tickled the boy, invented guessing games to keep him entertained. When Marie turned off the road into a long dirt driveway in darkness — her friends' farm — she invited Jamie to spend the night.

He stayed for weeks. Time swirled by as the earth warmed and the days lengthened. Jamie lifted hay bales, chopped wood, mucked stalls. He milked nannies, forehead pressed to their warm flanks, squeezed their teats between his fingers, and listened to milk hiss into the pail. He ate slabs of toasted bread and big bowls of lentil soup and goat stew.

At night he slept with Marie in the bunkhouse. At first she wanted nothing more than the warmth of his closeness, someone to play with her son. She'd seen too much to judge his uncertainty as anything more than kindness. But when Jamie began to explore her flesh with work-rough hands, she opened and pulled him in. Jamie was grateful, triumphant. Marie couldn't know what she'd given him. He wondered if he might love this small blond woman with a scar on her nose and her nervous, hopeful son.

Marie's friends invited him to stay as long as he wanted. They'd teach him to make goat cheese. He'd be the hired hand.

At night, curled around Marie, stroking her shoulders, he tried

to explain his plan. He didn't want to slide into another estab-
lished life the way he'd slid into Gramp's. He didn't want to chop
wood for someone else's stove. He tried to picture for her the log
cabin he'd build, the traps he'd set, the mountain ways he'd learn
up north. He'd make it good for her and Ian, and then they could
come and join him.

"Stay," Marie begged. She pleaded, cried, and then she grew
stony. "You'll never write. You'll never come back. I know."

Jamie began to see her need as large, as yawning as Gramp's.
"I'll send for you," he promised the day he left.

"Sure," she said. She gripped Ian's fist and turned away so as
not to see Jamie walking down to the road.

Then the rides were fewer, his feet freezing in his boots on the
side of the highways. Spring hadn't even started this far north,
it seemed. Jamie's equipment wasn't good enough for winter
camping—a leaky pup tent, an army surplus canvas pack that got
soaked. He spent a whole day standing at the side of the highway
and the only cars that passed either gave him the finger, or veered
toward him as though to run him over, big faces screaming out of
the windows about his long hair.

When he made camp that evening somewhere between Daw-
son Creek and Fort Nelson, a terrible achey lassitude came over
him. He had nightmares of bears bursting through the tent, footsteps crackling in the snow just beyond his head. In the morning
he went out to pee and nearly swooned with dizziness. He climbed
back in his sleeping bag. His flesh was clammy. Deep rattling
coughs wracked his chest. Two or three days—he wasn't sure—
he lay in the tent shivering, unable to get up, unable finally to even
go out to pee, so that the urine ran hot down his leg and froze in
yellow puddles at the edge of the tent.

Marie came to him and said, "Come back. We need you."
Gramp raised the splitting maul slowly, slowly, but the blade never
came down. "You do what you want boy. You're welcome here,"
Gramp said. "You should've told me," Pop chided. "You didn't
have to run away like that."

Jamie woke. His bag was wet, his limbs shaking. He knew he

was going to die there, on the side of the road, in his tent. It didn't seem terrible, just sad and stupid that he'd never even made it beyond British Columbia, never had a chance to step across the threshold.

A jeep pulled over beside Jamie, who was walking along the highway. Its tailpipe jetted frozen smoke. "Where you headed?" the driver asked, an old man with a bony face.

"I don't know," Jamie confessed. North or south? He'd lost his bearings.

The old man thrust open the door to the jeep. "Get in, for Christ's sake."

"Wait," Jamie begged the driver. "My tent. My pack." He looked around in confusion. All his gear was gone. He felt a terrible sadness at having lost them.

The jeep's heater blew hot air on his frozen toes—numbness followed by pain as ice crystals thawed to nerves. Tears ran down Jamie's frostbitten cheeks.

The old man turned to study him. A glass eye winked. The lean face grew familiar. "Gramp?" Jamie asked, joy filling his chest. "Jesus, Gramp. You saved my life."

"You're in over your head," the old man said. He drove Jamie sixty miles out of his way to a provincial health clinic. "You're just lucky Canadian medicine's free, Yank," he said, dropping Jamie shivering at the door.

Jamie wanted to cry, "Come back, Come back," when the jeep rattled away, Gramp's tools bouncing in the back.

They shot him full of antibiotics, put him in an oxygen tent, sucked phlegm from his chest. Mostly he slept.

"You had pneumonia," the nurse said. Her name tag read: Lucille. She leaned over Jamie to adjust his blankets, her perm the color of polished copper, the flesh of her fat arm swinging like the underbelly of a dog nursing pups. Jamie wanted to rest his head against her looming bosom. Lucille turned away to pull the blinds. "We've contacted your family, you know. They sent money for you to go home."

"I don't want to go home," Jamie protested. "I'm not going

home. I'm going to head south, back down to Vancouver and get
a job until it gets warmer and I can buy some gear. Then I'll start
all over again."

Lucille paused at the door. "Your father's dying. Go home,
eh?"

Jamie rode buses, sat awake in stations with pinball machines
pinging in eerie fluorescence: Billings, Bismarck, Minneapolis,
Chicago. Ma picked him up in Springfield. She cried when she saw
his skinny stork body, wavering with weakness, rising from the
bench.

"I knew you'd come back, Jamie." Pop grinned from the narrow wedge that had become his face. His big round muscles, his
beer gut, had withered away to parchment-covered skeleton. He
looked older than Gramp.

"I blew it, Pop," Jamie said.

"The hell you did. Just remember, you're a beautiful boy. You
were always perfect in my eyes."

Jamie lay on the couch in the living room in front of the tele-
vision under a blanket, recuperating. Cable programs blared while
Pop cried in pain in the den that had become his sickroom. When
he could, Jamie went down to the trestle, walked the rails, threw
stones into the filthy black water.

Pop called Ma into his room. Jamie followed. The covers had
fallen off and Jamie averted his eyes from the sight of Pop's
stomach—the flesh a transparent film barely covering the roiling
fluids of his rotted guts.

"You better take me back," Pop whispered.

Jamie supported Pop out to the station wagon and folded him
into the back seat. The trees were leafed out already, with the
palest early yellow-green, leaves that seemed lit from within.

Pop gazed about him, studying the oaks rising over the house,
the scarred maple he'd hit so many times by the garage.

"This is the last time I'll ever see any of this," he said.

When he died in the hospital two days later, he weighed eighty-
six pounds, a fact the pallbearers noted.

Gramp was there at the funeral, frail and palsied. "Well, well,

well," he shouted into Jamie's ear. "We got lots of projects waiting. You ready to come back?"

Jamie's eyes filled. He put his arm around Gramp's skinny coat
hanger shoulder. "Not yet, Gramp," he said.

The house had changed with Pop's death. Ma's shoulders relaxed and a peacefulness came over her face. She rang bells in a bell
choir at her church and volunteered for bake sales. His sister
Eileen came back to live at home after her husband broke her arm.
Rosalie, the baby of the family, was still in high school. Frank, the
oldest, was overseas in the Army, Midge married and living in
Springfield.

Every evening Jamie, Rosalie, Eileen, and Ma sat around on the
couch watching TV, eating cookies. They didn't want anyone else.
It was enough to have what they'd never had when Pop was alive,
enough to sit there and laugh at the dumb shows, stay up late
watching Home Box Office movies. Ma made breakfast for the
whole crew every morning, and made their beds, as if no one was
expected to be grown up when they'd missed so much as kids. But
it was never spoken of, not a word, as though Pop had never lifted
a beer. "I had a perfect childhood," Rosalie insisted, and Jamie
didn't have the heart to disagree.

He painted a few houses for friends of Ma's from her church.
He had no plans. He no longer cared about plans. He began
keeping company with one of Rosalie's friends, an eighteen-year-
old girl named Lindy who'd spent six months in girls' detention
as an "incorrigible child," committed by her crazy mother. They
sat on the trestle dangling their feet and Lindy leaned her head
against his shoulder. Sun glinted down, a golden shimmer rising
from her auburn hair. Jamie listened to her quiet breathing, matched
his breathing to hers. She didn't know how close in age they really
were. To Lindy he was the wise one, the one with experience.

Ma hung up the phone, teary-eyed. Gram had called, crying.
Gramp was in the state nursing home. She couldn't take care of

him any longer, couldn't drive up there to visit. She didn't think it was a good place for him but what could she do?

Jamie drove Pop's old Chevy wagon north. It was fall already and the clouds were scudding again across the Connecticut River Valley, casting shadows over the hills on the New Hampshire side. He turned off Interstate 91 at Putney and headed north on Route 5. He drove past the turnoff to Gramp's road just to look around, continuing through Shelby center. The black-shuttered, white frame colonials stood like sentries, sharp-angled, austere, facing each other across the road.

The produce stand down by the cattle auction house displayed shelves of artistically arranged squash: acorn, hubbard, crookneck, butternut, in orange and green chevrons. Pumpkins and tripods of cornstalks stood in doorways. Halloween cutouts filled windows. He passed the familiar dilapidated colonial down on the flats that never took down its Christmas display, but let Santa ride the eaves year round. The Jesus fanatics who lived in a commune by the bridge to Walpole were out in their yard cutting wood, the women in long archaic dresses and head coverings. All the kids, even the toddlers, were working, stacking logs. He turned around and headed back to Gramp's. When he parked the car in the driveway he hit the accelerator, revving once, to leave some gas in the carburetor as Pop always had.

Gram came out to the porch when she heard the car. "Thank God," she said. Jamie was embarrassed to see the tears in her eyes, Gram who never showed anything.

While she cooked supper Jamie chopped stove wood, his arms and back kinked at first but smoothing out, enjoying the rhythm of the rise and fall. He had a lot of wood to split for himself up at the sugarhouse if he was going to spend the winter. He'd left at least a cord and a half in four-foot lengths that needed bucking. His chainsaw wanted tuning, the spring digging out, and Gram's storm windows weren't put on. He would be The Man of a Thousand Projects.

Over supper Gram told him that Mitchell had joined the Navy, gone AWOL, got a dishonorable discharge—all in the past four months. "There's no one here to rely on," she said. "Marsha's busy taking care of my poor sick Annie."

"Doesn't Lowell come over to help?"

Gram screwed up her mouth in disgust.

"Well, I'm here. But I'm going to live in the sugarhouse from now on."

Gram nodded her head. "It's already yours. That and forty acres. We made it over in your name. It's what Gramp wanted. There's no tax, you know, if you give it away three years before you die."

"You're going to live a lot longer than three years," Jamie said. He reached out to touch Gram's hand, hesitated. She curled hers up to grasp his, held on. He figured he could find a lawyer, divvy the land up fairly. There was no need to talk about that now.

Jamie drove Gram up to the state home in Waterbury. The riotous crimson and orange maples on the hillsides seemed to mock their journey. Gram sat upright in the car seat, massaging her thick knuckles. "It's a pretty day," she said, looking out blindly at the hills.

They found Gramp in a large communal ward, lying on a metal cot with a sagging plastic mattress. He was curled into a fetal position, wearing only a diaper. When they greeted him, Gramp looked up, his one good eye cloudy, searching their faces for something familiar, then turned away.

"Was he this bad when he left?" Jamie asked.

"No, he just couldn't walk, and he forgot things, you know, acted foggy." Gram turned to him, her face a guilty plea. "I couldn't lift him anymore, or I never would've sent him away."

"Gram, it isn't your fault. But we've got to get him out of here."

A private ambulance drove Gramp to the hospital in Hanover that afternoon.

Jamie worked. He cut up the tops and stumps left by the loggers, dragged them into piles, doused the piles with gasoline and burned them the first time it rained. He bucksawed dead lower branches off the pine trees nearest the sugarhouse, so that the trunks rose smoothly fifteen feet up. He stomped down the ruts in the road, borrowed Gramp's weed whacker, and trimmed the brush so that when he looked out the sugarhouse window the trees stood out cleanly, one from another. He marked out the space for his garden. In the spring he would plant a lilac bush and cuttings from Gram's perennials: cosmos, phlox, feverfew.

He climbed the steep back stairs to the bell room over Gram and Gramp's garage. The bells were still there as Gramp had arranged them, his ticket to a distant world. Jamie raised a dusty cowbell, listened to its clapper's tinny clank. The jade bell rattled like heavy glass. The church bell was mute as ever. Without asking, Jamie spirited the camel bell back to the sugarhouse and set it on a high shelf next to the picture of Gramp.

He called Lindy from a pay phone in front of the General Store. Would she come up to live with him in the sugar house, he asked. It was his, it was where he belonged. Lindy said her mother was as crazy as ever. She promised to quit her waitress job, to come soon.

"Well, well, well, look who's here!" Gramp greeted them, his droopy face pulling up in a smile. He inched up a bit in his hospital bed.

"I brought you some sweet buns," Gram offered.

"That's fine, Eleanor, fine. How's everything at home? Did you get the chimney cleaned yet? That creosote's a devil, you know."

"Jamie brushed it out on Sunday. We told you yesterday."

"Right. What about the storm windows?"

"They went on last week. Remember?"

"They did?" Gramp collapsed back on the pillow as though all the wind had been sucked out of his lungs. "I'm losing my mind," he whimpered. Tears ran runnels down the lines of his face. "I'm scared, Eleanor, I'm scared. This place is going to be the death of me."

"Now, now, Horace." Gram reached out to Gramp just as Jamie was getting up from his chair. Accidentally, he intercepted her touch. The heat of her wordless love, all the love that had been pent up for a lifetime, jolted him with the force of an electrical charge. He moved his arm away as if scalded. Unaware, Gram leaned intently across the rail of the hospital bed, gripping Gramp's hand.

Jamie said, "I'm going downstairs to get a Coke," though neither of them noticed. He made it a long trip, strolling the halls, taking the stairs instead of the elevator, to give them time alone. When he got back, Gram shuffled out to get herself a coffee, and Jamie sat down again in the chair beside Gramp's bed.

Gramp whispered, "Jamie, boy. You got to help me get out of here. I got work to do."

"I can't, Gramp."

"Please, Jamie, help me."

"I can't."

Gramp sighed. "Don't get old, Jamie."

Jamie smiled. "I'll try not to." He folded his useless hands in his lap. Silence ticked by. The man in the next bed coughed behind the drawn white curtain.

Then Gramp sat bolt upright, pointed across the room. "Look. Jamie. Over there."

"What?"

"Did you see it? A heron."

Jamie hesitated. He glanced about. A wheeled tray table held a small bouquet of pink striped carnations. Down the hall an orderly pushing a cart delivered bland dinners. White nurse shoes squeaked by. Somewhere, somebody groaned.

"Sure, Gramp. What a beauty."

"Jamie, Jamie! I felt a nibble." Gramp clasped his hands together and jerked backward. "I got him! It's a big one. It's a big one, alright." Gramp turned, his one good eye wide and eager. "That's right, Gramp," Jamie said. "Reel out. Reel out. Play him."

Gramp's voice shook with excitement. "He's pulling hard. What are you waiting for, boy, they're biting. Get your line in the water!"

Jamie lifted his empty arm, swung it back overhead and snapped the fishing line across the hospital room. The ripples widened as the sinker fell. Along the banks of the river, small animals rustled in the bushes. Dragonflies swooped low, flitting iridescence. Jamie dipped a finger and water striders skittered away. He reeled in his line. It wouldn't matter what they caught. It was enough to be sitting with Gramp in the boat, casting his line as they drifted.

GATEAU

[Nancy, 1979]

AFTER SCHOOL, Nancy, the youngest Chartrain daughter, lugged her books up the hill from the bus stop, crushing fresh powdery snow underfoot. The only track was from her father's pickup going to milk at four this morning and Nancy's own footprints heading down for the bus at seven-forty. Gram wouldn't drive until the plow came through, and Jamie, who lived with his girlfriend in the old sugarhouse back in the woods, rarely had a car that was running, or money to put gas in the tank when it was.

Although Dad's tire tracks had preceded her own small trowel-shaped boot prints, Nancy imagined that his broad aggressive tread, straddling hers, could have run her over. And the fact that only their two tracks marked all that white, as fresh as when they'd left them this morning, made it appear that there was nobody but the two of them in all the world. Even after a day of noisy slush-filled school buses and classrooms, the thought made her shiver. Her toes were already numb.

It was one of those bright sharp February days after a snowfall, with big bleached clouds and bitter cold that pressed her nostrils closed and made her head ache. Fresh dry snow reminded Nancy of confectioner's sugar, the way it compressed softly to itself. She envisioned sifting it over the tops of Christmas cookies, or in a doily pattern over a lemon cake the way Gram had taught her.

She hoped Gram wasn't watching out the frosted window from her own side of the road. Nancy hadn't been by to visit for a couple of days. She hated going over there now. Ever since Mom died, and then Gramp, Gram had changed. She complained bitterly all the time, and made insulting remarks about Nancy's sisters, who were all gone from home, busy with their own lives. If Mitchell was mentioned, Gram only grunted with disgust. And once she got Nancy in her clutches, it was hard to get away. Let Jamie visit her, Nancy reasoned. Turning into her own driveway, Nancy stared down at the salt-stained toes of her winter boots, hoping to avoid Gram's vexed gaze.

When she stepped up to the door, a cardinal flew up from the milk carton bird feeders she had hung along the kitchen windows, gorgeous red against the snowy eaves. Nancy followed its flitting brilliance through bare branches, until it was swallowed by the dark of hemlock boughs. It seemed as though it was inviting her to follow it through the trees into some mysterious other life. There were always signs like that in the fantasy and romance books she traded back and forth with her sisters. In real life, she figured, these things never added up. She knocked snow off her boots against the doorjamb and stepped in.

Nancy placed her boots neatly on the throw rug she had set in front of the door to protect the floor wax and stepped into the slippers she'd left there. The linoleum was still new and Nancy took care to keep it shining. All the years Mom lived here, she had never had a linoleum floor, just scuffed and muddied plywood. It was only after she died that Dad had entered into a flurry of home improvement projects that his resentment hadn't permitted while Mom was alive.

Now the house was absolute in its emptiness, a hollow silence that filled Nancy with dread. Mom had always been there when they got home, and even when she grew too sick to teach second grade, when she was drugged and drifting, at least she was a breathing presence lying in a darkened room. Everyone else had left as soon as they could.

Nancy put on the radio immediately to fill the house with sound. She turned on the TV to a soap, with the volume low. The close-ups of huge flashing faces with their capped white teeth were ridiculous but comforting. Nancy set her history and English texts on the corner of the kitchen table, a precise pile she would get to later, while whatever it was she was going to make today browned itself in the oven.

The kitchen looked good. Nancy took pride in the immaculate formica counters, the crisp white and blue curtains she had stitched herself, the framed prints of floral arrangements she'd bought at Newberry's. She had scrubbed and polished and organized to a level of gleaming perfection that Mom's illness, and, before that, her defeat, had never permitted. At times Nancy pretended the house was her own, the present incarnation of the house she would someday live in—minus Dad—with fat little babies playing in the yard, deep perennial beds ablaze with carefully coordinated hues of pinks and purples, and an oven emitting the rich smell of bread and pastries.

Somewhere in her fantasy was a husband, clean and polite, who would disappear each day to earn their keep, who would buy her gifts—jewelry from inside the glass case, not from on top—and for whom she would make herself fragrant and beautiful.

Gary would do. The only thing wrong with him was his job. As a mechanic, he got greasy and his fingernails stayed black no matter how much he washed. But it wasn't anywhere near as bad as the stink of cow manure on Dad's barn overalls. And though Gary liked to party, he was no drunk. It bothered her a bit that she wasn't in love with him, not the way her sister Donna was crazy for Claude, but they'd only been going together a few months and it could happen . . .

Nancy opened the refrigerator to check on the materials for Dad's dinner: tonight would be meat loaf with potatoes and peas. When she had first started cooking in earnest, she tried baking delicacies for him, but Dad turned up his nose at anything fancy, preferring his greasy meat and potatoes drowned under catsup and gravy, and gooey sweet rolls or Hydrox cookies for dessert. Once she had added capers and olives to a meat loaf, and Dad had spit a mouthful back on his plate. Eventually she discovered a pleasure in secretly baking special foods and sneaking them out of the house. It was a way to hold a part of her life separate, out of Dad's reach.

Nancy opened the Craig Claiborne *New York Times International Cookbook* her sisters had given her last Christmas and studied the index. The names of the recipes entranced her—crème brûlée, coq au vin, zabaglione—as did the exotic ingredients: cardamom, saffron, marsala, marzipan, anchovy paste. She'd gotten Gary to take her down to Brattleboro twice to shop for special spices in more sophisticated stores than those she could find in Bellows Falls.

But what to make today, she wondered. It had to be something that would keep, as she wouldn't see Gary until tomorrow. He was working late on his cousin's GTO tonight. His boss often let him use the garage after hours, and industrious Gary always went for the chance to make extra bucks. It was another thing that made him unlike Dad, and therefore appealing; Dad, who could never get along with a boss, had been out of work, it seemed, half her life.

She decided that Gateau Bretonne would be perfect, because after baking it had to be kept wrapped in foil for twenty-four hours before serving. She checked her shelves for the ingredients: butter, egg, sugar, almond flavoring, orange rind, baking powder, flour, almonds, orange juice. Almonds. She knew she had walnuts. But almonds? Nancy searched the shelves, fearing disappointment, she wanted to make this cake so badly.

Found them! She only needed a quarter cup, and there, behind the molasses bottle, was an opened and resealed little plastic pack of slivered almonds. The recipe called for ground. Well, she'd smash them under paper with a hammer. Nancy laid out her measuring cups, donned her mother's old apron, turned up the radio.

She preheated the oven to 375. Then she creamed together the butter, eggs, sugar, and almond flavor, grated and stirred in the orange rind. She sifted the baking powder and flour, folded in the creamed mixture, the ground almonds, and a tablespoon of the orange juice. She loved that verb, fold, for the gentle mingling of separate ingredients into one substance. Baking was alchemy, the place where she'd found her own special talent, a way in which she could make things elaborate and perfect.

Nancy spooned the dough into a buttered pan, shaking it gently to spread it, then beat the last egg yolk with the remaining juice and brushed the golden mixture on top of the batter to form a light glaze.

The oven was up to temp and she popped the cake in, setting the timer for twenty-five minutes. She meant to do her homework then, but instead began to wash up. The phone rang. Nancy flipped dishwater from her hands, wiped them on her apron front.

"You alone?" Marsha asked. Marsha couldn't bear the thought of Dad being home when she phoned.

"Of course. It's only four."

"How you doing, honey?"

Nancy recognized her oldest sister's little mother voice—concerned, insistent. As much as Nancy loved her, Marsha's tone set her on edge, made her want to deflect the focus from herself. "I'm fine," Nancy said. "How's the belly?"

"Getting bigger." Marsha warmed at the mention of her pregnancy. "I'm huge!"

"You guys come up with any names yet?"

"If it's a girl, it'll be Anne."

Anne for their mother. A strained sorrow echoed between them. "Well if it's a boy, I hope you don't name it Horace for Gramp," Nancy joked.

"God, no. It'll be Eddie Jr. Or William, for Eddie's father."

"Nice." Nancy watched the soap opera faces shifting on the silent TV screen.

"He behaving himself?" Marsha queried. They both knew who *he* was.

Nancy shrugged, though her sister couldn't see her. "The

usual. He slops the floor with slush, gobbles his supper, and sits at the table all night with his beers whining about how everything's unfair until he passes out."

"You know you can come live with us, you don't have to stay with that pig," Marsha counseled.

"Like you really have room." Donna had made the same offer, but Nancy knew their husbands didn't want her there, they wanted their wives to themselves. Plus the two of them, Marsha, and now Donna since she'd married Claude, were straight arrows who would freak if they knew how Nancy liked her joints and beer.

"It's okay. I'm not home that much, just in the afternoons. I go out with Gary a lot."

"Well don't go out too much," Marsha bossed, shifting concerns. "You doing your homework? You're going to graduate, right?"

Nancy sighed. "Ye-es." Marsha could really be a pain. The lovely aroma of Gateau Bretonne billowed through the kitchen. Nancy glanced at the timer. Five minutes left. "How's Eddie? Must be busy with all the snow lately."

"Yeah, they're plowing round the clock." Marsha paused. "Sometimes I think Eddie is more like Dad than I realized."

"What do you mean?"

"Oh, you know." Her voice wavered. "He sure loves his beer."

"Is it a problem?" Nancy knew it was a problem, everyone knew it was a problem except Marsha.

"Forget it," Marsha said. "I'm probably just overreacting, 'cause of Dad." Her voice shifted to an urgent, cheery pitch. "My God, it's getting late. I've got to run to the store to pick up something for dinner. Be good. I'll call you tomorrow, honey."

"Okay. Bye bye." Relieved, Nancy put the receiver down, then rushed to the oven as the timer dinged. The cake was perfect: lightly golden, redolent of almonds and orange, something tropical and Mediterranean maybe. All she knew of the Mediterranean was the mural on the wall at Athens Pizza, where Gary took her for a double cheese pepperoni and onions once a week. In the painting, a couple in folksy high leggings danced with lifted arms, a whitewashed village in the background. Nancy imagined the place would smell like almonds and oranges—not that she had any urge to travel. It was enough to journey through foreign recipes; it would be more than enough to marry and get out of the house.

Nancy took the cake to cool in her bedroom, then opened the kitchen windows and the door to get rid of its fragrance. The shock of cold air immediately caused the oil burner to kick in. Cross ventilation whisked the sweet odors away.

It was time to make Dad's meat loaf. Wrinkling her nose at the chore, Nancy dumped cold raw burger into a mixing bowl, mashed in oatmeal and bread crumbs, but much less than her mother had used; those meat loaves of Mom's were three-quarters filling, one-quarter meat, and the meat only the scraps she'd ground from Dad's leavings. Nancy added tons of catsup the way he liked it, a can of peas, chopped onion. She scrubbed baking potatoes.

When the meat mixture was in a loaf pan, she set it in the still-warm oven on a low temperature and cleaned up the new mess. Through the window over the sink, it was almost dark. It was hard to believe that the days were getting longer when winter seemed so settled in, so permanent. The last western rays formed an ominous backlighting against the clouds; the sky glowed, as surreal as an acid trip. A feeling of dread rose again, a sense that nothing seemed quite familiar; she might step out of her body at any minute and watch herself, a paper cutout going through the motions. Nancy gripped a clean, wet mixing bowl in her hands, pinching its stainless steel rim, willing it to take on substance while panic rushed into her chest. A Carole King song was playing on the soft rock station: "You make me feeeel—you make me feeeel." Nancy focused on the rough grain of Carole's voice, its sad avowal of joy, until her chest eased.

She set the bowl in the drainer, avoiding a glance at the disturbing sky. Lately, these attacks came more frequently. Once she'd tried to describe them to Gary, but he hadn't wanted to hear. He drummed his fingers nervously on the steering wheel of his truck, made some joke about maybe she ought to lay off the grass for a

while, asked her what she'd like to do about dinner. Nancy understood—he didn't want her to be some crazy girl, he wanted her
cheerful, cute, someone the other guys at the garage would envy
him for. She didn't mention it again.

Now laundry. After emptying the bathroom hamper into a
basket, she checked Dad's room. She hated going in there. He
never bothered to open the curtains and it was always dank and
stuffy, rank with an odor of stale sweat and something overlying it,
cigarette butts, ashes, corruption. He dropped tissues in sticky
wads on the floor and she was afraid to think what they might have
been used for—Dad kept a stack of *Playboy*, *Penthouse*, and *True
Detective* magazines on the end table by his bed. She donned
rubber gloves when she went in to clean. Turning her head away
in disgust, Nancy whisked underwear off the floor into the basket,
undershirts, stained pajamas, damp towels. She ran two loads and
folded from the dryer.

At six, Gary called and said the hydraulic lift was busted so he
couldn't do the GTO. Did she want him to come get her?

Of course she did. It was best to be out of the house before Dad
came home and to return after he was already passed out. She'd
leave him a note about warming up the meat loaf, have everything
ready.

Nancy undressed quickly and slipped into the bathroom carrying her own towel, which she kept in her room so as not to
accidentally share one with Dad. She showered, scrubbing her
hair with a special blond highlight shampoo and expensive conditioner. Soaping her body, she ran a hand over her flat belly. She
thought she felt a fullness there. Was it just pre-period bloat, or
could it be more?

Every time she got her period she was almost as disappointed as
relieved. She wanted a baby so much she could see it already, a
beautiful little girl she'd sew bright dresses for—someone all her
own to love, and the one thing that would force Dad to release
her. Graduating from high school wouldn't be enough. He'd
expect her to stay on to take care of him. But when she was

pregnant, he'd have to let her go. It was February, and if only she got pregnant now, she could finish high school before anyone really noticed. A June wedding . . .

Nancy admired herself in the steamy mirror as she dried off. She'd been a homely, messy child, stuck with hand-me-downs, but she had blossomed, surprising everyone, to cheerleader cuteness, not that she had the time to go to tryouts. It was a cuteness she didn't fully believe in, but she was willing to use if it could buy her way out of here.

She puffed herself with powder and acne-proofed her face, taking comfort in the array of bottles and perfumes that proclaimed she'd risen beyond that girl with unraveling pigtails. As she tucked away the hair dryer she could hear Gary battling up the hill, his tires sliding in the unplowed road, and then his heavy work boots on the step, stamping and kicking snow. She had taught him not to sit in the driveway and honk his horn, but she rushed to the door, grabbing her coat and boots and hat, juggling her foil-wrapped Gateau Bretonne, so he wouldn't mess up her waxed floor by coming in.

Gary stood on the step grinning, all cocky smile and dark eyes, his shiny black hair without a hat despite the below-zero weather. His good looks always surprised her. Even though the girls at school told her she was lucky, something made her forget when he wasn't around.

He kissed her when she came through the door and she was suddenly happy to see him, grateful to be whisked away from everything that panicked her at home, to settle into the warmth of his truck, two six-packs between them on the seat, Gary's open can tilted against the steamy windshield.

As soon as they were past Gram's prying eyes, Nancy cracked a beer and guzzled greedily. "Sounds like you need some weight in the back," she said, remarking on his trouble getting up the hill.

"That and new tires. It's a pisser I couldn't do the GTO tonight. I could really use the bucks." Gary squeezed her knee. "At least I get to see you. What do you want to do?"

If he had no money for tires he had no money to take her out, so she suggested Mitchell's, where they often went to party. Since marrying last year, a month before his baby was born, Mitchell had taken a job on a dairy farm in Chester. Nancy settled back into the seat, confident in Gary's driving skills even on their steep, slippery hill, while he went on about the cars he'd dealt with today on the job and she pretended to listen.

The trip to Chester was slow, the roads slick where the new snow had been packed to ice. But snow blanketed the rooftops and the branches of the hemlocks were still laden, waiting for a wind to knock them free; the reflected glow of the lights on the white lawns softened everything, and for the time being Nancy felt cozy and at ease, with Gary's heater blowing on her legs and her own breath steaming up the window. Dreamily she inspected the passing colonial capes, white with black shutters, perfect in their symmetry, evaluating each as her future home. The rhythm of the tires thumping on the road sang: someday, someday, someday.

"Take your boots off out there, for god's sake, you slush mongers," Mitchell shouted cheerfully through the storm door.

In the plywood mudroom addition, Gary and Nancy stamped and heaved out of their footwear, stepping through snowy chunks in their socks to get into the warmth of the trailer. They never skimped on heat at Mitchell's. Oil heat came free with the job, as did the assortment of ratty old furniture left by earlier tenants. Once again, bluegrass jangled on the stereo. In the past few months, Mitchell had shifted his guitar efforts from blues to bluegrass and now he wouldn't listen to anything else. As with anything Mitchell did, he'd jumped in whole hog—at least for a while.

Red-faced from windburn and cold, Mitchell sat at the table in his long underwear. "What'd you bring?" he asked, reaching up to scoop the foil- wrapped package out of Nancy's hands.

"It's a Gateau Bretonne and you aren't supposed to eat it until tomorrow. It has to set or something."

Mitchell peeled at the foil and sniffed. "Mmmm. I know right where it can set."

Nancy didn't bother to protest. It would still be good, and she could always make another. The whole point was having people to cook for.

"Hey, guys," Corinne called out from the kitchenette. She was stirring something in a pot. Emily, Nancy's one-year-old niece, played in a cardboard box on the floor. Nancy stooped to pick up Emily and carried her to the sagging couch, placed her on her knees. They played "Ride a cock horse to Banbeurry Cross." Pony-riding Nancy's bobbing knees, Emily giggled and waved her fists. She was the sunniest baby, hardly a fuss ever. Nancy kissed her soft baby hair, her bump of a nose. Someday, someday, someday . . .

Gary plopped the remains of the six-packs on the kitchen table and sat down across from Mitchell.

"You guys hungry?" Corinne called out.

"I am," Gary said, "but Mitchell don't need much. Look at the gut he's getting. Jeez, you ought to be ashamed."

Mitchell put his hands on his growing belly and shook it contentedly. "All that free milk, it's killing me. I'm going to look like the old man if I don't watch out."

Corinne came in carrying an enamel soup pot and set it on a trivet in the center of the table. She hustled back and forth carrying bowls, spoons, napkins, butter, and bread. Nancy watched her curiously, amazed at the way Corinne had bloomed since having the baby. Nursing Emily had given her ordinarily flat chest a womanly swell, just as being a mommy had given her a life. Nancy envied Corinne having a husband, a baby, and a house, even if it was only a rent-free trailer with tacky green shag rugs that came with Mitchell's job at the dairy.

Corinne swept up Emily and carried her to the table, nursing her while they ate. Gary carefully avoiding looking. The baby's loud sucking was a match for the men with their slurps of soup and the crunch of the big chunks of bread they slathered with butter. Corinne expertly steered her own spoon to her mouth around Emily's head. The soup was beef and macaroni. Beef they got free, along with limitless milk, and vegetables in season. A little cooking sherry, Nancy thought, would add a lot.

"D'you hear about Leslie Marrett?" Corinne asked. Her face was eager—she loved gossip, perhaps because she was isolated on the dairy and had few friends. "She had a baby without anyone knowing and she stuffed it in a trash barrel at the rest stop on Route 91 near Shelby. Somebody found it but it was already dead."

"You're kidding!" Nancy was shocked. Leslie was the younger sister of a classmate. "How'd they know it was hers? What are they going to do to her?"

"I guess she confessed. She's lucky she's still a minor."

"Where'd you hear?"

"My sister that works as a dispatcher called me." Corinne switched Emily to her other breast.

Nancy couldn't tell if Corinne's smug look came from her pride in nursing, or from having something juicy to relate.

"Jeez-us," Gary complained. "We're eating."

They were indeed tearing into the Gateau Bretonne now, slicing it into big hunks, smacking their lips over its merits. The baby story would be in the papers tomorrow, she supposed. How awful, and awful for the girl, scared to tell anyone she was pregnant, doing something she'd feel guilty about for the rest of her life. She couldn't help picturing the tiny infant, blue with cold, stuffed in a garbage can. Horrible. If she got pregnant, she'd keep it for sure.

Corinne had more. "My sister said the nurses at the hospital cried when the cop brought the little dead baby in. It was all . . ."

"Nice dinner talk," Gary interrupted. "And they say guys are gross." He pushed his plate, littered with cake crumbs, to the center of the table. "Hey Mitch, did I tell you about that buck I saw up in the Goodell Orchard? Big sucker. Just wait until next fall. I'm going to keep my eye on him." Gary grinned. "You guys ready for me to roll up a number?"

"Let me put Emily to bed first," Corinne chided, lifting her daughter.

"Oh, yeah. Sorry." Gary took out his papers and his baggie of grass—nothing wrong with getting ready.

Nancy carried the dishes into the kitchenette and set them on the drainboard. She considered starting on them, but only for a moment. Dad would have left his own mess for her to clean at home. When she came back into the living room Mitchell was going on about how he was practically a son to Raymond these days. He'd be made dairy manager by next year, and since Raymond was an old bachelor without kids, if he played his cards right, he might even inherit. Nancy was doubtful. She'd seen it too many times. Mitchell was always like that, getting into something for a few months, full of excitement, the best employee any boss ever had, planning his whole life around it, and then something always went wrong and he walked. Still, it was nice to be around her brother when he was on an upswing.

"Yep, I'm going to be a professional dairy farmer, by Jesus. Just me and the girls." Even though he milked and shoveled manure and pitched hay for a living, there were library books all over the house — historical epics, fantasy, science fiction, even good literature, the kind of stuff they made you read in school, books Nancy wouldn't read unless she had to. And his wooden boat building magazines. Mitchell had ended up doing the same work as their father, but he needed to prove he was someone different.

Sitting on the couch with her beer, passing along a joint, Nancy felt a gentle affection for her brother coming over her. She was slipping into a soft place where the dread couldn't reach, a world without references to her mother's death, a place where she could be at ease.

"So last week Raymond hires on this new guy," Mitchell continued. "He's older than me, twenty-six maybe, and the guy's built like Schwarzenegger. Busting out of his shirts, he's so built. The guy carries two eighty-five pound hay bales at a time, one in each hand, no lie. And he isn't straining. They're living in the red trailer behind the barn. When I hear he's got a wife I figure I ought to see her, find out who he's married to. Last night I go over to ask him about this heifer with scours. I can't believe it. When I get to the door I don't even want to go in. I can see them through the glass. Mr. Universe is married to this three-hundred-pound sow, and they're having a fight. Damned if the pig woman isn't beating him up and Arnold is cowering in a corner."

Gary let out a loud, rattling snore.

Everyone laughed. Gary could fall asleep on a dime. He wasn't much for conversation, unless it was about cars or hunting, but he knew how to relax.

"I'm going to sleep," Corinne announced, yawning. "Keeping up with a baby just knocks you out."

Nancy smiled to herself. Corinne couldn't help waving that flag.

Mitchell stood up. "I better hit it too. I got a date with fifty girls with big tits at four in the morning. You guys can stay as long as you want." He raised a meaningful eyebrow at Gary and the couch.

"He's asleep," Nancy said.

Mitchell grinned. "It's easier like that. Have your way with him, he won't even notice. Corinne doesn't."

Nancy kicked at his long-john covered leg. "Get out of here."

But Mitchell lingered instead of following Corinne into bed. He picked up a beer can, glanced down inside the keyhole. "So, how's the old man?" he asked, eyes drifting away from Nancy toward the wall.

"Same."

"He ever, you know, ask about me?"

Nancy recognized the hope in her brother's face and it made her want to look away too. "Sure," she lied. "He always asks me how you're doing."

"Yeah?" Mitchell brightened. "He say anything about me keeping a job and all these days?"

Pity for her brother made her wince. "He's no one to talk about that," she offered, trying to shift the subject.

"Yeah," Mitchell said, his voice flattening. "A real world beater." But he cared about Dad's opinion, cared desperately. There was something between them, something the old man would always withhold that Mitchell would ache over forever.

"Well . . ." Mitchell stretched, turned away. "Got to hit it."

"G'night." Nancy sat on the couch next to sleeping Gary, sipping the last of her beer. When her can was drained, she nudged him.

"Gary, we should probably head home. It's late."

Gary yawned noisily, sputtered, shook himself, then reached up and pulled her down on top of him. "Mmm, you smell good." He slid his hands into her pants, under her shirt.

"Gary, it's too late. I thought you were working tonight so I didn't do my homework. I got to get home."

"Ah, c'mon, sweetheart. We got the place to ourselves."

"Not tonight. It's too late."

Gary pushed her off roughly. "All right already."

Nancy sighed. Now Gary would sulk.

The ride home seemed endless. Nancy drifted silently in the truck while Gary blared hard rock on the radio. Her usual dread returned as they fishtailed up the hill to her house. A light shone in the living room, but maybe Dad had passed out already.

Gary kissed her, though he didn't walk her to the door. He didn't want to confront Dad any more than she did. Nancy turned the knob gingerly, hoping. But there he was slumped in front of the television, shaking himself awake.

"Where you been?" Dad barked.

"Just Mitchell's."

"Hmmph." Dad sat back down in his lounger. "Raymond's got a lousy herd," he muttered.

"Was dinner okay?"

"Fine, baby, only you're out running around all the time it ain't no pleasure eating alone."

Nancy pretended not to hear, making a big show of shuffling coats in the closet as she hung hers.

"All them worthless kids running off, leave a man when he's all alone and down, life don't hardly seem worth living sometimes." He got up and pulled another beer from the refrigerator. His plate still sat on the kitchen table. He couldn't do that much for her, even carry his plate to the sink.

"You're my only one, now, sweetheart."

So he was in his sloppy sentimental mood. Better than surly, she supposed, but he wanted to talk more when he got like this.

"I got homework to do, Dad."

"Shoulda thought of that before you went gallivanting around, huh? It don't matter though. You ain't gonna be no brain surgeon, honey. You're gonna make some man happy, is all."

"I got to wash up and study, Dad."

"Hell with it," he muttered, as she escaped down the hall.

From her bedroom Nancy could hear the soft murmur of the television, louder when a commercial came on. He'd probably fall asleep and spend the night on the couch.

Nancy changed into her nightgown and washed up in the bathroom. Back in her room she sat cross-legged on her bed with her school books arranged at her knees. American History. All those boring dates. They were studying Manifest Destiny. She got under the covers and propped the book on her chest. Her eyes swam on the page. She was drifting off when she heard the knock on the door.

"Honey?"

She jolted awake. "What is it?"

"Just me. Can I come in for a minute?"

"It's late Dad, I'm studying." Quickly, she picked up the history text that had slid down her chest.

He pushed the door open, shuffled in, the beer like a cloud and the cigarettes stinking on his clothes. She didn't want his smell in her room. He settled himself on her bed. Nancy squooched over toward the wall, glanced at her father. His small features seemed to have drawn together in the center of his round pug face. Behind his glasses his eyes glittered.

"You don't know how lonely I get, Sissy," he said.

Sissy. That was her baby name. No one had used it for years.

"You're the only one worth anything. The only one who'd stay with your old man."

"Okay, Dad, fine, but it's late and I got to study."

"All those other kids run off and leave a man when he's down."

She would too, as soon as she could . . .

"No consideration. You always were the prettiest of all my girls, you know that. You always were my special little girl."

Nancy's chest started to feel funny and light, as though she might levitate out of the room. "Go to bed, Dad," she said, trying to be firm without getting him mad.

"The prettiest, my little blondie girl." He reached out and stroked her hair.

Nancy stiffened. Don't touch me, don't touch me, she silently mouthed.

"You got the best body of the bunch of them too. Oh, sure, your sister's got those big boobs, but you're a better all around package."

"Da-ad," Nancy groaned miserably.

"I get so lonely, sweetheart, so lonely. Don't you want to be a good girl and give some comfort to your old Dad?"

She cooked for him, she cleaned, she kept house, what more did he want? But she knew. How could she not know? Even as he spoke his hand slid down her shoulder and rested, as if casually, on her breast, spreading over the fabric of her nightgown, feeling her nipple.

"DAD! STOP IT!" Nancy jerked away. "Get out!"

"Hey, hey, easy there." The sentimental sweetness was gone now, replaced by his usual belligerence. "Don't go getting all worked up. You think you're some kind of holy virgin? You don't fool me. I know you're spreading those precious legs of yours for that grease monkey."

"GET OUT!" she repeated. She slipped between Dad and the wall and jumped up from the end of the bed. With her arms wrapped in front of her chest she stood panting.

"Hell with you," Dad slurred. "Just another little slut is all you are, like the rest of 'em." Amazingly, he sighed, rose, and shambled out. When he was out the door she ran over and clicked it shut. It had no lock, so she stuffed a chair under the handle the way she'd seen on TV. All the while her heart was pounding so hard she thought she'd be sick. She paced her room, shaking, then climbed back in her bed and pulled the covers to her chin. Outside a wind had picked up and the glass rattled in the windows.

Nancy lay rigid and wide-eyed on her bed, the light blazing, sure she wouldn't sleep at all that night. The room seemed to be closing in, the walls narrowing. She listened to the TV click off in the living room, the heater die as he turned it down, and then his heavy steps into his room. His door shut. She wanted to sneak into the living room and call Gary to come get her, but she was afraid of running into Dad. And anyway, she couldn't tell Gary. It was too shameful. She couldn't tell anyone.

Nancy shot out of bed again, paced the room. She had to do something, invent something, to forget, to force it away. She thought of her belly, where maybe even now a baby was forming, the baby that would free her from him. But as soon as she imagined her baby, she remembered the cold blue baby in the trash can, left behind, thrown away. No.

What then?

She climbed back in bed and lay there trying to make her breath even and smooth. When she closed her eyes the image of the Gateau Bretonne rose miraculously behind her lids. Grateful, she knew what she would do. She would build the cake again, from memory, in her head.

Carefully, methodically, Nancy gathered the ingredients and laid them out on the counter. Orange juice, orange peel, almond flavoring, flour, almonds, sugar, butter, eggs. She selected her bowls, spoons, egg whip. With a hammer and paper she crushed the almonds. Deliberately she measured, sifted, folded, poured, shook the pan, brushed on glaze. When it was in the oven, she pictured her cake taking shape as the minutes ticked past, molecules bonding as it rose, separate ingredients fusing. Eyes shut tight, Nancy watched her cake forming a structure so perfect she might live inside it, a structure so perfect it could never fall.

EASTER

[Marsha, 1979]

"EDDIE, SLOW DOWN," Marsha demanded.

"I'm only going sixty," Eddie groused.

"Well the limit is fifty-five. You know how those Massachusetts cops ticket."

Eddie stubbornly let the speedometer climb a few miles higher.

Marsha shuffled her enormous pregnant bulk in the seat and attempted a deep breath. Her inhalation caught halfway down; the baby was taking up all the room, pressing her lungs. Marsha looked out at the familiar landscape: fields not yet turned to green, the state police barracks just outside of Northampton, the big sign advertising a discount liquor mart at the first exit. Even here, sixty miles south of Shelby, none of the trees had leafed out yet. She hated this time of year as much as she hated November, dreary months when everything was held in suspension and you could almost believe the bareness would never end. She hoped the leaves would be started by the time the baby was born.

"I wonder if anyone else made a cherry pie?" she worried. "Maybe I should have stuck to apple."

Eddie didn't bother to answer.

In the back seat the two pies rested in their carrier: one for Aunt Ellen's dinner down in Holyoke, the other for Eddie's parents later tonight. Marsha's legs ached from standing to roll out the dough and weave the latticework crusts, but she wasn't going to be accused of not pulling her weight, even when her weight included an extra forty-three pounds of pregnancy.

The prettier of the two pies was on the bottom rack; she intended to save it for Eddie's parents, who were rich and had higher expectations. Eddie had refused to join his own family for Easter dinner. When Marsha heard the catch in her mother-in-law's voice, she'd explained that since Mom's and Uncle Jake's deaths, it was important for them to get together with Aunt Ellen's family on holidays, but that she and Eddie would love to stop by for dessert on their way home. Eddie hadn't yet forgiven her.

"I wish you'd just think about how they feel . . ." Marsha started in, but Eddie gave her an angry glance.

"I don't want to hear about it anymore," he said.

Marsha sighed. She just couldn't understand why Eddie didn't want to be around them. He was always like that, even when they were in high school. He could have gone into the family business like his oldest brother, gotten rich helping to run the wooden bowl and basket factory outlets that were so popular with the tourists. Or like his middle brother, he could have gone on to college and law school. *She* was keeping up her night classes at Keene State, along with her job as a receptionist for a dentist in Brattleboro; pregnant or no, she intended to get a degree and raise herself above her family. But all Eddie ever wanted to do was hang out with the town kids. He had no use for the wealthy, educated people from Boston and New York who'd moved up to Vermont, the ones with whom his parents now played golf. He hated the rich flatlanders for buying up the old farms to turn into country houses, blamed them for the destruction of what he considered the "real Vermont way of life"—poverty and desperation, as far as Marsha was concerned. He cursed his father, who no longer admitted that he'd grown up on a dairy farm.

Marsha wondered if Eddie's parents had left Shelby and moved across the river to a big colonial house off the green in Walpole, New Hampshire so their neighbors wouldn't see Eddie driving a

road grader or digging a ditch for the town. Of course, a Walpole
address offered more prestige.

Marsha loved Eddie's parents' house, with its elegant curved
staircase, oriental rugs, and fine old furniture. They might not
have been born to it, but somewhere along the line his parents had
acquired class, and she didn't see why she couldn't let a little of it
rub off. Although they'd been hard on Eddie in the past, ashamed
of his choices, they were making overtures these days. The baby
coming, she supposed. Why did Eddie have to be so obstinate?
With Mom dead, and Dad worse than useless, it was important for
their child to have grandparents.

"Hey, look," Eddie said as they passed the third Northampton
exit and continued south. Mitchell's rusted Ford sedan heaved
along in front of them, blowing burned oil out its tailpipe. Eddie
sped up and drew alongside. A lot of honking and waving ensued,
with Mitchell's toothy smile filling the window. Baby Emily sat
bundled up in the front seat between Mitchell and Corinne—not
even a baby seat for safety, Marsha noted, and probably the heater
didn't work. Dad sat alone in the back, puffing on a cigarette,
stinking up the car. Beside him stood Mitchell's guitar case. Mitchell
was probably hoping for a chance to show off his skills to the
crowd.

"Well, we won't be the last ones there," Eddie said, roaring
ahead, leaving Mitchell's weaving junker in the dust. Even with his
own kid on the way, Eddie still insisted on acting like a teenager.
Sometimes Marsha wondered if she'd made a mistake in marrying
him. But she'd forced him to wait so long, all those years while
Mom was sick, it hadn't seemed fair to back out in the end.

"Slow down, Eddie," she begged.

Eddie released the pedal an increment, but leaned over and
extracted a beer from the six-pack he'd set on the floor between
Marsha's feet.

Marsha closed her eyes in resignation. The baby—little William
or Annie—was bumping its elbow into her ribs. It had grown so
big there wasn't much room for it to move around anymore.
Soon, she thought, little sweetheart. Two more weeks . . .

Gently she massaged her belly, trying to picture the baby. Secretly she hoped it was a girl, although Eddie wanted a boy. A girl would be her best friend. She'd tell a girl all her secrets, just as she and Mom had told each other everything. Or almost everything, she corrected herself. Even as a little girl Marsha hadn't wanted her mother to be hurt or saddened. With Dad, and then the cancer, she'd suffered enough.

An image of her mother, skinny and wasted, rose before her closed lids and Marsha bit her lip to hold back the gasp of pain. It wasn't fair. Mom wouldn't get to see the baby. It wasn't fair that Mom wasn't with them now.

She couldn't understand how the rest of them seemed able to adjust and go on when she couldn't get over it. Sometimes she thought it was her punishment for being loved the most. Mom had told her that before she died, though Marsha had known it all along. Marsha was the only one Mom let see her bald head without her wig, the only one who could bathe her when she was too weak to do it herself, the bumps on Mom's spine standing out like knobs and her legs, always heavy as Gram's, whittled down to spindle sticks. Sometimes Marsha would climb in bed beside her and put her arms around her, silently begging her not to die. When Mom finally passed on, Marsha had wanted to die too, but all she had done was marry Eddie.

She'd never loved her husband as much as she loved Mom. Never. It had always been just the two of them, as though everyone else was background noise. Marsha remembered how they'd leave all the other kids at home and she'd accompany her mother to the laundromat in Bellows Falls to help wash and fold. She liked the sheets best, hot when they came out of the dryer, stretched between them, and that funny little dance they did, coming toward each other, folding, backing away, folding and meeting again, their eyes on each other's like lovers.

Marsha opened her eyes as Eddie slowed for the Holyoke turnoff. She hadn't even noticed their trip through the notch of the Holyoke Range, the spider-like blue water tower that stood guard over the valley on the east side of Interstate 91. They entered the grungy city of Holyoke, passing row buildings, bars, cheesy discount houses, closed five-and-tens. A left turn, a right at the bank, then down a street headed toward the river. Aunt Ellen's house was one of the nicer ones—nothing special, but nothing to sneer at. A hip-roofed white box with a couple of brushy acres in the midst of green and pink asbestos-shingled ranch houses with tacked-on additions.

The neighborhood was much worse than it looked, full of drug addicts. Marsha was sure that if Jamie hadn't come up to Shelby to live with Gramp he'd be one of them by now. Although she loved Aunt Ellen, Marsha thought she gave her kids too much free rein. Oh, sure, Midge was married to Burt and straight as an arrow, and Frank was a holy roller these days, but the rest of them, Jamie, Eileen, and Rosalie, were a bunch of acid-dropping potheads. She believed if it hadn't been for Jamie with his dope and his anti-school ideas, Mitchell might never have quit after tenth grade. Now Marsha had to worry about whether Nancy would graduate in June. Watching over everyone was exhausting. Wearily, she wrestled her way out of her seatbelt as they pulled into the driveway.

Aunt Ellen's house was crowded and boisterous, a swirl of floral church dresses. Nancy had ridden down with Donna and Claude that morning; Gram, who refused to ride in the same car as Dad, had come with Jamie last night. Sally wouldn't be there. She could only get half a day off at the horse farm in Virginia where she worked. Midge, a little replica of Aunt Ellen with her short, mannish haircut and good-natured loud voice, was there with her husband Burt and their spoiled brat Susie; Eileen and Rosalie flitted about with their cigarettes and shrieking laughter. Aunt Ellen was busy in the kitchen. The house overflowed with the scent of ham, the sound of doors slamming, phones ringing, shouts. Marsha had to admit the ham smelled wonderful. More than once when she was a kid they'd eaten venison roast on Easter, with no money to buy a ham.

First came all the talk of her belly—how big it was, how soon the baby would come. Then Mitchell arrived and little Emily drew the attention. The boys—Jamie, Mitchell, Eddie, Claude, and Burt—went out to shoot baskets in the yard. Dad ambled out behind them, a beer in hand. Not his first of the day, either, Marsha was sure.

"Can I help?" Marsha asked, tottering into the kitchen.

"Don't be silly," Aunt Ellen shooed her away. "Go sit in the living room and rest. Keep Gram company."

"I don't need company," Gram announced. She sat in an armchair in front of the turned off TV, straight-backed, grim.

Marsha leaned back on the couch across from her and raised her legs gratefully. Aunt Ellen's house was dark in a cozy sort of way, and although it was not elegant like Eddie's parents', it was full of old things: dark wood paneling, a staircase and bannister salvaged from a house in Bellows Falls, old furniture, and hand-painted Wallace Nutting photographs of Vermont. To the best of her ability, and with very little money, Aunt Ellen had managed to give her house a bit of the antique. Upstairs were high posted beds and a washstand from Great Aunt Gladys. Marsha wondered, a bit guiltily, if she'd inherit any interesting furniture when Gram's other maiden sisters died off.

Midge's daughter Susie came in and stuck a hand on Marsha's belly. "How come you're so fat?" she piped.

Marsha looked about helplessly. Was a four-year-old too young to know that babies grew in bellies? "I ate too many lollipops," Marsha explained. She poked a finger meanly into Susie's pudgy belly. "Same as you."

Susie stuck out her lower lip and flounced out.

"You having twins?" Gram asked, peering at Marsha's belly, disapprovingly, now that the subject had been raised.

"God, no," Marsha said, stung. It wasn't her fault she'd gotten so big. All her life she'd been tiny as a flea. The smallest of the sisters, only four-foot-eleven, she could barely wear junior petite sizes. It was why she looked so ridiculous now—a balloon on popsicle sticks. You'd think she'd get a little leeway, but Gram had gotten so nasty this last year. She supposed it was understandable. Parents weren't supposed to see their children die before them, and then to lose Gramp so soon afterward was a lot for an old woman. Marsha willed herself to forgive. "How you been feeling, Gram?" she attempted.

"Old," Gram muttered. "Not that you care much." She pressed her dress over her thick knees.

"Gram—" Marsha apologized. "I know I should get by more, but with my job and my classes and the baby and everything, I get so tired these days . . ."

Just then Dad came in and dug into the cooler in the hallway for another beer. He nodded at Gram. Marsha could see Gram's hands knotting in outrage. When Dad left, Gram said to the blank TV screen, "All my daughters married men that weren't worthy of them. Three drunks."

Although it was true, Marsha felt some need to contradict Gram's judgment. "What about Aunt Marty? Uncle Arthur's got a great job with IBM. They've got that nice Victorian house and everything up in Burlington."

"They're too fancy to come visit me, but he's still a drunk," Gram said. "My girls didn't learn it at home. Horace was a temperate man. You better watch yourself too, Missy, or you'll be in the same boat."

"Eddie's doing okay, Gram."

"Hmmph. Maybe so, maybe not." Gram worked her jaw angrily, chewing over some resentment. Finally she spat it out: "It never should've been my Annie that died so young, it should've been *him*."

Marsha gasped. She knew Gram meant Dad. A lot of times Marsha had thought the very same thing, but to say it out loud like that wasn't right. She picked up a magazine—*Vermont Life*—and pretended to read about maple sugaring in Peacham. After twenty years in Massachusetts, Aunt Ellen still pined for her home state and regularly subscribed.

Corinne came in, opened her shirt, and noisily nursed Emily. Marsha felt revulsion. The child was over a year old! Enough was enough, in Marsha's opinion. A few months back, Corinne had found her way into the La Leche League, and it was as though

she'd discovered religion. After a lot of prying Corinne had gotten
Marsha to admit that she intended to raise her baby on the bottle.
Now Corinne plied Marsha with La Leche brochures at every
chance. Nursing Nazis. It was easy for her to—Corinne didn't
work or go to school, she didn't care about improving herself, she
just sat around all day in that trailer on the dairy farm where
Mitchell worked, being the perfect mother. What Marsha wouldn't
admit was that the thought of anyone, even a baby, grabbing at
her, needing her body like that, made her sick.

A shout rang from outside: "Son of a bitch!" and then laughter.
Marsha flushed in shame at Eddie's voice. Gram stared at the
empty TV screen. In the kitchen and dining room the girls bustled
about—Nancy, Donna, Eileen, Midge. Rosalie was the round-
faced baby, the same age as Nancy, but too spoiled to even make
her own bed. She just sat at the table smoking and doing a high-
pitched, hysterical imitation of a Japanese pop singer named Pink
Lady she'd seen on TV. Eileen was pouring mixed drinks—rum
and coke—for whoever would take them. "You want one, Ma?"
Eileen called out and Aunt Ellen answered, "Well, maybe just a
little one." Marsha was shocked. She had assumed that all women
who married drunks wouldn't touch a drop; Mom never had. Out
of the corner of her eye Marsha saw Nancy and Rosalie headed
giggling upstairs to a bedroom, drinks in hand. Marsha started to
say something, but gave up. It was Aunt Ellen's house . . .

She worried about Nancy, home alone with Dad. She was spending too much time with her boyfriend Gary, and didn't seem to
give a hoot about her homework. She'd graduate near the bottom
of her class, if she graduated at all this spring. And Donna—she
seemed okay now, she'd been so wild as a teenager, that trouble
with the abortion and all—but since she'd married Claude and
left home she'd gotten too quiet, always clinging to Claude for
dear life. There was something missing in her that Marsha couldn't
identify.

None of them really cared about being *more*, they just wanted
to get out of the house and get by. Marsha knew she ought to be
glad that at least Mitchell was holding down a job now, even if it

was only slaving on a dairy farm, and that Sally was off doing the horse thing, not that Marsha saw much future in it. She couldn't understand it. You'd think she'd come from a different family than the rest of them. Maybe she had, the way Mom gave her all the attention, she reasoned guiltily. Her Intro to Psych professor had talked about that.

The door sprang open and in waddled Frank, Aunt Ellen's oldest, fatter than ever, with his wife Doreen. Doreen had a scared jackrabbit stare. Twitchy, as though she wanted to run out the door. Their little girls Jane, Jan, and Joanne, already looked weird in homemade dresses that didn't fit right, and wore peculiar pious expressions. Frank and Doreen were church crazy now, and didn't approve of these family gatherings where drinking went on.

Gram eyed Frank. "My. How stout you've grown," she said. "You ought to be ashamed."

Frank laughed with false cheer and massaged his belly. "I'm just trying to keep up with Marsha there."

"Well you're a *man*," Gram uttered in disgust. "You aren't pregnant."

"Hey," Frank asserted, "there's no difference between Jamie and me but metabolism. If I didn't have these glands, I'd be as skinny as him."

"That's a good one," Gram said. "When's the last time you bucked up a cord of wood?"

Aunt Ellen came out wiping her hands. "Call them in, will you Frank?" she said. "It's ready."

Frank groaned at the effort of raising his bulk from the chair he'd just settled into.

Midge shouted into Gram's ear, "I got to go up to Burt's parents' house for dinner, Gram. Good to see you though."

Gram shrugged.

"Kiss Great Grammy goodbye," Midge urged her daughter.

"No!" Susie crossed her arms on her chest and shook her head.

Midge leaned down to kiss Gram and winked at Marsha over Gram's head.

Marsha struggled to get up from the couch, as awkward as

Frank, and walked painfully into the dining room. Her feet were swollen and numb. Finally they were all seated, Rosalie and Nancy sharing a card table with Frank's little girls, the rest of them squashed around the big table. Donna sat twined around Claude as though she wanted to sit in the same chair. The boys were flushed and sweating from basketball. Eddie looked completely happy, a mixed drink beside his plate. Marsha panicked. When had he switched from beer? Dad pulled out a cigarette, thought better of it, and stuffed it back in the pack. He drummed his fingers nervously on the table. Pondering his own next beer, Marsha bet. Looking around at the faces, Marsha's eyes watered. She wondered if the rest of them were thinking it: Mom was missing, Mom and Uncle Jake and Gramp. If anyone cared, they didn't show it.

Frank wanted to say Grace.

"Well don't draw it out all day," Gram said. "We don't want a sermon like last time."

Frank sighed heavenward. Even when they were kids his favorite game was playing priest. But since he'd left the Catholic Church Uncle Jake had forced his kids to be raised in, Frank played at being a preacher now.

"Dear Lord," Frank began. "We thank you for bringing us together in your holy sight to bestow on us your blessings . . ."

Marsha saw Mitchell's and Jamie's eyes shift toward each other, smirks on their lips. More of those little secrets they'd always shared.

"And bless the bounty that we are about to receive. The fruits of the fields, the animals you have given us to subdue with the sweat of our brow . . . We thank you that we are fortunate, and not like those that suffer in deprivation in benighted lands across the sea . . ."

Eileen and Rosalie were having a hard time suppressing giggles.

Frank glanced about accusingly. "Yet there is deprivation of the body, and deprivation of the spirit, and there are those among us today who, though you have blessed them with all material gain, refuse to see the light of your ways. And they are as poor as the savage in the jungle or the beasts in the field . . ."

Aunt Ellen frowned.

Dad hawked a wad of phlegm, searched for a place to spit, then helplessly swallowed.

"We ask you dear Jesus to spread your light on this gathering and raise up the souls of those who . . ."

"Amen," Jamie interrupted.

"I wasn't finished," Frank protested.

Eileen and Rosalie snorted. "Give it up," Eileen whooped. "You're wasting your breath on this bunch of sinners."

"But . . ."

"Amen," everyone said quickly. Then came the clamorings, the plates clanging. Slabs of ham moved down the table, followed by mashed potatoes and glistening candied yams. Marsha felt remote from it all. She wasn't really a part of them, not anymore, not with Mom gone. She stared at her father and wondered, what did he feel? Did he miss her? Dad hunched over his plate silently, shoving a big forkful of pink meat into his mouth. Loud conversations criss-crossed the table.

"How's your job, Eileen?" Donna asked.

"Great!" Eileen shook her mane of wild blond curls. She was a pretty girl, but there was something tough about her face, and every few minutes she affected a thuggy accent she must have picked up working as a secretary in Springfield. "Some of the lawyers are pretty sleazy. Some aren't bad. One of the ones I work for? This little Jewish guy? He stops by the house all the time . . ." Eileen peered about quickly to see that Gram and Frank were occupied, "His wife is great too, we go shopping at the mall. She's got this cool red BMW, she drives about ninety frigging miles an hour—excuse my language, Ma."

Aunt Ellen rolled her eyes.

Eileen leaned forward enthusiastically. "The wife, she's far out. She buys me clothes, I provide her with a little . . . recreation. One hand washes d'other, if you know whad' I mean." Marsha shuddered. Eileen was dealing marijuana is what she meant. Beside her, Frank heaped his plate high with thick slabs of ham, drowned his potatoes in gravy, doused his salad with a cup of pink

Russian dressing. It was enough to make her sick. Metabolism, her foot.

Dad called out, "Pass the ham, Nancy sweetheart."

Nancy made a quick, cringing face before reaching for the platter.

Gram looked up. "Don't give that man a thing," she said sharply.

The table immediately hushed, forks hung midair.

"He killed my daughter," Gram explained.

"Mom died of cancer, Gram," Donna said flatly.

"I know good and well what she died of. But that man killed her, sure as shooting."

"Gram . . ."

"Hush now, Ma," Aunt Ellen said. "This is a holiday. Let's enjoy being together."

Dad got up from his chair, gave them all a wild look, and hurried outside. They could hear his shoes thumping on the steps, the door slam. Not one of his children made a move to follow him.

Aunt Ellen sighed. Her own eyes were wet with tears. "I thought we were done with scenes in this house," she said. She stood, lay down her napkin, followed Lowell outside. Voices mumbled beyond the door. Head down, Gram cut her ham into precise, angry bites.

Frank turned to Eddie and said clearly, as though everyone had been talking about just that thing, "My minister says all this rise in homosexuality lately is a form of witchcraft. It's just another chance for Satan to spread his influence. So, when you hear all this stuff about discrimination . . ."

"Why you telling me?" Eddie interrupted. "I'm not queer."

"But have you been saved yet?" Jamie asked. "That's what Frank really wants to know."

Mitchell snorted. "Eddie's been pickled maybe, but not saved."

"You shut up, Mitchell," Marsha said hotly, but the laughter rose up around her in a wall. They were all relieved to be laughing, eager to make a joke at her expense. The food platters started spinning past her eyes again.

After a while Dad and Aunt Ellen came back inside and took

their seats. They continued to eat as though nothing had happened. The phone rang.

"Oh, let it go," Aunt Ellen said. "It's probably just one of the girls' boyfriends. They ought to know better than to call now. They can wait."

"Remember how the old man never let us take calls during dinner?" Eileen said. "He wasn't going to have anyone disrupt his supper."

The phone rang on. "It might be Sally," Marsha broke in. "She said she'd call."

"Oh! Sally! Run and get it then," Aunt Ellen urged.

Donna jumped up and grabbed the receiver off the kitchen wall.

"Hello? Hey!" She called out to the diners, "It's Sally."

Then back into the receiver: "I can't believe they made you work today. I know. Did you get any dinner? Everyone's here. Of course Claude came. Yeah, we're all having a real good time. But . . ." Donna flipped the kitchen door closed and her voice was muffled behind it. Marsha thought she could make out the word "Gram." A few minutes later, Donna opened the door and called out, "She wants to talk to Dad."

Lowell fumbled over to the phone. The room quieted as everyone listened. "Fine, fine, yup. I'm doing real good. Now don't you go worrying. That's a shame, honey. Everybody misses you too. You're doing good down there, you just keep at it . . ."

Marsha saw Mitchell tense, listening to the praise he'd never received and she too winced at Dad's oddly tender tone. He was acting lovey with Sally because she was the only one who didn't hold things against him. Sally who never got mad.

"Now honey, don't cry," Dad mumbled. "Here, Ellen, you better talk to her."

"Let me!" Marsha said, struggling to push her chair back, but Aunt Ellen had already taken the receiver. She closed the kitchen door and they could only hear the muted rise and fall of her voice but not the words. A few minutes later she came back to the table.

"You didn't hang up, did you?" Marsha accused.

"She had to go," Aunt Ellen reported. "She was using her boss's phone and didn't want to run up the bill. Poor kid. She's lonely down there. She says hi to everyone."

Marsha was miffed. Her sister needed her and nobody even let her speak.

"Claude and me are thinking of driving down to see her in May," Donna said.

"If work isn't too crazy," Claude corrected. "I said we'd see. If I got a foundation or something then . . ."

"You *always* work," Donna pouted.

"You should be thankful for that," Marsha said sharply. She was jealous of Claude's ambition. She wished Eddie had more of it. Donna wouldn't be living in a rental house all *her* life.

"We ought to go down together to see her," Eileen suggested. "A girls' road trip. You, me, Nancy, Rosalie . . ."

What about me, Marsha fretted, forgetting for a moment the baby on its way, or that a trip like that would make her miserable.

"I wouldn't go without Claude," Donna said fiercely, running her hands through Claude's hair. "I wouldn't leave him all alone at home."

Eileen rolled her eyes. "He'd survive. Hey, it'd be fun. We could stop over in New York City, see d'sights, catch a concert, climb d'frigging Statue of Liberty . . ."

"That reminds me," Frank cut in. "I read an interesting article in the church paper about the Statue of Liberty just the other day. Did you know it was based on the figure of Mary Magdalene?"

"Oh, come on Frankfurter," Jamie objected. "That's stretching it."

"No lie," Frank protested.

Marsha tuned out as Frank went on with his long explanation of the statue's Christian significance, and the platters slowed their traffic as everyone but Frank, who could lecture and eat at the same time, got full.

They decided they'd wait for dessert. Gram stationed herself in front of the TV in the living room. *The Greatest Story Ever Told* was on, so Frank and his wife joined Gram. Marsha got up to help clear, but Donna chased her away. Corinne went upstairs to give baby Emily a nap, while Mitchell brought his guitar in from the car and sat at the table strumming intently. Bluegrass. He had ability, but the music was boring, Marsha thought. Worse than country music even. Dad smoked a cigarette at the table, listening. Encouraged by his father's presence, Mitchell strummed faster, more intricate chords and flourishes.

"It's too bad Sally ain't here to sing," Dad commented. "She always had the prettiest voice."

Mitchell abruptly put his guitar down and walked out of the room. Marsha felt a wave of pity for her brother. In her Intro to Psych class the professor said that kids who were never valued by their parents either gave up trying, or overcompensated by trying too hard to achieve. Mitchell was always doing one or the other. Marsha got up from the table and went into the living room. A minute later, Jamie, Mitchell, Eddie, Eileen, Nancy, Rosalie, and Claude decided they were going for a walk to the trestle.

Going to light up joints, Marsha knew. "Eddie," she called sharply. "Stay here with me, please."

"I'll be back in a few minutes, honey." He was jovial, happy with booze and company. "I got to walk off that great meal. Make room for some pie."

"We're having pie with your folks," Marsha reminded. "We'll have to leave soon to make it in time. We ought to . . ."

"For Christ's sake, Marsha, give it a rest," Edddie snapped. "I'm just going for a little walk."

"Let them go," Aunt Ellen counseled, eager to avert more outbursts.

"You gotta pamper her more, Eddie," Eileen said. "How'd you like d'have d'haul that friggin' belly around?" She was holding a travel mug filled with rum and coke and grinning.

Defeated, Marsha went back into the living room and lowered herself heavily onto the couch.

"Don't do the dishes, we'll do them when we get back," the girls called. Yeah, right, Marsha thought. They'd let Aunt Ellen do it all. If she weren't so tired she'd be in there helping now. Then everyone was gone in a rustle of jackets and slam of doors, laughter. Even Donna, who didn't like dope smoking either, had run after them. She couldn't be separated from Claude for a minute.

"Don't pay them any attention," Aunt Ellen said, standing at the opening between the dining room and living room.

"You know what they're going to do?" Marsha tattled.

"I can't control them," Aunt Ellen said. "It's their lives. I just don't let them do it in my house."

Gram stared at the screen and said nothing. Jesus was busy smashing the tables of the moneylenders in the temple.

"You just put your feet up on the couch there and stop worrying yourself," Aunt Ellen said. "You'll turn your baby into a worrywart."

She was used to it, Marsha supposed. All those years with Uncle Jake drinking. But Marsha wouldn't get used to it. When the baby was born it would be different. Eddie would come to see his responsibilities . . .

"You kids are sitting too close to that screen," Aunt Ellen warned.

"Shhh, Grammy," one of Frank's little girls said in exasperation. "Can't you see it's Jesus?"

Aunt Ellen headed back toward the kitchen.

Marsha lay back and waited. She tried to compute just how many beers and drinks Eddie could have had by now. And the grass. She hated even the smell of grass now, although there had been a brief period when she'd joined Eddie in his partying, until the time she tried acid. It was years ago, up in the sugarhouse with the rest of them. In fact, she'd loved it at first. The way everything moved and pulsed and was simultaneously itself and yet somehow not itself. An airplane flew overhead dragging the sky behind it like a great wrinkled blanket, and Marsha thought, that's right! It's always like that but you can't usually see it. She felt on the edge of some incredible realization. But then it started going bad. She panicked, and when she cried her tears turned to crystal and shattered on the floor in front of her feet. She felt her own self fracturing, breaking apart, and knew that nothing but luck held her together. When it was over, she decided it was wrong, never to be repeated. She suspected there was something already broken in all of them, something that could rupture and disintegrate forever, and none of them should take that risk.

The movie music swelled. Under it, Dad's voice droned on at the dining room table, talking to Aunt Ellen through the open kitchen door while dishes clanked in the kitchen. She supposed they were talking about their losses, sympathizing. For a rare moment, Marsha felt sorry for her father. After all, he had lost his wife. Then, during a lull in the movie, Marsha heard them clearly, Dad's voice wheedling, "Ellen, I been thinking we ought to spend some time together. You been alone here two years now, I know you got needs just like a man."

"Oh no," Aunt Ellen said. "Oh no, Lowell, you can just stop right there. You're my brother-in-law and I love you for it, but that's it. I don't want any of that."

"Don't tell me you don't never get lonely."

"No, I don't, Lowell. I've got my church, I've got this house to take care of, Rosalie and Eileen are still at home, I'm satisfied."

Marsha heard Dad rise from his chair and go into the kitchen. It got silent for a moment, then Aunt Ellen said clearly, "You just cut that out Lowell Chartrain."

Dad came out with his beer can, looking sheepish. Marsha burned. He wasn't thinking about Mom at all, just about getting laid. Mom's sister, too. It made her sick. Why couldn't she be at Eddie's parents' now, instead of with her own low-life family? She struggled off the couch, gave Dad a glare, and pulled her bulk up the staircase, headed for a bedroom where she could wait in peace.

The movie went on forever, it seemed, and then finally they were all back, slamming doors, laughing too loudly. It was almost dark outside.

"Who's winning?" Jamie asked of the TV watchers, and one of Frank's girls said, "God, silly."

Their laughter was hysterical, stoned.

"Eddie!" Marsha called. "Eddie, we got to go or we'll be late."

"Alright, alright," Eddie called back. "Get yourself down here."

Marsha sat up slowly. Her dress was probably all wrinkled by now. She should have taken it off, but it was too much effort. She felt headachy and weak, and the baby was pounding out a rhythm in her gut. They were too late to go home for her to change before going to Eddie's parents. Slowly, she made her way downstairs. Aunt Ellen proffered a bag of leftovers. Eddie held another beer.

"Don't you think that's enough?" Marsha hissed. She could imagine showing up at his parents with Eddie loaded. It was probably his plan.

"No harm in it," Eddie assured her.

"I'll drive," Marsha offered.

"You can't drive. You can't even see over your belly."

The goodbyes went on forever, but finally they were settled into the car. Marsha buckled herself into the seatbelt, tucking the waist strap under her belly as best she could. Eddie pulled out of the yard with a flourish of spinning tires.

"For God's sake," Marsha complained. "Grow up."

Eddie just laughed.

Instead of getting back onto 91 immediately, Eddie wound his way through downtown Holyoke and then onto back roads heading north.

"Aren't we late enough?" Marsha asked.

"Marsha, I've had a few and I got less chance of getting stopped than on 91, okay? I don't want to lose my license."

Holyoke, Chicopee, Northampton. The houses flashed by in the dark. It began to rain lightly.

"April showers bring May flowers," Eddie sang gaily. "It was a good time down there, wasn't it baby?"

"It was okay."

"You know." Eddie turned in his seat. "I don't get it. I like your family better than mine, and you like mine better than yours."

"I like mine," Marsha protested. "I love Aunt Ellen."

"Well I had a good time," Eddie insisted, "even if you didn't. I'm *still* having a good time."

Marsha didn't say anything. Rows of dark trees slid past the spattered windows. Eddie hit the brakes hard and Marsha threw her hand out toward the dashboard.

"Shit," Eddie said. "A cat. I missed it."

Marsha expelled tense breath. "Why don't you slow down?"

"Hey, you're the one who's so worried about being late."

Marsha didn't say anything.

"Let's play the alphabet game," Eddie offered.

Marsha laughed. There was hardly a sign to be seen, little traffic for reading the letters off license plates, and it was dark on these unlit roads. "Sure," she said, because the idea was so ridiculous. She relaxed into her seat. They were headed home, finally, headed to Eddie's parents. The car even felt cozy. She was willing to forgive Eddie, now that they were leaving Dad and the rest of them behind. Marsha squinted into the darkness for a signpost. Albert Connor, she read off a mailbox. That gave her an A, a B, and a C.

"I'm up to J," Eddie announced a moment later.

"You liar. You can't be."

"Yup. J for Jesus. Hey, that was quite a grace old Frank gave us today."

"I think they're crazy, Frank and Doreen and the kids."

"Pitiful. Promise me you won't dress our kid like that."

Marsha laughed. "Not if it's a boy."

Eddie reached over and squeezed Marsha's knee. "Gimme a kiss," he said. "Whoops." He swung the wheel hard, making the tires screech and sending the pie carrier flying across the back seat.

"Eddie! My pie." Marsha tried to turn in her seat to rescue it, but she couldn't reach.

"Sorry, baby, just went a little fast around that corner."

"Shit," Marsha said. She rarely swore. Sighing, she unhooked her seatbelt, turned on the overhead light, and laboriously swung around to reach for the pie carrier. It was nowhere to be seen.

"Damn it, Eddie, it fell off the seat. If that pie's ruined so help me . . ."

Marsha hoisted her big belly against the seat back and struggled to balance as she reached for the fallen wicker pie carrier. It was a gift from Eddie's parents, from their basket factory. But Eddie was already taking the next turn too wide. Headlights came toward him, directly in his path. Eddie swung too hard to the right and the tire went onto the soft shoulder mud.

"Fuck!" Eddie said as the car shimmied and lurched sideways.

Scrabbling for the overturned pie carrier, Marsha had time only to think: Damn, he ruined it—before she was flung backward against the shattering windshield glass and knew, for the first time, peace.

SILHOUETTE

[Mitchell, 1984]

IN THE MIDDLE of the night, Mitchell rolled over onto one of the kids. Carver, he thought, but maybe it was Emily. A tiny moan, and he rolled back fast against Corinne. There were legs everywhere. Little warm snuffling breaths, like sleeping in a pile of puppies. He reached out to Corinne to touch her back, but there was a small hard head in the way: Eli's. Mitchell lay there, breathing angrily in the dark of night, mind made up. If she'd rather sleep all five of them together, it would be four from now on. He'd sleep alone, until Corinne was ready to let go of the kids. Not that they didn't do it anymore, but it was always sneaking in a quick one while the kids were playing outside. In his own bed he'd been displaced by a heap of rug rats.

The moon was high and Mitchell's eyes adjusted so he could see Corinne's pale hair spread out, under and over the kids. He got up, careful not to step on anyone, shivering in the cold. Where was his sleeping bag stashed?

"Mitch?" Corinne called groggily. "Where you going?"

"The couch."

"What's the matter, can't you sleep, honey?"

"Not like this," he hissed. He hoped she'd pity him, though the reasonable part of his mind knew that anger never elicited much pity in anyone. Besides, Corinne had already drifted back into sleep, the pile shifting around her.

In the living room, Mitchell clanked open the door of the woodstove and poked around. The log hadn't caught, or had gone out. Damn. He never got his wood in early enough for it to dry. Cursing, freezing, bare soles on raw plywood, he crushed newspaper and paper bags, broke kindling, lit a match, then gave up. There wasn't enough split wood in the house to keep a fire going through the night, anyway. Hell with it.

After stubbing his toe on the place where the living room plywood didn't quite meet the kitchen subfloor, Mitchell found his old sleeping bag stuffed into a trash sack under a pile of junk in their "closet"—a metal pipe suspended across one corner of the kitchen. He lay his bag out on the sagging couch, slid into the icy nylon, rubbing his bare legs together to warm it. Through the doorless opening of the bedroom his children whimpered and snored, wrapped around Corinne. Sleepless, freezing, Mitchell stared through the frost-patterned glass of the living room window at bare branches holding crusty old snow.

The stupid thing was, he'd gotten used to it and now he couldn't fall asleep without them. Plus, he wished he hadn't spent half the day reading Whitley Streiber's *Communion*. That town in New York State was just a quick zip away in a space craft for a couple of ugly little aliens. To make it worse, he had to pee. It was dark out there and Corinne was asleep. He'd be the first to admit that his ease in the world depended on her waking presence. There were all sorts of bogeymen waiting to grab a hulking guy with a Navy tattoo on his arm who lived in a house without a toilet. He could almost feel aliens pulsing there in the darkness, like an evil-spirited aurora borealis. No way he was going outside.

Mitchell clambered up out of his sleeping bag, which had finally absorbed enough of his body heat to quit giving him goose pimples. He stubbed his toe once more, but cursed silently, so as not to alert hovering aliens as well as sleeping kids, and cracked the front door open just enough to prickle his legs with icy gusts. Thanks to the three cups of tea he'd consumed this evening, he managed to

pee just past his own doorstep. Very nice; the yellow stain would
be there in the morning. Wishing he'd installed a lock, he pushed
the door shut and scuttled back to his lonely sleeping bag on the
couch. Through the living room window, shadows of tree branches
crept menacingly over the moonlit snow. Mitchell squeezed his
eyes shut and used a childhood device, counting madly until the
meaningless numbers tricked him into sleep.

Three days later Corinne relented, as she always did. Mitchell
took the chainsaw and carved out a hatch through the living room
ceiling for access to the only insulated room in the unfinished
upstairs. There was no indoor staircase; he pounded a ladder together so the kids could climb up at bedtime and nailed up sloppy
sheetrock, not bothering to tape the joints. The kids would cover
it with crayons anyway.

That night he and Corinne lay alone in bed for the first time
since Emily was born six years ago. After some quick grappling,
Mitchell spread his arms and legs, luxuriating in privacy and space,
and let himself drift. Corinne tossed, sighed, nudged him awake.
She couldn't sleep unless they were tugging at her, breathing on
her. She'd probably be happiest if the whole crew were still nursing. She had breast-fed Eli until last year, when he was three and
screaming for his titty by name.

The irony of Corinne's earth-mother persona, in Mitchell's
opinion, was that she was so flat-chested. Which didn't make her
any less gorgeous—with her long, athletic legs, prominent cheek-
bones, and violet eyes, Mitchell considered his wife a knockout.
But the boob thing was a pitiful joke. He knew her too well not to
know what it was all about. Corinne, once the smartest kid at the
Union High School, had no idea of herself beyond motherhood.

"I miss them," she whispered.

"You can baby me," Mitchell mumbled, cuddling close.

"Mitch, let's make another one."

He jerked away. "Jesus, no."

Corinne leaned over the table to pour more tea into Mitchell's
mug. He spooned and stirred honey. Inside the woodstove, logs

whistled and snapped. The rug rats were quiet; Eli napped in the bedroom and Emily and Carver, cross-legged on the living room rug, wrangled over a worn out game of "Life" that Corinne had picked up at the charity store for a dollar. They couldn't read the cards and instructions so they made up their own rules and rewards: two blocks up the board, find a bag of candy; one block back, marry a mean old witch. Outside, the snow pressed itself onto the hillside, closing off the road, blocking any entrance or retreat. A pot of lentils simmered on the stove, raising its lid, dropping it with a clank, spewing a cozy, legume-laden steam.

Corinne sat down across from him. "They brought Ray Hilliard in last night."

"Again?"

"Yup." Corinne's face lit up with the telling. These days she worked as a receptionist on the tiny psych ward at the Bellows Falls hospital and got all the inside dirt. They liked to chew over everybody else's life, since nobody thought much of theirs. Even Mitchell's sisters wouldn't come up the hill to visit anymore. No one liked Corinne because of her terrible housekeeping, and because she was critical of everyone else's child-rearing methods since she had gotten involved with the La Leche League. As for Mitchell, nobody liked him because he walked off all his jobs and didn't care. Plus they were famous moochers, going down to his sisters' houses for showers or to use the phone. And their place looked like hell.

When Mitchell had thrown the house together, racing against winter, he only shingled about six feet up, as far as he could reach without a ladder. Five years later the tar paper flapped and the upstairs of the house, except for the one room the kids now slept in, remained an uninsulated storage space full of trash. Under the house there was no foundation; Mitchell had laid his joists on cement blocks, and hadn't bothered with a level, so the rooms resembled parallelograms instead of rectangles, and the windows all pitched at different angles. Frost had heaved the blocks and the house sagged, the roofline betraying the lack of a foundation. On the coldest days they froze with just the wood stove and got headaches from the kerosene heater.

Mitchell couldn't quite figure how it happened that he lived like the Culhanes on *Hee Haw*. He was more than that, he knew, but something was always pulling him down. The yard was full of garbage, stuff that had been used up or worn out or malfunctioned once and he couldn't be bothered to fix. When he was done with something, that was it—out it went, forgotten. And it was the same with the house: he knew he'd never finish it. First off, Gramp had put a curse on it, declaring he'd give no more land to Chartrains when Mitchell had asked, damning the whole family with his hatred of Dad. Mitchell had only gotten his piece from Jamie after the old man died. Jamie and Gram had worked it out—the girls got cash, the boys got land. Jamie had slowly bought up the pieces from his brother and Aunt Marty's sons. Mitchell knew he was never meant to have any.

Secondly, he had no follow-through. In long sessions of self-examination he pondered why, with all his energy and talent, he couldn't maintain interest. Now he was obsessed with photography, but before that, he'd practiced his guitar incessantly, then stuffed it under the bed for months. He threw himself into poetry, even placed a poem in the local *Town Crier*, then quit writing. He trained hundreds of miles a week on his racing bike and came in an impressive tenth out of a field of three hundred in his first race. Although it was no small achievement, it wasn't good enough. No matter how enthusiastically he started out, no activity could keep his interest once it failed to offer up that golden nugget of self-importance.

Thinking about his failures made Mitchell's mood sink and he took a big sip of the sweet, smoky Earl Grey—they didn't skimp on tea, their only luxury—letting it roll across his tongue, trying to regain that cozy feeling. "So Hilliard went on a bender. What was he, seeing snakes again?"

"Worse. This time he went down to Andrews Inn and started shouting about kicking all the perverts out of town. Broke some windows in the Catholic Church, screaming that the priests were perverts too. He wasn't even drunk." Corinne lowered her voice. "Turns out he came home yesterday, caught his uncle molesting his four-year-old boy, and knocked him in the head with a kiddie oven. The metal kind."

Mitchell tried to imagine how much damage you could do with a kiddie oven. More if the oven door was open, he supposed.

"When they brought him in he was raving about how he was going to kill every pervert in town."

Mitchell laughed. "That'd fill up the town vault fast. Be good work in the spring, though, digging pervert graves."

"Shhh," Corinne warned. They both turned to look at Carver and Emily, their blond heads shining above the tired green rug.

"They aren't listening," Mitchell said.

"Listening to what?" Emily spun around.

"Who's winning?" Mitchell asked to divert her.

"Me," Carver said.

"No way," Emily insisted.

"Yes I am. You said if you got down that red part there, then the first one who goes around that corner . . ."

"I didn't, I said you had to get three of the little cards first."

"You're a poop," Carver brazened. When no one reprimanded him, he giggled behind his cards.

"So, what happened with Hilliard?" Mitchell prompted.

"They gave him a shot of Thorazine and restrained him. They're sending him up to Montpelier for observation."

"What about the uncle?"

"He came into the emergency ward with facial lacerations and a possible fracture." Corinne liked using hospital lingo. She got up, stirred the pot, chopped an onion and threw it in, along with a carrot and a bay leaf. "Now Renee" (Corinne pronounced it Ray-knee, as was the local custom) "won't be so quick to put her nose in the air when she sees me in Buffums Market." Renee was Ray Hilliard's cousin, daughter to the deviant uncle, who'd married a chiropractor and taken on airs. "I feel sorry for the little boy, though."

Mitchell shook his head. There was plenty of that stuff around. First Donna's boy Jimmy getting pawed by his great-uncle up in Masonville one time, and then Mitchell had always wondered about Dad. The way Marsha hated him so bad, and how Dad went sniffing after everyone, even his nieces, after Mom died. Good thing Dad had remarried, to a woman who straightened him out. He'd quit drinking, something that pained Mitchell's sisters, since Mom never could get him to stop. The lure of regular sex, or the threat of withholding it, probably. Whatever worked, Mitchell figured. He drained his cup and poured himself another from the teapot. "What do you think about rabbits?" he asked.

"Rabbits? Like the Easter bunny?" Corinne was washing dishes now, with water heated on the stove.

"Like meat. Make some cages, raise them up, you know, get into the rabbit meat business."

"The kids'll get upset if you kill them."

"They won't be pets. It's a business. I read about it in *Mother Earth News*. You start out with two bucks and ten does, they breed like bunnies, and soon you got hundreds. Easy money."

"Where would you sell rabbit meat?"

"I got to figure that part out."

"I don't know anyone who eats it."

"The French do. Half the town's Canuck. Or we could ship it to New York. There's places."

Corinne shrugged. "I heard the males eat the babies if you don't separate them. Oh, I saw this thing on sea lions last night on the lounge TV. When they group up on these islands during mating season, only a few bulls get to mate, so the rest of the males get really frustrated, and they attack the babies. It was horrible."

Mitchell pushed his chair away from the table. "Jeez, it makes you hopeful about nature. Hilliard's uncle and murderous sea lions and baby-eating bunnies. In fact, it just makes me so disgusted with life I need some help getting my hope back." He pulled Corinne down onto his lap and leaned into her hair. "You want to help me get my hope back?"

She laughed, tilted her head toward the living room.

"Hey," Mitchell called out, "you kids need some fresh air, don't you? How come you aren't playing outside?"

"Dad-dee, we don't want to go outside," Emily explained with strained patience. "We're playing The Game of Life."

"It's a lousy game," Mitchell said. "The odds are against you. No way you can win."

"See?" Carver stuck out his tongue at Emily. "I told you it was a dumb game. I can't win 'cause you make up the stinky rules and then you cheat."

"I don't." Emily sighed. "C'mon, Carver, you can take two turns in a row if you want."

Mitchell pressed his nose into Corinne's back but she was already rising from his lap.

In February, Corinne walked down the hill carrying her waitress uniform, stepping carefully through new snow to keep it out of the tops of her boots. She was waitressing these days in Saxton's River, and she'd left the car parked nose to a snowbank, at the bottom of the hill when she came in from work yesterday. There'd been another storm last night but it didn't matter; the car hadn't made it up the hill in months. Mitchell poked the stove, sent Emily out for wood, wiped half-heartedly at the snow she tracked in as it quickly turned to slush.

Mitchell was official baby-sitter these days, after walking off another job. That made three in the past nine months. Nobody was better at finding work than Mitchell. He could talk the biggest line of bull, pushing his way in the door of a woodworking shop or onto a logging job or diesel repair outfit with slick talk and promises. And the thing of it was, he usually did well. He was a quick study and had natural talent. He'd start off full of manic energy, desperate to prove his worth. But once he was there, knuckling under, head in the noose, it worked on him. Either the boss turned out to be a jerk, or else he couldn't take the fact that he'd lied about his inexperience. The weeks would go by and he'd be so afraid of getting caught out by his ignorance, he had to walk just to make sure it didn't happen.

Mitchell turned on the water spigot over the sink and filled a pot for oatmeal. He had to turn the faucet off fast because the sink drained into an open bucket; he'd plumbed water into the house, but not out. While the kids ate their oatmeal he sat with his tea by the stove. He loved the way the light came into the house after a fresh snow, playing on the walls, bouncing off the backing on the insulation that he hadn't gotten around to covering. And outside a muffling silence, the only sound crows cawing and the woosh and thud of snow sliding off the roof.

He reread a letter from Sally, who was living in Alaska with her jerk of a husband Billy Devereau, who thought he'd make a bundle in construction. Sally wrote that she lived her winter days in half-light. Mitchell tried to imagine it: trapped inside an endless dusk, cold that could shatter ax heads or freeze the fingers off kids, locked inside the stillness of a thousand miles of land in all directions. No, thank you.

After breakfast, he bundled the kids into snowsuits, mittens, rubber boots, and pompom hats, and led them up into the woods. His camera hung from a strap under his down parka. The branches of pine and hemlock bent low under the snow's weight, springing free suddenly to dump a load on their heads. Chickadees cheeped and pecked in the sheltered lee of a bull pine. Every rock and stump was capped by a soft white pyramid. Mitchell broke trail toward the beaver ponds by the old orchard, but the snow was deep and Eli floundered. Carver started to whine.

"I hate the snow."

"C'mon, it's beautiful." Mitchell tried to imagine walking like this with his father and couldn't; no way he'd have dared complain.

They made it as far as Vesey Brook. Under a load of snow, the brook rushed about its business. Mitchell kicked a section clear so they could watch the water running under fractured ice. With a pang he remembered his mother quoting lines from a poem when he was little: "We minded that the sharpest ear the babbling brook it could not hear." He never understood the poem; no matter how deep the snow, you could always hear water if you listened.

She'd also read to him from a book called *Water Babies*. It was a funny, old-fashioned English book with line drawings, about a filthy, miserable little chimney sweep who fell in a river and drowned. But instead of dying, he turned into a water creature and lived a new life among beautiful naked water girls and waving fronds and fish. Mitchell could still imagine sinking beneath the water, giving up one sooty awful life and being granted another. Of course, predators existed, even for the water babies, though Mitchell couldn't remember what they were now. Otters maybe, or muskrats. There was no true escape.

Mitchell framed a rock poking through delicate layers of ice with his viewfinder—a planet, whirling in frozen rings in some far-off galaxy. When he snapped the shutter, he knew the picture wouldn't show what he saw.

"Where do the frogs go in winter, Daddy?" Emily asked.

Carver and Eli looked up from smashing their boot heels into the crust on the edge of the brook, waiting for his wisdom.

"They just burrow down in the mud and slow down their bodies so they don't have to eat. Pretty neat trick, huh?"

"What about the fishes?"

"They slow down too, but they don't sleep."

"How 'bout the mosquitoes?" Eli demanded.

"They die and new ones show up every spring."

"My mittens are wet and my hands are freezing," Carver whined. "Can we go home?"

At the house, boots had to be pulled off, socks and mittens and snowsuits hung on a rack by the woodstove, slippers insisted on. After a lunch of leftover soup and Saltines, all of them piled together on the living room floor and napped. When they woke it was back into socks and snowsuits and boots and mittens and hats.

Outside, the brilliant snow reflected sun into their eyes. Emily flopped backward into the powder and swung her arms in arcs. The littler kids followed.

"Carver stepped in my angel," Eli tattled.

"So make a new one," Mitchell instructed. "There's plenty of snow."

Carver touched his tongue to an aluminum ski pole left in the
yard and got it stuck; he had to be taken inside to melt it off.
Mitchell decided on a project. They nailed together strapping
wood for swords and had a sword fight, the three kids against him,
with lots of dying falls and Mitchell jumping off the roof of the
shed into a snow pile. Then Mitchell stamped out the outline of a
schooner and they all got in and sailed the hillside.

It was the boat he'd own someday when he moved them all to
Maine. He hadn't been back, not once since his aborted trip when
he was sixteen and had left his job driving the kiddie train at
Santa's Workshop. He'd wanted to sail even then, but who'd hire
a kid who didn't know anything, let alone a kid who had two black
eyes from being beat up by a chimp? He tried and failed to get
work on fishing boats, charters, in a boatyard. In Rockland, he
slept in a marine junkyard between peeling wooden hulls and
rusting machine parts—enormous pistons the size of his legs,
gears so large you could slide a hand between the teeth. They
made him feel like the incredible shrinking man.

By then it was late August, and the college kids were ditching
their summer jobs to party before the season ended. Back down
in Old Orchard Beach Mitchell got hired on at a tourist motel
called—no lie—The Passing Winds, where for $2.10 an hour he
cleaned toilets and made beds and picked used condoms and
soggy towels off bathroom floors.

In the evenings he walked the public beach. Even though the
docks were lined with graceful teak-trimmed craft, and out on the
indigo sea the sails filled with wind, Mitchell was landlocked,
ashore and adrift. Homesickness ripped at him; he'd never been
away before. He stepped over clam roll cartons and coke cups,
dipping his toes in the waves to convince himself he was really at
the shore. The water lapped quiet and icy and the briny low-tide
stench filled his nose, but it was all out of reach. The foghorn
might as well have been the sound of his own plaintive heart; the
calmed evening sea could be the green sweep of a Vermont summer pasture.

Mitchell quit one morning without a backward glance, and

made it home that evening. He snuck past the house and up to Jamie's cabin, and there he had stayed until he was old enough to join the Navy, which was another big mistake.

Standing on the deck of his stomped snow schooner, Mitchell let the swells roll beneath his feet. He needed the ocean, though he didn't know why. Nothing here was big enough, open enough for the tides of his imagination.

"Dad, Dad, I see a pirate ship!" Carver called out. "Dad, Dad, look!"

"Avast ye mateys," Mitchell ordered his crew, "Ready the cannons on deck. Look sharp now."

The kids scurried around, forming snowballs to bombard enemy craft.

"Ha Ha! Eli just stepped off the boat," Carver announced.

"I didn't," Eli lisped, standing one foot over the outline of the ship.

"He's drowned. Ha ha, ha ha."

"No I'm not." Eli rocked in his leggings and boots, red-faced from the cold, about to cry.

"Alright, all of ye, no arguing, you're my crew and we got enemy fire. Any insubordination and you'll walk the plank! Fire the cannons."

A barrage of snowballs flew in soft, overhand loops, smashing against tree trunks and sinking in the white waves.

"Shiver me timbers, I'm hit!" Mitchell clutched his heart, staggered, belly-flopped overboard.

"Daddy, Daddy, don't die," Eli cried. "Daddy."

Mitchell lay there for two beats, then lurched up. "Got ya!"

Screaming, laughing, the kids piled on in a spray of snow.

They kept it up all spring, through sugaring and mud season and into blackfly season: Mitchell babysitting, Corinne coming home with pockets jammed full of dollar bills and coins. She'd make more, she said, if she worked a dinner shift, and that would give Mitchell a chance for a daytime job while she watched the kids, but he wasn't ready to face another boss. Instead, when Corinne got home he took off with Jamie, down to Brattleboro or over to Keene for movies, or just to the sugarhouse to get a break from the kids. He imagined Corinne wanted the time with them anyway.

Jamie came up each night for dinner. He paid them $25 a week to share in Corinne's bubble and squeak or casseroles, and he rolled on the floor with the kids, swung them through the air, talked gruff and bought them presents. After his girlfriend got tired of playing Mrs. Daniel Boone and ran off, Jamie gave up hope of having kids of his own and concentrated on playing uncle.

Mitchell figured they got by okay, between Corinne's tips, Jamie's cash, and food stamps. He didn't need a job.

As spring wore on, though, the house filled with a refrain that got on his nerves. Corinne had made a friend whose brother owned the restaurant where she worked, and it was Judy Beal this, Judy Beal that all day. Never just Judy, as though she was too important for just one name.

"Judy Beal's going to Tortola with her boyfriend," Corinne announced as she lugged the bucket out from under the sink.

"Good for her." Judy Beal's boyfriend was a rich contractor-turned-developer who'd destroyed a hayfield in Rockingham, skirting the Act-250 antidevelopment law by selling the land to a proxy, and filling the field with ugly cedar boxes. Soon Mitchell was hearing as much about Judy Beal's brother as about Judy. The brother drove a Porsche and had his own Jacuzzi. "It holds six people," Corinne bragged as though it were her own.

"You've seen it?"

"No . . . Judy told me about it."

Mitchell bit his tongue. Corinne didn't have any interests outside of the kids, so he supposed he ought to let her enjoy herself, even if he doubted the depth of Judy Beal's friendship. Judy frequently asked Corinne to babysit her kid on weekends—always at her house—and she'd never once made it up the hill to visit. But when Corinne came home wearing Judy Beal's cast-off miniskirt (which she looked damn good in), and carrying a duped tape of

Robby Beal's favorite music (Pink Floyd's "The Wall"), which she plugged into their boom box, it was hard to keep quiet.

"Enough with the Beals, already," Mitchell complained as he suspended the wooden honey dipper over his fourth cup of tea. "Do we have to listen to that crap?"

"You don't want me to have anything!" Corinne exploded, getting up to punch off the play button on the tape deck. "We don't go anywhere, we don't do anything."

Bewildered, Mitchell dripped honey onto the side of his cup. He licked at the sticky porcelain. "You never wanted to do anything. What do you want to do?"

Corinne crossed her arms on her chest. "I don't know. Go out to a restaurant. Go dancing."

Mitchell was silent. She knew he didn't dance. Finally he said, "You think we got that kind of cash? The Toyota's not going to pass inspection next month without an exhaust pipe."

"You always go to the movies with Jamie."

"Jamie pays." The logic seemed obvious. Jamie was working full-time construction now, and living in the sugarhouse alone since his girlfriend ran off. With no bills, he was saving money by the handful, the way only a single guy could.

"Well, Judy Beal's invited me to go out dancing on Saturday and I want to go."

"Just the two of you?"

"And some other people."

"Like who?"

"Just people. Friends. Her boyfriend. Her brother."

"Didn't she invite me?"

"You don't dance."

Confusion shifted to anger. What was going on?

"Forget it," Corinne said. She sighed deeply. "You don't want me to have any friends."

"If Judy Beal was such a hot friend, she'd come over."

"You think I want anyone to see this dump? Just forget it."

"So go if you want to."

"No. Now you're making me feel guilty."

"Guilty for what?"

Corinne didn't answer.

Mitchell set his cup down on the table too hard; hot tea sloshed over the rim and scalded his hand. He jumped back, cursing. Something was starting to slip but he couldn't grasp what.

The first weekend in June Lowell got it into his mind that he and Mitchell should go on a father-son fishing expedition to Mooselookmeguntic Lake in Maine. Mitchell had made the mistake of talking about the trip he and Jamie took up there last year, fishing for landlocked salmon. He didn't want to go with his father. As long as he avoided Lowell, he could squelch the pitiful hope that something good might pass between them.

Lowell was early, which seemed designed to get them off to a bad start. He sipped from his to-go cup of coffee and stunk up the house with cigarettes while Mitchell threw water on his face and gathered his things.

"Your dad take you fishing?" Lowell interrogated Carver.

Hanging off the back of a chair, Carver looked skyward. "Um, sometimes."

"I used to take him when he was your age."

Right, and what a joy that was, Mitchell thought.

"Why don't you do something with that driveway so I don't break an axle trying to get up here?" Lowell groused. "I had to park halfway up, didn't want to risk it."

"If you weren't early I would've been down the hill waiting for you and you wouldn't have had to drive up," Mitchell said.

"Early bird gets the salmon."

"We aren't going to be fishing early with a six-hour drive."

"You want to can it? Is that what you're saying?" Lowell's voice rose up like a fighting kite, a sudden swoop from pleasantry to rage that always left Mitchell astounded. Lowell was a short, fat, wheezing little guy, but his emotional agility was amazing.

"I just meant we got a long drive." His own conciliatory tone curdled in Mitchell's ears.

"So let's get cracking. You kids like eating salmon?"

"Eeeewwww."

"I can see your dad ain't—isn't—raising you kids right." It irked Lowell that anyone might think he was the backwoods hick he was, now that he'd been civilized by his new wife, Helene.

"Have fun, you guys," Corinne offered.

Mitchell rolled his eyes and kissed her goodbye. He shouldered his backpack, which held his sleeping bag, pup tent, and fishing rod, and carried his tackle box and guitar. His father took short fast strides beside him.

"Quite a girl that can put up with this," Lowell said. "I never asked your mother to live without plumbing, at least I can say that."

Mitchell gritted his teeth. Mom had put up with plenty. "You're a better man than me, Dad," he said.

"Darn right," Lowell cackled. His laugh gave way to a sputtering emphysemic hack, complete with phlegmy choking.

Mitchell stood waiting for his father to catch his breath. How could it be that he wanted Lowell to choke his guts out and at the same time he wanted him to breathe forever?

Lowell's pickup, with the twelve-foot aluminum skiff tied on top (Mitchell wondered how his father had managed to hoist it up there himself) sat parked in a pull-off halfway down the hill. When Mitchell opened the tailgate to throw his pack in, his heart sank at the size of the load Lowell had packed. A folding table and chairs lay across bags and boxes. Helene's influence, he supposed. "Looks like you brought enough," Mitchell said.

"At my age you got to have your little comforts."

Gone were the days when his father would sleep under a plastic tarp, walk the Long Trail in the rain, hunt in freezing weather until he got his buck, even at the risk of frostbite. It saddened Mitchell to see Lowell turning into a wuss. It was disorienting, as though the earth had tilted a bit or the daylight dimmed. He closed the tailgate and got in the passenger seat.

"Did you have to slam it?" Lowell complained.

"Yup."

Mitchell had forgotten how much he hated the way his father drove. Lowell had no respect for the center line and lurched onto the shoulder whenever something caught his eye. He probably needed glasses but wouldn't admit it.

"You want me to drive?" Mitchell offered.

"I ain't that decrepit yet," Lowell snapped, forgetting his improved English, and Mitchell leaned against the driver's door, closing his eyes, figuring the best thing was just not to look, and maybe his father would believe he was catching some shuteye.

Oblivious, Lowell turned the radio up loud on a blaring country-western station and drummed his fingers on the wheel.

Mitchell sighed and opened his eyes, stared straight ahead as his father pulled onto Interstate 91 and veered in front of a semi. The driver blew his airhorn.

"They pay those guys far too much," Lowell commented. "Anyone can drive a big rig with all the hydraulics they got now. Just a bunch of fatasses who think they're cowboys."

As they headed north, the hemlock and pine forests gave way to spruce and the numbers of birch stands increased, as did the size of the wooded tracts and the dairy farms still in operation. "The way the state used to be," Lowell pronounced. "Before all these goddamn out-of-staters messed it up."

Though Mitchell agreed with his father in principle, Lowell's smug words irritated him. He didn't even live in Vermont anymore, but over in Claremont, New Hampshire, in his new wife's house.

They crossed the Connecticut River. Mitchell had never liked the Granite State. The soil was thinner, sandier, the people more redneck, and as soon as you entered something ugly struck you. Maybe it was the billboards, outlawed in Vermont, or the odd scraps of development in the middle of dead farmland, encouraged by New Hampshire's famous lack of taxes: a blue corrugated Butler building announcing a metal press operation, or a fake rustic factory outlet store set in the middle of a field gone to brambles.

Lowell drove erratically but slowly, making several pit stops.

Although he'd quit beer, he drank so many Pepsis now he still had to piss every hour. At noon sharp they pulled off at a roadhouse for lunch. It was more bar than restaurant, a dark familiar brown rectangle with no front windows, a separate "family" entrance, and several beer signs. Only two cars were parked in the lot.

"We're beating the rush," Lowell congratulated himself. "They used to make a decent cornbeef hash. We stopped in here with Walker once."

Mitchell remembered. They'd been on a fishing trip with his father's brother. Lowell and Walker hadn't spoken in years over the sale of Grampa Chartrain's sawmill, and the trip was a strained goodwill effort. They were headed for Maine, hammering beers all the way. Mitchell must have been twelve. When they ordered supper Mitchell asked for a Coke. They didn't have Coke on the menu, but for some reason he couldn't recall now, Mitchell had put up a fuss. Uncle Walker said, "Get one from the bar. They got to have 'em for rum and cokes, right?" The Coke was brought in by the barmaid. It had a little swizzle stick in it, and cost twice the price of the ginger ale on the supper menu. Plus, Lowell had to tip the barmaid a dollar. Mitchell saw his father's face pinching to-gether, the rage popping up under his skin, and the Coke turned into cough medicine on his tongue.

When the barmaid turned her back and slouched away, Lowell backhanded Mitchell across the mouth without a word. No one said anything, not Uncle Walker, not the couple with the baby in a high chair at the next table, least of all Mitchell, who sat there squeezing his eyes against hot tears while the Coke glass sweated beneath its plastic swizzle stick.

What happened when he got hit like that, Mitchell wondered now, as he crunched across gravel to a restaurant he didn't want to enter. Some blankness always came over him, a silence. He didn't experience rage. Nothing—just a shorting-out. How could he keep on being shocked about something that happened so often? He experienced a peculiar kind of daze that allowed him to keep loving his father. Sort of like electroshock therapy. You lost short-term memory, but you functioned again.

When they got to the door they read a note printed in wavery magic marker on water-stained pink cardboard announcing that since April 1, only the bar was open. Lowell led them back to the car.

"Nothing good lasts," he grumbled. "But we had fun that trip, remember Mitchy? Caught quite a few browns, though Walker couldn't get a bite. You landed a nineteen-incher, as I recall."

What made Lowell able to recollect the corned-beef hash and the length of a trout but not the whack in the mouth? He was rewriting his past to suit himself, recasting himself in innocence. Corinne, with her hospital know-it-all, said she thought the emphysema was cutting off oxygen to Lowell's brain. If so, it was doing it selectively as far as Mitchell could tell.

They ended up eating greasy corn dogs at a roadside stand and traveled the Kancamagus Highway. It was the first warm weekend in June, and all along the river there were cars parked in the pullouts and glimpses of kids splashing in the sunny flumes. The views, as they poked around the curves, were startling: the rocky peaks of the Presidentials loomed like some insurance company calendar. You had to give New Hampshire credit: its mountains dwarfed Vermont's. They passed camps and cottages and little rental bungalows, and rolled on into the big spruce forests of Maine, arriving at the lake in the late afternoon.

This far north the leaves were still pale and half budding, the blackflies hovering. The lake smelled cool and metallic, as though Mitchell could detect the minerals in the damp soil. The afternoon light cut an oblique angle on the water and the wind moved through the spruce like a lonely whisper that gave him the shivers.

It took three trips to ferry all of Lowell's junk to the island. Besides the folding table and chairs, he'd brought cast-iron frying pans, a large box radio, a cot with an air mattress, a Montgomery Ward canvas tent big enough for a family to stand up in, coolers, enough groceries for a week, a tablecloth, Coleman lamps, Coleman gas, charcoal briquettes, and several tackle boxes and rods. Last year when Mitchell came with Jamie, all they'd brought were their pup tents and the canoe. They lay on the beach with a bottle of Captain Morgan's and listened to the loons.

Setting up camp took two hours, with Lowell barking orders about which aluminum tent poles went where, the best way to stake it, how much firewood they needed. When they were done, Lowell wanted to cast a few flies, but Mitchell begged off with the excuse that he intended to take some pictures of the ruins of a sports camp he'd discovered with Jamie last year in the woods; the light would be perfect now.

Mitchell set off purposefully through stands of birch, and into the big darkness of spruce. There was no trail, but he remembered the camp's general direction in the center of the island. He walked fast for twenty minutes, breath ragged, as though he couldn't breathe easily until he'd left Lowell behind. Sun filtered through the boughs, lighting up the carpet of needles and bracken ferns. And the smell, somehow woodsier than the mixed hemlock/hardwoods at home, a balsam odor like those sachets he'd bought for his mother when he was a kid. For a moment he considered the possibility of black bears, but reasoned that there probably weren't any on the island. His steps slowed and he could feel his blood turn sluggish in his veins.

A familiar lethargy filled his body. When he came upon the stone chimney jutting out of charred timbers, he didn't have the will to frame a picture. He sat on a log with his head in his hands. Blueberry bushes and raspberry brambles grew thick here, filling in the clearing where the rich man's sports camp had stood. A mourning dove cooed its evening sorrow. He wanted to sink down into the acid soil and let the mosquitoes suck his will away with his blood. Being with Lowell was like sticking your leg in a steel trap, only he didn't have the guts of a fox that would chew its leg off to get away. Of course, what fox had ever loved its captor?

They trolled the entire next day while Lowell spun out home-made three-inch streamers he'd tied from deer hackle and feathers. Mitchell never liked trolling much because it was so boring. Cruising up and down the lake at a steady sputter, the grind of the outboard in his ears, swaying the pole to jerk the streamer. The gas mixture had to be enriched to get the six-horse Evinrude to idle slow enough; the stinking two-cycle exhaust billowed in his face. And nothing was biting. Not a tip on the pole bending, not a shiver. He sat with one hand on the red rubber grip of the throttle, making minuscule adjustments. Lowell occasionally reeled in to change lures and chided Mitchell for not bothering.

The flat expanse of the lake shimmered with noon heat, then caught afternoon shadows as they moved closer to the banks. It would be nice to see a moose come down to feed, but what moose would approach with the buzz of the engine? Mitchell missed the silence and slap of canoe paddles, the ring of Jamie's laughter.

Lowell droned on like the outboard. First it was the history of every distant relative's medical problem, one of Lowell's favorite topics. He loved to wallow in the details of cancer pain or hemorrhoids so bad they had to be bound with rubber bands the way you castrate sheep, or diabetes amputations. Since Mitchell had no phone, Lowell sent regular letters that began: "I've got bad news for you Mitchy. Your aunt/cousin/great uncle has . . ." Mitchell expected to receive a letter some day that said "I've got bad news for you Mitchy, I'm dead."

Then came the family stories, fishing and hunting trips of the past. "Your Grampa Chartrain was quite a fisherman. He could think like a fish, no lie, Mitchy. He knew when they were feeding, what they were feeding on, when they wanted to just hole up. He could see trout in water that reflected back my dumb face. He could hook a fish, let it go, and hook the same fish twice. He was a artist."

Mitchell settled into the family stories, sucking them up at first, wanting to believe he was part of some continuum, a chain of fathers and sons who honored each other. But as the hours wore on, Mitchell knew that Lowell wasn't sharing, Lowell was filling up the air to keep him out. That old longing worked him over: waiting hungrily for the moment when Lowell would ask something personal: How are you doing? How's Corinne and the kids? Does Corinne like waitressing? You taking any good pictures with that camera? Ask him if he'd taken a nice shit that morning, anything as long as it was about *him*. Frustration seized Mitchell as the hours passed and Lowell shifted to the history of logging operations in New England.

Mitchell lay back against the struts of the aluminum skiff, trying to decide if he'd rather have his square orange floatation cushion behind his back or under his butt, coveting Lowell's lawn chair. The boat was dented; he noted a small seep of water around the struts in the bow.

After nine hours, Mitchell reeled in his line, set his pole in the boat, and picked up his camera. He started framing compositions through the viewfinder: three spruce trees jutting above the line of alder; a half-fallen birch tilting over the lake. He trailed his hand in the chilly water and the sun shining through made shifting patterns like a giraffe's markings on his skin, triggering a flash of memory so clear it hurt like sun in the eyes: an outing to some state park when he was little, the shimmer of sand through a foot of light-filled water, and Dad playing Crocodile, crawling in the shallows with Mitchell and the girls clinging to his back. Shrieking with joy, demanding it go on forever because it so rarely went on at all.

Then Lowell said, "Hey, whoa, whoa, what's this?" lurching forward, yanking his pole hard to set the hook, then releasing the drag on the reel. He was onto something, the pole tip bending, and Mitchell leaned forward too. He could see a dorsal fin cutting an arc through the water.

"Oh, boy," Lowell crowed. "It's a beauty." The salmon was a fighter, rising to the surface, hooking left, then right, then diving again, Lowell playing it as the drag sang.

"Get that camera ready," Lowell ordered, his voice high with excitement.

Mitchell raised the Nikon to his face, steadying himself on his knees. Already he could see the hard curved lips and the open craw as the salmon was hauled from the water. Its flat eyes betrayed nothing as it entered a world of dazzling, hideous light. It shimmered silver, then dropped back under the surface and Lowell's line went slack. He'd lost it.

"Dammit," Lowell shouted. "Why didn't you get the net under him?"

"You told me . . ." Mitchell let the words die. He dropped the camera around his neck.

Lowell insisted on looping around for another two hours, sure he'd find the fish or another like it, and if it weren't for Mitchell's camera foolishness, they would have a twenty-six-inch salmon to grill. Instead they ate Dinty Moore heated in a saucepan and sat down at Lowell's table with napkins and china plates, the tablecloth fastened to the card table with specially made camping clips.

After supper Lowell smoked his pack of Vantages—he'd given up Luckies as a concession to Helene—under the light of the Coleman lamp while moths buzzed crazily about his head. There was no breeze now and Mitchell leaned away from the cigarette smoke. Lowell made his own stinking little mini-environment wherever he went, recreating their house. All he needed was a pail of lard and a deep-fat fryer for the full effect.

Mitchell took his guitar down by the shore and sat on a rock and strummed. He'd been practicing a lot again lately. Earl Scruggs. Flat-picking. After a while the music took over. Pinprick stars glittered in the still-light sky; a three-quarter moon reflected a thin line on the lake. Loons called across the water, a demented howl you wouldn't expect from a bird. Mitchell wondered what Corinne and the kids were doing and missed them with a stab to the sternum. He never could leave them for long.

In January, he and Jamie had driven all the way to Big Bend National Park in Texas, Jamie even paying for the trip just for his company. But regardless of all the months of big talk, the maps and *National Geographics* pored over, the hikes planned, the promised jaunt across the border into Mexico, Mitchell began to pine for them on the second day. By the end of three days, he had Jamie drive him to a bus station.

He bent to the plaintive music. He could almost hear that

lonesome whistle. Then Lowell's freight train emphysema breath chugged behind him. Lowell was listening. Mitchell rested his chin on the guitar, working the pick in between the strings, faster, with flourishes, hoping to impress his father despite himself. The sky was almost dark now, just the last tinges of changing blue, like that painting he saw once, *The Sleeping Gypsy*, with the lion standing over the man in robes, and the sky blending to darker and darker hues. A mosquito whizzed past his ears, and his fingers flew. He stopped, put his hand over the guitar strings, hushing their vibration.

"How come your flat-picking's so sloppy?" Lowell asked. "Don't you practice no more?" He threw his burning cigarette butt into the lake.

Mitchell heard the sizzle, though it might have been the snuffing of his own foolish hope. He stood, letting the guitar clatter on the rocks, and walked back, fast, to his tent.

"A hit bird always flutters," Lowell called after him. "You never did take care of your things."

When Mitchell woke to the clank of his father's skillet, he was sick with the need to see Corinne, like jonesing on heroin. Any moment he expected cramps and sniffles. He had to get back. Of course, Lowell was adamant that they fish. They'd come to fish, goddammit, and they hadn't caught anything, and he, for one, wasn't a quitter. He wasn't going to rush, either. While Mitchell sucked impatiently on a mug of tea, Lowell ate his breakfast slowly, smearing yellow egg across his plate with Wonder Bread and drowning his sausage in maple syrup. He smoked two cigarettes, then stubbed them out in sausage grease on his plate. He performed his morning post-cigarette phlegm hack, and spat into the dying campfire.

Mitchell stayed on the island, packing up their mountain of equipment while Lowell grimly trolled. When the tent was struck and folded into its sack, the dishes cleaned and boxed, the sleeping bags rolled, the tables and chairs folded, Mitchell paced the shoreline, oblivious now to the lap of miniature waves or the charm of birches crossing their slender stems. In Lowell's presence he could feel himself diminishing, like sand leaking from a torn burlap sack.

When Lowell finally conceded defeat at the hands of Mooselookmeguntic, Mitchell soaked his sneakers ferrying their three loads ashore. He put his wet shoes in the back of the pickup and got in behind the wheel.

"You can't drive like that," Lowell announced.

"Like what?" Mitchell rested the key in the ignition.

"Barefoot."

"You're kidding."

"Hell I am. It's illegal in this state, in case you didn't know."

Mitchell blew out breath and rested his forehead on the wheel. "I don't believe this."

"It's my truck and you ain't driving it barefoot. I'll drive."

"I'm not going to risk my life while you crawl along on the wrong side of the road. I want to get home today, not tomorrow."

"Don't you smart talk me." Lowell's hand flew up, then stopped midair, but Mitchell had already ducked. Silence ticked like an overheated car engine.

Mitchell got out, slammed the door, opened the camper back. He took out his soaking sneakers, put them on, and drove with gritted teeth and hunched shoulders. His father's hand kept flying up before his eyes like a bird in front of the windshield. He twitched at the memory of that shameful, reflexive cringe, proof of his cowardice. He drove without speaking, only stopping once to buy fuel. When Lowell got out at the gas station, he looked back over his shoulder suspiciously at Mitchell as if he suspected his son might steal the truck while he was inside pissing. On the road again, Lowell finished a pack of Vantages, blowing the smoke against the clouded windshield; somehow he managed to contain his bladder for the rest of the trip.

When they cut back over the Connecticut River into Vermont at Wells River, Mitchell felt relief. Home loomed nearer. At a gravel crossroad they passed a farm, and at its gate a kid stood with a staff in his hand, his expression as certain and secret as some biblical prophet. A herd of white Charolais spread across a rocky green field behind him. Something in that scene, lost already as they turned onto old Route 5 and bumped over potholed asphalt, made Mitchell want to weep.

Why wasn't that his life, he wondered. It could have been if Gram's farm hadn't been lost, if Uncle Ross hadn't been forced to drive all the way down to Shelby from the old house in Windsor every day to milk for Carlisle's dairy. They'd lost a farm so beautiful Maxfield Parrish had painted it, even though the artist had moved the stream from behind the house to the front, where a massive elm stood. Now the tree was dead of Dutch Elm disease, like all New England elms, and the interstate ran right by.

If he'd grown up farming, would things make more sense? Did family land that had been worked for generations give you some grounding that he'd never gotten? He ought to sell his house, forget sailing, buy one of those cheap farms in the Northeast Kingdom and raise the kids right.

What a load of shit, Mitchell decided, cutting off Route 5 and back onto the interstate. He'd still have the same father, still be himself. The kid with the staff probably wasn't satisfied anyway. He was likely dreaming of the day he could escape the milking parlor and go drive a truck for St. Johnsbury. He probably envied Mitchell and Lowell, zipping past in their pickup.

Mitchell made it to Shelby by four-thirty, still an hour before Corinne got off work. Lowell wordlessly let him out at the bottom of the hill, then backed up to spit out the window, "You're an ungrateful kid," before spinning gravel like a teenager.

The familiar ruts of the drive kissed the soles of Mitchell's damp sneakers. Home. He bowed his head, trudging uphill with his load, weighted by a good case of Dad hangover: the feeling of having been kicked in the chest by a foot that went right through his cardboard ribs, leaving him hollow as a paper lantern. He'd been suckered again, and still he felt guilty, as though the miserable trip was all his fault. He needed Corinne, needed to tell her the story and feel her sympathy smoothing the edges.

At the turnoff to the sugarhouse Mitchell could see Jamie's green '57 GMC truck parked ass-in, white-coned bumper jutting like a fifties sweater girl. He dropped his pack and guitar and tackle box at the base of a huge rock maple that once bore seven sugaring taps at a time, but now was cleft by a rot-hole a child could hide in. Jamie wouldn't let his trees be tapped anymore.

Jamie kneeled in his flower garden, his tee shirt hitched up, revealing his knobby spine and a wedge of pink sunburn. He looked up from spading peat moss around his delphiniums and wiped a smear of dirt across his peeling nose. "Where's my salmon steak?" he asked, grinning.

"Still swimming. Lowell got onto a good one but it was my fault he lost him. I was supposed to take a picture of Captain Ahab making the big catch and hold a net under Moby Dick at the same time. Failed again."

"Sounds like a good trip."

"A beauty. Want to run me over to Saxton's River to pick up the kids and meet Corinne? She'll be getting off soon."

"Can't wait 'til she gets home. That bad, huh?"

"I'll buy you a cone at the Real Scoop."

Jamie dropped his spade. "Well then."

At Corinne's mother's house, Mitchell sent Jamie in because his mother-in-law hated him. It was a known fact that he'd ruined her daughter's life. The kids came tumbling out, blond heads gleaming, full of hugs and reports of how Gramma washed their clothes before letting them sit on her couch. They were happy to ride in the back of the pickup with their dripping ice cream and a couple of bald tires.

They pulled into the lot at the restaurant ten minutes before Corinne's shift ended, Mitchell and Jamie still laughing about the barefoot driving rule, and the flat- picking compliment, and Lowell's bladder. The lot was empty except for employee cars as the shift changed. Corinne was probably finishing up, filling sugar shakers and marrying catsup bottles. Mitchell hurried to the door.

He peered through the screen. At first he couldn't see anything and then his eyes adjusted to the darkness inside. There, by the coffee maker, a man and a woman were hugging. The guy was grinding his hips and the woman was snugged up against him.

Somebody was having a good time. Mitchell started to shape the joke for Jamie but the woman sensed him watching and turned, snuffing his heart, flickering inside that flimsy Japanese lantern. Corinne recoiled and then glared as though Mitchell were an uninvited guest crashing her private party.

Mitchell jerked back. He leaned into the screen door again, just to make sure, but instead of Corinne he saw himself as she would see him—arms around his face to block the sunlight, in the pose of those chalk outlines cops draw on the pavement after someone's been shot or run over: the silhouette of a dead man.

GRAND CANYON

[Donna, 1984]

DONNA KNELT over the base of the notched rafter, struggling to pull it tight against the pencil-marked sill plate.

"Hold it right there," Tim ordered. "Okay, good."

Peched on staging, Tim reached up to fasten the rafter to the ridgepole. Every blow of his framing hammer reverberated through pale wood, a direct current into her flesh, almost a thrust. She closed her eyes and imagined the path from Tim's shoulder, through his biceps and forearm to his cracked carpenter's hand with its flattened fingertips. She was well acquainted with the shape of Tim's body, though she'd never touched him. She knew that under the grey sweatshirt Tim's shoulder separated into sinewy bands. She'd seen him in hot weather, bare-chested, glistening with sweat.

When the banging stopped, Donna pulled her hammer from her belt and toe-nailed her end into the sill plate. It took her a few hits too many, but the rafter stood.

Tim jumped down from the staging and picked up another notched rafter, lifted it up. "Hold it," he ordered again. Donna had long since given up the twinge of resentment that, in the midst of work, Tim never said "please." He commanded her like the laborer she was, although in fact, she signed his paycheck. Or

Claude did. It was an odd position, to be both peon and employer. Claude had been all for it, thinking of the money they'd save by not hiring a real carpenter's assistant, and because he knew that Donna was sick of hanging around their rented house with three kids under the age of six. It was cheaper to pay her sister Nancy, who happily stayed home with her own five-year-old, to watch the kids while Donna lifted boards.

Now she couldn't imagine living in this house. It would be just a grander version of her life before the project—before Tim. She saw herself pacing its new hardwood floors, rattling around the music room she'd insisted on for her piano, trying to escape the wet mouth of baby Melissa, the grabbing, greedy, needful hands of Jimmy and Beth. She wanted the building to go on forever and dreaded every finished step.

Thinking about the kids made Donna uneasy. From her stance on the plywood decking of the second story, she looked across rustling dry cornfields to where, half a mile north, the steeple of the Shelby Congregational Church shone white in the dazzling fall sunshine. The leaves were already past peak, many lost in the last rainstorm, spattered like brilliant quilting on the paved main street of town. The kids would have this view from their dormers. She and Claude would have the privacy of the large downstairs bedroom, not that they needed privacy anymore. Claude put in such long hours with his dozers and trucks that he never made it home before eight or nine, and was awake just long enough to wolf down supper and collapse in front of the sports report on TV.

Donna was twenty-six years old and she'd been with the same man for twelve years, the only man she'd ever slept with, a man so preoccupied with building a business that he didn't see her anymore, didn't see she was someone any man might want. A woman Tim wanted.

Donna knew it. At first she'd been intent on proving she could do the work—lift and haul and stack lumber, nail all day without whining—eager to garner Tim's approval, since he'd been reluctant to take her on. But soon they'd progressed to teasing banter, the sarcasm that passes for wit on any construction site, and then to something else, this hyper-awareness of each other's presence: a shoulder brushed by accident, the closeness of their faces over a corner joint, or the edgy familiarity of sitting in Tim's truck on the way to the lumber yard with their steaming styrofoam coffee cups in their laps. Now even the smell of Tim's sweat was dizzying.

Donna thought of him all the time. It didn't matter that Tim wasn't especially good looking. He was ten years older than Claude, already half bald, wiry and small, only his arms large from his labor. But he was thrillingly aware of the life that coursed inside her, life that Claude was stifling with neglect. When Donna lay awake beside Claude's snoring bulk at night, Tim stole out of the darkness, his calloused hands invading her bedroom, leaving her in a frenzy of bitter longing.

Tim jumped down from the staging and examined the row of rafters. "Looks good," he remarked.

"You talking about me again?" Donna put her hands on her hips and thrust out her chest in a parody of seduction.

"Now don't go distracting me from my work," Tim waggled his framing hammer at her, "or you'll get yourself into trouble, little girl."

She loved it when he called her little girl, the dumb intimacy. Let other women find it demeaning. Did they do a man's work all day? "What kind of trouble you talking about?"

Tim whistled and turned away to the pile of two-by-six collar ties. Donna laughed. A crazy game, pushing a little further each time. As though, stepping up to the edge of the roof, curling her toes inside her sneakers, she might dive right off and see if she could fly.

Donna poured herself another glass of spiked punch, her third in the past hour. Hitting it hard and fast, trying to ease her nerves, to keep the question—would he show up?—from ruining the party. When she'd had enough it wouldn't matter. Bull. Where was he? He said he might come. He said he'd *probably* come, but wasn't sure. She needed him to be here to see her in her costume, the harem girl outfit Nancy helped her sew. Donna pushed the ballooning velvet pants lower on her hips, beneath a belly still flat despite three kids. She adjusted her bikini top, knocked back the rest of her drink. Chiffon scarves swished from her clanking, braceleted wrists.

Under red and blue bulbs, Halloween revelers whirled to the music. The usual pirates and ghosts and witches and princesses, guys from Claude's shop and their dates, stomped and twirled. Smoke spiraled toward the ceiling. The bass pounded into Donna's skull. She stalked over to the boom box and shut it off.

"Hey? Wha . . . ?" The dancers lurched in confusion.

Donna ejected Bob Marley and popped in her belly dance cassette. Tim or no, she hadn't practiced with that video every evening for the past three weeks for nothing. Filigreed Arab music wound about the room. Donna put her hands up palm to palm and rocked her head. She swiveled her hips, rolled her belly, flashed her scarves. The partiers whistled and clapped. Through slit eyes she caught Claude grinning, half-proud, half-embarrassed, crouched by the beer cooler. Donna closed her eyes and let the music carry her.

She shimmied her shoulders, bounced her breasts, opened her eyes. And there he was, standing open-mouthed in the doorway. He hadn't even worn a costume. Sudden heat flushed Donna's cheeks. She made a veil of her scarf and swiveled behind it. She didn't care if Tim turned away, pretending that what he really wanted was a drink, afraid for Claude to notice him looking. From now on, even at the job, he'd see her like this.

Monday morning Donna waited at the house, but Tim didn't show. She sat on a box of nails, finished the last of the coffee in her to-go cup, glanced at her watch. It was a rainy November morning, so it was good that the roof was on, tar-papered and shingled. But it was cold when she wasn't working. There wasn't really anything for her to get started on without Tim's direction. Donna hugged herself and paced about the unfinished rooms. She listed the work left to do like a reassuring mantra: siding, insulation, wiring, sheetrock, windows, floors. Then all the finish work: cabinets to select and order, baseboard, trim, doors to hang. It would take them through the winter.

She liked the sight of her uncompleted house, the geometry of vertical studs slashed by horizontal headers and spacers. Pale rectangles of plywood subfloor muddied with footprints. The odor of fresh wood, the trail of white gypsum powder from the stacked sheetrock. Unfinished, the house was a monument to shared accomplishment—and proof of time left with Tim.

Where the hell was he? It was quarter to nine and they always started by eight. She peered out through the door opening. Paced some more. Got a broom and swirled sawdust around, but soon lost interest. Nine-fifteen. It dawned on her that he wasn't coming. It was the party. She'd pushed too far, scared him off. He didn't want to get in trouble with his boss' wife. No. That couldn't be it. He wouldn't just quit like that. Would he?

Donna climbed the staircase to the second story and huddled in the eaves. Rain pattered down softly on fresh asphalt shingles. She was freezing. She caressed her biceps through her jacket. Hard and strong. She'd dropped ten pounds since she started working, not that Claude noticed. Through the dormer hole she could see the last of the leaves ripped from the trees, the branches bare. Winter was coming. She was always afraid of winter, the darkness, short days, the numbing cold and grey skies that didn't let up until March or April. She hadn't been afraid of winter this year, barely thought about it, so intent was she on winning Tim, so busy with their project. Hunched with her knees to her chest, Donna started to cry.

With Tim gone she'd have nothing. Her sisters thought she had it so good with Claude pulling in the money. But something was wrong, had always been wrong. No, not always. She'd been crazy about Claude for half their years together. Starting when she was just fourteen, sitting in his lap, sliding down Precourt Hill in a flying saucer. His truck idling at the bottom of Gramp's road, waiting for her to sneak back home after one of their sessions in the tenant house on his parents' farm. Claude beaming beside the hospital bed, gripping a toy bulldozer, while she held Jimmy to her breast.

The kids had changed it. Before the kids she'd been proud of Claude's ambition. She used to go with him to the jobs—bring lunches, drive the gravel trucks. Then she was stuck at home with a post-partum depression that wouldn't quit. And a horrible secret: she feared she didn't love Jimmy enough. She'd wanted a little girl to dress in bows, not some squalling boy who always peed in her face when she tried to change him. A child born angry. She blamed the fact that he was a high forceps baby, a traumatic birth that kept them from bonding. It might have been better with the girls, but she already had Jimmy sitting under tables, screaming, or banging his head against the wall. He threw tantrums and turned blue, tore the curtains off the windows. Nancy had no complaints about him when Donna went to pick up the kids at five-fifteen each day. But as soon as Jimmy got in the car he was whining, hitting his sisters, creating a fuss, as though it were Donna's fault. She wanted to be a good mother. Babies were precious gifts. But who could love that?

Donna heard the rumble of a truck and leaped up. Hope fluttered at her breastbone like a bird against a window. Please, please let it be Tim, not Claude. Through the dormer hole she saw Tim's pickup bouncing over the ruts. She hurried down the stairs, relief giving way to fury. Tim backed close to the front door. A load of sheetrock and rolls of insulation filled the truck bed, protected by a tarp. Tim climbed out of the cab, his beige felt hat spotted with rain.

"Why didn't you tell me you were going to Tenney's?" Donna accused. "I've been sitting here freezing for an hour and a half. I could've stayed home. Or I could've gone with you."

Tim calmly placed his hat on a nail box. His wet, wispy hair stuck to his neck and collar and he wiped a drip of rain off his nose. "I thought I told you I was gonna stop by there on my way in. Sorry. Their delivery truck didn't show for an hour. You aren't crying are you? I didn't know you were *that* eager to work."

Donna sniffled. "I thought you weren't coming."

"C'mon now. You think I'd walk out on a job like this? For ten years I been stuck building barns, and now I get my first house, you think I'd just drop it?"

Donna turned away. "That's all you care about."

"What?"

"The house. What about me? Don't you care about me?"

Tim smiled. "Of course I care about you. You're a damn fine peon."

Donna whirled around. "It's all just a joke to you."

Tim shook his head. "I wish it was. You were incredible the other night, in your little "I Dream of Donna" outfit."

Donna wiped her nose on the back of her sleeve. "Do you?"

"Do I what?" Tim asked.

"Do you dream of me?"

"Oh, jeez. You aren't going to let it rest, are you? I been trying to keep clean here, Donna, but you're making it real hard."

Donna laughed. "Making what hard?"

Tim grabbed her by the upper arms and pulled her to him. Her eyes closed at his touch, at the eager, angry press of his mouth against hers. There. Now she could disappear into his touch like cream poured into coffee, like sheetrock dissolving in rain.

"Damn," Tim moaned, burying his lips in her throat. "I really liked this job, too."

You can only keep a secret for so long, though Claude made it easy. Nancy covered for her, keeping the kids later, feeding them supper, so Donna could spend an hour in Tim's bed. When Donna came to pick them up their smudgy little faces accused her. They grabbed at her all the more as if to say, don't leave us. Sometimes they didn't seem real to her, little strangers telling her with their eyes that she was a terrible mother. She needed to escape them and yet, sometimes, she wanted to hug them to death. She did love them, she really did. It's just that they were suffocating her.

"You sure you know what you're doing?" Nancy cautioned.

"No, but I don't care," Donna said.

Donna and Tim went on building the house as though nothing had happened, as though they weren't stopping from time to time to have at each other, on the floor, upstairs, trusting they'd hear a car approach in time. She came home with sawdust under her sweater, in her bra, not even showering, leaving a trail like bread crumbs to lead Claude to her crime. He never noticed.

She dreamed of Claude catching them. Then she'd be cast out of this safe, sure life, forced into Tim's cramped, dirty apartment, with its splitting naugahyde couch and dented aluminum pans. Every winter, except this one because of the house job, he took time off, went to Mexico with friends, collected unemployment. He was almost forty and lived like a kid. Why hadn't he ever married, had children? Why should she care when his touch left her all but weeping? Tim traced her angles and curves as though she mattered, told her she was the most passionate woman he'd ever known.

"Stay home today," she begged Claude. "Just today. Don't go in. I need you here."

Claude sat at the end of the bed and drew on his socks in early winter darkness. "Don't you want to work on the house?"

"I can skip a day. We'll leave the kids at Nancy's and be to-gether."

"I can't do that hon. I signed a penalty contract for the Bennett job, and I'll owe a fine every day I'm over. When work slows down . . ."

"It never slows down," Donna said petulantly.

Claude rested a hand on her hip. "You should be happy business is good. It can turn around any time. This building boom won't be here forever."

"I might not be here forever either," she muttered. Although she could hear the baby crying, Donna hid under the blankets, turning away from Claude's kind, square, puzzled face. He didn't ask her what she meant, the bastard. If he asked, she would tell him, and then he could save her from herself.

For a week Donna had to stay home with the kids because Nancy was off visiting Gary's parents in Florida. All the energy she dispelled with labor, with Tim's caresses, built up inside her like a toxin. She could actually feel her skin itch, stretched taut over her muscles and bones, as she stomped through the cramped rooms of her rented house. She ate fistfuls of cookies and hated herself.

Tim called twice a day from the market at the Shelby bridge.

"It's no fun nailing siding without you," he said. "And it's slow. I thought of hiring the Harrington kid to help me, but the coffee breaks wouldn't be the same."

"Mmmm. I guess not."

Jimmy danced about her legs, whining.

"I can't wait until your sister gets back."

"Me too," Donna said.

"Who is it?" Jimmy demanded. "Is it Daddy? Tell Daddy to bring me caps for my cap gun. Daddy, don't forget . . ." He tried to grab the phone out of Donna's hand.

Donna pushed him away. "It isn't Daddy."

"Who is it?"

"I've got to go," Donna said into the phone. "It's hell here." When she hung up she turned on Jimmy, grabbing him by the arm. "Don't you ever bug me again like that when I'm talking."

He yanked his arm free. "I didn't do nothing."

"You did too. Don't lie to me."

"You're the liar. I hate you. I hate you."

"And I hate you!" The vicious words plummeted from her lips.

Jimmy kicked his Lego superhighway across the room.

"You just cut that out, you little brat," Donna shrieked. "You just come back and pick them up."

"No! No!" He was down on the floor, banging his head. "NO! NO! NO!"

The baby set up a high-pitched wail from her crib, and four-year-old Beth, cowering in an armchair, started to cry.

"Jesus Christ, I can't stand it. Cut it out. All of you." Donna hurried into the baby's room. Melissa's face was puckered and red, her mouth open, her cries maddening. Donna grabbed a terry-cloth baby towel and, without thinking, jammed it into Melissa's screaming mouth. The baby's face stiffened in rage but the sound muffled enough for Donna to hear her own beating heart. Christ, what had she done? She yanked the towel out and ran into her bedroom.

"Mommy?" Beth stood at the door. Behind her Jimmy's rhythmic "No's" mingled with the baby's screams. "What are you doing Mommy?"

"Go away. Mommy's sick. You hear me? Sick."

"Mommy? Mommy! Mommy! What's the matter?"

Donna jumped up and slammed the door. She couldn't stand it. Couldn't stand it another minute. In the mirror over the dresser her distorted face, curly hair wild, eyes glittering, leered at her. Horrible. She grabbed the jewelry box and slammed it against the mirror. The glass shattered in long, spiky shards. Donna picked up a slice from the mirror, then threw it across the room. She wrapped her arms about her knees and rocked, keening and sobbing, until Claude came home and found the kids dirty and hungry and terrified, and Donna still swaying on the bedroom floor.

Then it was the whiteness of a hospital room. She hadn't known she was so tired. She lay still, allowing the nurses to rustle about her, sitting up only to slop her fork in a bowl of bland macaroni or to hack at a leathery Salisbury steak when she had no appetite. Nancy, Mitchell, Jamie, and Claude loomed out of a grey haze, as though fog had entered her room. Maybe they'd drugged her. She wanted Sally, an older sister, but Sally was still up in Alaska. It was really Marsha she needed, bossy Marsha who knew all the rules, but Marsha was gone now too. Each time Claude came in, stiff and frightened, massaging his knuckles until they cracked, she started to cry. Why did he look so concerned when she'd cheated on him, mistreated his kids? She deserved punishment, not moony cow eyes, not talk of how they'd work it all out when she came home.

She got up only to go to the bathroom or call Tim.

"Oh, baby," Tim said. "How you feeling?"

"Weird." It was a weekday morning, she realized. What was he doing home on a weekday? "Are you still working on the house?"

"Are you crazy?"

"I'm not sure. Maybe."

"I didn't mean it like that. Claude came by and told me to get the hell off his land. I can't really blame him. It was a lousy thing to do."

"I know."

"We probably shouldn't be talking about it right now, huh?"

"What *should* we talk about? Tim, do you still want to be with me?"

"Of course I do. Donna, listen. I don't care about the house. I just want you."

"Then come see me. Come visit."

"In the hospital? I don't think that's a good idea."

"Tim. Please come." She was crying again.

"Sweetie, don't do this to yourself. Just rest. We'll work it all out."

Work it out. Like a kink in your muscles. She didn't have a kink in her muscles, she'd hacked herself into two halves; in the middle was a gaping hole. She lay in her bed on the tiny psych ward of the Bellows Falls hospital and glanced back and forth at the two walls like one of those plastic cat clocks with the swinging tail and the eyes that clicked left, right. Go with Tim. Stay with Claude and the kids. Take the kids and go with Tim. Claude probably wouldn't let her have them; Tim probably wouldn't want them. She didn't even know if *she* wanted them anymore.

She spun out scenarios: Mexico with Tim, lying on a beach under palm trees, a thatched hut, his lips running along her salty flesh. Just thinking about it made her tremble with longing. But it would mean leaving everything that came before, her babies,

Claude, her sisters and brother. She'd have to walk away from her own, true life. And, if she stayed, she'd be condemned to terrible aloneness, stuck in the house, in danger of hurting herself or the kids. Either way she'd lose.

The Bellows Falls hospital only let her stay a week. After that she had to go home or get admitted to the real psych hospital down in Brattleboro. They sent her home with a supply of mood elevators for depression. Claude came to pick her up. She walked out of the hospital shakily, as though all her strong house-building muscles had atrophied in just a week. "Where are the kids?" Donna asked when she saw the empty car.

"At Nancy's. She's going to bring them over in about an hour." Claude guided her down the steps. An early snow was falling, big sloppy flakes. The world had lost all its color while she was sick; she was living inside a black and white movie.

Claude drove slowly, as though afraid to get her home. He stopped in the driveway, turned to her with the engine still running. She looked away from his grave, grey eyes, refusing to absorb the pain there. When was he going to turn the car off?

"Donna, it's pretty hard to talk about what happened." Claude paused, and his mouth twisted. "When I think about you and that asshole . . ."

Donna stiffened. Here it comes.

Claude sighed, composed himself. "That's not what I wanted to get into. Honey. I know it was partly my fault. I thought I was doing the right thing, working all those hours to get things going for us. But I see now I left you alone too much. I didn't realize you were so unhappy. I'm going to change, honey. You just tell me what you need."

Donna patted Claude's hand. He was so kind. Some other guy might have taken her to court. She was lucky, lucky. She didn't deserve such luck. But the car seemed stuffy, claustrophobic. She cracked the door handle, sucked in damp cold air. Claude turned off the ignition.

"Is it okay if I call Nancy and ask her to keep the kids another hour, so we can have a little time together?" he asked.

"Okay." Donna climbed the poured cement steps, grasped the wrought iron railing. It felt cold and wet under her grip. She had a moment of terror at the door. She didn't want to go into those cramped, dark rooms. But Claude was on the step behind her and she kept moving.

Inside, he put her bag down and she turned to him. Claude raised his arms, hesitated, and Donna pulled him close. It felt strange to be hugging such a large man again; she only came up to his breastbone, while she was used to standing eye to eye with Tim. No. Don't think about Tim. She grabbed Claude tighter and he responded eagerly. She wasn't quite sure if this was what she meant to do, or if it was only an apology, but she'd got things going and it didn't seem right to stop.

Claude pulled her into the bedroom, onto their bed. He touched her hair, her face, searched her eyes, but then he was pounding his way inside her, too eager, angrily, as though he could drive out the memory of Tim, and she was flying away, drifting up on the ceiling, watching them the way some bird might, flying over a winter field. She was a bird, cruising above stalks of dried grass and cattails sticking up through new wet snow. She'd always been amazed by how beautiful winter weeds looked, their dried tendrils as delicate and distinct as India ink sketches. In summer the profusion of growth made nothing recognizably itself. But in winter they stood out in isolation. Beautiful. Brittle. She was as brittle as a winter weed; she could turn to dust between someone's fingers. Claude's fingers.

He was finished. Donna rolled over, face in the pillow.

"I shouldn't have done that," Claude whispered. "I'm sorry."

"Don't worry about it," Donna droned. She deserved it. Into the pillow she silently mouthed: Tim. Tim. Tim.

She was getting better. She was sure of it. She hadn't talked to Tim in almost two weeks. She was busy cooking, baking bread, sewing curtains for the new house—as domestic as Nancy. She even decided to paint the walls of their rental. So what if it was only a few months before they moved out, why live another day with dingy paneling? She painted the bedrooms and the kitchen. Or part of each. She had so much energy now it was hard to focus on one room at a time. The happy pills raced through her bloodstream like pure amphetamine. The only problem was she couldn't sleep. It wasn't really a problem, though, if you didn't need sleep. It amazed her that people wasted a third of their lives in bed when there was so much to do.

True, lately she was seeing funny patterns, arrays of floating diamonds, flickers of light that danced a foot in front of her eyes, but it didn't really matter. They were interesting. And Claude was happy. How could she have taken that kind of chance? They had a future together. Things were definitely improving every day. They were seeing a therapist now and she was doing better with Jimmy. Claude was going to let her buy a horse as soon as they moved into the new house. He'd hired Mitchell and Jamie to finish building.

Donna put the kids in the car and drove down to see the house for the first time since the hospital. Jimmy and Beth ran inside, where Jamie and Mitchell were hanging sheetrock. Donna carried baby Melissa in her arms. The boys came down the stairs.

"Hey, hey. You come by to bang some nails?" Mitchell asked. "We need *someone* with experience around here."

"No way." She hugged Melissa to her chest as she paced the rooms. The whole downstairs was sheetrocked, though it wasn't taped yet. It looked different, bigger but blanker, with the framing geometry hidden behind white plasterboard. It wasn't the same place she'd worked on with Tim. Not at all. "Yup. I learned my lesson," Donna announced. "I really have. I'm staying home for good." She thought she caught Mitchell glancing at Jamie, a raised eyebrow shared between them, and she frowned. Mitchell had taken up residence on her couch last summer when he and Corinne were having their troubles and she'd never gotten snide with him.

"Always glad to see a happy ending," Jamie said. His curly hair was white from sheetrock dust.

"You guys are really moving fast," Donna said. She sat crosslegged on a stack of sheetrock and offered Melissa a bottle.

Jimmy started banging a hammer on the subfloor.

"Jimmy! Quit it . . ." she caught herself. He wasn't doing any harm. She had to be gentle, a good mother from now on.

Beth kneeled in a heap of sawdust. The wood shavings clung to her tights. Donna started to tell her to get up out of there, but a glimpse of old memory broke through the insistently hyper present that was all the happy pills allowed—she used to play in the shavings with her sisters. Back when they lived in Masonville, at her grandfather Chartrain's sawmill. They made nests out of shavings and pretended they were baby birds. Cheep, cheep, cheep, come feed us, they called, opening their mouths wide, certain they'd be taken care of.

Stretched across Donna's lap, Melissa sucked at her bottle. Donna traced Melissa's fine blond eyebrows, stared into her pale blue eyes. It wasn't Donna who'd stuck a towel in this beautiful baby's mouth. It had to be someone else. "I can't wait until we move in," she declared. Seeing the house hardly hurt at all.

In the middle of the night, sleepless, wild with sudden urgency, Donna climbed out of bed and dressed. She tiptoed from the bedroom, through the hall, and out the door the way she used to when she was fourteen, trying to escape her dying mother, her father's drunken snores. She turned the key in the car's ignition, the starter grinding in the cold. She was terrified the battery had died overnight, but finally the engine caught and roared. Without bothering to scrape the frosted windshield, she drove straight to Tim's apartment in Bellows Falls. She stood in the frozen shrubbery and rapped on Tim's window, pressed her face against the slivers of frost on the black pane, let them chill her lips until a light came on.

Claude took the kids to stay at his sister's house and a few days later Donna was back in the hospital, talking suicide. She didn't know what came over her, what made her do it. She couldn't stop weeping. She could feel the heat of the tears running down her face but didn't know why they kept falling. She imagined them carving tracks like water on rock, as though, when she wasn't with Tim, drunk on his touch, her body hardened into something ancient and brittle, eroded by the force of emotions that weren't even hers.

She was brought home; she sat in her living room and stared out the window while the kids played quietly on the floor. The baby was still spending days at Claude's sister's in deference to Donna's "condition." When she walked around the house her arms and legs felt stiff and robotic. Some alien will had subsumed hers. Beth and Jimmy glanced up from their games; when she noticed them staring, they looked away. They were scared of her, she realized. But she couldn't blame them. She was scared too.

First the endless, mindless drive through Massachusetts, Connecticut, New York, Pennsylvania. They'd left at three in the morning to "get a jump on it," Jamie said. Black trees and crusted snow, a crescent moon riding the empty sky. Walls of dark forests, birch and fir giving way to warmer species, more oaks as they headed south. They drove straight through, two days: Kentucky, Tennessee, Arkansas, Oklahoma, and finally Texas. The further west they traveled the more physically disoriented Donna felt, a magnetic imbalance, as though the east coast of the continent pulled at her the way the moon pulled at the tides. Road markers and signs advertising Stuckeys' pecan logs blurred with cups of coffee. The land so flat and dull. All of it passing by like static on the radio, visual white noise. Before she left, Claude said, "I hope this trip does you good. Because this is it. If you go back to him again, we're finished. You better think long and hard about what you want."

How could she think of anything else?

The first night she stayed awake even when it was Jamie's turn to drive. She asked, "Why'd you let me come?"

"I was worried about you. All that suicide talk."

"Weren't you worried I might try it out here?"

"No." Jamie squinted at the road. "I just figured nobody could be unhappy inside the Grand Canyon."

What did *he* know? What did he *know*?

Jamie hit the brakes, veered off the road and made a U-turn.

"What's the matter?" Donna peered anxiously into the blackness.

"Javelinas. Wild pigs. Look, see their eyes. There they are." Jamie's voice shook with excitement.

She saw them: squatty little things huddled together on the side of the road. It was a mystery how anyone could care that much about something just because it was alive.

At night they set up their two separate tents. She didn't even know where they were—they'd arrived at Big Bend National Park in the darkness. In the morning she couldn't tell Jamie, but Big Bend horrified her. He'd said, when she asked to come along, "Okay, but no whining even if the hikes are hard. This is my vacation and I don't want you to slow me down." She didn't know what she'd expected from the desert, knowing it only from Road Runner cartoons. She'd wanted a landscape she could lose herself in, but this was a place of little shade, of dirt and rocks and spiky century plants where your self was always with you.

Plus, the park was filled with old people in RV's who spent the winter here, hiking energetically with their leathery legs and their bolo ties and sunhats and nose guards. They rode three-wheel bicycles to the little park store. Everyone thought she and Jamie were a couple. Let them. It sounded too weird to say they were cousins. No one would understand.

Jamie hiked her to a hot spring right on the Rio Grande. Over the dry hillsides and down into a lowland of tall reedy weeds, like bamboo. The tub was built up of stones, and beside it ran the Rio Grande. It was filthy, full of pollutants. Across the river, a stone's throw away, the scrubby hills were Mexico. Tim said he was going to take her there. It was absurdly close, not foreign at all. No more foreign than this whole dried-up wasteland. Donna leaned back and let the hot water steam her pink. She thought of lobsters, boiled alive, their antennae waving, waving, little frantic messages that no one heeded.

Then they were driving again, north. Stopping for overnight hikes. She followed blindly behind Jamie's long, thin legs with the skinny calves that never tired. Head down, watching for scorpions, cacti, rolling loose rock, leaning into the straps of her borrowed pack. She wouldn't complain. There was relief in the mindless exhaustion. Making camp, tending to her blisters demanded the whole of her attention. But in the middle of the night she woke in her tent weeping.

As they moved further north, it grew too cold to sleep in separate tents. They needed the warmth of each other's body. The coldest winter in fifteen years, everyone said. Donna hunched in her sleeping bag, talking on and on between sobs.

"Quit thinking and go to sleep," Jamie finally said.

"I can't."

"Just breathe. Breathe with me."

So she leaned into her cousin's long, lean back and breathed in unison, in innocence, until their breath condensed on the tent ceiling; in the morning it fell in their faces as thin sheets of ice.

They passed through the mining ghost town of Jerome, red rock Sedona. In Flagstaff the temperature wavered at zero. They drove under an impossible cloudless blue sky. On a high plateau between Flagstaff and the Grand Canyon, an expanse of scrub and sage, Jamie pointed out the remains of a development that had failed before it got off the ground: empty streets carved out of sand, tilting street signs, one faded, sagging model home. And nothing for miles and miles and miles. It spoke to her of useless hope and ambition. She'd always thought such emptiness was a mental state, not something made tangible by sky and land.

The canyon felt terribly wrong.

They drove up through a sparse ponderosa pine forest into a complex of snack bars, ranger stations, an enormous old-fashioned log hotel, and charming tourist cabins. A steam train chugged past, a larger version of the one her brother had driven at Santa's

Workshop back in Vermont, blowing its whistle and dragging a plume of condensation. And there, behind the apparent normalcy of trees and man-made structures, the earth fell away as though you couldn't trust any surface. All the buildings on the planet might as well be false-fronted sets—the real truth was a gargantuan, gaping hole.

The Canyon was an expanse beyond comprehension, an abyss swimming between rocky tiers, the material evidence of time revealed in pink striations. Geology as mockery. Supposedly it was created by the action of the Colorado River wearing away stone, but Donna didn't believe it. This hole had always been there.

At the rim, the lookouts were crowded with sightseers, many of them foreign, leaning back, snapping cameras despite the bone-chilling cold. The donkey trail wound below, icy, treacherous. Donna remembered a record her mother played when she was little: the Grand Canyon Suite, a thunderstorm and the donkey's symphonic hee-haws. The memory of her mother's music gripped Donna's heart. Fingers on piano keys, a wavering, cheery soprano. And then the cover slamming down as Dad's truck lurched into the yard. In the vast abyss of the canyon, Donna felt her mother's presence, or rather her absence, in the molecules of space between rock walls. Her mother floated out there, in some limbo of fitful souls; she wasn't waiting up in heaven for the joyous reunion as Donna's sisters imagined.

"You're killing her," Donna's oldest sister Marsha had accused when Donna was fifteen, sneaking out to be with Claude, and her mother kept sacrificing parts of her body to cancer. But Marsha died too, and even before Mom or Marsha there was the baby, Donna's first. Only a fetus, they said, but she knew. She allowed them to suck it out of her insides because she was only fifteen and she was killing her mother and didn't know what else to do.

In this great void her dead floated, all of them angry. It gave her vertigo, drew her to the rail. She imagined plummeting through space and remembered that corny thing you heard about the Empire State Building, how people felt themselves drawn to the edge. She'd always been drawn to edges, lying spread-eagle on the interstate as a girl, rolling away just as the cars bore down on her, honking and swerving . . .

Beyond the lookout, ravens played loop-de-loop along the rim, and a canyon wren called out its odd spiraling song, a child's imitation of a dropping bomb. It might as well be the sound of Donna's body, falling and falling.

That night, Jamie conceded to renting a cottage at the top for the luxury of bed and bath. Tomorrow they would head into the Canyon's backcountry, for a week-long hike. It didn't seem right to Donna to start on top and descend. You were supposed to climb to the summits of mountains, look down at the world spread below, a tapestry rolling off Vermont hillsides, miniature fields and farms, and the distant slices of ski runs. Here she got an upside-down vertigo: afraid of depth, not height. She feared descending into something she might never come out of, and she called both Claude and Tim.

"How's it going?" Claude asked warily.

"Good. It's really cold out here. Jamie says it's usually much warmer. There's a lot of snow."

"I guess he blew it, trying to escape a Vermont winter. The kids miss you."

Donna sighed. "Tell them I love them. I'll bring them presents."

"Jimmy wants to say hi to you."

"Okay."

"Mom. Mommy, is that you?"

"Yeah."

"D'you see any cowboys yet?"

"Not yet honey, but I bet I will soon. I saw coyotes at Big Bend."

"What are you going to bring me?"

"It's a surprise," she lied. She hadn't bought anything.

"C'mon, tell me, Mom. What'd you get? Mommy, tell me." His voice rose to a desperate hysteria that made her tired even from this distance. Claude disengaged Jimmy from the receiver and came back on. "You think you know what you want yet?" he asked. As though he were discussing gifts too. He wouldn't say Tim's name. Donna sighed. "I've got to go, Claude. Someone's waiting for the pay phone." A second lie.

"Right. Okay. Have a good one . . ."

She wanted to shout him back on, cry come get me, don't leave me out here, but she couldn't. Claude was angry.

She dialed Tim.

"Donna? God, it's great to hear you."

"Yeah."

"You having fun?"

"I'm cold and tired all the time, but it's beautiful."

"You come back and I'll take you to Mexico and warm you up. We'll lie on a beach."

"I don't know, Tim. I don't know. I don't know."

"Easy, little girl. You don't need to get all worked up."

"I've got to go, Tim. I'll call you soon. After we come up out of the canyon."

"I'll be waiting."

That night an old, recurring dream from childhood invaded her sleep. She was standing at the kitchen window with her mother, looking out at the afternoon sky, when suddenly a big yellow fireball hurtled toward them. Donna turned to her mother but her mother was gone, the room empty. She woke panicked, a weight pressing all the air out of her lungs, her heart beating painfully in her chest. It wasn't the fireball but her mother's desertion that scared her. What did it mean that she'd dreamed it over and over, even before Mom got sick?

Across the room Jamie breathed rhythmically, every now and then emitting a sputtering snore. The radiator rattled and the room felt dry and stuffy, although her feet were chilled on the linoleum floor. Donna went to the window. Beyond the roofs of the tourist cabins, stars glittered in the sky, their tiny lights vibrating. She'd always been afraid of stars, afraid of being whisked away into a frigid, meaningless space. In the darkness, she could feel the Canyon waiting. Wind rattled the windowpane and in its low moan she heard the Canyon's voice. It said: you are nothing. You've always been nothing.

Tim, she whispered, but Tim could no longer offer the illusion that she mattered. Touch was only touch, and when they'd burned up all their heat they'd float away from each other, like scattered debris from a dead star. There wasn't enough in Tim's loose life to hold her. She needed to be tethered to the planet. She needed Claude, the kids, her sisters, Mitchell, Jamie, the house, cars, clothes, the town of Shelby—all the accumulated mass of her existence.

Standing at the edge of the great abyss, Donna longed for Shelby as she'd longed for her lover. She craved a place where time was revealed not by geology, but by tumbling stone walls and the rise of a white church steeple. The earth was just a spinning hunk of rock, but its core was fiery. Maybe, if she was careful to stay on the surface, she might call it home.

DEALING

[Mitchell, 1985]

MITCHELL BUMPED through muddy ruts with the kids in the Toyota, steering a jerky course between two lines of tumbling stone walls. Behind the walls, purple tubing ran from maple to maple. Mitchell missed that old drip drip drip you'd hear, the sap pinging in the galvanized buckets. Now it was just a steady seep through plastic piping, silent and distanced. Of course it was easy to be nostalgic, since he didn't have to hump those buckets like when he was a kid.

Ahead, an orange town backhoe balanced over the roadside ditch, idling with bucket up, a yellow grader pulled up behind it. Three men lounged beside the vehicles: the Shelby town crew taking a coffee break, sucking up a bit of March sunshine.

Mitchell slowed as he pulled abreast. Faces lit up when they saw him: Grease Gun Munn, nearly twenty-one by the time he made it out of high school, who used to strong-arm smaller kids in the halls; Augie West, who'd sat behind Mitchell in homeroom and called him Shit Train instead of Chartrain—a reference to the kiddie locomotive Mitchell used to engineer at Santa's Workshop—and his former brother-in-law Eddie Wells, who had driven Marsha to her death on a rain-slick road. Waving and grinning as though Mitchell was their own personal delivering angel. Mitchell skidded to a stop.

"Hey, hey how's it going, how you doing, Mitch?" they cho-rused, all smiles as though they were great old pals. Mitchell took it in like a cat stretching in sunshine, the warmth of popularity that had always been denied him. He knew why they were so glad to see him, but he didn't care. He was willing to take whatever attention he could get.

"Good to see my tax dollars at work," Mitchell jibed, tilting his head toward the parked heavy equipment.

"You get what you pay for," Augie West struck back. Everyone knew Mitchell was iffy on taxes and had fed his family on food stamps over the years.

"So I hear. So I hear." Mitchell could afford to be good-natured. Augie West would lick his boots to get what Mitchell carried in the zipper pouch under the car seat.

"You got some inspiration for us?" Eddie Wells inquired. He was holding a bottle of his usual, cheaper inspiration: Miller at ten A.M., and not his first. Eddie leaned against the passenger window, poking his shaggy, bearded head in the car. The bags under his eyes could carry mail. Clearly on a downward spiral, the poor sucker. "Hey kids," Eddie greeted. Only Emily, Miss Sunshine, smiled back at her uncle. After Marsha's death Eddie didn't come around anymore, couldn't face the family, and the boys barely knew him.

Augie was getting antsy. He glanced at the kids, back at Mitch. "Hey Chartrain, you want to do some business or what?"

"Well . . ." Mitch paused to stretch it out, flex his muscles a little, then relented. "It looks like I got a civic duty here, gotta help you guys get those machines moving before Easter. Just let me pull off the road." He backed through the ruts and parked behind the grader so the kids wouldn't see the transaction.

"Daddy, how come we're stopping here?" Emily wanted to know.

"You kids hang on. It'll only be a minute. I got to talk to these guys," Mitchell said.

"Don't take *too* long, Daddy," Emily requested reasonably.

"Ohhhhh. Darn." That was Carver, always the disappointed

one. He crossed his arms on his chest and flopped against the back seat. He reminded Mitchell of himself. His old self.

Mitchell reached under the driver's seat and pulled out the zipper pouch. "You guys be good," he warned, "or I won't take you to Newberry's." He closed the door and started off, looked back over his shoulder and smiled—Carver and Eli were already punching each other in the back seat. If he was his father, he'd be rushing back there to slap them for disobeying. But he wasn't Lowell Chartrain, and never would be.

Mitchell laid out the lines on a mirror set on the hood of the orange backhoe. They all leaned in to block the light breeze. Big white fluffy clouds sailed in a bright March sky, birches scraped against each other, and the branches of the maples, with their swollen purple buds, reached up as pretty as a *Vermont Life* magazine cover.

The three men shouldered in, anxious as dogs at a food bowl, quietly measuring, searching out the one line that might be a speck bigger than the rest. They took their turns with a plastic straw.

"Whooeeee," Eddie said, "Mmmmm goood."

Augie West was silent, though his shoulders twitched.

Munn wiped his fingers over his lips and nose and licked them.

Mitchell grinned and took a share of his toot. He liked to remind them that he was the lucky bastard who could do it at will. Snoof. Snoof, one per nostril. Whooo. Slick on the back of his tongue and against his teeth, faintly metallic. And then the little rush that pleases.

Munn shook his oversized head in wonder. "I don't know how you keep from snorting up all the merchandise."

"Self-control," Mitchell said. "Some guys got it." A joke. He was famous in town for having no discipline at all, for never holding down a job, a perpetual loser. But that had all changed. His chest expanded with pride: it was he who brought the good times on Clavell Brook Road, he who sparked up their day.

Some discreet bucks changed hands and Mitchell was back in the Toyota, bumping along over washboards. The town crew didn't do such a great job grading the road as they used to, he noted.

Mitchell parked the Toyota at the bottom of the hill. It was mud season, and you couldn't drive up. You couldn't drive up in winter either, and in summer only between thunderstorms, and then you still risked ripping out your muffler. He'd carved the driveway with a rented dozer but he hadn't ditched or crowned it, and already it was half washed out, a track of deep ruts and jutting rocks veering away from the old town road, cutting a switchback up the hill.

The kids ran ahead, whooping, happy with their purchases. They'd gone to Newberry's in Bellows Falls and then to the video store in Walpole. Emily had a china horse to add to her collection, Carver a pack of baseball cards whose statistics he would memorize by morning, and Eli brandished a green squirt gun that he promised he wouldn't fire in the house. Mitchell carried the bread-baking machine he'd bought for Corinne, another of the many gifts he'd lavished on her since she'd almost left him last summer.

Once the money started coming in from dealing, he'd bought and bought, desperate to keep her. The shed held matching racing bikes and cross-country skis for all of them. Corinne, a master of the thrift shop bargain, now owned brand new hiking boots and an expensive down parka. They might live too far from the road to afford electric poles, but they had a generator, a VCR, and a TV with a twenty-nine-inch screen. They also had the remains of Mitchell's good intentions about improving the property. The yard held rolls of linoleum, big cotton-candy wheels of pink fiberglass insulation, a toilet, in the event that he put in a septic system. Cedar shingles lay in bundles, for when he got around to covering the tar paper.

Mitchell had held a sheetrocking party this winter with coke as incentive, and all the guys who suddenly wanted to be his friends had come. They'd spent the night snorting and banging, but nobody thought about the taping part of it, and used every tiny little scrap, so the walls were a patchwork of rectangles and triangles that would be impossible to tape. Already, the unpainted sheetrock had yellowed from wood smoke, and one of the walls had a big hole where Mitchell had put a fist through it.

He knew he'd never finish the house. It wasn't just the fact that Gramp had never wanted him to have the land; Jamie made him feel unwelcome, even if he cast it as a joke. Always bugging him about cleaning up his garbage, or bitching about the big trees he cut for firewood. Always judging.

If he just got them off this cursed land, if he could keep Corinne distracted until he had a fresh start, he could finally make it. As soon as he saved enough money dealing he was going to get them out of there. They would buy a boat and sail, spend their winters in the Caribbean, their summers in Maine. Just because he was born in Vermont didn't mean it had to be his dream. Meanwhile, he didn't mind that coke had turned him into the town big shot.

Mitchell stepped through melted snow and mud and soggy trash: a gas range with plugged jets, a bicycle with a bent wheel rim, moldering books, broken toys, glass bottles, kids' clothes, and smashed windows littered the yard. Mitchell didn't even see them.

As he approached the house, his mood soured; he'd lost the swell of good times he'd garnered with the road crew down on Clavell Brook. At the door, his neck stiffened and Corinne's bread machine grew heavy in his arms. He resented the bribes, even as he bought them. The whole business was eight months past, but he couldn't stop picturing her with that other guy, the owner of the restaurant where she'd waitressed. He suspected she'd only come back to him because the guy wouldn't take her with three kids.

Mitchell had taken her back, of course, despite his fury, because he couldn't imagine life without her, and during their endless recriminations, she'd opened his eyes. It was interesting to learn that she couldn't stand the way they lived another moment, or that he'd ruined her life. He was a dish-washing, gift-buying fool these days.

In the kitchen, Corinne stood over the table slapping sandwiches together while the kids displayed their prizes. Her long honey hair fell forward, her lean shanks and slender back flexed as she bent over bread and peanut butter. Mitchell couldn't help looking at her with other men's eyes now, couldn't help being anxious about what they saw. She was a mystery, a ticking time bomb.

Corinne glanced up, betraying nothing. "Hungry?"

Mitchell shook his head and set the box down on the table.

"Look Mommy, it's a surprise!" Emily announced. "Daddy got it for you at Whitehead's."

Mitchell winced at Emily's eagerness to make them happy with each other. She was only eight, a little girl busy offering a carrot stick to the china horse beside her plate.

Corinne eyed the package. "It's just like the one Gary bought Nancy last year. Thanks." She licked the jelly knife and set it in the sink. "You know, I didn't really mind kneading by hand. It let me work off my frustrations."

Mitchell frowned. Which frustrations was she talking about? *He was a better lover, she'd said.* "Throw the damn thing in the yard if you don't want it."

"No, it's nice. It'll be a lot quicker."

"And we all know quicker is better, right?"

Corinne rolled her eyes.

"Hey!" Carver shouted in outrage at his smaller brother. "Look what you did, you dorkhead."

Eli looked up, grinning, sandwich in hand. He'd dripped a bloop of jelly on Carver's baseball cards, which were spread across the table. "I didn't mean to." He reached down to smear it off.

"Mom!" Carver protested. "He's ruining them."

"Well don't put them where he's eating," Mitchell snapped. "What do you expect?"

Corinne rolled her eyes. "Come on, you guys, chill out. I made oatmeal raisin cookies while you were gone."

"Mmmm. Cookies!" Emily and Eli smacked their lips.

Carver kicked the table leg. "I hate oatmeal raisin."

"Then don't have any," Corinne said. She gathered Carver's cards into a deck and set them out of harm's way.

"It's not fair," Carver whined. "You always make the kind I don't like."

"That's enough. You kids go eat outside," Mitchell ordered. An unpleasant echo of his father's voice reverberated under the static in his head.

"Mitch-ell. It's okay," Corinne objected.

"They've been in the car all morning. They can use the air."

"They can use a little patience," Corinne said softly.

Grumbling, the kids struggled back into their jackets and trooped out, sandwiches in hand, Emily entrusted with the baggie of cookies. In a moment there were hysterical shrieks as Eli brandished his water pistol.

"You didn't use to snap at them like that," Corinne admonished. "You used to play with them, Mitchell."

It was true, he used to, but now he was too busy, too stretched. Dealing kept him running and the coke kept him edgy.

"I'll play with them later," he said. "Why don't *we* play now?" Corinne glanced at the closed door, bit her lip.

Mitchell laid out the lines on the table from his pouch.

"It's kind of early," Corinne protested. But she was down there already, snarfing it up, a guzzler.

When she looked up, Mitchell pressed his mouth to hers hard, resentment mingling with desire, lips numbed by white powder. Over Corinne's shoulder he saw Carver's small, unhappy face pressed against the window.

At eight, Mitchell left Corinne reading the kids to bed under gaslights and walked down to the bottom of the hill, slipping as ice hardened up again in the nighttime chill. The fenceline maples loomed ghostly along the remains of the old town road. He hated to admit it, but he was still afraid of the dark. He never should have rented that vampire movie last week. Now he expected Dracula to jump out at any moment. Blood red eyes, a flash of incisors . . .

He heard footsteps and froze. Then the black lump of his neighbor's labrador took shape, sniffing the snow, running deer, probably. The dog deserved a bullet between the eyes, but Mitchell was so relieved he called the dog over and petted the soft ears, let the wagging tail whip his thighs, the wet neoprene nose push into his palm.

Mitchell pushed the dog away. He hadn't liked dogs since Lowell made him shoot his border collie for barking when he was twelve. Anyway, he had a party to get to.

The flashlight picked up the yellow reflectors of the Toyota's sidelights. Mitchell put his zipper purse under the seat and sat shivering while the engine turned over and caught. Cold air blew through the defroster. He bumped down the dirt road and hooked onto Route 5, headed for Jerry Rawley's on the Shelby/Putney line.

Rawley was a dentist in Brattleboro who'd come up from New Jersey five years ago and sunk a lot of money into a contemporary house in the middle of what was once a working hay pasture. The house was a prow-fronted glass and cedar monstrosity with a view to New Hampshire, jutting off its "executive lot," a three-acre building site that sold for ten times what the acreage had cost a few years ago. Agricultural land was a goner.

The huge angled windows glowed merrily and through them Mitchell could see figures moving. They'd blow coke without a shade drawn because Jerry believed in his privacy; he actually thought he was living in the country.

Mitchell parked between a Volvo station wagon and Rawley's Jag and crunched up the peastone gravel path. The door flew open before he even knocked: that's how welcome he was. Jerry, wearing one of those big print Bill Cosby sweaters, reached out a spongy little hand and drew Mitchell in.

"Mitch, Mitch, great to see you. How's it going? Everybody's waiting for you."

He bet they were. He followed Jerry into the kitchen, which had glittering white tile and the fluorescent feel of a dentist's office; all it needed was the chair and the drill.

Annette Rawley turned from mixing drinks to smile at Mitchell without meeting his eyes. She was a small, tense brunette wearing pleated wool pants and a beige wool sweater with a lot of feathers and fur and glitter glued on. It looked like something you'd pull out of a pack rat's den, only it probably cost a week's wage at Putney Paper. The Rawleys hadn't figured out yet that New Jersey style didn't go over well in the land of L. L. Bean and compost.

Mitchell took a Chivas and soda and wandered into the living room where, reflected back in the huge windows, a small party had gathered.

"Hello, Mitchell, how are Corinne and the kids?" Judy Morris graced him with one of her brilliant insincere smiles.

"Fine, fine." Mitch took a burning sip from his drink and smiled just as insincerely back. When he was driving school bus Judy had tried to have him fired because he'd put her juvenile delinquent eighth-grade son off the bus for dangling some little girl's gerbil out the window and for calling Mitchell a shitbrain local too dumb to do anything but drive bus. Judy was a therapist in Brattleboro, which made perfect sense. She wore girlish bangs and her greying blond hair hung in a ponytail. He'd always taken her for the Birkenstock type, but here she was, beer in hand, coke hungry, ready to let bygones be bygones. And there in the corner was her husband, a semi-retired stockbroker who worked out of his home by computer. Arthur Morris had traded in his business suits for Icelandic sweaters and the gentlemanly art of sheep raising. He talked about his losses at lambing time as if they were the Dow Jones average.

Mitchell glanced about. The rest of the guests included Jerry's hygienist, the assistant principal of the Shelby Middle School, who'd threatened to bring the state on him for keeping Carver at home when he didn't like his teacher last year, a furniture builder, a Brattleboro lawyer. There was a time, oh, maybe six months ago, when a place like this would have left Mitchell intimidated, wondering if his fly was down, aware of the dirt under his nails. He would have felt like they were all teachers and that he was being called in front of class to answer question for which he didn't have answers. Now he had the upper hand; he could look them in the eye.

Sure, it was only the fact that he delivered the best coke in the area, straight from the source, with less cut than anybody's, that made him welcome. But what the hell. Now he could see their foibles, their unhappy bullshit. Oh, they'd stumble over themselves to buddy up to him now, when before he was an object of their contempt. They probably didn't even like each other, but coke made strange bedfellows.

Mitchell lay lines out on the shiny surface of the chrome and glass coffee table. For an instant he saw his own shock of blond hair and startled lashes reflected in the glass, and experienced a momentary disorientation—What am I doing here?—then he handed the rolled bill to Annette, who giggled like a schoolgirl. Jerry leaned over, too eager to pretend to be the good host, muscling Judy Morris out of the way.

Soon, conversations in the room took off with a roar like a jet at Windsor Locks airport, shimmering up to bounce off the beams of the cathedral ceiling. An hour later, Judy Morris had cornered Mitchell and was giving him some line about getting his GED and going back to school. He couldn't tell if she was showing professional concern or flirting. Everyone got horny with blow.

"There's so much more you could do," Judy persisted. "With your energy, and intelligence . . ."

There's so much more she could do, like suck his dick. Who'd she think would deliver her good times if he "furthered" himself? What a load. Just another version of the putdown, acting like she cared what he did. Still, the remark about his intelligence was flattering. What got him was that he believed it—oh, not about going back to school, but that he was able, bright, talented. He deserved a destiny that went beyond coke courier, if he could just get his hands on it. Another line, and he'd feel it, that swell of possibility . . .

A series of sharp raps on the door broke the mood. Anxiety

circled the room like a waft of old sweat. Mitchell eyed the coffee table spread with coke and measured the distance to the back door.

Shrugging as though he didn't have a roomful of coked up guests, Jerry went to answer.

"Hey Jer, how's it going, man, saw Mitch's car, figured I'd drop on in." The boom of Teddy Kendall's voice made Mitchell smile.

"Well, sure, come on in, Teddy," Jerry feigned welcome, trading one source of alarm for another. Teddy pushed through the door and headed straight for the coffee table. Behind him, Jerry rolled his eyes at Annette but Annette's gaze was riveted on Teddy's barn boots, which were dropping cowshit on her creamy rug.

Teddy was a famous coke slut, a mooch and a brawler who, like his brothers, was busy sticking his father's dairy farm up his nose. Teddy used to deal to Jerry before Mitch got into the business, but now Teddy was so facey he couldn't keep his nose out of his stuff, and he cut it so heavy it was too beat up to sell. Teddy was into everyone for money. He owed Mitchell five hundred and Mitchell knew he'd never see it, but he didn't care. Teddy and he went back.

When Teddy settled down for a toot, Jerry grabbed Mitchell and drew him into the kitchen. He whipped out a roll of bills. "Here's what I owe you, and here's an extra fifty. Do me a favor, Mitch," Jerry glanced over his shoulder toward the living room, where Teddy's weird high giggle reverberated, "just get him out of here."

Mitchell closed his fist over the money. Who did Rawley think he was—better than Teddy, but not by much? It was a question that didn't bear too much examination right now if Mitchell wanted to keep that happy feeling. In the living room, Teddy sat leaned back, knees spread, legs jiggling, surveying the scene with a smile. The table looked as though it had been licked clean, and Rawley's guests huddled in various corners. Mitch sat down next to Teddy. "Hey Kendall, there's nothing going on here. You want to split?"

"Whatever." Teddy was like a hound on a bitch in heat; he

could sniff the coke in Mitchell's jacket and would follow him anywhere. He clambered up from the couch, leaving a smudge from his greasy clothes on the pale plush. "Bye, folks," Teddy offered, backing out the door with a wave. "It was real."

Outside, Mitchell laughed. "I don't think they like you Kendall. Rawley gave me fifty bucks to get you out."

"Then you owe me twenty-five, you fuck! I was just looking for you anyway. We're having a little thing over at the house and we run out of supplies. You want to swing by?"

"No," Mitchell said, "but I will." Parties at Kendall's were always lively, and Mitchell wasn't ready to go home.

"You know Mitch, I don't think I like them folks neither." Teddy picked up a piece of gravel and drew it against the gleaming Jaguar's black finish, down low where it would take Rawley a few days to notice. "There, looks better that way, don't you think? A custom job."

"Jesus, Kendall, let's get the fuck out of here."

Teddy's famous giggle floated down the hillside to settle over the icy scrim on the river.

Mitchell got into his Toyota. He could almost hear the collective sigh as Rawley's crew resumed their party. They'd keep on all night, too. One thing he was sure of: he wouldn't want Jerry Rawley sticking a dentist drill in his mouth tomorrow morning.

Mitchell followed the red beam of Teddy's single taillight back into Shelby. Fuck Rawley and his buddies. Mitchell could blow the town apart if he wanted to. He knew which teachers, which school principal, which dentist bought his coke, who was at the parties. It was the only time you'd find farmers with cow shit on their shoes socializing with professionals—as long as the farmer still had coke to deal. Coke, the great equalizer. Mitchell decided he ought to run for mayor, the way he crossed constituencies.

The lights were blazing at Kendall's farmhouse and the stereo blared U2. "Where's the old man?" Mitchell asked as they entered.

"Asleep upstairs. He don't hear that good no more. That's what fifty years sitting on a tractor will do to you. Pretty soon I won't be able to hear your whining voice no more, neither, you piece of shit!" Kendall thumped him good on the arm.

The Kendall farm was marginal: dirty cows, mucky fields full of stumps, and the house was a wreck. The old man said he left the place looking like shit to beat the taxes. Before the old lady died, they'd kept it up. When they were kids, Mitchell envied Teddy for living on a farm his family owned, while Lowell only milked for other farmers, and never for very long. Mitchell used to try to talk like them, not correct like his school-teacher mother insisted. Back then Mitchell thought the Kendalls had everything—all the dogs they wanted, tractors and trucks they could drive before they were old enough for licenses. Now they still had the place, but no pride except in their toughness, and almost all the farms his father had worked on were gone.

The Kendall farmhouse needed paint and plaster fell from the walls inside. The kitchen held two old wood cookstoves and two broken-down gas ranges. Grease and trash coated every surface. But at lunchtime everyone sat down together—family, friends, hired hands, whoever was around—at the two picnic tables in the center of the room, and they ate a meal, by god. It was still a farm, even if the boys were doing their best to destroy it.

Mitch took a proffered beer. The party included two of Teddy's younger brothers, Marvin and Bert, and his sister Jeannie, who'd been a good-looking girl when they were in school together. Now she had a mean, wasted look. She'd gone the skinny route instead of the fat one, and her wiry body had shriveled down to little boy hips and bumps under a blouse. Thick orange makeup covered her cheeks. Mitchell had seen her at parties, trying to pick fights with men, just like her brothers.

One of Jeannie's kids, about two years old, leaned against a cabinet wearing a droopy diaper, puffy-eyed and sucking his thumb. A dirty plaster cast covered one arm. Mitchell hoped Jeannie hadn't slid that far.

"Joey fell through a heat register upstairs," Teddy explained. "It was under the rug, we forgot all about the hole. Landed right on the counter. You hardly even cried, huh tough guy?" Teddy tossed a fake punch at the child, who batted his uncle's hand away and glared.

"See?" Teddy grinned. "He's a Kendall."

Teddy popped a beer and recounted how Mitch made fifty bucks to get rid of him, and everyone had a laugh.

"Yeah, we could be just as rich as that fuck Rawley if we sold the land," Marvin said. Marvin was smaller than Teddy, but just as scary in a bar fight. He didn't have his brother's good humor either.

"You hear the Precourt farm is for sale?" Teddy said. "They want three hundred thousand. Just for the view. The house is selling separate but it's shit."

The Precourt farm had the most beautiful land around, big swooping hayfields on a hillside with a view to Mount Monadnock in New Hampshire, at the end of a town road. The house was nothing, a box covered in asbestos shingles, but the fields . . . Mitchell and Jamie used to toboggan there. The Kendalls had cut hay on those fields for twenty years.

"We could probably make that much selling ours," Marvin interjected. "We got more road frontage."

"We ain't gonna sell it," Teddy said. "No way. We might lose it, but we ain't gonna sell it. Har har har."

Not as long as the old man was still alive, Mitch figured. But who knew what would happen when he was gone? You could buy a lot of coke with executive lots.

Mitch laid out lines and they got down to business. When Mitchell snorted his own, he accidentally took half of the one beside it.

"Jeez," Teddy exploded, "what you got there, 'Train, a vacuum cleaner for a nose?"

Mitchell laughed. "Yeah, I got a Hoover growing out of my face, why do you think my nose is so big?"

So then he was Hoover for the rest of the night.

Gary, Mitchell's brother-in-law, appeared at the door and was welcomed in. Gary and Nancy lived down the hill from Mitchell in the house Mitchell grew up in; Lowell had sold it to them for almost nothing. Gary used to complain when Mitchell and Corinne came down to use the phone or take a shower, but since Mitchell had started supplying the parties they were buddies.

"So how's it going?" Mitchell asked his brother-in-law. "What did the doctor say?" Nancy and Gary were taking their daughter Michelle to some specialist in Boston. Her first grade teacher said she couldn't skip, which was apparently some important developmental marker.

Gary shrugged. "It's probably nothing. You know doctors. Got a license to steal. Hey, how 'bout some of that booger sugar?"

Mitchell laid out more lines. Bert bragged loudly about how much timber he'd cut this winter. The Kendalls were always logging. Clearing more pasture, keeping enough soft maple cut for the sugaring arch, Bert selling cordwood on the side.

"You ought to get yourself a team of horses like Henry Weeks," Mitchell said, just to bug him. "They're more efficient than a skidder on a small lot and they don't make the mess." As though erosion and skidder marks would matter to a Kendall.

"Bull," Bert countered. "What's so efficient about something you got to feed whether it's working or not?"

"So? You got the hay cheap enough."

"I don't care. I don't like hayburners. Give me a Timberjack any day." Bert made a diesel roar and grinned. "I like to feel hot steel throbbing under my seat, smell that good exhaust. Mmmm. I don't want no shitty horses' asses in front of my nose."

"Don't tell that to Henry Weeks," Mitchell said.

"Well, he's something else," Bert admitted.

"He sure as shit is," Mitchell declared. "I ever tell you about the time I was cutting cordwood for him and his horses fell? Old Henry, drunk as skunk every moment of his life except when he's working in the woods, but he's some kind of magician with those horses. He never raises his voice and the horses trust him like God. One time we were hauling logs down an embankment on Carroll's land and the lead horse, a big Percheron named Prince, went down, pulled the other horse with him. Here's these big feet thrashing around, two tons of horsepower ready to splinter your skull to smithereens, and Henry jumps right in between them, knife flashing, slicing through all that harness like a goddamn ninja. Just watching nearly made me piss my pants. Those horses got up like nothing happened. 'Shoulda saved the harness instead,' Henry says, 'worth more than the damn beasts.' You know he didn't mean it. If one of his horses broke a leg, he would've cried like a baby."

"See, didn't I tell you?" Bert argued. "You won't have that kind of trouble with a skidder. Course we did get into quite a jam there on Darcy's hill that time. Remember Teddy?"

Bert went on with his own logging story, but Mitchell didn't listen. When you got coked up enough all you wanted to do was talk—listening took too much patience. He went off on his own internal riff while Marvin's mouth flapped. Henry Weeks was a goddamn hero. Any kind of courage impressed Mitchell. He'd pegged himself a coward since childhood for breaking in the face of Dad's beatings. Corinne said you couldn't blame a kid for that, but it didn't help matters.

"You whore!" Jeannie's meth-addicted, truck driving husband accused loudly across the room, interrupting Mitchell's flow. When had he come in?

"Shut up, Riley!" Jeannie screamed back.

"What about you, Chartrain? You fucked her, right? Tell 'em, she's a whore." Riley turned his manic meth gaze on Mitchell.

Mitchell blanched. He'd slept with Jeannie once, fifteen years ago. He sure didn't want to fight over it.

"She might be a whore but she's our sister," Teddy said pleasantly, "so shut your trap Riley or I'll have to push your face in."

"Do it!" Jeannie urged.

The child slept on the couch, oblivious to his parents, already an expert at self-protection.

Teddy and Bert strong-armed Riley out the door and everyone did a few more lines.

But after Riley came back in and attempted another fight with

Jeannie, and Teddy and Gary arm-wrestled to a standoff, it got to be that point in a party when the fun was over but you just kept hitting it, hoping to stave off the crash.

Teddy came up to Mitch, standing too close, eyes darting like minnows. "Cut me in on your supplier, man. I got to get back in the business. My connection's gone bad."

"I can't. I swore to Lenny I wouldn't pass it on."

"Shit," Teddy spat. "Lenny Garber. That little New York geek. Comes up here and shoots a doe on our land. Spray paints the trees orange so he can find his way back to the fucking house. And he don't want me in on it?"

"He's paranoid. He doesn't want it traced back to him. What can I do? He's a friend."

"Ain't I your friend 'Train?"

"Sure you are. That's why I'll tell you, you can't handle it Teddy. You get some money together to buy an eightball, you'll blow it all yourself. You'll never make the sales."

Teddy stuck out his chest, ready to fight and then collapsed like a stepped-on puffball. "You know, Chartrain. You're right. I can't deal no more. Shit, forget it. You're my guest. You got good stuff, too. I got some people want to do business with you. I'll send them on up to your place."

"Don't send anyone to the house, Teddy. I don't want to do business with anyone I don't know."

"Ah, they're okay. Met them at Nick's or some damn place, can't remember right now."

Great, at a bar. "Don't send them, Teddy."

"Okay, okay. Whatever. Let's do some more, hey?"

Light filtered in through the windows. Jeannie and the kid were gone, Gary had headed home to get ready for work, Bert snored cheek down on the table, and Marvin, possessed by manic energy, was engaged in burning great loads of kindling in the cookstove, although it was already way too hot in the room. Mesmerized by the cracks in the picnic table, Teddy ran a fork through the greasy openings as though they might yield lost grains. Mitchell was gathering himself together for the drive home when the old man, all stooped shoulders and grim visage, came thumping down the stairs dressed in barn overalls. Dan Kendall surveyed the scene bitterly. He knew what was going on but he wasn't able to do a thing about it, since he couldn't tend sixty Holsteins himself.

"Wake up your brother," the old man ordered Teddy. "We got chores." He turned and slammed a coffee pot on the stove.

Mitchell headed out. He was glad he didn't have to drill teeth or milk cows this morning. All he had to do was figure out how to fit his soul back in his body, because right now it was only an illusion that he was in one piece, crunching on frozen crust out to a frozen car. The ice breaking under his Sorel boots could be his nerves snapping. Across the road the lights went on in the milking parlor. Mitchell shivered at the thought of Teddy moving down the line of cows, cleaning udders, hooking up the milking machines, the suction going like the sound of Mitchell's spirit being drained out of his body. It was just sleep he needed, only it would be hours before he could come down enough to crash, and he was due in New York by noon.

Mitchell was getting twitchy, worried about missing his exit and landing on the wrong side of the Triborough Bridge. He had a gut-wrenching fear of getting lost down here, ending up in some toxic garbage dump in New Jersey with two thousand bucks just waiting to be ripped off, or breaking down in the Bronx where he'd get eaten alive. Of course, the real nightmare would be getting busted, but he couldn't even think about that. There were some risks worth taking.

He hated the way New York drivers veered toward you, as if their whole lives weren't already crowded and they couldn't get close enough. Signs whipped by announcing Manhattan. Mitchell made a series of fast lane cuts to the exit and on through the toll booth, where everyone fought over the shortest lines.

On the FDR Drive it was easier, only the next thing to be scared about was Artie, his connection. Would he show up like they'd arranged? Would he give good weight? Would he take Mitchell for a ride and cut his throat? The thought of ending up dead down here made him want to cry. He yearned to be back with Corinne and the kids so badly he could taste it. Better not to think of Corinne—he didn't like leaving her behind, not even for a day . . .

Red brick buildings zoomed past, the project maze of upper Manhattan on his right, a strobe-fast glimpse of cross streets dead-ending at the highway—women leaning out windows and clots of men in bright clothes gathered on the street, hanging around, their sweeping gestures enough to make him wonder about a life of graffiti and fumes—and then they were lost as the brownstones of the hundreds and upper nineties gave way to the white concrete of the seventies. The river flashed almost pretty on his left, despite the poisonous water. Descending toward the southern tip of the island, Mitchell's Toyota banged over the potholes. Fucking pot-holes on a major thoroughfare! He wondered what the New York City road crews snorted off *their* trucks.

Mitchell turned onto the cheap wide colonnade of Canal Street and cut west. Big signs announced army surplus; shoddy wares spilled from tiny street-front shops: watches, gold chains, elec-tronics. Trucks choking exhaust, people running right in the mid-dle of traffic. At a light, a guy with filthy dreadlocks jumped out and sloshed a squeegee on the Toyota's windshield. Mitchell stared straight ahead. He thought he knew what poor meant, but this guy flapped with rags. He'd weep for the poor fucker if he wasn't so scared of him. Plus the guy wanted money for messing up the windshield with his dirty slop. Mitchell stared straight ahead through the longest light in the world. The squeegee guy smashed a fist on the hood, his crazed face filling the streaked windshield. The light changed and Mitchell's heartbeat eased as the Toyota spun rubber and jerked forward.

He found Delancey Street and, miraculously, a parking space that he thought was far enough from a hydrant. He'd already punched down the door locks on the FDR. Mitchell waited. Where the hell was Artie? The Toyota's green Vermont plates waved like a flag: I'm up to no good. He didn't look like a tourist.

Pedestrians walked briskly past, heads down as though they were leaned into a stiff wind. Then three black men sauntered by like they had no business in the world except pulling him out of the car and grabbing his cash. They didn't even give him a glance, though, laughing with their loose high voices as though they owned the world. He was ashamed that dark-skinned people made him uneasy. Too many cop shows as a kid, maybe. There sure weren't any living in Shelby.

Just last week he'd made a fool of himself at the Shelby Quick Mart, a garish new convenience store serving the interstate trade. He got caught between two black guys up at the register and he got so nervous he stepped on one guy's toes and before he could apologize he'd bumped his six-pack into the other's nuts. "Jeez, I'm sorry," he'd mumbled, and all they could do was shake their heads at his sorry honky ass.

On Delancey Street, a pair of old-fashioned Jews in fur-brimmed hats, long black coats, and messy beards crossed the street in front of him, gibbering in their strange language. Hasids—Lenny Garber liked to point them out, do imitations. He could, being a Jew himself.

It was a lot easier when Mitchell had bought directly from Lenny. All he had to do was to park in Lenny's fancy neighborhood and the doorman would carry him up to the apartment Lenny's mother's boyfriend owned. He could sleep on Lenny's couch, order in Chinese food, blow some toot, and maybe they'd go out in the middle of the night on what Lenny called "a job"—racing uptown red lights flashing in Lenny's fake unmarked police car, to watch a fire announced on Lenny's police radio. Harlem, Spanish Harlem, the Bronx. Mitchell had seen it just like in the news: a fireman climbing out a window with a child in his arms. Hatchets crashing through doors. Real heroes. Lenny loved them.

Lenny had a fake police badge and a NYC police department jacket. When he came up to Vermont he drove ninety; he flashed his badge at the state troopers who stopped him, told them he was on an extradition case, and they even offered an escort. All with several thousand dollars worth of coke in the trunk of his car. Lenny was hard to figure—he was fearless negotiating the streets of Harlem, but afraid of getting lost in the woods.

Lenny was the little rich kid whose parents had built a weekend mansion up in the orchards above Gramp's land. Lenny used to drift down to play, and later to race dirt bikes and hold hands with Donna. His real pleasure was setting fires and detonations. He was a funny little kid who wore a cap all the time because he had a nervous habit of pulling hair out of his head. After Lenny's father blew his brains out and his mother sold their country house, Mitchell rode the bus down to visit Lenny in the city. They dropped water balloons on pedestrians from Lenny's mother's Fifth Avenue apartment and took cabs to fires. Even then Lenny had the police radio tuned in all night. Finally a UPI photographer told him to get a camera because he always got to the fires before they did. Now Lenny had a good news job and a bad cocaine habit, which made him eager to sell a direct line to his connection for only five hundred bucks—five grams of coke up his nose.

Yeah, buying off Lenny was clean and neat, but Lenny wanted a bigger cut and Mitchell wanted more profits, and the deeper Lenny got into his addiction the more obnoxious he became—manic and aggressive, when before he was just hyper and funny. It wasn't Lenny who brought the first coke into Shelby—that probably came along with the city refugees—but he sure made it easier for Mitchell to get into the business.

Where the hell was Artie? A uniformed cop swaggered by. A couple of squat men in leather jackets speaking something foreign, Russian maybe. What if Artie didn't show? What if he had to get a new connection? He'd have to beg Lenny to set him up again. He couldn't think about going out of the business, being dumped back down into poverty and nobodiness, not even for a little while. Mitchell's guts tightened. Maybe he had the wrong corner? Should he go to a phone booth and call? In his experience, the phones never worked on New York streets. Somebody always trashed them for the change. A growing claustrophobia seized him. The dreary cement and brick blocks were closing in.

Mitchell drummed the steering wheel. Five more minutes and he was out of here. Then a face appeared in the passenger window—Artie, rattling the door handle. Mitchell leaned across and pulled up the knob. Artie had grown a mustache since Mitchell's last trip. He wasn't sure what Artie was. Italian or Puerto Rican or something, maybe nothing, just a guy with black hair and a taste for pointy shoes.

"Hey, man, let's drive," Artie said.

"I was just about to take off. Figured you weren't coming."

"I got into something I couldn't get out of, if you know what I mean." He winked, like Mitchell was his biggest pal.

Artie probably thought Mitchell was a stupid hick; it would be so easy for him to pull a gun and rip him off. But that didn't make sense, Mitchell tried to reassure himself; Artie would lose a good customer, an expanding northern market. "Where to?" Mitchell inquired.

"Tribeca."

Mitchell looked blank so Artie, with heavy patience, instructed, "That way."

They cruised across town and into a neighborhood of five-story office and industrial buildings; no little parks here, no vendors or street sellers, no restaurants, no pedestrians.

"I got good stuff for you, man," Artie said. "No shit."

"Good."

"Pull over there." Artie pointed to a space under a sign that read: NO PARKING, DELIVERY ZONE. Mitch pulled in.

Artie slid a box out of his shopping bag, flipped the cover to reveal folded undershirts. And beneath them, a baggie of pink Peruvian rock. "Check it out, man." Artie cracked the ziplock seal.

Mitchell slipped a finger into the powder that had rubbed off the rock and pushed it up inside his nose, casually, all the while looking for the cop or citizen ready to notice. The streets were empty. The rush hit him: pure and uncut, like opening the throttle on a Harley, sheer low-end torque. Whooo. Mitchell reached under the seat for his money. Artie stiffened; he wasn't sure of Mitchell either, suspecting some country cowboy going to pull a knife. Mitchell smiled and handed over the envelope. Artie counted down in his lap, smooth now.

"Must be nice up there, huh," Artie crooned. "Birdies going tweet tweet. You got the right idea, just come down to the big shithole for business, you got a nice place up there I bet."

"It's okay," Mitchell lied.

"Cool. Yeah, I'm going to get out too soon's as I get enough money together. Move to Miami. Sit on a beach with a pina colada, a babe in a bikini. Live like Scarface, ha ha. You seen that flick?"

"I've seen it. Guys cutting each other up with chain saws. Real nice."

"So." Artie tapped his arm. "You give me a call when you're ready." He opened the door and was gone, the only proof of his presence the undershirts sitting in their box on the seat.

Mitchell headed east and found his way onto the FDR. He had to force himself not to speed, because all he wanted was to get out of here fast. He had to look normal, just your average tourist in a bashed-up, rusty Toyota, taking in the sights. What he really wanted was to stick his finger back in the bag. But he was brightening already as he headed north, another little success, two thousand bucks worth to be divided and multiplied. He'd done it, made his way through New York like someone who knew what he was doing.

In Connecticut he decided he was thirsty and pulled into a drive-through McDonald's for a king-size soda. Half an hour later Mitchell had to piss. He had to piss bad, but he had a horror of public bathrooms. There weren't any bushes along this stretch of highway, just smooth grassy flanks leading to a chain-link fence. Ten minutes further up the road he was biting his lips because he had to go, and he had to go now. He spied the empty soda cup on the floor. Why not? There weren't any cars around.

Mitchell scooped it up. With a foot lodged on the accelerator he lifted his butt, eased down his zipper, and wrangled the big fella out with one hand. He slid the cup under and let go. Sweet relief! He was feeling pretty smug as the wax cup filled. Now to get rid of it. He considered dumping it out the window, but it would only blow back in. He'd just pull over and pour it out. Mitchell steered right and hit a pothole. The cup tipped, soaking his crotch. Cock-sucking bastard! It was all over his lap like he'd pissed his pants, running down into his shoes. Jesus fucking Christ. What a loser.

Then he remembered. He had a box of good times at his disposal. A bag. He wiped his hands and opened the baggie, scraped off a flake and rolled it between thumb and forefinger, then lifted the powder to his nose. Pissed himself. Jeez. Jamie would really laugh at this one.

At dusk moist air settled over the river. The trees lining the banks merged into a dark wall, muffling the sound of the cars running up and down Route 12 on the New Hampshire side. The June darkness was a soft warm blanket rolling down from the hills. The canoe cut the faintest vee; Mitchell's paddle lapped through velvet black just enough to keep them headed downriver. Jamie liked to drift while he cast and as dusk gave way to night they held to the center, staying away from the snags along the best pools.

Sitting in the bow, Mitchell listened to Jamie's reel spinning psheeeeeeeee and then the distant clink of the bass lure before it sank. Jamie was an energetic fisherman, casting and reeling constantly, changing lures, charged with the thrill of pursuit; Mitchell no longer cared if Jamie caught more or bigger bass than he did. He just wanted their time together.

Jamie snapped his rod back. "Shit, lost him."

"Bull. You can't lose what you never had," Mitchell jeered.

Jamie reeled in and set his rod in the canoe. "I had him. He got my favorite humpback razorback, the bastard."

"You mean some snag got it."

Jamie stood up carefully to piss into the river.

"Watch you don't lean over too far. That big bass you're lying about just might take a bite of your wienie. Course he'd need a magnifying glass to find it."

"Hey, it's so big I been using it for a paddle. Sending up a hell of a wake."

Jamie sat back down and dug around in his tackle box. He pulled out a candle and lit it, made a few drips on a middle thwart and stuck the candle into the soft wax. A little globe of light lit the blackness. On the cooler between them sat a mirror, and on it white powder laid out in big rails. It was from Mitchell's private stash, the pure stuff, before he cut it to sell. The cooler held a six-pack and a bag of State Line potato chips, which they'd never bother to open.

"Remember that time Dad took us fishing up on Knapp Pond and wouldn't let you eat any potato chips?" Mitchell laughed.

"Lowell." Jamie whistled. "He's a beauty."

Mitchell must've been eight and Jamie twelve. In the morning when they were packing lunches, Lowell asked if Jamie wanted chips and he said no. At noon when they were starving and Mitchell offered to share his, Lowell wouldn't let him. Jamie'd hadn't wanted any that morning; he wasn't going to get any now.

"The best part," Jamie reminisced, "was the way he'd make us fish until dark even when we hadn't gotten a bite all day. We'd come to fish, goddammit, and we were going to fish. Twelve hours sitting there in a rowboat bored out of our skulls. He really knew how to take the good times out of fishing."

Lowell took the good times out of just about anything, like those hunting trips to deer camp up in Masonville. Despite Mitchell's nine-year-old excitement at being included with his father and uncles, his pathetic belief that this time he'd do things right and his dad wouldn't get mad, each trip ended in his father's black rage because Mitchell had done something unforgivable like forgetting the alarm clock or standing in the light while Dad was cleaning his gun at camp. He always had some excuse to make Mitchell feel worthless.

One time, though, just once, he'd been praised.

He and Dad were unloading the truck at the dump. Seagulls whirled above the bulldozed trash. Mitchell always wondered what they were doing there, so far from the ocean. The smoky odor of burning tires filled his nostrils with their exotic stench. He was edgy, excited, happy to be off doing something alone with Dad but scared too, because it could go sour at any moment. They backed the pickup up to a pile and threw off the junk, Mitchell struggling not to hit the tailgate or side fenders with anything that might scratch and bring down Dad's wrath. While Dad paid the attendant, Mitchell cruised around through the piles of junk, checking out bicycle wheels, bureaus, strollers. He turned over a pile of cardboard and discovered a bashed-in metal tool box. A set of shiny Snap-on socket wrenches nestled inside.

"Look what I found Dad!" Mitchell held up a fistful of wrenches.

"Quit screwing around and get . . ." Lowell saw Mitchell's prize. "Well what do you know? You got damn good eyes, just like your Grampop Chartrain. That set's worth a hundred bucks. Some fool probably don't even know he dumped it. And I'm missing quite a few. Good for you, son."

The unfamiliar words of praise filled Mitchell's chest with a joy that nearly made him faint. He had good eyes, just like Dad's father! Dad had called him son! He turned back to the trash piles, eager to repeat his triumph, sure he would find something equally valuable, maybe better, that would garner more praise.

Dad honked the horn. "Get your ass back in the truck," he shouted. A father and a boy unloading the trunk of a blue sedan next to Dad's truck glanced up—the son scared, the father disgusted. Mitchell averted his eyes and hurried over to the pickup, the brief praise drowned by new shame.

Psheeeeeeeeeeeeee. Jamie's line reeled out and the canoe leaned as his weight shifted.

"You know what I been wondering?" Mitchell ventured.

"What's that?"

Mitchell let his own line trail in the water, unattended. "I been wondering if Mom wasn't so innocent after all. We always blamed

Dad for everything, but I was remembering, just last night, how when we were doing the foundation and I was, I don't know, maybe ten, and my job was to fill gallon jugs with water for the cement. Mom came up from the hole and told me to fill more and I said we didn't need anymore. We didn't. But she ran down into the hole to tell Dad I'd disobeyed her. He came up and hit me so hard with a length of PVC pipe he knocked me out of the bed of the pickup. I always hated her for that."

Jamie expelled breath.

Mitchell dragged his fingers in the tepid water. He wished he hadn't started in. This was a touchy subject between them. Although Jamie had witnessed the worst of Mitchell's childhood, he thought Mitchell should just get over it, that he was dwelling on the past; he considered it weak to blame your parents for your failures.

Sure, Jamie's father had been a sloppy drunk too, but not a mean one, and since he'd died an ugly cancer death like Mitchell's mother, Jamie insisted he'd put it all behind him, as though you weren't allowed to be mad at a dead person. There was something about Mitchell's persistence in talking to Jamie about his parents that reminded Mitchell of the stupid blind way he was always trying to get something—praise, recognition—from Dad. He needed Jamie to know this part of him yet he feared his judgment. He'd always set Jamie above him. If Jamie lived poor as he did, without electricity or even water in Gramp's old sugar-house, it was a choice, not a failure like it was for Mitchell. All the time, living on the hill, he could feel that undercurrent of Jamie's disapproval. Jamie wanted the land to be a monument to Gramp.

"Lowell's a real beauty," Jamie repeated.

Mitchell gave up. That wasn't the point of the story. What was Mom doing? Nobody, none of his sisters, would hear a word against her, but what the fuck was she doing that day, or any day, letting Dad beat the crap out of him all the time, even letting him beat the crap out of the poor dog?

Jamie set his pole on the floor of the canoe and leaned forward over the white powder, blocked one nostril, and inhaled through a bill. "Aaaah," he exclaimed. The candle glow lit Jamie's face from below, a sudden monstrous image of dark nostrils and white speckled beard. "Good stuff."

"Look at you go, big fella," Mitchell said, though his heart wasn't in it. He wished Jamie would talk about how bad his own Dad was, just to even things up. The only thing that evened things now was how eager Jamie was for Mitchell's blow. The coke habit Jamie was getting made him dependent on Mitchell in a way he'd never been. Even that didn't sit well with Mitchell. As much as he wanted to triumph over Jamie, he didn't like seeing him diminished. Everyone needed heroes, didn't they?

Mitchell watched the moon rise over the New Hampshire hills, a glowing white disc. Above Dorsey's fields a nighthawk swooped and mice huddled in their holes.

At dawn, Mitchell stripped off his wet fishing jeans and slipped into bed with Corinne. She huddled under the quilt, back to him, facing the wall. What did she dream of, he wondered. Everything about her—her posture, even her ragged sleep breath—seemed to exclude him now. Risking waking her, he snuggled close, but she only shifted and whimpered a little, like one of the kids. Mitchell touched his lips to her slippery hair, wishing that he could penetrate the firm shell of her skull, come to live inside her again, the way he used to, back when it was the two of them against the world.

Until last summer, he'd never questioned their alliance. She'd set her sights on him when she was just fourteen, a fat shy friend of Nancy's. By seventeen, she was willowy and Mitchell had started to notice. Her father was a timid postal employee who lived by the credo: "I woulda, I shoulda, I coulda . . ." so Corinne had found Mitchell's outlaw ways romantic. For years she never bitched when he walked off jobs, grew pot for cash, kept them freezing on the hill. And then she took that waitress job . . . He wanted to shake her awake now, demand she make it not have happened, insist that things go back the way they were. The coke energy still coursed through his body. He ran a finger down Corinne's spine, kissed the back of her neck gently, hoping to ease her into something that would prove her his.

"Wha . . . ?" Corinne startled awake.

"Shhhh, nothing." Mitchell slid his hand down her thigh.

"No." Corinne pulled away, sat up in bed. "Mitchell, there were people here last night."

"What are you talking about? Who?"

"I don't know. Some guys drove up around ten. Hooting and honking and calling for you. They wanted to buy coke. They said Teddy Kendall sent them. They woke the kids."

Mitchell sat up too. "Fucking Kendall. That fucking idiot. I told him not to send anyone up here. You didn't know them? You've never seen them?" His mind rapidly turned over the possibilities. Strangers. All he needed was bar talk about where to buy blow. Why not just call Deputy Fairbanks and get it over with? Fucking asshole.

Corinne shook her head. In the pale morning light her blue eyes loomed large and frightened. "They wouldn't go away for half an hour. I was afraid to go to sleep. And the kids heard the whole thing."

"Don't worry, I just got to be real careful about who I sell to. You didn't tell them I had anything, did you?"

"Of course not. Mitchell, I think it's time to get rid of it."

"Get rid of it? Are you nuts? I just got to get it out of the house."

"I think you should quit dealing. We agreed it was only for a while, just to get a few things. It's too dangerous."

"I *told* you I'd get the stuff out of the house!"

Corinne looked miserably down at her bare legs. "I don't want to live like this anymore."

"Goddammit." Mitchell slammed his hand on the mattress. "You don't want to live like this. You didn't like the way we lived

before, either. You like the money, don't you? What do you want
me to do?"

Corinne crossed her arms on her chest.

"Jeez, you really know how to yank me around." Mitchell
leaped up from the bed and loomed over Corinne. "There's no
way I can make you happy, is there? What you really want is that
restaurant jerk, isn't it? Admit it."

Angry tears filled Corinne's eyes. "That isn't it. That's not what
I'm saying. You don't even listen, you bastard. You never listen.
We said we wouldn't talk about him anymore."

Mitchell knew he was skating on thin ice. He was wired and
under it lurked real fear about the strangers who'd showed up.
They could've broken into the house, forced Corinne, stolen his
stockpile, hurt his kids. Yet all his anger flew toward her as though
she were an anger magnet. "You put me in a fucking bind, Corinne.
I notice you don't mind your occasional toot."

"I don't get high every day like you do."

"I don't do it every day." He didn't, did he? So what if he did?
That wasn't what they were fighting about.

Corinne turned toward the wall. "This just isn't working,
Mitchell."

What, the dealing? Or their being together? He drew on his
fishing jeans with their soggy legs. "Fine, Corinne. You do what
you have to do." He didn't mean it, any of it, but he couldn't help
upping the stakes, bluffing. There was no way out. He left the
bedroom. He took his zipper pouch out of its storage space in the
inner pocket of a winter parka hanging in the closet, and carried it
to the shed. There he found a twelve-inch length of iron pipe with
threaded ends and twisted on two caps; he opened one and shoved
his stash inside, screwed it back on. Airtight, watertight, he'd find
a hiding hole up in the woods and no one would know. Mitchell
opened the pipe again and removed a small plastic baggie from the
cloth zipper bag—nothing wrong with a little private supply. He
tucked it in a pocket before closing up the tube again.

Outside the shed, Carver and Eli stood watching. They wore

shorts and no shirts, their bare summer legs scabbed and scratched, their arms wrapped around their narrow chests to ward off the morning chill. Sometimes his children looked foolish to him, Eli with his round pumpkin head and thick straw hair and silly grin, Carver's constant pouting disappointment. If you mixed love with pity, it came out precariously close to contempt. Mitchell walked past them.

"Where you going, Dad?" Carver asked.

"Nowhere."

"Nowhere?" Eli giggled.

"I just want to take a little walk by myself right now, okay?" Mitchell stalked off.

"Can't we come?" Carver trotted behind.

"No." Mitchell stopped. "Go back to the house."

"Why not? Pleeeease can we come?"

"No. Go on."

"Awww." Carver threw a rock into the bracken ferns, close enough to his father to show his resentment, not quite close enough to be punished. "You're no fun."

Mitchell spun around. A frightening surge of anger left his hands trembling. No fun. He shook his head and continued walking.

In the afternoon, Mitchell sneakily removed his private stash from the toe of a winter boot and headed down the hill to visit his sister. Maples stood over the recently dried road in a shower of pale new leaves; behind them hemlocks blocked the light, growing over the toppling stone walls. Frost had taken its toll on somebody's long-ago labor. A chunk of quartz glowed in the ferns. Generations before Gramp bought his hundred acres, this land had been some farmer's dream. Clearing and humping, pulling stumps, lifting stones to make walls that would someday run senselessly through woods instead of pasture. Mitchell had seen a framed picture in the town hall, of Shelby in 1800—nothing but bald hills, fields sliding down to the river. All that work, for what? The looming darkness of the grown-up forest was more beautiful, he thought. As though beauty mattered.

Hadn't there been a time when he'd found solace here, even magic? As a kid he'd slept out at night, built forts with Jamie, played in the snow with his sisters. They made angels and shaped little snow cars over their laps; they carved deep dangerous tunnels in the bank left by the plow. He used to stand on frozen Vesey Brook until the pieces of ice broke off and slowly sank beneath him, or gave way with a sudden thrilling explosion that submerged his boots. Something cramped in his chest at the memory of soggy mittens leaving woolly lint on his palms, the steamy warmth when he came in with soaked leggings, and then the harsh intrusion of his father's voice: "Take off your goddamn boots."

He had to get them out of here, away from this land swarming with memory. There was ruination in the dark seeping mulch under the ferns, the bones of deer dragged home by dogs, baby rabbits run over with a lawn mower, crowding saplings, relentless brush, tangles of scratching blackberry vines, mosquitoes whizzing past his ears.

Mitchell crossed the culvert under the road and a glimpse of the clear rill of Vesey Brook splashing over stones was enough to make him cry. Something was spoiled, something that had mattered back when he confidently set sticks afloat to the ocean, when things were still new enough to be washed clean and imagination could lift him beyond what he knew would greet him when it was time to go home for supper. He needed an ocean now, open sky and water, where grey was all there was to look at, and the rising and falling would be waves and not his own choked breath.

Mitchell sat down on the wall to snort a line. No rush, he noted, just a slight easing of the crimp in his chest, a momentary escape from the willies. He got up and trudged on.

The trees opened when he hit the graveled town road at the intersection that led to Tuckerville. Tucker had bought fifty acres from Gramp back when the old man was in his eighties and terrified he couldn't make his taxes; Tucker had turned it into a little development of trailers and ranch houses that fortunately couldn't be seen behind the pines.

Down the hill, Nancy's low green ranch house sat surrounded by new lawn. Across the street was Gramp's place, bought by a minister after Gram died. The realtors had said Gram and Gramp's wasn't worth much because it was paneled in knotty pine. Then the minister turned around and sold it the next year for twice what he paid and put in a house for himself in Gramp's woodlot.

Nancy's yard looked impossibly tidy compared to when they all lived there with Mom and Dad. Even the pigs Gary raised were kept out of sight in the gully; Nancy wouldn't stand for them in her yard. Siberian irises waved over her perennial beds. In another month her garden would bloom with lemon lilies, day-lilies, phlox. Nancy wanted to put a false pitch on the roof, turn the squat ranch into a colonial cape, but Gary drew the line. And now money had to be saved for the doctors.

Mitchell climbed the poured concrete steps—not that wobbly cement block they'd grown up with—and peered through the glass. Nancy sat at the gleaming maple table with a coffee mug. An open catalog lay before her, but her body was turned away to watch her daughter. Michelle lay stretched out on the couch in the living room, her kitty curled on her chest, the remote control clutched in her fist. Mitchell stood there and watched his sister watching her child, and wondered if this was a bad idea. His youngest sister's grief altered the atmosphere, thickened and weighted it so that being in her house was like living on some strange planet with more gravity. Well, he had a remedy in his pocket, at least for a little while.

He knocked and Nancy spun around, motioned him in without getting up. Her thick honey hair hung stringy and unwashed, and baggy sweats replaced the cute little outfits she used to wear. Michelle waved from the couch. It was still impossible to believe what the experts down at Children's Hospital in Boston said: Michelle suffered from a rare genetic disorder that caused something in her brain to quit growing. A disease all the more awful because it allowed kids to seem completely normal for five or six years, and then took everything away from them—walking, speech, thought—before they died, usually in less than two years. When the diagnosis came in April, a lot of crying went down in Shelby, even up in Alaska, where Sally was, but now months had passed and people had to get on with their lives. Nancy survived on Xanax, though she swore she couldn't sleep anymore. Even the sound of Gary's breathing kept her awake.

Mitchell went over to his niece, who lay on the velour couch against ruffled pillows, beneath framed prints of nineteenth-century flower illustrations. Everything in Nancy's house, except for Gary's trophy deer heads, which she made him hang in the basement, was a dream of pastel and lace. Nancy thought she could lift herself from the sorrow and disorder of their childhood through housekeeping; it had worked, until now.

"Hey tiger," Mitchell said.

"Hey," the little girl answered. She had wide, black-lashed green eyes and the full, pouty lips of a model; she would have grown into a beauty.

"I wasn't talking to you, Chelly Belly. I was talking to Kitty. What's her name? Bluffpinkwall?"

Michelle giggled. "Puff-blink-ball."

"Oh, Buffwinkpall."

"No! Dummy!" Michelle grinned. She'd lost a front tooth like any regular kid. It was enough to break his heart.

"Hey gap-tooth. Tooth fairy bring you a quarter?"

"A dollar," Michelle bragged.

"A dollar? You got it made." So that's how it would be, more money for lost teeth, bigger presents, a pitiful display in the face of what the little girl didn't know was coming. Except for the odd way she gripped the remote control, her fingers curled inward, clawlike, she seemed perfectly normal. For a moment Mitchell experienced a terror for his own kids, but pushed it away. They were healthy little devils. He left his niece to blaring cartoons and sat at the table with Nancy.

"How you doing?" he asked.

"Not as good as you're doing." Nancy lowered her voice. "She can't make it up the front steps now. She complains her bones hurt. Yesterday she asked me if she was going to die."

"Oh, Jesus." Mitchell wasn't ready to hear this. "What did you say?"

Nancy flipped a page of her flower catalogue. "I said 'everyone dies, honey.' I just didn't tell her in our family it happens sooner."

"And not always to the right ones."

Nancy let that go without comment. She got up and set a perfect homemade coffee cake between them. Neither touched it. Mitchell took out his baggie. "You want a little bump?"

Nancy glanced around at Michelle, who was engrossed in a "My Little Pony" cartoon. "I shouldn't with the pills. But . . . who gives a shit."

"Considering."

Nancy pulled a compact mirror and a dollar bill from her purse and set them on the open flower catalog. Mitchell poured out a small pile and used an envelope to cut it into lines. Nancy leaned over, pressed a nostril shut, and inhaled through the rolled dollar. When she sat up her blue eyes widened for an instant, as though she'd seen more world than this one, visited the illusion of reprieve. She shimmied her shoulders and exhaled. Mitchell looked away.

When she was just fifteen and Mom was dead and Dad gone, they'd had a party in the house, Sally and Jamie and all of them. It was Nancy's first time drinking and she got looped and collapsed on the couch. Sally tried to put her to bed, but she was too far gone herself. Mitchell had carried Nancy into her room and dumped her on the bed and covered her. She struggled to get out of her clothes and Mitchell laughed at how silly she looked, fighting with quilts and a sweater, but when he got to the door, she fell out of bed. He turned back, and there she was, completely naked, a beautiful fifteen-year-old girl, and he was choked by a mix of emotions: embarrassed for her, attracted despite himself and shamed by it, but more than anything, pained by her vulnerability. Above all, he'd wanted to protect his baby sister from any future harm, a task as hopeless as saving the dairy farms, as it turned out. Not that he'd really tried.

"Gary's over at Kendall's all the time now," Nancy said. "I guess it's easier than talking to me. He wants to pretend nothing's happened."

"Corinne isn't talking to me either."

"I thought you two were doing okay now." Nancy wiped at her nose.

"Oh, some guys showed up looking for blow last night and scared her, and now I'm a shit."

"Well," Nancy said deadpan, "she's got that part right."

Mitchell smiled. Any little touch of sarcasm was a triumph, a breach of Nancy's recent zombie state. He started to lay out two more lines when the roar of a car pulling in stopped him. Damn. Through the window he saw Donna's red Saab turbo in the driveway—Cormier Trucking was doing well these days. Regretfully, Mitchell closed the flower catalog on half a line. Even though she was younger than Mitchell, Donna had appointed herself the grown-up of the family after Marsha died. She might do a belly dance at a party, but Donna had no tolerance for drugs.

Dark curls jouncing, eyes sparking with indignant energy, Donna pushed through the door with a *Brattleboro Reformer* held high. "You guys hear?" Donna demanded.

"Hear what?" Mitchell said.

Donna snapped the paper open on the table. "Look." She waited, hands on hips, while Mitchell read the banner headline: FEDS UNCOVER COKE RING IN SHELBY.

Early this morning, local authorities, the FBI, and the Bureau of Alchohol, Tobacco and Firearms, working in concert, made two arrests after a month of undercover operations. Gerald "Jelly" Brown, 31, and his brother Sheldon Brown, 28, both residents of Shelby, were apprehended at 4:00 A.M. in their Shelby auto body shop and charged with narcotics and firearms felonies. The operation began in March when Donald Jensen of Hartford, Connecticut, allegedly the Browns' supplier, was arrested and turned informant. The brothers are accused of trafficking in guns in exchange for cocaine, and the sale of narcotics. Sheldon Brown threatened federal agents with an automatic weapon before being overpowered and is being charged with resisting arrest and armed assault as well. Authorities are continuing the investigation into widespread cocaine dealing in southern Vermont and possible links to organized crime.

Mitchell's heart clanged in his chest and his mind shifted into overdrive. Organized crime, what a load of horseshit. But this bust was for real, not just one of Deputy Fairbanks's hornblowing exaggerations, like when he found a couple of pot plants in someone's back yard and claimed he'd uncovered a dope ring. Jesus Christ, Jelly Brown, that stupid lardbutt. Running guns? Jelly was a motorhead with a dream of owning his own auto repair shop, the shop that coke built down on the flats. Everyone knew about it. They didn't share the same customers, run with the same crowd. Still, Jelly probably knew about Mitchell's business. Why shouldn't he talk?

Donna rattled the paper. "They'll be put away forever. They already confiscated their shop and house. You better be careful, Mitch. What about your kids if you get arrested? And what about Gary? Don't you think Nancy has enough troubles without you bringing this down on us?"

Nancy sighed. She had bigger problems.

Mitchell's mind raced on. Those guys last night wanting to buy coke . . . no one knew them, where they were from. It could've been a setup, part of the investigation. Possibility shifted to certainty. They were already after him! He had to get the stuff off his property, move it, hide it, wait until everything cooled down. If there was no evidence, they couldn't convict him. He'd just lay low until it blew over; the important thing was to move it now before they caught him.

"I gotta go," Mitchell muttered, lurching from his chair. Breath chugging, blood roaring in his ears, he hurried up the road. He remembered that he'd seen Deputy Fairbanks's cruiser on Gramp's road last week. He assumed Fairbanks had pulled off Route 5 to take a piss, but now it all made sense. They were after him, playing him like a fish, waiting for him to make a mistake. They might be up the hill already, waiting. And he was carrying! Mitchell left the road and cut through the woods, stomping through ferns, thankful now for the thickness of the willow and alder brush. He hid the baggie from his shirt pocket under a rock, noting its location—a few paces from the big oak, beside a bull pine with elephant trunk branches—and rushed off again. He stopped, spun around. Hell with it. Mitchell dug up his baggie and quickly snorted the last of it straight from the bag, wiping his nose and mouth madly to remove any powder. There, his mind was sharper now. He had to think.

Just this morning he'd buried his big stash in the right angle of two stone walls that formed the boundary of a clearing. He had to move it up into the woods somewhere, off his land. Maybe that old barn falling down in the orchard? No, it might draw hikers or kids. Just in the woods somewhere, in one of the old fencelines. Then when things cooled down, it'd be there, his future . . . He could sneak up once in a while just to keep himself going.

Instead of following the logging road that led straight to the clearing, Mitchell kept to the woods, sliding past birches and beech, climbing ledge, until he was above the spot and could drop down. He heard voices and froze. They couldn't have found it already? And then he recognized the sweet high voices of his kids. A rush of relief, followed by mind-numbing fury. Emily, Carver, and Eli sat cross-legged on a green carpet of moss, and in their midst lay the stash pipe, uncapped. The zipper pouch was open, a plastic baggie of coke spread out, and the three children leaned over, poking stalks of grass down into the precious powder and up into their noses.

"Wow, what a rush," Carver mimicked, waving his grass stalk about. Glancing up he spotted his father bearing down on them, and smiled foolishly, before his expression gave way to alarm.

Mitchell loomed over them. "What do you think you're doing?

You little sneaks! You followed me up here this morning, didn't you?"

"We're just playing," Emily said fearfully.

"Who told you to go into my stuff? Did you put that up your noses?"

"We only pretended," Eli said. "Honest."

"So what?" Carver groused. "You and Mommy do it."

That was it. Mitchell wasn't going to take any more lip. He grabbed Carver above the elbow and lifted. He could feel his fingers biting in, knew he could squeeze forever, snap the puny little bones. He raised his other hand and saw his son cringe, the glazed shock in his eyes. It didn't matter. Something was set in motion, a rage that demanded release. Mitchell watched from a distance as his father inhabited his body.

"Daddy, stop it!" Emily shrieked. "Daddy, don't!"

Carver hung from his grip like nothing, no weight to him at all. A ghost child. A child he loathed.

"Daddy," Emily cried, grabbing his arm. "Please Daddy, don't! We were just playing."

Mitchell whirled to shake her off, but the sight of Emily's terrified face stopped him. And hanging from his grip, his son cowered, hand up to block a blow. Mitchell recognized that pose—his own, as Lowell hit him and hit him and hit him. His kids had never feared him. Never. Slowly, the world tilted back into focus. Mitchell released Carver's arm and sank to his knees. Carver scuttled away.

Lowell had singled Mitchell out from the girls to punish, and now Mitchell had singled out Carver. Because Carver looked like him, because Carver was angry, because he was the kid, like Mitchell, who at the Easter egg hunt couldn't find even one egg, while the other kids raced about scooping up prizes.

Once Mitchell had taken Carver fishing. He got onto a big walleye and handed his pole to Carver, who was only three. The little boy fought that fish for a long time. And when they landed him, Carver was confused and incredulous. "Did I really catch that fish, Daddy?" he kept asking, unable to trust his good fortune, his accomplishment. A little boy who never believed in anything good.

But Carver had been his favorite, too. When he was tiny Mitchell used to bring him along on his weekly breakfast with Jamie at Miss Bellows Falls Diner, where they ordered eggs to match the blind cook's eyes: yolks shot with white. Carver wore little leggings and a woolly pompom hat. Mitchell set him in his lap, let him play with the silverware, pulled wadded napkins from his mouth. He'd been proud that he wasn't like Lowell.

"Carver, honey, I'm sorry," Mitchell whispered.

Carver watched him silently, lip trembling.

Mitchell covered his face with his hands. Every nerve in his body jangled, as though wire-brushed. He'd come so close to stepping over the line he swore he'd never cross. His heart beat kaboom, kaboom. He ought to have a heart attack, die right here, punished for what he'd almost done. Heart attack—it hit him like tinfoil on a filling—the coke might have killed them, one snort could have stopped their small hearts. The noise that came out of him was more like a gag than a sob.

"Daddy, are you okay? Don't cry, Daddy," Emily whispered.

He wasn't crying. He never cried, not since he was their age. Not when Marsha or Mom died. Not for Michelle.

"It's okay, Daddy," Emily reasoned. "We know you didn't mean it. You just wanted to scare us for being bad. Isn't that right, Daddy?"

Kids believed what they had to. They reinterpreted ugliness so they could keep on loving the only parents they had. Just as he'd kept on loving. And now it was over. All of it. In a minute he'd get up and pour the entire zipper bag of powder into Vesey brook. He'd tell them it was bad, bad stuff that made people do bad things. He'd blame the drug and hope that they'd forgive him. Together they'd make a ceremonial dumping. And as it melted and flowed away into the cold clear brook, everything would flow away with it: his business, his money, maybe Corinne, the dream of a boat in Maine, his status in town, his powdered pride.

Mitchell leaned forward and pressed his face into the cool green moss. He could see the little flower-like spores straining upward just as everything—trees, brush, ferns, flowers—grew upward, all of them struggling to leave the earth, yet inexorably rooted. Shouldn't there be comfort in knowing that, through all the striving, you couldn't escape the part of you that grew down into the dirt? No comfort, Mitchell decided.

"Daddy?" Emily implored. "Daddy?"

"I'm here, baby," Mitchell replied. "Right here."

WATERCOLORS

[Sally, 1990]

SALLY CHARTRAIN DEVEREAU met her next-door neighbor Mel one freezing morning in December when the Pinto
wouldn't start. The girls were belted into the back seat, lunch
sacks clutched in their mittens. Sally turned the key in the ignition;
she heard a low, grinding growl, and then a click. She turned the
key again. There was no growl this time, just a click. Sally blew out
a hard rush of frozen breath that leaped onto the windshield and
spread. The thought of being late and risking this, her first job
since she'd put the girls in the car and snuck away from Billy
Devereau in the middle of the night, made Sally cringe. A repair
bill could break her.

"What's the matter, Mommy?" Jenny leaned forward in her
seat. At five she was already attuned to any hint of problems.
Molly, three, was still oblivious. She hummed a Sesame Street
tune, her tiny snowboots beating accompaniment through the
seat. Sally resisted a desire to lean her forehead against the steering
wheel. "Please God, don't let it be the starter," she whispered.
"Or anything else expensive."

"Mommy, what's the matter?" Jenny implored. "Mommy?"

"I'm cold," Molly piped up, alerted by her sister's anxious
tone.

"Hey, you guys, take it easy," Sally said firmly. It was important that the girls believe she was in command. She got out to lift the hood. Looking down into a tangle of grimy hoses and wires skirting an acid-crusted battery, Sally wanted to cry at the confusion of it all. It wasn't fair that something as important as a job could hinge on something so cheap and rusty as an overage Ford.

When Mel cracked the aluminum storm door and crossed fifteen feet of yard to ask if he could help, he didn't look like much of a hero. Gangly, with a dark ponytail, wispy beard, and hunched shoulders, he appeared too young to be the defeated guy she'd seen loading his own three kids into a rusty green Malibu or wrestling grocery sacks from the trunk while his wife ordered him about in a loud, aggrieved voice: "Mel, I told you to get Tiffany's ass in here right now. Mel, are you listening?"

Their two houses, mill-era Victorians broken up into apartments, shared a driveway on Bulcher Street in Bellows Falls. Sally's second-story living room looked down into Mel's first-floor kitchen. Witnessing his wife's bullying, Sally felt contempt for Mel rather than pity. She considered it as shameful for a guy to be pussy-whipped as for her to have been married to a man her sisters called "the Animal," a man who'd left layers of bruises across her breasts.

However, that morning in December when Mel placed his daisy mug on the Pinto's fender and went off to find his jumper cables, what registered with Sally was that Mel looked kind.

Their two cars sat in the driveway nose-to-nose, engines exchanging power, while Mel shyly commented on the state of the Pinto's tread and the benefits of dry gas in freezing weather. He brought out a couple of powdered doughnuts to occupy the girls and made a big deal out of learning their names and ages. He even got Jenny to giggle by addressing her as "young fella."

The Pinto held the charge long enough to get Sally to a garage, where a new battery cost a third of a week's take home pay at the grocery. The rest of the winter, when Sally ran into Mel she waved and smiled—except when his wife was there; then she only nodded. He was a nice enough guy and she didn't want to add to his problems.

On a Saturday in March, Sally sat in the window seat in the living room, flipping through her sketchbook. The pages were filled with bright floral arrangments she'd drawn in pencil and then watercolored, overlapping washes of pinks and purples, copies from flower catalogues and botany texts she took out from the library. She hoped someday she could afford an apartment with garden space; until then she painted the flowers she'd plant in her perennial garden.

She knew her paintings weren't good yet, but she was proud of them because they were hers and because she'd bothered to make them, just as she was proud of her job behind the meat counter, the fact that she'd only been on welfare for eight months after leaving Billy, that she had managed to construct and support a world for herself and the girls.

The problem was that whenever she had a moment to breathe, the girls were gone, the apartment empty. According to the terms of separation, Billy got the girls three weekends a month. So it was Sally who had to nag them out of bed in the morning, rush them through breakfast, dole out slaps, while Billy got them on lazy Saturdays; he was the one with time to play games and buy presents. As often as not he missed his child support payments, yet the court was convinced that he loved his children and deserved partial custody. And much as it made her crazy to think of Billy driving drunk with the girls in the car, she had to admit it. In his way, Billy loved them.

Sally opened to a new page and looked out at the fresh wet snow clinging to the rocky face of Fall Mountain. It loomed up so steep and close it was hard to believe that it wasn't right there in Bellows Falls, but across the river in New Hampshire. She tried to sketch the mountain in charcoal, shaping the gash of the power line, the facets of rock, but it came out too soft and smudgy. She wanted to catch the way snow made shadows out of every place it didn't fall: the darkness under rock outcroppings, the undersides of trees.

There was something compelling about that high-contrast, etchy black and white that she couldn't name. It always reminded her of Fairbanks in winter. Before the girls were born she had lived in Alaska with Billy. They'd gone north because Billy was convinced he'd make his fortune, but it turned out that construction was slowing down and Billy couldn't get hired. He finally found a road crew job holding a stop sign. The wages were twice what he made at home, but he couldn't get over his humiliation and Sally bore the brunt of it.

They lived in a log cabin chinked with pink fiberglass insulation outside Fairbanks. The only color was at night, when the aurora borealis swirled in the sky. The snow fell and never melted; it creaked under her boots, and frost lined the inside of the windows, even the windowsills. Sally waitressed, and when Billy lost his job he accused her of cheating on him. He slammed through the cabin breaking things and wouldn't stop until he'd cracked her jaw. Then he got down on his knees, crying, begging her to forgive him. And all the while the snow, the lack of color, cast them into something black and white, an old photograph or a TV show, a sense that this couldn't be her life.

Sally looked away from the window. Toys littered the throw rug, beds were still unmade. Sometimes she thought she stretched out the housework to make it last all weekend, a way to fill up the emptiness when the girls were gone.

In the afternoon, when Sally was hauling two laundry bags up the stairs, Lydia, who lived beneath her, stuck her head out her door. Lydia's husband Joe worked at the die-cutting plant in Springfield. Lydia didn't work, and had let it be known more than once that it was only the bad luck of an uninsured fire that made them have to move out of their mobile home and take a rental.

"D'you hear about next door?" She half-whispered, as though whoever it was about might be listening.

"What?" Sally wanted to get the laundry upstairs and unpacked before the stuff that was still damp wrinkled so bad she'd have to iron it. She'd run out of quarters on the last load.

"Joanne. That one with the boots, waitresses in Saxton's River?

She up and run off on him. Left him with the three kids and took off with some guy works over t'Claremont. Poor guy's probably going nuts."

"You mean Mel?" Sally dropped her duffel sacks of laundry and sat down. She pulled her cigarettes out of her purse and lit one.

"You better watch them ashes," Lydia warned. "Take it from me, fires can happen any time. And unless you got your own renter's policy, you don't get a damn thing if the building goes up."

Sally thought about it while she was folding and putting away the clothes. She remembered Mel's kindness the day he jumped her car, and the grating voice of his wife. It couldn't be easy for a guy, managing alone with three kids—it was hard enough with two. In the late afternoon she considered baking cookies for Mel, but decided on something more substantial—a macaroni and cheese casserole. She brought it over hot, gripped in oven mitts. Coat over her shoulders, she walked through wet snow in her sneakers. She had to push the bell by the storm door with an elbow. No answer, although she could see a TV flickering within. Finally a small boy, about Jenny's age, came to the door. He stared through the glass.

"Is your daddy home?" Sally asked.

The child shrugged and turned away.

Sally waited a moment and pushed the door open. Electronic laughter and applause issued from the living room.

"Hello?" she called. Mel couldn't have run off and left the kids alone, could he? Who would she call to report them? What if Lydia was wrong, if Mel's wife was back, and she was walking into something she had no business in? She decided she'd just put the casserole on the table and leave. She peeked past the kitchen door. Mel sat slumped on the couch in front of the TV. A little girl about Molly's age lay curled up beside him; a toddler in a drooping diaper wandered about gripping a soggy bread slice; the boy who'd answered the door sat right in front of the tube, which was blasting the "Newlywed Game."

"Mel?"

He spun toward her voice, a look of hope wavering, then he collapsed back on the couch. His dark hair hung long and greasy around his bony face. She'd never seen it out of a ponytail.

"I guess you heard," Mel said. "I guess it's news all over town by now." His eyes were red-rimmed.

Sally shifted weight from one wet sneaker to another. "I thought maybe you and the kids could use something hot to eat. I made a macaroni and cheese."

"Like for a funeral," Mel said. He grinned lopsidedly, and his mouth quivered.

Sally thought he was going to start blubbering right there. That was something she just couldn't handle. "I think the little one there needs a diaper change," she suggested.

"What? Yeah, I guess it does kinda stink. This whole thing's got me spaced.

"Don't worry about the dish," Sally offered, although casserole dishes were probably not high up on Mel's worry list right then. "I'll get it sometime during the week." She backed toward the door.

"Hey, thanks," Mel called plaintively as she fled.

Billy brought the girls back three hours late on Sunday. They were supposed to be home before supper, but the spaghetti water had long boiled out, the sauce splattered itself over the stove, and still they didn't come. Sally had phoned her sister Donna twice to ask if she should she call the cops. And then Billy came clomping up the stairs at ten after nine, Molly in his arms, Jenny running in front of him clutching a new doll.

"You're late," Sally said. "How do you expect me to get them into bed now?"

"Daddy says we can go to bed whenever we want," Molly insisted.

"Well, Daddy has his rules for his house, and we have our rules here." She wasn't going to make a scene. She wouldn't rise to Billy's bait, expose the girls to any more of what they'd lived through. Sally reached out her arms to take Molly. Billy held on a second too long before releasing the child.

"Daddy says we don't have to listen to you at all," Jenny announced gravely. She wiped her runny nose with the back of her hand and looked from her mother to father.

"Mommy, I got a stomachache," Molly moaned.

"I bet you do." Sally glared at Billy. "What did you feed them?"

"Whatever they wanted."

"Dammit. Jenny's getting a cold again. You've got to make them wear clothes when they're at your house. That place is too drafty to let them run around naked all the time."

"Since when did you get so hung up? You shook your bare ass around that place plenty." Billy grinned.

"Why don't you just go so I can put them to bed?" Sally muttered between clenched teeth.

"Sure, babe. But don't forget, you're still my wife. And I got my rights." Billy leaned back and blocked the door, arms crossed, chin lifted, looking down at her under his long pale lashes. "Tell me you don't still want it."

"Get out," Sally hissed.

"Hey." Billy raised his open palms. "No problem. Bye, sweeties."

"Bye, Daddy," the girls chorused. "Bye! Bye!"

Sally sat too long on the couch with Molly in her arms, struggling to calm her own ragged breathing by pressing her lips into Molly's curls, until Molly wriggled to get down.

When teeth were brushed, faces washed, a tantrum averted, and Sally was tucking them in, Molly asked, "Mommy, why can't we sleep in your bed? Daddy lets us sleep in bed with him."

"I told you honey, we've got our rules here, and Daddy's got his rules. I like sleeping by myself. That doesn't mean I don't love you just as much as Daddy does." She kissed Molly's nose and moved on to Jenny, who couldn't fall asleep unless she ran the edge of the top sheet over and under all ten fingers like a ribbon woven through a basket.

Jenny whispered, "Mommy, sometimes Daddy bothers me."

Sally's breath caught but her voice came out even. "What do you mean bothers, honey?" He couldn't have. She'd steal them away. She'd go underground like those mothers she read about in *People*, the ones who found safe houses, who went to prison to protect their kids.

"Well," Jenny explained in a tiny voice, "he keeps talking about you having boyfriends."

Sally sighed with a relief that shouldn't have been relief. She could just imagine what kind of crap he was inventing for them, but even so, it could've been worse.

"Honey, you know I don't have any boyfriends."

"I know, but he keeps saying it."

"Well, then that's just Daddy's problem, isn't it?"

"I guess so." Jenny sighed, rolled over, careful to keep her fingers laced in the sheet. Sally made circles on Jenny's narrow, flannel-covered back until Jenny's breath deepened and she shuddered into sleep.

Sally sat in the window seat, smoking cigarette after cigarette in the dark. Across the driveway, in Mel's apartment, the kitchen light blazed. He probably wasn't sleeping too good either. Sally lit another. She could almost hear the heavy spring snow melting and sliding down the rock face of Fall Mountain.

Tuesday night when the buzzer rang, Sally was leaning over a bathroom sink full of hot water, head under a tented towel, steaming her pores. She jerked up, face flushed, condensed steam running down her cheeks. Billy? But it was only Mel, shivering in the doorway without a jacket, holding a clean casserole dish. His eyes slid downward from her face to the bathrobe wrapped around her chest, then away in embarrassment. Sally shrugged inwardly. So he was a man too.

"I brung it back," Mel offered. "Sorry it took 'til now." He looked nervous and dazed.

"Oh, that's okay. C'mon in. Wait, I'll just go get dressed."

"I don't want to bother you or nuthin'."

"It's no bother." She was only a little annoyed at having to get dressed again when she was ready to flop around the house in a nightgown and slippers.

Molly and Jenny looked up from the TV, Jenny's face forming a question.

"You girls know Mel from next door. He helped us with the car?"

"Doughnuts!" Molly shouted, remembering.

Jenny stared. "You're Rusty's daddy."

"Right," Mel answered. "And Melinda's and Tiffany's. What are you guys watching?" He squatted down to talk to them at eye level.

"Tele-vision!" Molly crowed.

"He knows that, dummy," Jenny huffed.

"No I didn't," Mel protested. "I thought you were watching the toaster oven. That's what I always watch."

Jenny clicked her tongue at such silliness, but Molly collapsed in giggles.

"Did you leave your kids alone over there?" Sally called from the bedroom as she pulled the dirty jeans she'd worn at work back on.

"They're with my folks. I got to go pick them up pretty soon."

Sally came back in the room, combing wet hair. "So how's it going?"

Mel shrugged.

"How about the kids?"

"It's hard. The girls keep on crying for their Mommy. Rusty don't cry, he just keeps asking when she's coming back."

Sally sighed. Wasn't that the way with them, they'd pine for any mommy or daddy, no matter how unworthy? She softened. "You want a beer? Or some coffee or something?"

"Coffee, I guess. Or tea. You got tea? My stomach ain't been doing too great lately."

"I've got Salada," Sally said. She went into the kitchen to put on the kettle and Mel followed. He hunched his shoulders and popped his knuckles.

"I didn't go to work yesterday." Mel spoke in a rush, eyes averted, the words tumbling out as though he was afraid Sally might dodge them. "I called in sick. I feel sick, but that ain't it. I don't know what to do with them. Joanne worked nights, and I got a regular shift at Beacom's, and we just traded off. My folks took them today, and but they can't do it every day. My ma's too old to be changing diapers."

"You'll put them in daycare, like I do." Sally was surprised by the brusqueness of her tone, as though she'd been doing it herself more than a few months, but she detected something in Mel that needed telling.

"Well, Rusty's six, he goes to school, but what about from three to five-thirty, before I get home?"

"You'll pay a baby-sitter. You got to go to work, you got to start paying for all of them on one salary. Look, I'll give you the number of the lady who takes Jenny and Molly. I think she's got room for more kids."

The kettle shrieked and Sally poured out a cup for Mel, threw in a tea bag, and pulled a beer from the fridge for herself. She leaned against the counter.

Mel sat at the table swirling his tea bag. When he looked up his eyes caught her. In his narrow, angled face, they loomed large, green, moistly stricken. She felt pity, a familiar emotion that grabbed her gut, yet repulsed her.

"I guess you been through all this before," Mel said. "I bet you had your own hard row. That was real nice, you bringing food over for us and all."

Pity gave way to discomfort. Sally saw again what she'd seen the day Mel jumped her car, something in him that was willing to go outside himself—kindness mixed with sorrow. It made her like him, and it made her nervous.

*   *   *

Sally drew her thick hair away from her face with a head-band. She buttoned an old flannel shirt, her painting smock, over a tee-shirt and jeans. She gathered her pad, brushes, and paints into a shopping bag. She was on her way to her third watercolor class at the YMCA and Mel was babysitting. He'd offered. The kids got along good, and as Mel said, what was the difference betweeen three and five? He wasn't going anywhere.

Sally ran back into the bathroom to put on lipstick. Not that there was anyone in the class to show off for, old ladies, mostly, and the teacher, although he flattered her with talk of her talent, wasn't what you'd call a catch—a bearded fat man with a cane and a pathetic little red scarf tied around his jowls. But just going to class made her feel festive.

Sally stood before the mirror sliding the waxy pink over her lips. Her eyes stared back, glinting dark above her short nose and broad jaw. She'd never been pretty so much as cute, but cute was something she figured didn't wear well. Sally pulled her lips into a smile, watching the laugh lines fan around her eyes. A friendly face. "Remember," she asked her reflection, "when that used to be you?"

She threw the lipstick into her cosmetic basket and turned off the light. In the sudden dark, light glowed across the driveway in Mel's bedroom. She could see him lying on the bed, head propped on a pillow. Rusty, Melinda, Jenny, and Molly jumped wildly on the bed, mouths open, probably screaming holy hell. And Mel just lay there peacefully, baby Tiffany stretched out on his chest as the kids bounced. Sally shook her head. In the darkness, she smiled for real this time.

Whenever she needed something, Mel was there, saving her fifteen bucks by changing her oil, or wielding needle-nose pliers to dislodge the screw end of a light bulb that she'd broken off in the overhead lamp. He was always ready to take the kids bowling down in Brattleboro, or to the rec center pond in Saxton's River.

He showed up with pizzas. Each time he talked less of Joanne, more of Sally. He wanted to know what she'd been like as a kid, and pored over her photo album with so much care it made her squirm. "Look at you!" he'd exclaim at some ordinary snapshot of Sally in pigtails blowing out birthday candles, or riding her pony in the backyard. "Why didn't you stick with it?" he demanded, studying a picture of her in breeches and boots and hunt cap, astride a thoroughbred at equestrian school.

Sally turned away. The riding photos saddened her. She'd wait-ressed three years to earn the tuition, and then quit her first job at a stable after Marsha's death. She'd told herself she left Virginia because her family needed her, but it was just an excuse. She couldn't stand the cold-hearted competition, or being forced to kowtow to the rich. Horses were an old dream and a dead one, as dead as Billy's Alaska fantasy. What mattered now was getting along, making a home for the girls. Anyway, she didn't want to share her history with Mel, because then she'd have to ask about his. She didn't want to get that close.

Billy called up crying.

"If we don't get back together I'm gonna kill myself," he threatened.

Go ahead, Sally breathed, go ahead. "You're blackmailing me, Billy."

"I love you, Sally. Please. You got to give me another chance."

Someone knocked on the door, then Sally heard Lydia yelling some crap about one of the kids' bikes in the hallway.

"Just a minute," Sally called out, covering the phone. "Billy, there's someone at the door. I got to go."

"You got somebody there?" Billy screamed. "Some guy? I'll kill him, you slut bitch. I'll kill you."

Sally ruled that any time she spent with Mel couldn't be at her apartment. She didn't need the girls gabbing about a man at

Mommy's, or snoopy Lydia downstairs making some comment when Billy came to pick them up. "He's not a boyfriend," Sally explained carefully to the girls. "He's just Mommy's friend."

"You're still scared of him," Mel argued. "You had the guts to leave him, you shouldn't let him run your life."

"It'll be different after the divorce comes through," Sally insisted. The hearing was July 2nd, only a few weeks away. She didn't want to give Billy ammunition. He was convinced, if crazily, that eventually he'd be awarded full custody, and she cringed at the thought of what he'd say about her at the hearing to try to make that happen. But it wasn't just that. Mel wanted them to be a couple, but Sally couldn't see it.

"Sally's got a fella," her sister Donna sang.

"Jesus," Sally protested. "I told you, it isn't like that."

Donna was lathered with suntan oil, her oversize sunglasses pushed up on her head. They lounged in chaises while the kids splashed and shrieked in Donna's pool. Sally glanced around in admiration at the flower beds bordering the patio, the redwood lawn furniture, the aqua glow of chlorinated water.

Claude's back-breaking work had paid off. Now Donna went skiing in Vail and spent a week in the Caribbean every winter. She had a new house, a snowmobile, a minivan, and a labrador retriever.

Nancy held her daughter Michelle's rigid body across her lap while she tried to spoon in some goo she'd whipped up in the blender. Michelle could no longer chew; her head lolled back and her spastic fists clenched. At six Michelle had been a cheerful first-grader, drawing pictures, learning to read. At nine she lay in a special wheelchair, head flopping. The only thing that made her respond anymore was the mention of her cat's name.

"C'mon, you know you love power shakes," Nancy crooned, staring deep into her daughter's unfocused eyes with the absorption of a mother looking at her newborn.

"You want me to hold her for a while?" Sally offered.

"Never mind." Nancy deposited Michelle in the special chair the state had bought her. She wiped Michelle's face with a wet face cloth, arranged her stiff limbs. "Michelle's going to practice diving in a minute, aren't you honey?" Nancy made jokes, but she couldn't sleep any more.

"So tell us," Donna urged. "What's he like?"

"There's nothing to tell," Sally said. "Mel's just a nice guy. He helps me with things."

"So?"

"So nothing. It's not like I'm real attracted." She couldn't explain why it was that she didn't feel romantic about Mel. Maybe because she'd seen him the day that Joanne ditched him, looking so lost. Or because he was always around, being so insistently nice. Maybe it was his gawky body and skanky long ponytail, how young he was, or the way he talked so ignorant, saying "don't" when he should say "doesn't," and "nohow" and "ain't."

Donna picked up her iced tea. "You don't know how to like someone who's good for you. I read about that. It's because of Dad. You're addicted to excitement. You think someone nice is boring."

Sally laughed. "Mel *is* kind of boring. Besides, it's hard to respect a guy whose wife pushed him around."

"What about you and the Animal?" Nancy broke in.

"It's different for a woman. And anyway, I left."

"Well, you're lucky Mel babysits," Nancy said. "I can't leave Michelle with Gary for a minute, just so I can go shopping or something. He puts her on the couch and goes outside. It drives me crazy. He doesn't even look at her anymore. I need to talk about it, and he just wants to pretend nothing's happened."

Michelle started to cry, a keening animal wail. She always cried when they talked about her.

"You want to be in the conversation?" Nancy asked. "Michelle? Chelly!" She picked Michelle up out of her chair and held her in her lap, a long skinny monkey. Michelle's anti-convulsion medicine made thick black hair grow on her arms and legs. "I bought lupines and columbine for my new rock garden, the one I put in by the steps," Nancy announced, dandling Michelle. "You ought to come over and see."

"Lydia downstairs gave me some strawberry begonias," Sally said, eager for the change of topic. "I'll never have them again. They're messy plants, alway shedding. Messy, messy, messy."

"Mo-om," Jenny squealed. "Jimmy's dunking me again."

"Jimmy, you cut that out right now," Donna shrieked, "or you can just go inside."

Jimmy, who was the same age as Michelle, climbed out of the pool, came over beside Nancy and took one of Michelle's twisted hands. He gently tried to straighten her fingers.

"Jenny, come out of the water and have a sandwich," Sally instructed. "You too, Molly."

The girls climbed out, Jenny still pouting, Molly all smiles inside her little blow-up flotation ring.

Sally reached into the cooler for peanut butter sandwiches.

"I don't want peanut butter," Jenny whined, although peanut butter was her usual favorite.

"Well that's what you're getting. And I want you to sit in the sun for a while, honey. Your lips are blue."

The phone rang and Donna leaped up. She came back wearing a terry beachcoat. "That was Claude. He wants me to come to the shop to join him for lunch."

Sally and Nancy exchanged glances. They never gave voice to their envy, their longing. Donna and Claude had their problems, but they'd made it through.

"What about me?" Jimmy looked alarmed. His two sisters were still splashing at the far end of the pool.

Donna turned away. "You stay here and swim with the girls."

"Aw, shit," Jimmy mumbled, then glanced around fast to see if he was in trouble for swearing.

Nancy leaned over Michelle's head. "You ought to give Mel a chance, Sal. Believe me, the sex stuff doesn't count that much. Look how things turned out with me and Gary. You want someone you can talk to."

Sally shrugged dismissively.

"You think you're going to get something better?" Nancy demanded. "In Bellows Falls?"

Friday Mel called, his voice shaky. Joanne had showed up at Beacom's tire store that day without warning. After three months she had decided she wanted to take the kids for the weekend. Of course, he'd let her. She was coming to pick them up in a few minutes. Would Sally come over after?

Sally agreed. Mel needed moral support, and anyway, Billy already had the girls. She watched from her window seat like a spy when Joanne walked up the driveway. She couldn't see her face, only the top of Joanne's blond head where her hair was pulled up in a pineapple ponytail. The screen door opened, then Melinda popped out and grabbed her mother's legs. Joanne, with her skinny little boy's ass, bent over to hug Melinda, then disappeared inside. Sally waited long minutes, smoking. Maybe Joanne's boyfriend had dumped her and she wanted Mel again. The weekend with the kids might be a ruse. Sally's chest clenched with alarm. Joanne couldn't come back. Sally depended on Mel.

As soon as Joanne emerged with Tiffany on her hip, Melinda in hand, and Rusty trailing, turning back to look at his dad, Sally was on her way downstairs. She waited by the front door until Joanne's dented Camaro coughed, caught, and pulled out, and then she was across the driveway. Mel was wearing a new button down shirt, still creased from the package. He'd even cleaned the black dirt from under his nails, the ever-present dirt that came from changing tires at Beacoms. All for Joanne.

"Don't you look spiffy," Sally commented.

Mel shrugged, embarrassed. "I don't want her to think I went to the dogs just 'cause of her." He pulled two beers from the fridge, gave Sally one, and they sat at the kitchen table.

Sally said, "My sister Donna thinks I drink too much just because I have a few beers after work. She'd drink a few too if she had to live like us. So? How did the kids take it?"

"The girls were real excited. I think Rusty felt bad leaving me. Poor guy, it must be awful confusing."

"How about you?" Sally fished.

Mel sighed. "Kicked in the guts again. Her boyfriend don't want the kids around, but he's visiting his folks this weekend so suddenly she got interested in playing Mommy."

"Bitch," Sally pronounced with satisfaction. She took a long pull on her beer.

"God, it hurt to see her."

Sally peered at him. He had that old stricken look. She felt ashamed. All she'd been thinking about was what she might lose instead of what this was doing to him. She reached out for Mel's hand. "It really sucks, Mel."

He sniffled. "What about the kids? What if this is just a one-shot thing and she don't want to see them for another three months? We all got used to it and now everything's up-side down."

Sally didn't know what else to do but sit there holding his hand. Mel blinked, shook himself, sighed. "Jesus." He gulped at his beer. "So how was your day?"

Sally couldn't believe it. Even now, she could count on Mel to ask questions about her life, to care about the answers. "Oh, the usual crap," she said. "They hired a new guy in Meats, and started him at six, a whole buck more than me, and I been there half a year."

"You ought to complain."

Sally started to say, yeah, like you do at Beacom's, but hushed herself. He'd had a rough enough day.

Mel tapped his empty beer can. "Sally? You want to go out for supper or something? It's so lonely here without the kids."

Tell me about it, Sally thought, but just said, "Sure."

At home she put on a clean pair of jeans but then pulled them off and changed to a skirt. Mel had never seen her in a skirt. It was a bit too short, and she'd put on a few pounds over the winter, so it was snug on her hips. At least she had good legs. She tried on a few tops before she decided on a low-cut pink tank that showed off her breasts. Then makeup: eye shadow, mascara, the works. She knew she was setting a trap, competing with Joanne for what she didn't really want, but what the hell? It was a long time since she'd dressed up for anyone.

Mel whistled when she returned. "Wow. Look at you."

It was Sally's turn to be embarrassed.

They drove the twenty-four miles down to Brattleboro and Mel bought supper at the Via Condotti. Sally drank sweet cream drinks and they ate garlicky veal parmesan. Mel confessed he was splurging. He'd intended to take the kids down to the Water Slide in Massachusetts on Sunday and now he was using the ticket money.

Sally looked at him across the table and tried it on: this is my boyfriend. This is my boyfriend Mel.

They danced to a loud rock band at the Mole's Eye. During a slow song Mel's hands slid down to her butt, then up again, as though reprimanded. Sally wanted to tell him to leave them there, but felt too embarrassed. They came back looped and without really thinking, she allowed Mel to lead her into his apartment. When Mel started kissing her she let him. He pulled her to the bedroom. They flopped on the bed and he slid her tank top up, unhooked her bra, and stopped to admire her breasts, running a finger between their sprawl.

"You're a wonder of nature," Mel breathed.

Sally rolled away.

"What's the matter?"

She found her purse on the floor and pulled out her cigarettes. She lit one and smoked it, staring up at the ceiling.

"The first time Billy took me to meet his parents? We walked in the door, took off our coats, and Billy said, 'See, Dad, doesn't she have great tits just like I told you?' I went in the kitchen and cried. Billy's mother said, 'Don't let that bother you, honey. They got some strange ideas but they're good boys.'"

Mel leaned on an elbow. "I ain't him, Sally."

Sally crushed out her cigarette. "I know. It's just I haven't been with anyone since I left, so it all kind of comes back." She reached out to embrace him, feeling the hard bones of his back, the skinny plates of his hips, the trailing ponytail. She tugged on it gently. "Why do you keep it long?"

"I dunno. I was too young to be a hippie, but I kinda wished I was one. I would like t'gone to Woodstock."

Sally snorted. "Hah! How old are you?"

"I ain't telling. You'll think I'm too young." He paused. "Twenty-six."

Sally was thirty-four. "You guys started early."

"She got pregnant. The usual story, I ruined her life."

"And now she's paying you back."

"Oh, I dunno about that. But there was a few things I would liked to've done before I got the kids and all." Mel lay back on his pillow. "You know what I use to dream about?"

"What's that?" Here it comes, she thought. Guys always wanted to tell you their dreams.

"You'll laugh."

"No, I won't."

"Well . . . I always wanted to collect exotic animals. You know, peacocks, boa constrictors, baby crocodiles, llamas. I wouldn't have no big cats or wolves, things that gotta run, 'cause I think it's cruel to keep them caged. But I'd have this little farm for kids to come look, maybe even a petting zoo with some goats and bunnies and such. Just a little backyard deal. I know you couldn't make no money on that kinda thing, but I woulda liked that, building the cages and feedin' them and all and showing them to kids."

Sally was astonished. "I didn't know you liked animals. You don't have a cat. You don't even have gerbils."

"Rusty's allergic to fur, and Joanne said animals was a waste of money when you got kids to feed. I had a pet bull snake, though, when I was little."

Sally smiled, picturing Mel surrounded by cages. It was funny to think of such a modest guy wanting to own show-off creatures like peacocks. Exotic animals. He'd probably be good with them, though, like he was with the kids. "Come here," she said, suddenly tender, pressing her lips to his.

Mel rolled over on top of her, his weight unfamiliar. He stroked her hair off her face, kissed her throat. "She said I weren't no good in bed," he said shyly.

Don't tell me this, Sally thought. Not now.

"How could I be, thinking about her doing it with other guys?"

"I'm sure you're good," Sally lied. His lips felt scratchy, his hands awkward as he stroked between her legs. When Mel thrust inside her she felt numb. With Billy it was different. Scary, ugly, but exciting too. Above her, Mel scraped his lower lip under his upper teeth in concentration, giving himself a goony expression. She shut her eyes but tears squeezed out. She was crying for the memory of Billy's hands on her. How could she be so stupid as to mourn for that bastard, with all the things that had happened, the things he made her do in that lousy shack of a house in Ludlow, with his brother, his friends? Billy had covered her with a skin that wasn't hers, until it was; she'd never get over the shame. And now she was crying for him, idiot, asshole.

It went on longer than she would have expected, considering that Mel hadn't been with anyone for months, and when he began to come, she faked satisfaction for his sake. Mistake, she thought, lying awake while Mel slept, mistake.

Sally slept fitfully, waking again and again, panicked to find herself in a strange bed. Early in the morning, just as it was getting light, she woke to Mel's hands making circles on her breasts. Sleepily, reflexively, Sally pressed against him. When Mel slid inside her she arched, pulled him deeper, matched her breath to his. They rocked together while light began to shape the room. Just don't think, she told herself, let this happen. Didn't she deserve some comfort? Didn't she deserve a life?

"You're beautiful," Mel repeated, over and over.

She wasn't. She knew what she was, what Billy had made her, but she could have cried for Mel's kindness.

Mel came out of the bathroom grinning. "What do you think?"

Sally was speechless. He had cut his ponytail—cropped his hair close to his head unevenly, and shaved his wispy beard. He didn't look weasely anymore, he was almost cute in a bony-faced way, but he'd done it for her, Sally thought resentfully. Spineless.

Steve, the manager of the meat department, came into the freezer to announce that Sally had a visitor. Mel, she thought, pleased. It was nice to have an excuse to get out of the cold that seeped into her bones, reddened her fingers, and gave her sniffles year-round. Mel was probably doing his shopping. It was Saturday and he was off, but she had decided to pick up some overtime since Billy had the kids. She finished stacking trays of plastic-wrapped lamb chops, slammed the freezer shut, straightened her bloodied apron, and stepped out through the swinging doors. Billy, not Mel, stood there, the girls at his sides. At the sight of Sally the veins in his neck went taut.

"Hi Mommy!" Molly called. "Hi!"

Jenny glanced worriedly up at her father.

"Hi, sweeties," Sally said, feigning cheer. "You having fun with Daddy?"

"I called you 'til three in the morning last night," Billy hissed. "Where the fuck were you?"

An elderly couple comparing hams in the meat display straightened up and shared a glance.

"Go away, Billy," Sally begged. "You want me to lose my job?"

"You wouldn't need a job if you'd stayed home where you belonged." His voice rose. "Don't think you can fool me. I know what you're up to, you fucking whore."

The old couple quickly wheeled their cart away.

Sally felt the tears come into her eyes. She wouldn't cry here, not at work, not in front of her girls. "Get out, Billy. What I do is none of your business. I'm not your wife anymore."

"Yes you are!" he bellowed. "We're still married. I still love you, goddammit."

Steve came over. "Alright, alright, that's about enough of that. You got some trouble here, Sally? You want me to call security?"

"Mind your own business, asswipe," Billy counseled. "This is a family matter."

"Okay," Steve bristled. "I'm calling security now."

Billy started to say something else, thought better of it. He gripped the girls' hands. "Just you wait," he called over his shoulder as he yanked them away. "You aren't fit to be a mother."

Sally shut her eyes against the image of Jenny's mouth shaping a frightened O, Molly starting to cry. She collapsed against the rail of the meat bin. She felt drained of energy. "I'm sorry, Steve. That's my ex. We're separated but he can't accept the . . ."

"Hey, I don't want to know about it," Steve broke in with a grimace. "Just keep him out of here."

Sally didn't cry until she was back in the locker, hefting frozen slabs of flesh, wiping her eyes with the sleeve of her bloodied smock.

Mel flipped through her sketchbook, carefully studying the watercolors she brought over. He paused at her own favorite, modeled after a postcard he'd bought: a white farmhouse on the side of a winding road, hills, the dappling of light in summer leaves, banks of flowers.

"My teacher's been showing us how to do the leaves, shading the different colors," Sally explained.

"It's great. I mean it, you really got talent."

Sally shrugged. What did he know? The only art in his place was a Grateful Dead poster. "Billy laughed at me when I told him I wanted to paint," she said, placing a clean sheet of paper over the picture. "He bought me a paint-by-number set for a joke."

"I told you before, Sally, I ain't Billy."

"Right." Sally sighed, sat down on Mel's lap. The TV was on, volume low. On the screen, a sitcom family ate breakfast in a perfectly appointed kitchen. The TV family's teenage son strolled into the room sporting a green Mohawk haircut. The father leaped from his seat, spilling his coffee. Miniaturized hilarity buzzed from the laugh track.

Mel rested his head on Sally's back. "What would I do without you?" he said softly.

"Go back to Joanne, if she'd let you?"

Mel leaned away. "Sally, why you want to talk like that?"

Sally didn't know. The nasty words had just slipped from her mouth. She didn't even know they were lurking there. "I'm sorry," she said. "I didn't use to be like this. Honest. You would've liked me better before."

"I like you fine," Mel said. "I love you."

Sally sat very still. If she didn't move the words might not be real, and she wouldn't have to feel so angry, so scared.

Sally came home from picking up the girls at the babysitter to find the door to the apartment battered and hanging off its hinges. She knew it was Billy. The TV and stereo were intact, nothing taken, but drawers were pulled from the dresser and clothes strewn around the room. He'd been looking for clues, probably, sniffing around for a boyfriend.

"What happened, Mommy?" Jenny whined. "Who did this?"

"I don't know, honey," Sally lied. She bit her lip so she wouldn't curse Billy in front of the girls. They didn't need to know how sick their father was.

Molly said, "Somebody was ba-ad. Somebody ba-ad was here."

"You got that right," Sally said.

Lydia appeared on the landing outside Sally's ruined door, hands on hips. "He was making some kind of a ruckus," she complained. "I nearly called the cops."

"You should have," Sally said, and slammed the tilted door.

"I'm gonna call the landlord to get you out of here if it doesn't stop," Lydia screamed from the staircase.

"Suck wind, you old bitch," Sally shouted back.

Downstairs, Lydia's door whammed shut.

"Mommy! You talked bad," Jenny chastened.

"I know, honey, I'm sorry. Mommy's just mad right now."

"At Lydia?"

"Not really. At whoever did this." Sally squatted down to gather her underwear off the floor. She discovered her new nightgown— something lacy she'd bought because she didn't want to wear a coffee-stained housedress in front of Mel—lying in the corner, ripped in half. She pressed the torn aqua satin to her lips and waited until her breath stopped catching in her throat before she continued picking up panties and bras.

The girls were afraid to go to bed, and Molly woke with nightmares about the "bad man" coming to get her. Sally had her own fears to contend with; even more than the bashed-in door, the torn nightie felt like a violation.

"Get a court order," Donna instructed over the phone. "Call your lawyer. Report it to the police. You've got to document it all for the hearing."

"Move in with me," Mel urged later that night, stepping back to survey his work. Once again the door swung on its hinges, although the frame was splintered from Billy's blows. "I mean it," Mel continued. "You'll save money on rent; everything will be easier for you."

Sally flopped down in an armchair. "Are you crazy? Don't you see that will make him worse?"

Mel stuffed a screwdriver into his back pocket, came over and squatted in front of her chair. "How come he's still running your life, Sal?"

"I suppose you want to run it instead?" she snapped. They were all—Billy, Lydia, Mel—pushing her to the wall. She reached for her cigarettes, lit up.

"I just want to help. Listen, when the divorce is final, I think we ought to get married."

Sally avoided his earnest green eyes, their hungry intensity. "You mean you want a mother for your kids. What's the difference between three and five, right?" She knew she was being unfair. She hated herself for this quick new cruelty, despised Mel for letting her get away with it.

He gripped her by the knees. "Sally, I love you."

Sally drew hard on her cigarette. "That's what Billy says."

At the hearing in Springfield, the weary judge said to Billy, "You realize, you aren't married to this woman any longer. You've got no right to invade her privacy."

Billy gazed off toward the windows.

"Do you understand?" the judge persisted. "Your only connection is the children. From now on you will pick them up in a public place agreed upon by your lawyers. You are not to go to her house or anywhere near her. Do you understand?"

Billy swung around to look at Sally. She dropped her eyes to her hands, which were clutched together on the maple table beside her lawyer's stacked notes.

Annoyed at Billy's silence, the judge leaned forward over the bench. "Answer!"

"Yeah, I understand." Billy shaped the old lie used on principals and parents. He added a sullen "Whatever."

And then, with an absence of drama, it was over. Billy's lawyer led him from the room. Sally felt dazed. Her own lawyer, an elderly man in a crisp bow tie who she believed disapproved of her, solemnly shook her hand and began tucking his papers away. "We'll talk next week," he said.

Donna kissed her cheek. "Thank God that's finished. You want to go somewhere, have coffee?"

Sally looked at her watch. "I better get back. Mel's baby-sitting."

"Well, you call me if you feel bad or anything. I know how these things are. I've read about it. No matter how awful the marriage was, you still have to go through a period of grieving when it's over."

Sally wanted to laugh. Grieving over Billy was the last thing she'd do.

Sally drove the eighteen miles back to town slowly, choosing Route 5 instead of Interstate 91. The interstate would get her home too soon, before she'd had a chance to assimilate what had just happened. She wound along the cracked asphalt paralleling the Connecticut River, past farmhouses in need of paint, a jungle growth of summer green, and slowly it sank in: she was free. She hadn't really believed it was possible to escape him, but they were divorced now and Billy didn't have a legal right to step in her yard, let alone the apartment. If she only had full custody things would be perfect. At least she didn't have to dread the hearing anymore.

For months she'd been afraid of what Billy might say about her, yet it had all passed in a swirl of legalese, with none of her secrets revealed. She was surprised that Billy had seemed so quiet, almost subdued. Maybe his lawyer didn't want him to hurt his own custody situation by bringing up the ugliness out there in the shack in Ludlow. After all, Billy had been the ring-leader; it was his kinky weirdness that Sally had tried to placate and satisfy. Group sex had never been her idea of fun. Fucking voyeur.

When the shameful memories rose, Sally shook them from her head. It was all in the past now. She could divorce herself from them just as she'd divorced Billy. She could be a different Sally, not the empty-headed, lonely girl who'd married him because she got pregnant, gotten pregnant because she wanted a child and Billy offered to support her that summer. She was no longer the idiot who thought he was sexy because he talked dirty, because he put his fingers around her throat to show her how easily he could hurt her; in the beginning, he never did.

A wave of sadness replaced the shame. She wasn't grieving the marriage. No, she was grieving that girl she'd been back then, the one dumb enough to marry him.

Sally dug in her bag for cigarettes with one hand, pushed in the lighter button on the dash. She wanted one good memory so that she wouldn't have to judge seven years of her life a complete waste. Something to make it comprehensible that Billy was the father of her kids.

The only memory that came to mind was the day Jenny was born. Billy had wanted a boy so badly. He talked about his son every time he touched her pregnant belly. He even bought a little football and a tiny football jersey, jokingly referred to her belly as "Butch." But he never showed a second's disappointment at the squalling, red-faced little girl that Sally presented to him. He loved Jenny from the very first moment, loved both his little girls, insisting on their perfection, even Molly who was undersized from the start.

She could see him now, holding tiny Jenny in her blankets, cooing at her, in what was still their first year together. If he just hadn't given in to the booze . . . if he wasn't so miserable with himself . . . No. Dammit. She was being a jerk. That was her problem after all, not being too mean like she was to Mel, but too soft. She'd been a softie all her life and where had it gotten her?

Okay. So Billy had one redeeming quality. It didn't mean she had to forget all the bad things that had happened. One good thing didn't wipe out a million bad. Other guys loved their kids and didn't break jaws or bash down doors. The hell with him.

Sally tried to concentrate on the landscape sliding past. Off to her left, a farmer tedding hay marked a field with sweeping windrows. She breathed in the sweet aroma. How pretty it looked, as distant as a postcard from the life she lived now. It was funny, she'd grown up near the river, on the edge of her grandfather's hundred acres, but since she'd moved to Bellows Falls she'd lost all touch with the land.

Maybe it was the way they lived out there at Billy's shack, their only electricity an extension cord running from their house to Billy's uncle's, no toilet or running water, the tar paper exposed, no phone. Living like trash, the way Mitchell lived on Gramp's land with his family. Somewhere along the line the country had become synonymous in Sally's mind with deprivation, and even an apartment in a run-down house on Bulcher Street seemed better.

But now, free of Billy, driving past hayfields and white clapboard houses with blazing perennial beds, the river a glimmer between the trees, she missed this. How had her life narrowed down to just the apartment, the store, driveway cookouts, the cracked sidewalks and empty factories of Bellows Falls? She might as well be living in New Jersey.

On impulse Sally took the next left, a gravel road that led to the river. She parked the car and fought her way through brush to the riverbank, keeping an eye out for poison ivy. The river looked flat

and placid here, backed up above the dam in Bellows Falls. Overhead, maples and alders rustled and whispered, catching a higher
breeze. The trees on the New Hampshire side swayed. The water
looked steady, soothing. She ought to try to paint it sometime.

She didn't want to sit on the muddy bank because she was
wearing a good skirt, her court clothes. But she wanted to feel the
water. Sally slipped off her pumps and waded in, holding her skirt
above her thighs. She wasn't wearing stockings. The water lapped
cool against her bare legs. Mud squished between her toes.

It was too bad the Connecticut River was dirty. It would be nice
to slide in, sidestroke all the way across to New Hampshire. She
wouldn't mind having such a goal: challenging, but simple.

Sally smiled, remembering. Once, when she was thirteen, she
had swum her buckskin Dusty across the river. She'd been riding
bareback, following cow paths through the fields that ran beside
the river. It was terribly hot, July or August, almost too hot to be
riding. The grass was alive with insects. They leaped out of Dusty's
path and the grass rustled around his forelegs. At a break in the
brushy alders, she guided Dusty down to the river for a drink. He
stepped out into the water, guzzled, lifted his head to look around,
the droplets falling from his whiskered chin. His dark-tipped ears
flicked forward and back, alert but relaxed.

When he was done, without thinking Sally urged him forward
with her heels. He stepped out knee-deep into the river, hesitated
for an instant when the water rose to his belly as though asking,
"Are you sure?" then leaped forward. Water rose above her waist,
a sudden chill. She floated up off Dusty's back as they both became buoyant. She gripped his mane, feeling the powerful surge
of his forelegs, the rise of his chest up out of the water with each
stroke.

That day the current was running strong. The distance across
seemed vast. Halfway, with the opposite shore still far off and
Dusty's breath a series of snorts, Sally realized that they were
being pulled southward despite how powerfully Dusty pumped.
She wondered how long he could keep it up if she turned him
downriver with the current. It made her feel powerful to think

that he would probably just keep swimming, doing her bidding, until he sank with exhaustion. Of course she'd never ask that of him.

They landed a quarter of a mile south of where they'd started. Sally was almost disappointed when Dusty gained his footing again and gravel crunched under his hooves. But they'd swum far enough. Dusty's sides heaved and his breath came in gusts. When he lowered his head and shook water from himself, she nearly went flying from his slippery back.

Sally rode home across the bridge, reins loose, enjoying the hollow clopclopclop of hooves on suspended asphalt. Water ran down her bare legs, drained off her cutoffs. The heat struck her face, shoulders, and knees, but it was cool where her shorts and tee-shirt were still wet, cool on Dusty's damp flesh. Cars slowed as they passed. Sally tilted her head back, smug with the knowledge that she'd swum her horse from Vermont to New Hampshire. She felt awed by her own achievement, satisfied with a world that had offered itself up to her whim.

Standing thigh-deep in the river, Sally slapped a mosquito. Her girls were waiting. She had to get home. She splashed back to the bank, thrashed her way through the brush to the car. She felt refreshed, cleansed, as though she'd swum the river herself.

Driving south again on Route 5, she looked at her face in the rear-view mirror. She didn't look any different yet. But everything was different. She would take the kids hiking. She would sign up for an oil painting class at the Community College this fall. She would lose ten pounds and quit smoking. Her new life had begun. Anything could happen without Billy to drag her down.

The Fourth of July in Saxton's River: in the middle of Main Street, the Grafton Volunteer Fire Department battled the Saxton's River Volunteers with firehoses and a soccer ball. Soaked men with hairy thighs shouted and splashed. Water sprayed up over the shrieking spectators.

Mel pushed Tiffany's stroller with one hand, holding Melinda's hand in the other. Sally held onto Molly as they wove through the crowds. Jenny and Rusty ran ahead, then came back to beg for cotton candy and hot dogs. Mel bought everyone balloons, tying Tiffany's onto the stroller.

They passed face-painting booths, tables selling ice cream and pies and tee-shirts, a Middle Eastern wagon dispensing falafel— spicy smelling, drippy things in pita bread that Sally had never tried. A snaking line of tie-dyed dancers wove through the street, gyrating to the accompaniment of congas and cowbells. Tourists— well-heeled elderly folk mingled with the inn-hopping bike tour people, sinewy in their black stretchy cycling gear—looked on from wicker chairs on the porch of the Saxton's River Inn. Sally recognized the amused condescension in their smiles. Still, she wondered if they might wish, for a moment anyway, that they lived here in this little village with its white steepled church, its black-shuttered, clapboard colonials, instead of in far-off New York or Boston. She wouldn't mind living in Saxton's River herself. Well, maybe not Saxton's River. Like Putney, it was full of people who'd moved here from away, snobs who looked down on locals. But Westminster or Rockingham or Shelby.

Maybe, just maybe, if she and Mel moved in together, they could afford to get out of Bellows Falls. Maybe they could find a rental with a yard, some land where she could plant a garden. With their two salaries, perhaps they could even find a little house to rent instead of an apartment.

Her reverie was interrupted by the sight of Nancy pushing Michelle in her special chair across the street. People stared or glanced away fast from Michelle's rigid body, her lolling head. Nancy ignored them. She was used to it, a girl who should have been drawing attention for her blond hair, her nice legs. Her husband Gary looked less comfortable. He walked a few feet behind Nancy and kept ducking his head nervously from side to side to see who was watching.

Sally shouted "Nancy!" She waved, then turned to Mel. "There's my sister. Let's go over and say hi. I'll introduce you."

Crossing the street with Melinda clutching the stroller, Mel reached for Sally's free hand and she let him. She felt so fucking normal she could cry.

On the grounds of the elementary school people spread blankets and lined up for barbecued chicken served by the fire department auxiliary. Reggae music blared from speakers. Sally sat spraddle-legged, hunched over a plate of chicken and cole slaw, licking her fingers while the kids tumbled about on the grass. She grinned at the sight of Mel's chin smeared with sauce and passed him a napkin.

"Hi, Daddy!" Molly announced.

Sally looked up fast to find Billy glowering down at them. He wore a muscle shirt; his sunburned shoulders loomed big and pink, his crossed forearms thick and veiny. Behind him his brother lurked, a leering backup. Sally's heart plummeted. Why did he have to show up now? It wasn't fair.

"Hi, Daddy," Jenny echoed softly.

"Well isn't this a pretty picture?" Billy said. He stepped forward onto the edge of the blanket. "Isn't this a pretty picture," he repeated, zeroing in on Mel. "Only thing is, that's my place you're sitting in, bud."

"Hi Daddy, Hi Daddy, Hi!" Molly sang, grabbing her father's leg. He reached down and scooped her up, hugged her fiercely.

"Look, we're all having a nice time here," Mel said. "Why don't we try to keep it that way, huh?"

"Why don't we keep it that way," Billy mocked in falsetto. He set Molly back on the ground. "*I'm* not having a nice time. Wanna know why?"

Sally threw down her piece of chicken. It wasn't fair that Billy should catch them like this: Mel made small by the fact he was seated on the ground, the smear of sauce on his face no longer endearing but ludicrous. Towering over them, Billy possessed an advantage and knew it.

"Billy, leave us alone," Sally protested. "Remember what the judge said? You aren't supposed to come near me."

"I don't give a shit what the judge said." Billy crossed his arms again. His lower lip pooched out like a pouting kid's, only more dangerous. "This guy's sitting in my place. He's got my wife. He's got my little girls. I don't like it."

"I'm not your wife!" Sally hissed. As much as she wanted Billy to simply disappear, to have this not be happening, part of her longed for Mel to leap to their defense, to seem larger, more imposing. She wanted a super-Mel who would knock Billy into tomorrow. Not this scrawny guy who just sat there. Why didn't he do something?

"What's the matter, can't your boyfriend talk for himself?" Billy smirked, as though reading her thoughts.

Rusty looked from his father's face to Billy's, questioning.

"Look," Mel said reasonably. "I don't know why you want trouble. Nobody wants trouble here."

"You shut up, shithead!" Billy shouted.

"No, you shut up!" Sally shrieked. Behind her, a family picked up their food and blanket to move away.

"Don't start with me Sally," Billy said. "I'm warning you." He raised a hand as though to cuff her.

Mel started to clamber up but Billy put a hand on his shoulder, pushing him down. For what seemed like forever, Mel struggled to get up and Billy pushed. When Billy let go suddenly, Mel lost his balance and fell backward onto the blanket.

Billy laughed. Then he turned away and ambled off to join his brother. "I'll catch you later," he called back.

"Bye, Daddy," Molly called softly. "Bye."

Sally stared at the ruins of the afternoon. The chicken knocked over, sauce staining the blanket. Mel's pale face. The kids silent, scared.

"What an asshole," Mel said. "Jesus."

"You coulda taken him, huh Dad?" Rusty said. "Couldn't you?" Hope and doubt mingled on his face.

"Shit," Mel said. "Fighting's no way to fix things, Rusty, I already told you."

Even if it was true, Sally thought it sounded lame. A coward's excuse. It didn't matter that Mel had tried to get up when Billy raised a hand at her. He'd been humiliated and so, by extension, had she.

"But you coulda taken him, if you weren't sitting down," Rusty said, trying to convince himself. Then he turned to Jenny and Molly. "Your dad's an asshole," he taunted. "My dad said."

"Okay, that's enough," Mel warned.

"But you said it." Rusty's voice quavered with tears.

"Your dad's a shithead," Molly retorted. "My dad said."

"All of you! Stop it! Right now!" Sally screamed. She was shaking. She closed her eyes, opened them. Shocked by her tone, the kids sat open-mouthed, stilled. "I want to go home," Sally said.

"Sally," Mel implored, scooping spilled coleslaw back onto a paper plate. "Don't let him win. Forget it. We were having a good time."

She looked at him in astonishment. Right. They could really just go on like before, pretending. He was lamer than she thought. "Look, I'm tired and I want to go home." She stood up. "Jenny, Molly, we're leaving. Now."

"What about the fireworks? We haven't seen the fireworks yet!" Jenny complained.

"Aren't we going to stay to see the fireworks? Dad?" Rusty demanded angrily.

"We'll come back," Mel said.

"What about us?" Jenny cried. "That's not fair."

"If your mother says . . ." Mel began.

"Just forget it," Sally snapped, her voice rising precariously. "I'm not going to have you girls here with your father acting crazy. And that's that." She stood, gathered up her purse and blanket, grabbed Molly's and Jenny's hands. Mel and his kids followed her back to the car. They drove home in silence, the kids too scared to whine.

"Stop at the drug store," Sally commanded as they pulled into Bellows Falls. "I want to buy cigarettes."

"Sally. You haven't had one in two days," Mel chastised.

"Mel, just stop." Sally felt close to hysteria. If she didn't keep her voice under control she might lose control entirely. She gripped the dashboard.

Mel pulled over and backed up. Sally climbed out. Inside, sliding two dollars to the cashier, she went weak with sudden exhaustion. She fought an urge to rest her head on the counter, to just lie there and not get up. Who was she kidding, quitting cigarettes? What difference did it make? She was so tired of it all, Billy surfacing again and again like a bad dream, as though the divorce didn't mean a thing. It had all been some stupid fantasy to think she could escape, just a dream like the idea of moving in with Mel, of finding a house, of thinking she might love him.

They parked in the driveway on Bulcher Street. Sally got out, trailed by the girls. Mel started to follow. Sally turned around.

"Look, Mel, I'm tired. I'm not in the mood right now."

"What about Mrs. Alfred? She's coming at ten, remember?"

"Oh, shit." She'd forgotten. They had an overnight babysitter lined up. They'd planned to go to the dance party at the rec center pond after bringing the kids back from the fireworks. Now all Sally wanted was a long shower, a beer or two or three, the girls in bed. She wanted silence. Down the street someone was letting off M-80's, the firecrackers shattering the quiet with repetitive booms. "Cancel her," she said.

Mel reached for her arm. "If you don't want to go to the party, I'll take the kids to the fireworks, and then we can just put them in my house and let the sitter watch them. We can spend some time alone."

Sally looked at him as though he were crazy. "The girls aren't going back there with that asshole running around, and I want to be alone with myself tonight, okay?"

"Okay."

Sally despised his forlorn tone.

"Maybe I'll keep the sitter and go myself if you don't want to go," Mel said bravely.

"Fine. Go." What did he think, she'd be jealous?

Mel lingered. "Sally, don't let Billy do this to you. To us. C'mon."
He put his hands on her hips.

"It's got nothing to do with Billy," she insisted, shaking him
off, though of course it did. But it wasn't just Billy. It was how
Billy had made her feel about Mel. Billy had won. Sally turned and
headed in the door. The screen door creaked open, then snapped
closed. The girls thumped behind her up the stairs.

"I love you, Sally," Mel called.

Sally pretended she didn't hear. Lydia probably had, though.
She was probably standing right there at her open window, the
snoopy bitch. Upstairs, Sally dropped her purse and the blanket
on the floor and collapsed in the armchair. She pulled out her
cigarettes, lit one, stared at her toes, filmed with dust in her san-
dals.

"Are you going to stay home tonight, Mommy?" Jenny asked.

"Yeah."

"Good. I hate Mrs. Alfred."

"You always liked her before," Sally said wearily.

"I never did." Jenny put her hands on her hips, ready to argue.
Molly interrupted, "Mom? I don't feel so good. Ooooh."

Sally turned just in time to see Molly, clutching her belly, vomit
a stream of pink cotton candy and hotdogs onto the living room
rug.

"Yuck!" Jenny declared, clamping fingers over her nose.
"Peeyoo."

"That's enough Jennifer," Sally ordered. Perfect. A perfect finish
to the day. Jesus fucking Christ. Sally let out a sigh. "C'mere baby."
She scooped up Molly and headed for the bathroom. "Let's get
you cleaned up."

At first she thought she was dreaming the steady pounding.
Then, fuzzily, she wondered if it was her head pounding from the
beers she'd had after she got the kids to bed. But the knocking
persisted and she heard someone calling her name. Billy, she

thought fearfully, leaping out of the bed in a frenzy of adrenaline. Then she recognized Mel's voice, and her fear gave way to annoyance. The digital clock read one-sixteen.

"Sally, open up. Please."

That's all she needed now, another drunk guy making noise. Sally drew on her bathrobe and went to the door. "Go away, Mel."

"Wait, Sally. Please."

Downstairs Lydia's door opened. "What the hell is going on up there?" Lydia shouted. "I'm gonna call the cops."

"Sally, I'm bleeding. Open up."

Sally opened the door quickly and Mel stumbled in. His face was swollen lopsided, one eye blackened and shut. Blood seeped from his nose.

"Oh, my God. What happened?"

Mel collapsed in a chair. "They jumped me when I was going to my car. Billy, and some others. There was two or three of 'em. I think my nose's busted. And they kicked me bad, in the kidneys and ribs."

Mel looked ready to cry and Sally could feel tears welling in her own eyes. "Oh God, I'm sorry, Mel. I'm sorry. I could just kill him." She knew it was her fault. Poor Mel, dragged into her own rotten drama.

Sally wet a towel, broke ice from freezer trays into a plastic bag, and left Mel propped in the armchair. She roused the girls and carried them, whimpering, across the street to Mel's house, where the sitter was sleeping. She woke Mrs. Alfred and explained to the frightened old lady that she was taking Mel to the hospital and not to wake his kids. Then she drove Mel to the emergency ward. In the darkness, firecrackers shot off like distant gunfire and shadowy teenagers ran through the streets as though Bellow Falls was under seige, a mini Lebanon.

It was a busy night at Rockingham Memorial because of the holiday. They had to sit for a long time in the waiting room on hard plastic chairs under the glare of fluorescent lights. Sally held Mel's hand while he pressed the icebag to his battered face. Down the row of seats, a kid burned by a firecracker moaned over his wrapped fists. A too-young mother, chewing the inside of her cheek, held a silent child in her lap. Sally glanced away from the sight of the child's black eye. On Sally's left, a woman in curlers methodically cleaned and polished her nails. The acetone reek of nail polish remover filled Sally's nostrils. She lit, then stubbed out, her cigarette.

"Maybe I never shoulda gone there, but I just didn't want Billy calling the shots," Mel mumbled. "I didn't like him ruining our plans."

"Never mind," Sally comforted. If only Billy would die, she thought. If he'd die, she'd be free. Every day people got cancer, died in car wrecks driving drunk. Why not him?

A nurse finally led Mel to an examining room. Sally sat alone, smoking. She started up, then sat down again, when the double doors swung open, but it was only a man in a wheelchair being rolled back to his wife, the woman doing her nails. The wife glanced at her unfinished pinkie, then tightened the cap on her polish bottle with an annoyed frown. Sally put her hands over her face and tried to still the panic rising in her guts.

She'd been here before, in this very emergency ward, though not for years. Once when she'd broken her arm falling from her horse; the second time with her mother, after her father strapped Mitchell in the face with a dog leash and the metal snap flew out and cut his eye. An accident, her father kept saying, as though strapping a kid in the face with a leash was okay, it was the metal part he hadn't intended. Her mother had cried the whole time, as much out of shame as sorrow, and Sally had comforted her though she was only twelve.

Later they'd spent time in the hospital waiting room, not here in this ward, but upstairs, while her mother was dying of cancer. All those months when Mom was moaning in pain, Dad had hardly ever showed up. Don't be mad at him, her mother begged the girls, he can't handle hospitals, he means well. Later, after Mom was buried, they heard the stories: how while Mom was sick,

Dad had propositioned Jamie's sister Eileen as well as Eileen's mother, their aunt. He had even tried to hit on Mitchell's girlfriend. And all that time she'd pitied him, just as her mother requested—their father was a lonely man distraught at losing his wife. A man had needs that had to be fulfilled.

But it was he who was sick, sick as Billy. Always accusing everyone else. He'd gone after Jamie with a shotgun, saying Jamie and she were screwing, just because they were friends. And then accusing Jamie of screwing her mother. And now her father was married again and sweet as pie, his new wife able to whip him into a shape her mother couldn't manage despite all the tears.

A loud rustling caught Sally's attention. She looked up to see an enormously fat woman in a white tank top and purple stretch pants settling into the seat beside her.

"I'm waiting to hear about my boy," the woman announced. "He drove smack into a tree on Route 5."

"I'm sorry," Sally said. "That's terrible. Will he be all right?" Go away, she silently pleaded, leave me alone. She didn't want to share anyone else's tragedy right now.

"Don't know yet. DWI. Not the first time, either. Just like his father, the bastard. Don't know how I'm gonna pay these bills." She snapped open a can of Orange Crush and guzzled soda.

Sally covered her eyes again. She hoped the woman would get the hint without being offended. A rebellious thought stirred her soul—so what if this woman was offended? Why was she always so worried about other people, as if making that woman comfortable was more important than how she felt herself?

Sorry. Sorry. She was always sorry. Sorry for her mother, dying so terribly. Sorry for Mitchell, taking the brunt of their father's wrath. Sorry for Nancy, stuck at home alone with Dad at sixteen, now with her wasted child. Sorry for Billy. Donna was right, this crippling pity was something they'd learned from forgiving Dad all the time. And here she was, pitying Mel.

It dawned on her that Mel could have driven himself here. He had wanted her to see him and feel sorry, wanted her to know what Billy had done. For all she knew, he'd gone to the rec center party so this very thing would happen. Fury made her hands shake.

By the time Mel came out with an I-shaped bandage across his nose, Sally's rage had settled into a cold, congealed lump.

"What did the doctor say?" she asked perfunctorily when he walked up.

"He said I got beat up pretty good." Mel attempted a sheepish smile. "As long as I don't find no blood in my piss, I'm okay. Broke my nose though. I'll look real pretty now."

Sally turned away from Mel's forced humor. He'd scared the shit out of her, manipulated her pity for a broken nose. Outside it was turning light. Sally drove the short distance back to Bulcher Street. Refuse from blasted firecrackers, soda and beer cans littered the empty roads. Mel rested his head on the back of the seat.

"Jeez, I'm sore," he said.

Sally didn't respond. She pulled into the driveway. When she shut off the ignition, she could hear birds chirping frantic territorial messages across the dawn. No matter what the species, that's all anyone seemed to be saying: get outa here, it's mine.

"I s'pose we might as well leave the kids with Mrs. Alfred for the rest of the night," Mel said. "No sense waking everybody. Mind if I come up?"

Sally stared ahead through the windshield. "Look, Mel. I know this isn't a good time for you, but I got to tell you, I can't do this anymore."

"Do what?" Mel sat up in the seat.

"This." She spread her hands to indicate the whole sorry mess of their joined lives. "I can't do it. I can't."

"What are you talking about, Sally?"

She turned to face him. "You wanted me to see you beat up. Admit it. You wanted me to feel sorry for you. Well I don't, Mel. I can't feel sorry for anyone right now. I'm sick of feeling sorry. I can't take this."

Mel expelled breath. He touched the bandage on his nose as though to adjust it, then dropped his hands. "Okay. Maybe I did want you to feel sorry for me. Maybe I wanted you to see I weren't scared of that prick, and it backfired. So what if I showed up at your door? Ain't that what people do when they're close? They help each other last I heard."

"I don't want to take care of you," Sally wailed.

"Hey, Sally. It goes both ways with us. It always has."

But it didn't. She was the one shouldering the load.

"Don't you see," Mel implored, "it ain't me you're mad at, it's Billy." When Sally didn't respond he slapped the dashboard. "I won't give you up. Not 'cause of him."

"That's just it," Sally exploded. "You guys are such assholes. You both think you have me. I don't want anybody to have me. I'm telling you, Mel. I can't do this anymore." She hunched over the steering wheel and broke into sobs so ragged she thought her heart would rip.

"Hey. Okay. Okay." Mel patted her shoulder hesitantly. "Look, I'm sorry, Sal. Just forget it. We'll do whatever you want." He opened the car door. "I just want you to be happy."

For an instant she wanted to cry out—come back, don't leave me weeping in the car—but when he climbed out and shut the door after him, she felt bitter relief. Done.

"I'll have Mrs. Alfred bring over the girls when everyone wakes up," Mel said through the open window.

July passed slower than she ever remembered. The days weighed as heavy as the heat that wouldn't break, the humidity choking, a slimy film appearing on her skin the moment she stepped out of the artificial chill of the grocery store and into the swooning heat of the parking lot after work.

Thunder rumbled in the afternoons but didn't give way to showers. How could it be that the air could hold that much moisture and refuse to let it go? It was a drought, the worst in twenty years. The girls splashed in their plastic wading pool at the end of the driveway, and Sally slid back inside when she saw Mel's car turn into the drive. It hurt to hide from Mel's kids. Once she

saw little Melinda standing in the driveway, staring up at her window with her head cocked like a dog.

Routine reasserted itself: dragging laundry bags up the stairs;
the reprieve of Donna's pool with her sisters for company; delivering the girls to Billy at the agreed-upon meeting spot—Athens
Pizza—with Donna there to help avert trouble; Billy's lateness in
bringing them back at the end of the weekend, so regular it might
as well have been part of the arrangement.

Eventually Sally stopped ducking at the sound of Mel's Malibu
thundering up the road. She realized he wasn't going to bang
down the door or call up weeping like Billy. He hadn't fallen apart
without her. She was relieved at first, then annoyed. It irked her to
see Mel continuing on with his life as well as he seemed to be
doing. His car came and went, blowing blue smoke. He lugged
groceries and kids into his apartment. The nose bandage disappeared and his black eye faded. One night a couple of the guys
from Beacom's Tire Shop came over with beers and she heard
their laughter mingled with music echoing up from the open
window of Mel's living room.

She was spying on him, she realized with shame, a nasty habit.
And dumb. If anyone was spying, it ought to be him. After all, she
was the one who broke up. He probably hated her by now, anyway.

It was strange. After she first left Billy, she was so happy to be
on her own that she only felt lonely when the girls were gone,
but since Mel she felt lonely all the time. She rattled around the
apartment, switching channels on the tube, opening and closing
the refrigerator, starting painting projects she soon abandoned,
checking on Mel from behind the curtains of her living room.

A Friday evening, and Billy had the girls again. The apartment
was so hot and stuffy Sally thought she would faint. It was going
to be one of those nights when the only way to sleep was to wear
a wet shirt to bed and point the fan at herself. She couldn't afford

an air conditioner, not when she was still paying off the lawyer for the divorce. This week she didn't even have the bucks to take herself to an air-conditioned movie. She wasn't about to go to her sisters' houses on a Friday night, either. They had their own families, and anyway, it was too pathetic.

She heard a car pull into the drive, and looked out to see a beat-up Camaro blocking Mel's Malibu. Great. Sally watched from the bathroom while Joanne climbed out, lanky legs unfolding in short shorts. No cellulite there. The old jealousy clutched at her, but she shoved it away. Why should she care if Mel's wife came back? Still, Joanne's staccato knock hammered Sally's heart.

Sally moved into the kitchen. She ducked her head under the faucet and let cold water run down her neck, under her halter, between her breasts. She thought of running a cool bath but stalled. Not until Joanne came back out with the kids and packed them into the Camaro did Sally breathe relief. Just another one of Joanne's erratic visits.

She decided to work on a watercolor of the river. She set up her box of colors, water jar, and pad on the window seat, pointed the fan at her damp throat. She sketched out the far bank, the outlines of trees, and the hills rising above them. She couldn't figure out what perspective she wanted—as seen from the near bank, or including the near bank, a birds' eye view? She sketched and erased, sketched and erased. When she finally started painting, she couldn't get the colors right. The river looked blue when you drove over the bridge on a cloudless day, black sometimes, or camouflage green. She painted, mixing blues and lavender and black, painting over it, until the paper underneath began to get spongy. Still, the river eluded her.

She switched to the trees for a while and had better luck, but then a big drop of sweat ran off her forehead, blurring a delicate dappling of dark and light greens. Sally tossed the pad onto the floor. The hell with it. It was too hot to concentrate in this oven.

She knew it wasn't the river she was trying to capture, really, but the way she'd felt that day driving back from the hearing, standing thigh-deep in water, and later, that night, the first night she'd let Mel stay over, when it had seemed possible that they might be a family. Things had really gotten loused up. It was all some trick of shadows and clouds, anyway, nothing she could pin down; feelings changed as swiftly as the river shifted color under her gaze, and hope kept sliding away with the current.

She heard the creak of Mel's screen door, and then the scrape of an aluminum lawn chair in the driveway. She stiffened, as though he'd caught her peeking at him instead of just sitting in her window seat working on a painting. A ring snapped on an aluminum can. Tires whirred over hot pavement as a car turned the corner and chugged on.

Sally sat stock-still on the windowseat, trying to decide what to do. She wanted to go down there, but either way she'd lose. There was the shame of rejection if Mel refused to talk to her. But if he was happy to see her, she'd judge him as weak. They were both trapped in a cage of her own making.

Goddamn. Who made those rules, anyway? Who was to say that strength wasn't just going on with your life, taking care of your kids, remaining kind when life kept coming along to kick you in the ribs?

Sally went into the kitchen for a beer, sidetracked into the back closet, picked up her folded lawn chair, grabbed her cigarettes. She thumped barefoot down the stairs, afraid that Mel would be gone by the time she got there. Outside the air was moist and heavy but cooler, the sky a darkening blue gone to dusk. The screen door slammed behind her. Mel looked up but didn't say anything, his eyes a flash of startled green in his bony face.

Sally approached. The concrete driveway radiated heat under her bare feet. She set up her chair beside his, sat down, cracked her beer. "Hi," she said. It came out too high, a bleat.

"Hey." Mel shifted uncomfortably in his seat.

"Joanne got the kids?" Smooth now, pretending weeks of silence hadn't passed between them.

"Yeah." Mel paused. "Her fella's out of town again."

"Same old story."

"Uh-huh." Mel took a swig from his can.

He didn't ask her how she was. Sally lit a cigarette, breathed in deeply. She was an idiot, coming down here like this. "It's too damn hot to stay inside," she said angrily, embarrassed.

"You got that right."

They sat in silence. Sally focused on the point of her cigarette lighting the near dark. She didn't know what to talk about. What could she say, how was life while I was avoiding you?

Mel set his empty can on the driveway. She feared he'd get up and leave.

"Mel?"

"Yeah?"

"I'm . . ." The familiar words stuck in her throat. "I'm sorry."

"Hey, forget it. It don't matter." His voice sounded flat.

"I never should've said that stuff."

"Well, sometimes people say things."

She sensed him shrugging her off and stared straight ahead. She didn't know how to save this, didn't know how to erase what had happened. A loneliness deeper than any she remembered hollowed her chest.

"Mel, I miss you."

"Sal-ly . . ."

She heard the catch in his voice, its ragged ache. His chair scraped as he stood up. He was going to go inside, Sally realized. He didn't even want to sit outside and share a driveway with her. Well, could she blame him?

Mel walked around behind her. She braced herself, waiting for his departing footsteps, the slam of his door, to know he was really gone. She flinched in surprise when she felt his hands on her shoulders, then sucked in breath as Mel began to rub. Silently, he kneaded her shoulders, her neck, the base of her skull. His breath blew soft on her face as she leaned back, letting him take the weight of her head in his hands. He stopped rubbing, gently cupped her head. She closed her eyes in gratitude. She was so tired of holding herself up. It felt like floating to be held like that. She imagined she was on horseback, swimming across a river so wide she couldn't even see the other side. She wanted to just keep floating. As soon as she reached the other side it would be over and she'd have to wake up to her life.

When Mel rested his hands on her shoulders, Sally reached up and put her hands over his. "Now what?" she whispered.

"Nothin'. Everythin'. Whatever you want."

What did she want? She wanted freedom. She wanted things not to be so hard.

"Mel?" Sally said. "You want to go swimming?"

They crossed the Vilas bridge to Route 12 in New Hampshire. Sally clutched her towel in her lap, allowing the hot rush of wind past the car window to mimic a breeze. The moon was nearly full and rising. It splayed beams over the Connecticut River, then it was lost as they turned left onto Route 123. Corn rustled faintly in the fields. They bumped over rough gravel under a bower of trees paralleling the Cold River.

"Is it really cold?" Sally asked.

"Probably not with this heat," Mel answered.

A few miles along Mel pulled onto a turnoff. He lit their way by flashlight on a path through brush, across a few planks bridging a swampy spot, then down a steep embankment twisted with roots. She could smell the water, or maybe it was just the cooler air settling over the water.

The moon shone through the opening where the Cold River widened into a pool lined with boulders and ledgy cliffs. The water was black, and silvery where the moon reflected off its surface.

"There's some poison ivy in the rocks there," Mel cautioned.

Sally peeled off the shorts covering her bathing suit. She made her way in a crouch down the steep rocks. The water felt cool but not icy. She slid in and paddled across. It was deep here, dark, way over her head. She grabbed a rock on the other side, found a place to sit on an underwater ledge. Water lifted her breasts, their buoyancy a relief to her shoulders, one of those burdens she was so used to carrying she didn't even notice until it was gone. Mel stood naked on a high rocky outcropping. His narrow ribs, white in the moonlight, looked familiar enough to touch.

"Whooeeee!" he shouted, and dove. The water flew up sparkling. Sally waited for him to surface, anxiety rising, and then his face popped up like a seal's.

"Great!" he shouted in that overloud voice people use while swimming—from joy, or having your ears filled, or maybe it was just the water itself, carrying sound so efficiently.

Sally could hear him breathing, fifty feet away as he clambered out. Upstream the river tumbled, coursing rocks before it pooled, shaping the distance between them. It moved on, drawn toward the Connecticut River and the sea by a force more powerful than any she could fathom.

Balanced on ledge, Mel wavered in moonlight. "Not bad, huh?" he called out.

Sally smiled, although she knew he couldn't see her in the shadows. "Not bad," she replied, slipping back into the silky coolness, slicing through distance with every stroke.

CARDINAL

[Nancy, 1991]

NANCY POURED protein powder in the blender and added a scoop of Ben & Jerry's blueberry cheesecake. Ice cream was one of the few things left Michelle could, or would try to, swallow. While the blender whirred, Nancy filled a second cup of coffee for herself and set it on the counter, then lifted Michelle from the couch, where she lay propped by pillows. Michelle needed a diaper change. Nancy turned off the blender.

"Hey Stinky," she said, smiling into her daughter's unfocused eyes. She lay her on the changing pad on the floor.

"What do you want to do today, honey? Want to go to Aunt Donna's house?"

Michelle no longer struggled against her diapering efforts, but lay with her skeletal legs drawn up, her hands frozen into claws by her shoulders. It was the reverse of how it had been ten, eleven years ago: first your little baby lies still for changes, waving toes in the air, and then when she starts to crawl she's insulted that you want her to stay on her back. Michelle had been like any baby, twisting and wriggling, crazy to be mobile. And that impulse to be upright. Fall down twenty times and never get discouraged. Nancy wondered how it was that people lost that ease with themselves, began to think that everything they couldn't do right off

meant they'd never do it. You never heard babies say, "Damn, I'm
no good, I'll never learn to walk."

Then it was all in reverse, the humiliating return to diapers as
Michelle lost control of her muscles, her insulted struggles, and
then the passivity that came with what everyone else considered a
"vegetable" state. But there was somebody home in there, Nancy
was sure of it. Only Michelle's intractable muscles wouldn't let it
show. The few times Nancy left Michelle with Donna or Sally so
she could have a moment to herself, they said if anyone spoke
Nancy's name Michelle would wail. She still knew enough to
know her Mommy.

The doctors said two years, tops, and Michelle had hung on for
five already, though she was down to a wisp of nothing, and had
been in the hospital three times this month with seizures. The next
time, Nancy would sign the form that requested "no heroic mea-
sures."

"You're the hero, aren't you sweetie," Nancy said, swabbing
Michelle's bony groin with a baby wipe. Although she was down
to forty-five pounds, enough hormones were coursing through
Michelle's body that she'd begun to sprout wisps of pubic hair on
her crotch and a few black curls under her armpits.

She used to smile, even last summer she still smiled, but now
she cried half the day. The doctors said it was just some neurologi-
cal misfire, that she couldn't feel pain anymore, but how would
they know? Nancy begged them for painkillers, but all they pre-
scribed was valium.

She taped the oversize diaper around Michelle's hips and pulled
her upright, then carried her to her room, where she pulled off the
nightie and dressed Michelle in lavender appliqued overalls, a
white jersey, and the paint-on sneakers she'd made for her last
week.

"Don't you look gorgeous."

Michelle's head lolled backward. Nancy cradled her in her arms,
carried her into the kitchen, and locked her into her wheelchair.
She set the blender whirring again, stopped it, and poured into a

sippy cup. When she tilted the cup to Michelle's lips, Michelle sputtered and gagged.

Damn. She was losing the ability to swallow. The next step was a feeder tube. Nancy set the cup down and spooned tiny mouthfuls into her daughter's clenched jaw.

Despite the malnutrition, Michelle's auburn hair continued to grow thick and glossy, full of red and gold highlights. Nancy cut it short now because if it fell in Michelle's eyes or nose or mouth it might bother her and no one would know, but it was still a glorious shiny cap.

Nancy turned on the tape player, an old Joni Mitchell album, sipped her coffee, picked at a piece of sour cream coffee cake she'd baked yesterday. Her mind turned over the trivia of the day. The tree was out in the yard, yellowing, the needles already vacuumed out of the carpet, and not one strand of tinsel drifted about. Nancy decided she'd throw out the cards today and be done with Christmas. She gathered them off the mantel and pulled them down from the refrigerator, where they were pinned by magnets beside a newspaper clipping about Michelle's visit to a fifth grade class to teach them about "the handicapped," a faded first grade drawing: "Our House," signed Michelle, and a homemade Valentine.

She'd do laundry. Floor mopping. She always mopped on Mondays and Fridays. If Michelle conked out from the valium, she'd work at her sewing machine. In the afternoon she'd load Michelle into the car and carry her to her sister's. On Fridays, Donna and Sally and their friend Lisa sang together and had their weekly tea party. They were members of the Shelby Congregational Church choir. Nancy didn't have much of a voice, but she could go and listen and eat cookies. When she got back she'd make supper: tonight would be Szechuan beef in the wok. When Gary came home she'd go to aerobics at the gym in Bellows Falls. He'd leave Michelle on the couch with the TV blaring while he went out to work in his shop, but she had to get her exercise. It wasn't like she could even go out for a walk anymore. They'd eat supper, watch the tube, and that would be the day. Over and done.

If she acknowledged the sameness, the boredom, she'd go mad. Days and weeks and years went by, marked only by the small degrees of Michelle's degeneration, and by Nancy's growing disgust with Gary. But it wasn't forever. Everything was bracketed by the unspoken future: when Michelle died. When Michelle died, she'd leave Gary. Gary with his coke and his drinking and lying and bullshit. She'd leave this house that had turned to ashes around her and walk into some new life she couldn't even put a name to. She was still young. She could have other children with somebody else, somebody who wasn't a genetic land mine.

Nancy rinsed her coffee cup. Chickadees were hopping about her seed feeder. A flash of red caught her eye: a cardinal sweeping across the snowy bank of her perennial bed.

Michelle was choking. Rigid in her chair, gargling lung fluid, her twisted hands thrashing the air beside her face. Another seizure.

Call 911, call 911, Nancy ordered herself, but she couldn't lift the phone. She watched her panic from the outside, considering. Not another trip to the hospital, where she knew they'd end up inserting a feeding tube, or keep Michelle locked to machines. Instead she grabbed a dish towel and rushed to the chair, unhooked the waist and chest belts that kept Michelle from falling out, and lifted her down to the floor. She stuffed the towel into her daughter's mouth so she wouldn't bite her tongue. Michelle's bony body shook with convulsions.

"Look at me," Nancy ordered. "Honey, open your eyes, see me. Mommy's here."

But another voice broke in: Let go. Michelle, baby, let go. It's enough now. Fly away, little bird.

Michelle thrashed, her green eyes rolled wildly, met Nancy's for one panicked instant, begging: help me help me.

"Let GO," Nancy ordered. "Mommy's here. Mommy's here."

Michelle shuddered and went still.

Nancy stroked her head. "There. We didn't need the ambulance, did we. Not that scary ride again."

Michelle's eyes stared and her clenched hands went limp. Nancy straightened her daughter's long thin fingers, the nails painted red just yesterday. "You might have played the piano," Nancy said.

She kissed her daughter's shiny hair. She knew Michelle wasn't breathing. She knew she'd have to get up and call 911, but not yet. Not yet. She rocked her wasted daughter in her lap. Outside the chickadees cheeped and chirped and knocked seeds to the ground. A cardinal flashed red feathers through a dark tunnel of hemlock branches as Nancy's child turned into a husk in her arms.

UNDER THE BRIDGE

[Lowell, 1991]

LOWELL PARKED Helene's shiny black Buick between Jamie's ancient pickup and Sally's rust-cankered Toyota. Only Donna drove a decent rig, a late model Saab. He never would've guessed she'd be the one to rise to the top, hitched to that workhorse Claude Cormier, who built a fortune out of a dump truck. Lowell pulled so close to the brush lining the south side of the Bellows Falls cemetery that Helene had to struggle to open her door. Gamely, she fought her way out. Beyond the brush the ground dropped away precipitously; good drainage, Lowell observed.

He fumbled with the cigarette pack in his breast pocket, caught Helene's quick shake of the head "no," and sighed. He brushed donut crumbs from his slacks and took Helene's arm.

It wasn't a good day when you had to plant your little grand-baby in the ground. He'd already outlived a wife and a daughter, and now this. They'd held Michelle's body in the town vault all winter until the ground thawed enough to dig a hole. They'd had the memorial service back in January; now there wasn't much of a crowd. Gary, his soon to be ex-son-in-law, looking bleak, stood off on the other side while Nancy huddled with her sisters. The minister and a couple of grave diggers lurked about on a May day so pretty it seemed like they should've been having a picnic.

A robin redbreast struggled with a worm beside a granite headstone. Lowell didn't want to think about the birdy bones rattling around in that polished steel box. On the other hand, it was a blessing to see the baby go after all these years, just wasting away to nothing, and taking Nancy's life with her. He never came to visit because he couldn't stand it, seeing his little blondie girl, his own baby, lugging that dying child around in her arms year after year. She was nearly thirty years old now, and almost every day of her fun years had been given up to that. You got to wonder what'd happen now. Some people, they got free, and others fell apart.

Not so different from him, after Anne finally died. All those years of her suffering had kept him drinking, he hated so to see it. And then after, grieving her. She was a fine woman, too.

What no one understood, what he never could put into words, was that when Anne died, she didn't just take herself away from him, but she took the part of himself that only she knew, the better part. Only she could remember who he'd been in the early days, before all the sickness, back when she wanted him the way a man wants to be wanted. They were kids in Masonville, ready to break all the rules. Shocking everybody, her the teacher and him just a dumb hick kid who dropped out of school. He had a 1949 Buick Roadmaster that'd been wrecked. He beat out the lumps and got a paint job on it and took her cruising. They used to go out to Hickman Falls. She liked falling water—he even drove over to the Berkshires once cause she'd heard of Bash Bish Falls and wanted to see them.

Later one of the kids told him some fool theory that falling water creates negative ions that makes people feel good, changes your body electricity or something. Well it all sounded like a lot of hippie horseshit to Lowell—that's something they'd seen a lot of around these parts in the past twenty years. Stores selling crystals and granola. There even was some kind of lesbo parade in Brattleboro, made all the papers, a bunch of turned-around women prancing down Main Street with no shirts—not just braless, mind you, no shirts a'tall—because they got it into their twisted heads that it wasn't fair men could go bare chested in summer and they couldn't.

But anyway, Anne and him used to cruise the waterfalls. Hickman wasn't too far away. It was a scary place. There was a wire crib stretcher hanging off a tree year-round for pulling out bodies, cause fool kids were always trying to go in the upper pools, with the water washing right over a forty-foot fall, and knocking their brains out or drowning. But Anne, she liked that place no end. Made her feel some kind of "possibility" she said. He never understood what she meant there, but her family, they were different from his. That was a cause of a lot of the problems, truth be told. They had notions. Her old man was a plumber, but he had a bunch of old maid sisters gone down to Smith College and got their fancy degrees, and they had to have their opera in Boston and their Weston Playhouse in the summer, and one of the girls, Marty, they sent on up to Middlebury College, where she learned to keep her nose stuck in the air. None of 'em backwoods folks like his own.

Lowell's papa had told him he'd be miserable every day of his life if he married a woman smarter than him, but that wasn't it. It was her old man started the trouble. Never could do nothing right for him, being his servant in the business, giving them that land to build on, and making him know he was beholden every day.

Well, no use getting riled now, Lowell cautioned himself. It was all water under the bridge, just water under the bridge. He closed his eyes. The minister's drone faded as May sunshine sparked memory against his lids, a shower of sunlight on greeny water:

She took off her clothes under the bridge, stepping out of her skirt, her legs milky white with the sun dazzling and the pale green pulse of her veins, a vein in her breast, the pink crinkled aureolas like Rose of Sharon blossoms, her behind plump and her belly swelling with the first of the babies, Marsha. The plop and circle of ripples as she dunked into the pool, into darkness of unseen rocks, trout bumping their blunt snouts against her shins and her hair winding across her throat like fingers. Even here, in the cemetery, desire came so sudden, so real, that it ran through Lowell's body like a shock, desire for a dead woman, it made him ashamed, with Helene at his side dabbing her eyes for a grandchild that wasn't even hers, and Anne's poor bones moldering under the moss only fifteen feet away. And still he wanted to slip into that water after her, wanted the coolness to close over his head, to reach out underwater and hear her giggle as he grabbed her foot, feel her thrash, only pretending she wanted to get away.

The sob caught in his throat and came out as a phlegmy hack. Helene gripped him tighter, squeezed forgiving fingers.

Lowell glanced up, embarrassed, and caught his son's hard eyes. Mitchell looked away.

The boy'd been snubbing him ever since the memorial service back in January. At the reception, at Donna's house, Lowell had taken all his kids into a bedroom to talk.

He said, "I never told you kids I'm sorry that things weren't like they shoulda been when you were coming up."

The girls crowded around to embrace him, but Mitchell said, "What do you mean?" in a tone Lowell didn't like.

The boy was ruining it, cramping the moment, and Lowell had to struggle to keep from snapping. "You know, things were tough, we didn't always have money to buy what you kids wanted and all."

"Is that all? What about the rest?" Mitchell demanded.

"What are you talking about?"

"Don't you remember lining us all up in the basement so the girls could watch you beat me with the belt?"

"I never hit you kids. Never." Where did he get off with a story like that? He never.

Mitchell gaped like a hooked bass, then walked out.

In the cemetery now, Lowell shook his head. Those kids didn't even know what hitting meant. And worse than hitting. When he was only seven his father had taken him into the woods and showed him a dug hole. Maybe it was going to be a foundation for a shed or something; it looked like a big grave to him. Lowell couldn't remember now what his crime was, forgetting to shut off the hose, maybe, or knocking over the ash bucket. Dad said, "You climb down in there boy." Lowell went rigid with fear. "Do as you're told." His father grabbed his wrist and lowered him, too scared to even kick, until his bare toes touched the cold, dank bottom. Then Dad let him drop. The dark walls rose over Lowell's head and the tendrils of a chopped root reached out for him like fingers. A spray of dirt sifted down from where his father's boots poked over the edge. All Lowell could see of him was the holes of his big nostrils.

Dad said, "You're gonna stay in there cause you're dead and don't even know it. Nobody cares about you boy, remember that." And when his father walked off into the woods and left him, Lowell knew it was true.

But he got over it. Kids get over everything.

He wasn't even a bad kid. He did his chores fair enough and he even had some crazy, noble ideas. Those times they went to Hickman Gorge when he was a kid he'd see the basket hanging there and imagine himself a hero, the guy who would carry it down on his back or lower it on ropes to save the drowning person, or the one who fell and hit his head. It was only later that he figured out it was used to carry up the bodies of those who had died. And that's the way it had been in this family. Nobody had ever been rescued. It was just body after body after body, and instead of bringing them up, they kept lowering them into the ground.

It was funny, Lowell thought, as the minister quit and the mourners mingled and the gravediggers began grinding their hydraulics. He'd always thought when he was a kid that he wanted to be a hero. But maybe that wasn't it a'tall. Maybe, instead of saving the ones that'd fallen in, what he really wanted was to be the one saved—to ride in that wire casket, be raised up and given a second chance.

LIVE LIKE A
BACHELOR

[Jamie, 1993]

AT FIRST Jamie thought it was the sun waking him. Sara rented the loft of a converted barn; the big triangular window in the eaves faced east. Jamie shut his eyes and snuggled close. They were still beat from the trip. They'd driven through freak winter floods the whole way back from Texas, with the windshield steamed opaque and drowned raccoons and snakes lining the interstate. Every night they stopped in cheap motels to make love and drink Kahlua from the bottle they carried through customs. Halfway home, with the wipers sluicing and the old truck without shocks rocking like a hobby horse, they agreed to head up to Quebec City one day to get married. Maybe they'd even have kids, something Jamie had given up on long ago, but with Sara everything seemed possible.

They'd been back in Vermont two days and Jamie hadn't even gone over the hill to his cabin, or seen anyone from his family. He didn't want to get out of Sara's bed. As long as he stayed here they were still on their trip, inhabiting a landscape of their own. But it wasn't the sun that had woken him. Someone was knocking, and then he heard Mitchell's familiar voice.

"Hey. Hey Romeo. I got to talk to you."

Sara groaned. "Who's that?"

"My cousin."

"How'd he know you were here?"

Jamie smiled. "They all know. Someone must've seen my truck."
He yelled down the stairs, "Just a minute," then nuzzled aside a
spread of sandy hair and kissed Sara's freckled shoulder regretfully,
because he wanted them to wake up gently and slide together as
fervently as they'd been doing all month—in a tent in the Canyon, in a Chihuahua fleabag, in the hotel shaped like a ship over-
looking the sea in Topolobampo, where a fisherman pulled up in
his skiff each morning with a fresh catch of shrimp and crab for
their omelettes. But Mitchell was waiting, so Jamie got up in the
early March chill, yanked on clothes, and went down to let him in.

Mitchell grinned through the glass, sweatshirt hood pulled
over his head, red down vest puffy. "You must've worn the little
feller down to a nubbin by now. Better give it a rest," he said as
Jamie opened the door.

Jamie laughed. It was good to see Mitchell again; it had been
two months. After the first night he spent with Sara, Mitchell had
warned, "A girl from New York, you better worry about AIDS."
Then he added, "In your case, though, it'd probably be worth it."
It was no joke how long Jamie had gone between girlfriends.

When Jamie had told everyone he was seeing a woman from
West Shelby, the land of trust fund hippies, the guys he worked
with wanted to know if she had hairy armpits and ate tofu. His
cousins worried that Sara would change him; would he still wear a
rasta wig and dance like a maniac at Donna's parties? They were
afraid of Sara, someone with an education. They couldn't know
he'd never felt so at home in his life.

"Well, I really did it," Mitchell announced as they climbed the
stairs.

"What's that? Quit pulling your pud?" Jamie wondered if
Mitchell would smell the funky odor of love in the room. Sara
padded about barefoot, making coffee; the covers had been thrown
over the bed.

"Exactly. I put a deposit on an old 1940's sloop I saw advertised in *Wooden Boat* magazine. Fifty-footer."

"Whoa." Jamie realized it wouldn't matter if he and Sara were roasting human flesh up here; Mitchell was wound up in his own reality and Jamie smiled at his cousin's excitement. So he'd bought himself a boat, the crazy fucker. "This is Sara," Jamie announced. "Sara, my cousin Mitchell."

Mitchell nodded; he was off and running. "The deal is, I'm selling out, everything, the land, the house, the whole shebang. If you want it, you better act fast, because I'm out of here in two weeks. We're moving to Maine, big fella. I just wanted you to have the first shot before I turn it over to Howie Vesey to sell."

Jamie sat down. Jesus. He felt himself being yanked, unwillingly, out of the cocoon Sara and he had been living in, and he stalled. "You're going to stay on the boat? All five of you?"

"Well, maybe not the first few weeks. The cabin is pretty rough. It's basically an empty shell, but that's why she was so cheap. We'll camp or something while I put in bunks and a galley. Next winter we'll take her down to the Caribbean." Mitchell couldn't sit still. He paced Sara's apartment, touching her things, glancing at a study for a book cover on the easel. "You didn't think I'd ever do it, did you?" he demanded, turning back to Jamie.

Jamie's heart lurched at the sight of Mitchell's toothy grin, his shock of blond hair falling on his forehead, his open face begging for approval. He hoped to hell Mitchell knew what he was doing. Once that money was gone, the house would be gone too, and there'd be no coming back. And now Jamie had big problems, because he didn't want to let any more of Gramp's land go out of the family, so he'd have to buy Mitchell's land, and he'd just blown two thousand dollars on a trip to Mexico.

"Well, I better get going," Mitchell informed them. "Got lots to do. Let me know if you want first dibs. Vesey said he could get me $19,000 for the whole thing as is, but then I'd have to get a surveyor and a lawyer and I want to get out of here fast. The boat costs fifteen, so if you can manage it, the place is yours." He turned to Sara. "Nice to meet you."

Sara cocked an eyebrow as Mitchell hurried downstairs.

"I'll be right back," Jamie said, following Mitchell. They stood outside the barn, watching the landlady's mare blow steam from her nostrils and nose wisps of hay on the frozen mud. Behind the pasture, the bare branches of purplish soft maple and lightning forks of silver birch climbed the ridge. A few miles away, on the other side of the ridge, was Jamie's land, and Mitchell's, land that had been Gramp's, land it would break Jamie's heart to lose.

There were trees on the property, enormous rock maples whose every bole and rothole were as familiar as his own freckles and scars. Back in the years when his nerves were shot, when he was all tangled up in fury at Pop and fear of eternal damnation, when he ran from home to live with Gramp, they'd sheltered and sustained him as much as the old man had. Jamie had spent days lying in the ferns, losing himself in the sway of their sun-dappled canopy; he'd stretched his arms around their massive bulk and touched his lips to the tough nubbled skin of their bark, dry as any communion wafer. They were his body and blood, his cathedral, his salvation.

"I'll come by this afternoon to talk about it," Jamie said wearily. The Mexico trip was definitely over.

"You don't know what it's been like here this winter." Mitchell shook his head. "No snow, just ice and brown dirt, the water lines freezing all the time because there's no cover. Fighting the kids for the last Cheerio. I was starting to feel like that guy in the Dylan song who puts seven shells in his shotgun for his wife and himself and his kids." He laughed, because now his desperation was over: he'd bought a boat.

"I hate to see you leave the hill," Jamie said.

Mitchell climbed into his bank-owned Mitsubishi and grinned expansively. "Next winter you'll visit us in the Caribbean."

"Sounds good." Jamie thumped back up the stairs. Sara was sitting at her little round butcher block table with a cup of coffee and a book. She looked up.

"He didn't seem very interested in meeting me. He never even asked about your trip. Doesn't it bother you that he only talked about himself?"

"No," Jamie said. He wasn't in the habit of measuring conversations to see who was talking more. "That's just Mitchell. He's pretty high right now."

Sara returned to her reading. "You didn't tell me he was good looking."

Jamie had planned to take it easy for a while, not jump back onto a construction crew when they returned. Before he left for his yearly Southwest journey, before he sent Sara a ticket to join him, she'd given him a book to read on his trip. It was Turgenev's *Sketches from a Hunter's Album.* He'd told her he liked Russian writers. When they met he was reading *The Cossacks* by Tolstoy. She said it was a minor work, though Jamie loved it. Sara had all the school definitions; he just knew how he felt.

But she was right about Turgenev. After reading it he called her from Big Bend. It was dusk; a coyote ran across the road, backlit by desert sun, while Jamie stood at the pay phone outside the campground store. Jamie told Sara he'd had enough of humping boards in zero weather; he wanted to live like Turgenev's narrator, wander the countryside, simplify his life.

Sara replied, "Turgenev was a rich nobleman who didn't have to work. And your life is pretty simple already."

He detected a note of alarm. Sara was hooked into the achievement thing. But that was okay, he admired her achievements—the row of books on her shelves that she'd illustrated, her own deft sketches and large, bizarre acrylics. In any case, there'd be no Turgenev wanderings for him now. He'd have to hustle to make this land thing happen.

Jamie took ten thousand dollars in savings out of CDs, paying the penalties, borrowed another two from his mother, and agreed to owe Mitchell three. Just as he promised, Mitchell was gone in two weeks, leaving behind everything that didn't fit in the car, including all the furniture, their skis and winter clothing, and nine hundred and fifty-three pounds of garbage from inside and outside the house that Jamie bagged and boxed and trucked to the dump. He decided he'd fix up Mitchell's house well enough to sell as a camp since he couldn't afford to keep it, giving it only enough acreage to make a lot, and keep the rest of the land that bordered the sugarhouse for himself. Sara offered to support him while he worked on the house; he'd pay her back when it sold.

The first step was to finish shingling the tattered tar paper walls. Jamie shook his head in amazement at all the supplies Mitchell had purchased and never used: the bundles of cedar shingles, floor tiles, even a molded plastic shower, lay strewn about the hacked-out clearing that served as a yard. When he was done shingling, Jamie ripped out the yellowed patchwork sheetrock that had never been taped and stuffed insulation into the walls. He propped up beams and doubled headers to make the house stand a few more years. The real problem was that it needed a foundation to keep it from sagging and crumbling, but that had to wait for the ground to thaw. The weather stayed cold and he wondered how Mitchell's family was making it up there in Maine.

Sugar season passed, and mud season; the trees leafed out and the pastures greened and all the things that made people want to run from the state in endless winter gave way to vibrating beauty, tempered by blackflies so you wouldn't find it too sweet. Sara planted a garden beside the sugarhouse and worked it in the afternoons when she was done with her illustrations. The sight of Sara bent over weeds or tying up snow peas on Gramp's land made Jamie unreasonably happy. She even agreed, when her lease was up in June, to move into the sugarhouse with him.

It was time to put a foundation under Mitchell's house. Jamie couldn't sheetrock until he finished jacking it up. When he went to the bank for a loan, he was shocked to learn that he couldn't borrow a few thousand dollars because he had no credit. He had always paid with cash, which was worse than bad credit, apparently, since Mitchell continually borrowed on cars that the bank repossessed. Jamie's only option was to mortgage his entire property, which he'd never do, so he decided to dig the foundation hole himself and pour the footers by hand.

He began, jacking up an eight-foot section of sill at a time, digging a hole, pouring cement he mixed in a wheelbarrow, and setting in pressure-treated plywood. It was a massive operation; half the time he thought he was crazy for trying, or that he'd never finish. But he and Sara had a plan now. When they sold the camp they'd invest the profit into another fixer-upper; Jamie would have his own renovation business and could quit working on a crew.

Toiling on the foundation, his mind wandered. He thought of Sara and how most of the time she was so sweet to him—bringing him coffees and treats, sketching pictures of his labors, even carrying buckets of cement some afternoons when she was finished with her own work. She slept with her arms wrapped around his neck. But other times she'd want him to listen to tales of her parents' crimes.

When she was in these moods he'd have the same uncomfortable feeling he got when Mitchell complained about Lowell. He wanted to snap, "That's over and done with, just get on with it." Sara accused him of rejecting this part of her, of drumming his fingers on the table when she talked or getting up to do something else when she was trying to tell him who she really was, what she had come from.

"You keep saying how much you love me but this is me too and you don't accept it. You don't want me to get angry because you're afraid of your own anger, like that thing with your old girlfriend," she'd say.

Jamie resented her amateur psychoanalysis, the way she could turn around a confidence to use against him. But she was right, too. There'd been more than one bank in which he'd made a nasty scene when they wouldn't cash his checks—he'd always had bad bank karma—and with Lindy he'd gotten out of hand. It had taken two years of her running to the bars and sleeping around before he snapped. All he'd done was slap her in the face once, but he never thought he could hit a woman. The force of his anger sickened him, and for years he didn't even want to try being with anyone.

Now he thought it best just to concentrate on the things that pleased him. And Sara pleased him; maybe not every part of her, but he didn't ask that she love all of him, and he knew for a fact that she didn't. She was quick to correct him if he mispronounced a word he'd read but never heard, and on the way back from Texas she nearly had a breakdown over the fact that he'd bought a MAD magazine at a truck stop. She couldn't believe he could be amused by such juvenile crap but he bought it anyway and had to laugh when she read it cover to cover, blaming highway boredom.

She was a funny one, full of insecure questions: How much do you love me? Do you think I'm pretty? And he'd answer he loved her THAT much, or that she was so pretty that if a caravan of big rig drivers was speeding toward a free whorehouse, they'd all stop just to admire her. *Why do you love me?* she'd demand. She'd badger him for answers and then be dissatisfied when he couldn't put it into words. He didn't want to measure and analyze everything. He loved her because she was his beloved, because she walked the woods with him studying cellar holes and liked to drive the back roads commenting on lovely old houses; at night she held him close and told him that the first time she met him he seemed more there than anyone she knew. He loved her because he loved her and thought it should be enough. And it was. Each day the whine of Sara's Subaru climbing the hill quickened his heart, and he was up and out of the foundation hole, wiping cement off his hands, feeling blessed.

On a Sunday in early June Sara helped Jamie wrestle Corinne's old blue bureau down the stairs of Mitchell's house and hoist it into the truck. They'd promised to bring it over to Bellows Falls for Sally. They were driving through the flats, past the house where the Jesus freaks lived, the river bottom fields stretched left and right, black and mucky and rich where they were turned over, striped green where they'd been planted in rows. Jamie lay his hand on Sara's knee and she leaned into his shoulder. The moist heat of June filled him with a wave of desire and raw ripe happiness and then Sara said, "Isn't that Mitchell's car?"

Ahead, the familiar brown Mitsubishi tooled toward them, loaded to the gills, with the kids' bikes tied on top.

"Uh-oh," Jamie said. "That doesn't look good."

"Shit," Sara said.

As they came abreast the kids waved madly in the windows, but Mitchell sat grimly at the wheel and Corinne stared straight ahead. Jamie and Sara continued on, hauling away Corinne's dresser.

Sally, wearing an oversized tee-shirt and cotton leggings, was waiting in her tiny yard outside the run-down Victorian where she lived with the kids. In the driveway, her boyfriend Mel hosed and soaped his junker. He turned off the water and took over Sara's end of the bureau. When they'd hauled it up the peeling, rickety staircase into the hot apartment and Sally was pouring them glasses of Kool-Aid she'd made for the girls, Jamie said, "Guess who we just passed on the flats?"

"Not that fuck Billy?" Sally always thought of her ex first, was still obsessed with him, in Jamie's opinion.

"Nope. Mitchell and his crew with everything they own."

"Oh no." Sally shook her head. "Maine didn't last long. No surprise. I hate to say this. He's my brother and I love him dearly, but he's got to get his shit together one of these days."

Mel wiped his sweating forehead. "You got to give the guy credit for trying."

Sally sighed. "So where are they going to live now?"

"That," said Sara, who hadn't spoken since they'd passed Mitchell's car, "remains to be seen."

Mitchell's family-size tent glowed orange beside the sugarhouse. Mitchell sat, bent over his guitar, on a lawn chair.

"Where is everybody?" Jamie asked.

"Corinne took the kids over to her mother's," he said. "For good, for all I know."

Sara looked from Jamie to Mitchell. "I got some things to take care of at home," she said, backing away.

"Okay, I'll be over later." Jamie waited until Sara reached her car, then he sat down in the grass beside Mitchell. "So what's going on?"

Mitchell shook his head bleakly. "Everything's fucked up. Corinne hates living on the boat. We can't afford dock space so we have to moor in the harbor, and the kids are going nuts stuck aboard. All Corinne talks about is Judy Beal and how I've ruined her life by tearing her away from her only friend and how she wants to be back in Vermont. Like she was so happy here or something. Every time she mentions Judy Beal it's like she puts a fishhook down my throat and yanks. Okay, it's tough on them right now, but if she'd just stick it out I could make something happen. But if I run with it I'm going to lose her. She already proved that."

"Jeez," Jamie said. "That's really tough." He pulled a blade of grass and chewed the sweet white end. "Was the boat coming along at all?"

"Yeah, slowly. I got a galley in and some bunks, it's rough still, but I was working forty hours a week building stone walls for a guy in Camden to get the money to put into the boat, so it's not like I had all day to fix her up."

"That's really tough." Not surprising, Jamie thought, given the way Mitchell's great ideas always went, but tough.

"Fuck." Mitchell let the guitar slide between his knees to the grass.

"So what do you think you'll do?" If it came down to choosing between the boat and Corinne, Jamie figured Mitchell would crumble.

"I don't know . . . I guess I'll have to take the house back."

The old familiar sickness grabbed Jamie's stomach, the way he used to feel in school when he didn't know the answers, the way he felt when Lindy was running around—helplessness and something he didn't even recognize as rage. A headache leaped up into his temples, pressure and pounding like a distant thunder-storm. "I don't know, Mitchell. I've done a lot of work on it already."

Not to mention the fact that Sara had been supporting him while he did it.

"Don't worry. I'll pay you for the house and the work."

"With what? Are you going to sell the boat?"

"I can't sell it until I own it. I still owe the guy three thousand. I could pay you over time."

"I got to think about this one. I know you're in a hard place and all, but Sara and I have plans."

Mitchell looked stunned. Jamie could see his cousin hadn't expected for a minute that he wouldn't just give the house back. As though all Jamie's savings and three months of his work meant nothing. Sometimes Mitchell got so involved in his own disasters he couldn't see anyone else's life.

"I got to think about it," Jamie repeated.

Mitchell picked up his guitar and headed for his tent.

Head aching, Jamie drove over to Sara's apartment. She was just starting out for a walk. He shortened his long stride to match hers and they followed the dirt road that led back into Happy Valley, an odd assortment of cabins built by a farm wife to rent to hippies—one shaped like a Dutch barn, another an A-frame, one made of planks hacked by a chainsaw. They cut through a stand of evenly-spaced planted pines and into a mowing gone to weeds and brambles. At one end was an old cellar hole surrounded by twisted fruit trees, at the other a series of terraced beaver ponds. The hills rose up on the field's perimeter like encircling arms. It was a beautiful piece of land. On other walks he and Sara had fantasized about owning it, building here. It belonged to a young coke dealer on the lam who was letting the juniper scrub and saplings invade its edges. A good brush hogging and lime for the acid soil could bring it back. Jamie wanted to slide into that innocent fantasy, forget Mitchell's request.

He sat down on a mossy spread and pulled Sarah down onto his lap. "Mitchell wants the house back," he said into her hair.

"I knew it." She struggled in his grip and spun to face him. "I knew it. What are you going to do?"

"I don't know. He says he'll pay me back if I finance him."

"Oh, sure. Like he'll ever pay you back. You might as well just give it to him, if that's what you want to do. But I can't believe you'd throw away all our plans because of his whims."

Jamie put his hands against his aching temples. "I didn't say I was giving it to him. I said I had to think about it."

"What's to think about?"

"Sara, he's my cousin, he's in trouble. He's got a wife and three kids and no place to live."

"So? I didn't have a place to live until I rented one."

"We go way back, Sara. Look, this is getting too crazy. I think I'm going to go down to my mother's for a few days to think it through."

"Fine." Sara got up and stalked off.

Jamie wanted to follow her, but he was too exhausted. He lay his head on the moss and watched an ant dragging a dead beetle through a jungle of grass. The pounding in his temples could have been African drumbeats in a bad old movie.

Ma slid a slice of strawberry rhubarb pie onto Jamie's plate. She stirred Coffee-mate into her cup. She preferred it to cream, but now as a concession to cholestrol she used the lite version. She pushed her glasses up on her nose. "Don't give it back," Ma said. "It took all your savings to buy it. Everyone's been picking up Mitchell's messes for years. It won't help him any."

Jamie forked a load of pie into his mouth, but even that dazzle of tart and sweet couldn't ease his heart. He just wanted to spend a week on Ma's couch watching HBO movies.

Donna called from Shelby. She said, "Mitchell's been spouting off how it's Sara's fault you won't give him the house back, but I want you to know, nobody blames you. We don't want you to give it to him. It's time he got it together, Jamie. Don't cave in."

All the voices were making him sick. He went down to the trestle like when he was a kid running away from school. He skipped rocks and walked on the rails and crossed the river listening for a train. He kept seeing it from both sides, Mitchell's desperation, Sara's and his plans. In the end it was Gramp who decided. Jamie knew the old man would've been relieved to see the garbage cleaned off his hill. There were still more dumps back in the brushpiles that Jamie hadn't gotten to—a junked washer, bikes, broken storm windows. Mitchell had no respect or affection for the land Jamie loved. It was just a place he'd gotten for free. He would never be happy there and he'd trash it again before he left.

"I can't do it," Jamie announced.

Mitchell's face pinched together. For the first time, Jamie could see the resemblance to Lowell. "Boy, she really turned you around," Mitchell said.

"Sara had nothing to do with it. I made my own decision. Sure, I have other responsibilities now, but she didn't decide for me. You guys can stay in the sugarhouse a few weeks while you find a place, until Sara moves in. Of course you can camp on the land as long as you want."

Mitchell slumped. "I don't know what I'm doing anyway. I don't know if we'll even stay together. What's the point, if I'm just going to be mad at her all the time? Maybe if we don't, I'll just go back up there and live on my boat, at least until I lose it."

"What about the kids?"

Mitchell shook his head. "Who knows?"

"Mom cries all the time," Eli announced. He'd come up to watch Jamie work on "the Project." That's what they called it now. Sara didn't like Jamie referring to it as Mitchell's house anymore.

"Sometimes grownups get sad too," Jamie said, swinging his pick into the hardpan soil under the house.

"I know," Eli said, kicking through the rubble Jamie had shoveled out of the hole. "Hey, there's the head to Emily's old Barbie!"

Mitchell was too demoralized to get a job. He and Corinne lived out an uneasy truce in the tent behind the sugarhouse, and spent their days lolling around Donna's swimming pool, until one day Donna came home from Claude's shop at lunchtime and the sight of Mitchell's kids dripping wet bathing suits through her house pushed her over the edge. Jamie heard the story from Mitchell the next morning. Donna seized Mitchell around the neck and pushed him up against a wall, screaming, "You've got to shape up. You can't live like this." Then Corinne grabbed Donna and hauled her off. If it had come down to a real fight, Jamie would've staked his money on Corinne, but Donna let go and now none of them were talking.

Sara moved out of her rental and into the sugarhouse, but having Mitchell and his family living behind the cabin in their tent drove her crazy. The kids' kitten pooped in her garden and the boys played football in her beans. "There's forty acres," Sara whispered in bed. "You'd think they could pitch their tent a little further away."

Jamie's stomach ached from the tension.

"This isn't working," Sara announced one night in early August when they were sweating in bed. "I need more privacy."

Jamie felt as though he was on a ladder that had slipped—a half-inch heart attack they called it on a job site, only this fall might go on forever. "We can rent you a studio to paint in," he suggested.

"It's not only being interrupted. I can't get dressed without someone walking in the door. One-room life just doesn't work for me."

"I told you I'd add a room on eventually," Jamie snapped, "but I'm balls to the wall here with the Project."

"Jamie. I know how hard you're working. I just can't take all the people around all the time, okay, I'm not from a big family like you, and it makes me uncomfortable."

"Well I want to live that way. I want an open door." When he was growing up with Dad drunk every night, he was too ashamed to have anyone over. Long ago he'd decided when he had his own place it would be different.

"Anyway," Sara continued, "it isn't just people in general. It's Mitchell and Corinne, right there, hating me all day."

"Sara. C'mon. They're fucked up at the moment." Jeez, she could be hard. "Alright," he said, not meaning it, "I'll tell them to leave. I'll kick them off, if that's what you want."

"It's not just them. I can't live like this. I said I'd try it and I have. One room, no running water, an outhouse, kerosene, it's okay for a while but it's your dream, not mine. I'm sorry."

"I don't believe it. We're getting along fine and now you want to break up?" He glanced over at Sara's pale profile, set with a certainty he feared. He slid a hand onto her belly, sweaty under one of his tee-shirts, hoping that somehow touch could carry them back to a familiar ease.

"I don't want to break up," Sara said, grasping his hand. "I want to be with you, I just don't want to live here. I found a Putney rental that begins in September and I'm going to take it. You can move in with me if you want."

"Goddammit." Jamie drew his hand away. She'd been out searching for rentals without telling him, a betrayal as bitter as if she'd been cheating with men. "I want to live on my land." Didn't she understand what it meant to him to wake up every day under the shade of Gramp's huge maples, or at night to stand outside in a clearing he'd made by hand, peeing under the stars? What about the rhododendrons he'd planted, the lilacs and flowering quince? "I lived at your place all spring," he protested.

"That was your choice. You didn't have to."

"You have all the answers, don't you?" Jamie knew he was sliding toward the land of no return, he had to get back under control, but everything was leaking out, his voice clamped down into a duck quack so he wouldn't shriek. He slammed the barn-board wall behind Sara's head and his framed drawings rattled.

"Cut it out," Sara shouted, scrambling up out of bed. "What are you going to do next? Hit me like you hit Lindy?"

It was as though she was trying to force him over some edge so she could prove he was the asshole she always thought he was instead of hearing what he'd been telling her all along. How he'd learned from the Lindy thing, how he'd changed.

Jamie got up. "I'm out of here."

"Jamie!"

He pushed past, catching a glimpse of the anger on her face shifting to fear, pale legs under the tee-shirt and her sweaty hair wrapping her throat. He stomped on up to the Project, where he spent a bad night on gritty plywood wondering how the hell it had gone so sour. In the morning when he returned, half angry and half contrite, hoping they could make some sense from it all, Sara's stuff was gone from the cabin.

"I saw a loaded Subaru pull out of here fast," Mitchell said, standing in front of his tent with a mug of tea.

Mitchell couldn't help gloating, and for a moment Jamie hated him for that. Jamie got in his truck intent on finding Sara, but he didn't know where she'd gone. Back into the stranger's world of West Shelby, he supposed. Her rental wasn't starting until September; she must be at a friend's. Or maybe she had taken off, gone all the way to New York to blow off steam. He drove over the hill to West Shelby and cruised a few back roads, then gave up. He wasn't sure what he'd say if he found her. Better to let things lie until he knew his own heart better.

They left at three in the morning, Mitchell sheepish because Jamie had to wake him. A week earlier, Jamie had agreed to help

Mitchell move the boat to a cheaper mooring in another harbor and he kept his word. On the five-hour drive to Maine, neither of them mentioned the house or Sara; they both wanted this to be a regular outing. In silence, Jamie turned the fight over and over in his mind. Sometimes it looked like Sara was a terrific bitch; other times he knew he was an asshole. He gave up and let the roll of dark highway lull him to sleep while Mitchell drove.

When they reached the coast, the sweep of pointed firs jutting over rocky shoreline filled Jamie with an urgent and surprising longing—maybe he had made the wrong choice, opting for maple trees and pastures over the graceful utility of trawlers and lobster boats, the briny ocean smell, and that beautiful grey that shingles turn only in proximity to salt air.

In Devin Bay, seagulls complained overhead or sat on pilings, turning a cool yellow eye. A bell buoy tolled. The steep, low-tide ramp to the docks rattled underfoot. They rowed out to the mooring in the patched and shaky dinghy someone had lent Mitchell—"the dink," he called it. Hands on peeling thwarts, Jamie felt the coolness of the ocean drawn through wood. "There she is." Mitchell pointed.

The sloop was impressive—a sleek low hull, freshly painted, with a towering, varnished mast. You had to give Mitchell credit, as Mel said; he dreamed big. Once they clambered aboard Jamie was a bit surprised that Mitchell hadn't gotten further with it. The cabin was still rough, and although fifty feet sounded large, much of it was unusable; it really wasn't much bigger than a dog run for a family of five. It was easy to see why Corinne and the kids would go stir-crazy stuck on aboard.

They planned to motor out of the harbor and then sail in open water, but the boat's battery was dead. Mitchell had to row ashore, take the battery out of his car, and row back with it. It was ten o'clock before they got the old Perkins diesel rumbling. They putted out past moored sailboats, stinkpots, fishing craft, shingled houses tucked into the shoreline fir, piles of rocks marked by buoys. Morning clouds shredded thin, blue seeping through, a

perfect summer day in Maine. The angle of the sun just low
enough to skitter across the water. Seals lolled on a rockpile, as
though they'd been ordered up by a TV nature show.

They motored around a point, and left the harbor; out in the
open water the sea rose up in swells. Mitchell killed the engine and
raised the sails. They flapped madly, and then filled with a whoosh
as Mitchell pulled in line. The boat leaped forward. They flew
through swells so big the boat reared into the air, then slid down
the troughs like a toboggan. Jamie hand-over-handed it to the
bow and gripped the rail as the sea splashed up and the bow
dipped under water. He couldn't believe that they were sailing,
that Mitchell, who'd never skippered more than a rented Sunfish,
was pulling it off.

Jamie shouted into the thrilling roller coaster ride, and then he
felt the rail under his grip begin to give way. He grabbed a stay and
steadied himself. The fucking rail wasn't screwed down. Shaking
his head, he eased his way back to the aft deck and sat on a bench.
For an hour Mitchell stood at the wheel, intent on the horizon,
which was dotted with rockpiles and islands. The rigging and mast
creaked and squeaked, the ocean slapped at the hull, the pathetic
little dinghy leaped and skittered behind the boat. Jamie leaned
back, grinned into salty breezes. It was too good.

Gradually he became aware of the breeze lessening. The sails
fell slack and luffed gently. The boat slowed, then simply bobbed
up and down in what were still considerable swells.

"We could wait for the wind but we got too much to do today,"
Mitchell advised. "We better motor in. I guess we had our sail."

"It was a good one."

Mitchell lowered the sheet and turned the key and the Perkins
diesel rumbled to life. They plunged through the swells for twenty
minutes, spewing diesel fumes, yelling to each other over the
engine's noise, and then the Perkins quit.

"What the hell?" Mitchell exclaimed. He climbed down into
the engine compartment and came back up five minutes later,
looking green and gulping fresh air.

"I can't believe it," he said, shaking his head. "For the first time in my life I'm getting seasick. I can't stay down there. You want to take a look at it?"

"You're the one who took diesel mechanics in the service," Jamie objected.

"They don't teach you anything in the service."

Jamie climbed down into the stinking engine hole and stared at the block. It was pretty sickening down here with the swells and the close quarters. He fiddled with the injectors to no avail, then checked the stick in the gas tank. Empty.

"We're out of gas," he announced, climbing out of the hole.

"No." Mitchell lay stretched on deck. "Can't be."

"You crawl down there and check."

"No. No. I believe you. Oh Jesus."

They drifted.

"There's got to be some wind eventually," Mitchell said. "This is the fucking coast of Maine."

Jamie shrugged. You'd think so. It was funny how the ocean looked blue from the beach, but up close the water was greenish, divided into little hexagons of flecked foam, and full of litter: twigs, floating snags, a styrofoam coffee cup. A gull flew up and hovered, then veered off. An hour passed. Jamie noticed they were drawing closer to a dark, fir-lined island. Good-size breakers were forming a hundred yards offshore, and quieter water lay beyond them—evidence of a nasty reef. Jamie flashed on a Sunday afternoon TV memory—Australian lifeguard competitions on "Wide World of Sports," teams of brawny men mindlessly running down beaches, lugging rowboats into shark-infested surf.

"I don't suppose you'd have some kind of radio on board?" he asked.

"Nope."

" 'Course not."

Twenty more minutes. The tide—it had to be tide, since there wasn't a breath of wind—was pulling them toward the reef. Jamie began to figure his chances. He was a strong swimmer, but even if he made it over the breakers without getting too banged up, there was the temperature of the water to consider, and the fact that once ashore he'd be soaked. Exposure was a real threat. It seemed too stupid to imagine drowning or freezing to death out here under marching blue clouds (there must be wind somewhere, up there in the ionosphere or whatever) and riding the beautiful swells. Definitely, he'd made the right choice. Maple trees, pastures. If he could only get back there . . .

"There's a lobster boat," Mitchell said, gazing through binoculars.

"Let me see." About a mile away, a little white square-housed lobster boat bobbed with its stern to them. "You got something to signal with?"

"Airhorn." Mitchell ducked into the cabin and came up with a horn attached to a canister of compressed air. He pushed the button and it made a sad little bleat like a sick lamb: Bleaaaa. Bleeaaaaaaa. It was out of air.

"Well that ought to get them over here fast," Mitchell said, tossing the airhorn down. He whistled through his teeth, shouted "Hey!"

"Why don't I throw the anchor?" Jamie suggested. "We'll just sit it out here until the wind comes up and we can sail off."

"Oh, don't do that," Mitchell said.

"Why not?"

"I just don't want to do that."

"Then what?"

"Look," Mitchell rallied. "I'm going to get in the dink and see if I can pull her around that reef."

"You got a life jacket, Mitch?"

"Nope."

"'Course not."

Mitchell pulled the dinghy alongside and gingerly lowered himself into the pitching little boat while Jamie held the painter, then Jamie hauled the dinghy up to the bow. Jamie threw Mitchell the sloop's bow line, which Mitchell tied to the pathetic dinghy's stern. He started rowing. There were ten tons of lead in the keel to keep the boat upright, and as hard as Mitchell rowed, they made no progress. Jamie feared the sailboat might just yank off the dinghy's stern. They were close enough to the reef now to hear the breakers booming.

"I'd sure hate to lose my boat," Mitchell shouted.

"Forget the fucking boat. What about us?"

"I don't know about you, but I don't figure I'm worth too much right now."

"Well that's true."

"Knew I could count on you," Mitchell said.

"But what about me?" Jamie met his cousin's pale eyes, the crazy sick grin, and he shook his head.

In the distance, the lobster boat picked up its traps and putted off.

Jamie sighed.

Smash—boom.

And then, as suddenly as it had diminished, the wind picked up. Mitchell rowed himself back to the stern and climbed aboard. They raised the flapping sails, winched and cleated, and Mitchell grabbed the wheel. They were sailing again. They managed to just slide by the tip of the island, close enough to see the surf smashing, and they were free, the boat running up the swells and gliding back down like a surfer, and they were laughing, slapping each other's back, as the island grew small behind them.

"Jeez, that was close. I didn't think we were going to make it," Jamie said.

"I didn't either."

Riiiip. They both froze at the sound of pants splitting, pants for some giant, the biggest pair of pants you can imagine, about the size of a sloop's sail. The patched and mildewed canvas had torn from mast tip to boom.

"I don't believe it," Jamie said.

"I think I'll just go down into one of the bunks and curl up and die," Mitchell said.

"I'll throw the anchor and we can just wait to be rescued," Jamie offered.

"Oh, don't do that."

"Why not?"

"Just don't."

Jamie threw up his hands. They drifted again. Eventually they realized the tide was carrying them toward the mainland. Slowly they drifted across open water and then into a reach as they marked the distant progress of fishing boats, tankers, a ferry. They lay on deck eating the only food they'd had since seven A.M., a bag of chips, wondering where they'd end up, wishing they had some cookies, or at least water.

As if hauled by a giant fishline, the boat cruised in on the tide, swept past a stone jetty, silent houses and docks. They entered a harbor—not the one they'd intended, but the one from which Mitchell had bought the boat three months ago.

A hundred yards from the docks Mitchell leaned off the bow and caught the ball of an empty mooring. "I'll row the dink in," he said. "If anyone gives you any trouble about using their mooring, explain the problem."

"Why can't we drop anchor here?"

Mitchell looked sheepish. "No anchor line."

Jamie just shook his head. Mitchell removed the battery and lowered it into the dinghy. He'd have to row to the dock, hitch twenty-three miles down the coast with a battery, before he'd be back with the car. Jamie stretched out and went to sleep. When he woke Mitchell hadn't yet returned. The sky had clouded over and Jamie was cold. He surveyed the scene—tattered sail, engine out of gas, unfinished cabin, sleek, fresh-painted hull, varnished spar. A boat without a radio or life jackets or radar or an air horn that worked. And all around them the heartbreaking beauty of a Maine coast town: shingled houses, docks, boats lolling on moorings, the hollow toll of a bell buoy.

There it was, the perfect image of Mitchell's strivings. His breadth of ambition and bravery and foolhardiness. He'd nearly drowned them both out of ignorance and laziness, yet he'd taken Jamie for an incredible ride that Jamie didn't regret for an instant. Mitchell had tried to remake himself. He just hadn't tried hard enough or well enough, Jamie wasn't sure which. His own dreams were so much smaller and more manageable: hiking the Grand

Canyon or the Long Trail, living on his land, being with Sara, having some kids.

If Sara would even have him anymore. He remembered a line his former boss said one day after the boss's wife had left him: "Live like a bachelor, stay a bachelor." And how Gram, after Gramp died, surprised everyone with her bitterness and her complaint that Gramp always did whatever it was he wanted and that she never got to do anything. She'd always wanted to travel, but it was he who went to Honduras. With Lindy, too, Jamie'd had everything his way; he was ten years older and she didn't have any opinions. They lived in the cabin and she painted houses alongside him in the summers, until she grew up enough to rebel and want her independence, but not enough to go after it any way except by drinking and screwing around. Jamie knew he'd have to bend for Sara, learn from his mistakes.

On the way back to Shelby Mitchell and Jamie were giddy with exhaustion and relief. Over and over they recounted their adventure, hitting the high points, imitating the airhorn that sounded like a sick sheep, joking about the anchor.

"I don't suppose there's any chance I could convince you not to repeat this story, is there?" Mitchell asked, wolfing a Big Mac.

Jamie licked catsup from the side of his palm. "Ha. Not a chance in the world."

Later, Jamie decided his trip with Mitchell was like a divorced couple spending a sexy night together. It was good but too late; something had already changed between them.

In September, Jamie moved into Sara's Putney rental and tried to contain his bitterness about not living on his land. At least he was there every day, finishing the Project. When the walls were sheetrocked and painted white, he brought Sara over to see it.

"It looks great," she said. "I can't believe it's the same place. It's almost a shame to sell it."

"I don't want to sell it. Not if you'll live here with me."

He turned away to the new indoor staircase, afraid to see Sara's face if she was going to say no. "There's no electricity yet, but there's running water, and lots of rooms and white walls." That's what she'd said she'd wanted, long ago, on one of their first dates, when he'd asked what was at the end of her rainbow, and she'd surprised him with the simplicity of her answer: her own house with lots of white walls.

"How can you afford not to sell it?" Sara asked, fingering the new pine trim around the windows.

"I can't afford to sell it if you'll live here. Will you?"

Sara put her arms around Jamie's waist and leaned her head against his back. He felt the imprint of her cheek and held his breath. Far down the hill the top of one maple flamed with early color.

Jamie didn't exhale until Sara said, "I will."

Mitchell found his own rental in East Putney, a little frame house covered in asphalt shingles patterned with brick. The ceilings were so low Jamie had to duck. "Easier to heat," Mitchell said, putting a good spin on it. "Warm it with a candle, fart and smell it for a week." Mitchell took a job working at the fancy window-building shop in West Shelby, a place where they made huge installments with fanlights for rich people in Connecticut and New York. He had to keep the job now that he paid rent. He was still struggling to sell the boat and recoup some of the twelve thousand he'd already paid. When Mitchell got a phone he put an ad in *Wooden Boat* magazine, and some guy gave him a check. Mitchell ran out and bought a TV, a VCR, and put a down payment on another car (his Mitsubishi had been reclaimed by Vermont National Bank). And then the check bounced.

Mitchell just gave up. He returned the boat to the guy who had sold it to him, and the bastard didn't even give him a penny back, not for the paint job or the galley, just kept Mitchell's $12,000 and put it up for sale again.

Jamie occasionally went to visit Mitchell over at the rental that winter. He didn't go often because he was working so hard to finish the house for Sara while living in her rental. Sara's New York friends came to visit often. Taking them cross-country skiing on weekends and being with Sara didn't leave him much time to visit. For a while, Mitchell talked about trying to buy the little asphalt-shingled house. In the spring he put in an enormous garden. When Jamie dropped by to visit in June, the peas hung down in the dirt, unpicked. Mitchell hadn't bothered to stake them. Jamie imagined the scenario—Mitchell's sudden enthusiasm for gardening petering out. It wasn't a dream anyway; he was just spinning his wheels.

Sara said, "You did the best thing for him. Now he's buckling down, holding a job for the first time. You've helped him learn responsibility."

It was true and not true. Something was lost in Mitchell that Jamie had always loved, something Sara couldn't know.

One day Jamie drove past Mitchell's shop at lunchtime and saw him eating at a picnic table with other workers, hunkered over his sandwich. Years ago, when Jamie was courting a Putney girl, he used to see a bent-backed man trudging up the hill from the Putney paper mill every evening, head down, lunch box in hand, and every time Jamie saw the poor old fucker he wanted to weep. Something about Mitchell in the worker's lot made him feel the same way.

Jamie was going to stop, or at least honk, but he didn't. Mitchell's hair was shining in the summer sun and it was the only thing about him anymore that glistened.

THE VIEW FROM
THE END OF THE
WORLD

[Donna, 1993]

THE WEEK BEFORE Donna's thirty-fourth birthday, Claude asked her to come with him to "look at heavy equipment," then drove to a livestock auction barn in Massachusetts and offered Donna any horse she liked. Gripping Claude's hand, Donna bid highest on a little grey mare, only fifteen hands, with the compact build and delicate dished face of an Arabian, though she was a grade horse, unpedigreed.

"She's a little small," Claude said. "You sure?"

But Donna didn't want a big horse. It had been twenty years since she'd ridden and she was afraid to fall from too high off the ground. After so much time, she was afraid that she might not have the courage to ride at all.

The mare, whom she named Jasmine for the princess in the Aladdin movie, had plenty of spunk. The first week, Donna came home each afternoon from her job at Claude's shop and in the waning October light worked her mare in circles through her neighbors' cut hayfields and stubbled fields stripped of corn. The mare pulled against the bit, eager to run, but Donna held her to a quick trot, the choppy stride of a short-backed horse. It would take some work to bring her back to a slower, more comfortable gait. Donna was cautious, a little tremor of fear in her chest when the mare half-reared and spun at the flap of a plastic bag blowing across the grass. It had been a long time.

After cooling the mare, she curried and brushed her, reacquainting herself with the roundness of a hoof in her palm while she rested the delicate knee against her thigh and scraped out dirt, the mystery of how a horse's leg could be thinner than her own yet carry so much bulk, the oily richness of leather tack, the gratifying way the mare lowered her head while Donna brushed her face. Leaning into the familiar pungency of horseflesh, she inhaled an odor that carried with it a hint of something she'd lost.

She didn't even know she was grinning when she went inside to face a house full of hungry kids.

On a cold and overcast Saturday, she tacked up and headed out for a trail ride. It was the first time she'd ridden alone in her life. She'd always had a sister to go with and it made her nervous to go on her own. She followed a paved road up from the village, hooking on to the trails cut into the Boys' Home forest with their poignant little powwow circles, peeled log benches, and stacks of hand-sawn firewood, and then on to the old logging roads above Gramp's land where she'd ridden as a girl.

The leaves were mostly off the trees already but crisp on the forest floor, still bright before the November rains rotted and blackened them. A luminous carpet of dun and rust that rasped like the sandpaper blocks from grade school music, so loud she couldn't have heard a companion speak if she'd had one. The dead leaves lit the forest floor, made every beech and maple and birch trunk stand out as distinct as an etching.

The ferns had yellowed and curled, decayed to brown. Donna wished she'd had the mare in summer, when the forest was full of vast spreads of bracken ferns with the occasional rarer Boston. She loved the way the greeny sweep of ferns was sometimes hit by a tiny breeze and only one out of the whole expanse would spin and wave as if possessed, like a Shaker at a worship service, the first to feel abandon.

Over the years she'd spent her outdoor time perfecting her perennial gardens or hanging laundry or sitting by her pool. Oh, once a summer she and Sally might take the kids for a hike up Mount Monadnock or Mount Ascutney, but that was mostly about urging the kids on, ignoring their whining, applauding their scrambles up the rocks. Donna hadn't really spent time in the woods for years. Not since she was little, when she and Mitchell played house in the mossy room in Masonville—she winced at the thought of Mitchell, who hadn't spoken to her for over a year—or when she rode with her sisters over hell and gone. Being in the woods like this was strange now. Half of her alert to the jumpy little mare beneath her, half of her attentive to her past.

The landscape was familiar, but familiar in the way of things you didn't know you had forgotten, a grove of beech with the smooth grey skin of elephants, the same crumbling roof of an old hunting camp that had been built without a foundation and rotted inch by inch into the ground; the rusting gas can from a long-ago logger who'd given up, stumps that were mossy and broken down that she recalled as topped by flat pale circles, the chainsaw's mark.

What wasn't familiar was how much the forest had filled in. Some trees had fallen, of course, but there were many more new ones: birches in silvery clumps and the feathery dark green of hemlock where she remembered brush. But the shape of the old roads, their maze of cutoffs and turns, the crazy runs of stone walls securing nothing, she knew instinctively, like a map tattooed on the back of her brain.

When the ground was smooth enough, Donna trotted the mare, but the leaves obscured the rocks and ledge that could trip them or slip under iron-shod hooves. The mare flared her nostrils, champed on the bit, spewing foam, tossed her head, and pranced.

The fear kept nudging up at Donna like an insistent dog that she tried to swat away. What if she fell here all alone? No one would know. She could break her neck and lie here rotting. Where had the fear come from? She'd never been afraid as a girl. And it was ruining everything. Besides, horses were sensitive and picked up on your every mood. She couldn't let Jasmine feel her fright or the mare would lose confidence in her. Concentrate on the landscape, she ordered herself.

They crossed a new embankment created by generations of beavers, ponds on each side, and across the murky water a green heron standing on one foot. Moose country these days. They emerged from a bower of brush into the lower part of the old orchards. The apple trees with their odd right-angle branches were bare except for a sparse display of shriveled clinging fruit. The leftover apples glowed red against the brittle bare branches like Christmas tree bulbs. Donna's nose ran from the cold.

Up through the orchard she let Jasmine canter on the grassy swale between trees, standing up in the stirrups to peer ahead for woodchuck holes and to hold the eager mare back, her biceps sore at the effort. Jasmine tossed her head in annoyance at Donna's tight grip, and Donna decided she'd have to get her a tie-down if she didn't want to end up with a broken nose.

She saw the flock of crows rise up in a great black flapping before she could think, before she could feel the mare jump sideways, much less respond, and then Donna hit the ground with a familiar whump that left her gasping. She looked up at the sky with that old curiosity, how did I get here? Jasmine stood over her; the reins were still in Donna's hands. Shit. Her back was tweaked, her hip sore, but her fingers and toes moved. Gingerly she got up. At least she'd held onto the reins. It would've been a long walk home if she hadn't.

She mounted and slowly they walked off, both of them blowing, neither of them fit. Only then Donna tasted the adrenalin, that queasy seep of chemical fear on her tongue.

So she fell. Got dumped. Thrown. It wasn't a big deal. You had to fall to ride. Okay. Nobody had to know.

She cut through an opening in the fenceline brush and up onto the broad stretch of gravel that a long-gone landowner had put in as a runway for his Cessna so he could commute to Boston. The tattered windsock hung limp above apple trees. Donna walked the mare the full length of the abandoned runway, letting her rest, catching her own breath.

At the end of the strip the land fell away like the end of the world. Below, she could see the Boys' Home, which was now a Girls' Home too, the ugly expanse of the new gymnasium like the flat roof of a shopping plaza, the old Victorian buildings replaced by new modular constructions. Beyond them, the spire of the village church, the miniature roof of the house she had worked on with Tim and lived in with Claude, and across the ribbon of river, the hills rising up in New Hampshire to match their mirror images in Vermont. New houses dotted the hillsides, farm fields turned to lawn. On the flats in Shelby there were new self-storage units and outside Walpole a strip plaza was growing, but you couldn't see them from here. It was still a spectacular view.

Then, as though someone had pulled the string on a louvered shade, the sky darkened. A gloomy black mass rushed down from the north. The old windsock flapped wildly. The mare's mane lifted in the sharp breeze and they were enveloped in a sudden squall of snow. The ground hissed where the flakes hit bare dirt. A whiteout. The mare stomped nervously as the flakes melted on her hot skin, the reins dark in Donna's bare red hands. The apple trees, dried goldenrod, and open milkweed pods with their half-blown silk were immediately camouflaged by clinging white. The world became colorless, stripped of its familiarity, strange.

An old panic gripped Donna. She was lost in a place she knew and didn't know. Disoriented by the obscured view, the blanketing white. As though someone had taken her up in an airplane to point out her home far below, only she knew it wasn't her home, never had been, never would be. She gasped as her breath blew out of her lungs.

And then it was over, as fast as it had begun, only a late fall snow shower that dumped its insignificant load and moved on. The clouds broke apart. The world regained its familiar shape. A beam of sun shot down from the sky like God's word. The little mare fidgeted, eager to move on.

Donna turned Jasmine to face the stretch of gorse-covered

runway. It wasn't something she planned, just an impulse. She dug in her heels. The mare shot forward, streaked low, flattened into a wind that felt as though it might lift them both. A crazy, un-expected happiness coursed through Donna, like coming home from sledding all day with pink cheeks and frozen hands. She hung on, thrilled, the stinging wind on her snow-wet cheeks like a slap that would wake her from a life-long dream.

SAILING

[Maine, 1994]

MITCHELL GOT UP to make another cup of tea. He'd just been completely humiliated by Carver and Eli on the Super Nintendo. He was Star Fox the flight leader, given the task of infiltrating enemy ships and destroying their cores with his Sonic Nuco II blasting missile. He attempted to reach the mother of all ships, but his comrades in arms failed to alert him to the fact that there were thousands of baby ships in the way, all with the fire-power of the Starship Enterprise. One of his electronic comrades, Slippy, went smoking by and a message appeared on Mitchell's screen: "Help, Fox! Help! There's a bogey on my tail!" Mitchell tried, he really tried, but he just couldn't hit the bastard and Slippy died. Another crewmate, Falco, flashed a message as Slippy's ship erupted into a ball of flame: "Oh, way to go Fox, way to go." Then his face came on the screen and he scowled at Mitchell.

At this point, Mitchell's little communication screen started flashing messages from his remaining flight companions: "What's wrong Fox? Bad move, Fox. Where are you going, Fox? No, Fox, NO! I think we should turn back, Fox. We need a new leader. Fox is an asshole. Fuck Fox, let's get out of here!" Though the last few didn't appear on the screen, Mitchell knew what his men were thinking.

The whole business was very unnerving, especially with Carver and Eli sitting right behind him, guffawing and pointing, interjecting comments such as "You're so stupid, Dad. Even a moron could've killed that one." And then the chant: "Dad's going to die, Dad's going to die." The worst part was watching the boys do everything they told him a moron could do and then some.

When Mitchell was at the helm it was like he was sitting in a bubble with everything in the universe heading for him at light speed. He killed one enemy ship, only to find it was the type that blew up in your face, taking you with it on the way out. It was probably a godsend he did die, because with all that firepower coming for him at warp speed he might've had a heart attack if it had gone on much longer. He walked away from the machine with eyes agog and hands shaking. A dangerous game, boy, a dangerous game.

"Isn't it time to go pick them up?" Corinne asked from the couch, where she lay on her back with knees up, reading.

Mitchell glanced at the wall clock. "Must be." But instead of rushing off, he sat down beside Corinne and ran a finger along the smooth inverted V of her bent leg, bare above her shorts. He wanted to put his face against the familiar sleekness of fine blond hairs and hide there. Corinne put down the book she was reading and patted his hand. "Don't worry," she said. "It'll go fine."

It was only a short spin across the bay from the island; they could have taken the ferry, but Mitchell owned the runabout and this was his weekend to play professional seaman hero. Captain Mitch. Carver wanted to come so Mitchell let him. It was a mistake, of course, because there were seven of them waiting on the beach. Thank god Mel's kids were off with their mother and Nancy's Rob had to work this weekend or there would have been ten. Mitchell already had to make two trips, but the truth was he needed the moral support.

Carver nagged, "Let me drive, Dad," until Mitchell surrendered the slick wooden wheel of the runabout, and he was cheered by the sight of Carver's silly grin under the bill of his Red Sox cap, spray baptizing his new teenage pimples. The old wooden motorboat pounded the small chop. Evening light cut an angle over the mainland, tinged the shoreline rocks with seaweed gloss, silhouetted spruce tops. It was so fucking picturesque Mitchell wished he hadn't sold his camera. And it was home. He'd never been one for sandy Cape Cod beaches, never wanted to go in that warm water, swim where sharks might reside. Better to skitter across the cold surface like a skipped stone, seeing how many hops he could make before sinking.

Carver throttled back expertly and slid her into the town dock. The spectacle of his family standing on gull-spattered boards, with their clam rolls and backpacks and grinning faces, was enough to churn Mitchell's stomach. Because as much as he wanted them here, he didn't. He needed them to see his new life and he was scared to death they could steal it from him just by their presence, because they knew what nobody on his island knew: who he'd been before.

This is how it happened.

He was working in the wood shop in Shelby, living in that low-ceilinged rental house. It was a lousy job. They had all kinds of rules, like you couldn't talk about anything that wasn't work related or you'd get cited, supposedly for safety, but they were pushing so hard the foreman made them take the guards off the saws to speed things up. And the boss, who'd moved up from Connecticut a few years ago because "the values are so much better in Vermont" would come by with his sailboard tied to his Land Rover, bragging to his peons that he was heading over to Lake Winnepesaukee to catch some breezes. And then Mitchell cut the tips of three fingers off with the dado.

That put him out on workman's comp for three months and when the screaming pain subsided enough that he could think, he realized here was his chance. If it wasn't his fingertips, it would have been his balls they'd chop off sooner or later, better to go while he was still largely intact. The settlement was three thousand, one per digit; he would've got more if he'd taken them down to the knuckle, but three was enough for Maine.

He and Corinne made a deal. Mitchell would go up and get a

job and find a house to rent, and when everything was in order, she'd come up with the kids and "give it a try," whatever that meant. Right away, Mitchell found work in a boat shop on the island repairing diesels for a ponytailed old Peace Corps veteran named Duke who ran a charter schooner business in the summer. He rented a decent little shingled Cape. Corinne joined him after a month. Just as he'd figured, once they got back to Vermont Judy Beal had made herself scarce, and Corinne had to face up to the fact that it wasn't Maine or Shelby, it was just them. Nobody liked them, period. And that was the funniest part of it. Because once they got here on the island, everyone liked them a lot.

They were invited to potlucks and parties; Corinne got involved with the school and took dance classes. When Mitchell's stubs healed fully, he played the guitar again with two other guys, a hit at parties. Everyone treated them like they were normal. The islanders, united by their resentment of summer people but hungry for fresh blood in the winter, made the mistake of seeing them as hip, cool people with beautiful kids instead of a couple of lowlife losers living on a Vermont dung heap.

Mitchell worked his butt off at the boat shop. When his boss, Duke, started to praise him, Mitchell warned him off.

"I got a history," Mitchell said.

"What do you mean?" Duke hunkered down beside the engine hatch of the Egg Harbor Mitchell was working on. All Mitchell could see above the hatch rim were Duke's bent hairy knees in cutoffs, the tips of his worn Weejuns.

"You didn't murder anyone, did you?" Duke asked, like it was all a joke.

"No," Mitchell said, determined to be honest for once, "I mean I got a pattern. I do okay at a place for a while and then I walk."

"Well, let's see if we can work around that. I want you here." The hairy knees unfolded, the Weejuns withdrew.

Mitchell was so grateful he was willing to make Duke into the perfect daddy and lie down at his feet every night like a goddamn golden retriever. He would've brought Duke his slippers in his teeth, but, as he should've known, after a while Duke's slippers started tasting like they might have stepped in shit. Duke worked Mitchell a lot of overtime without pay. When Mitchell finally mentioned it, something you shouldn't have to do, Duke cut Mitchell a deal. He'd pay it off in trade, a trip on the schooner with all the fixings—lobster dinner, crew service—for Mitchell and whomever he wanted to invite.

Okay, Duke could be a jerk, calling him up on weekends to fix his kid's car. But a year had gone by and Mitchell was still there, showing up every morning. Lately Duke had been asking Mitchell to help him move sailboats from one cove to another for summer people. He was talking about bigger sails, bringing a sloop from Cape Cod up here, and even a trip to the Dominican Republic this winter. Mitchell couldn't complain.

"Jesum Crow, Mitchie," Jamie shouted, putting on the old Vermont farmer voice, "where'd you find this antique beauty?" Raving about the wooden runabout that Mitchell had picked up for nearly nothing, made some repairs on, and refinished. Jamie was crazy for anything old and wooden and Mitchell expanded with his cousin's envy.

Behind Jamie, Sara stood big-bellied pregnant. No love lost there, but Mitchell didn't want to do anything that would alienate Jamie, and Sara was part of the package. Sally's girls looked awed by Carver's marine knowhow; Mel just awed to be out of Vermont, probably never seen the ocean before. Sally, ripe as summer melons in her tank top, and Nancy, tawny and tanned in white, shuffled coolers and paper sacks full of goodies on the dock.

It was a slow chug back in the boat with the first load, slapping through the ferry wake, everybody oohing and ahhing, and just for a moment Mitchell felt his heart open like the spread of sea stretching beyond the islands, that clear vista you never got in the cramped little hills back home.

❁

Tents were staked in the yard. Upstairs Emily indulged her younger girl cousins in a nail polish orgy. Carver and Eli hunkered over the Nintendo, easily defeating Mel; bubbling space noises competed with the lusty pleading of Eric Clapton's "Layla."

Sipping a boring glass of non-alcoholic sparkling cider, Sara wandered between the kitchen, where Sally, Nancy, and Corinne gossiped about Shelby people she didn't know, and the living room, where Jamie and Mitchell gabbed by the CD player. No one had set out to exclude her, but that's how she felt. Even if she weren't pregnant and able to drink, she doubted she'd know how to be here. She sidled up to Jamie and waited for a lull in the conversation.

"Hey, old man," Mitchell razzed. "I hear tell if you're losing your hair in front, around the temples, it means you're a great thinker. And if you're losing it in the back it means you're good in bed. But if you're losing it in front and back, it means you *think* you're good in bed. Where's that put you?"

Jamie rubbed his growing forehead and thinning skull cap. "It's a sad thing to realize my kid will never know me in my true glory."

Sara had never known him in his full glory either.

"Of course, being young and virile with a full head of hair," Mitchell added, "I wouldn't know much about it." He ran a hand through his own blond thatch.

"And I heard that vasectomy took all the fun out of it," Jamie countered.

"Ooh, it hurt, I'll admit that. I pissed blood for days."

Sara nudged Jamie's arm. "Listen. I'm tired. It's late. I want to go to bed now."

"Go ahead," Jamie suggested. "I'll be out in a little while."

Sara frowned. "Won't you come with me?"

"Sara, it's only nine-thirty. You go on. I'll be out in a while."

Of course he wouldn't. He'd party all night, and it wasn't fair to expect him not to. Still. Sara bit her chapped lips. A woman at the post office insisted chapped lips meant she was carrying a boy. But Sara wanted a girl. Stupid tears filled her eyes. She blinked angrily.

Mitchell glanced at Jamie. "Uh-oh. You got to watch out for those pregnancy hormones."

"Scary stuff," Jamie agreed, laying an arm over Sara's shoulder. She shrugged it away in annoyance.

"I got to tell you, Jamie boy," Mitchell said, cackling like an idiot, "it does my heart good to think of you in that birthing room."

Jamie had let everyone know that he wasn't eager to encounter the mystery of life up close, but Sara had let him know he better be by her side when the time came.

"You ought to talk," Sara turned on Mitchell. "I heard when Eli was born you got so involved in the book you were reading you forgot to coach Corinne."

Mitchell shrugged. "Hey, it was a good book. Anyway, being mad at me helped her focus. She went through the whole thing chanting 'Son of a bitch, Fucking bastard.' She didn't even need Lamaze."

Sara gave up in defeat.

❀

"So, Mitchy," Jamie said, watching Sara pilot her pregnant bulk toward the staircase that led to the bathroom, refusing to let her mood dampen his evening. "Winter pretty bad up here?"

"Oh, it's brutal. Every time you walk outside it's like you get hit in the face with a wet towel. They got this ice fog here, it's wicked. 'Course I can't complain too much, because nobody listens. They seem to think it's just as cold for them."

Jamie laughed.

"The thing of it is," Mitchell continued, "I can't know how anybody else experiences anything, I can only know what I feel, so it's safe to assume that nobody else feels anything as deeply as I do. But if I go around saying this, everyone gets an attitude and quits listening, so I can't complain. But it's cold, Jamie boy, believe me."

❀

Nancy cracked another ice tray and filled the red plastic cups lined up on the wet counter, then poured several inches of rum into each. She divided a liter of Coke between the glasses. She always played bartender at these gatherings and was famous for making strong ones.

Sally leaned on the counter, scrutinizing the kitchen with its hanging pots and butcher block counter, its cheery curtains Corinne had sewed. "It's really nice," Sally said with surprise. "They're keeping it up. I could live in a place like this. Not here, of course. I mean it's pretty on the island, but I'd never want to live far away from Shelby."

"Me neither," Nancy agreed.

"Or away from you guys." Sally dragged a soggy corn chip through a coke puddle. "You know, I feel guilty. I do. I just wish Donna could be here with us. I wish they'd make up so we could all be a family. It isn't right. If Mitchell could just get over it, we could all be here together."

All of us, Nancy reflected. As if Donna's presence would complete the picture. All of us that are left would be more like it. No one mentioned Marsha or Mom or even Michelle anymore. No one wanted to revisit those losses. And Dad didn't count.

"It's not just making up," Nancy said, wiping the counter with a sponge, sweeping away the sodden corn chip, "Donna wants Mitchell to see Dad and he won't. He won't go through the motions. I don't know why she wants to force him."

"You got to forgive sometime," Sally insisted. She lowered her voice. "Mitchell's just being a dink."

Nancy watched Sara come down from the bathroom and head out the door with that sway-backed pregnant swagger; a prickle of jealousy shamed her. What she remembered, what she missed most, was the feel of a baby falling asleep on her while rocking.

"Ocking" Michelle had called it when she was two. When the squirming stopped and lids closed, spiky lashes resting on curved baby cheek, arms falling limp, breathing steadied. Rocking, hypnotized by the damp breath against her chest and the hot head beneath her lips, the sweet heft and heat and moisture, astonished by that trick she'd played again with the simple fact of her body—making a baby believe she had safety to offer, even when it turned out to be a lie.

Rob was willing, he could be tested to see if he carried that gene, one in ten thousand chances, what did that add up to with two different men? But there were so many other things that could happen. She hadn't thought of them fourteen years ago, but now she knew the way the chances could work against you, how you could be the statistic, the one whose baby doesn't wake in the night, who chokes on a slice of hot dog, who carries a recipe for destruction in her genes.

Everybody managed to live as though nothing could ever happen, as though death weren't waiting around each slippery wet corner. Even her brother and sisters, who'd known car crash and cancer and the slash of the belt and a bad spin of genetic roulette, all of them going on in their attempts to wrest some little bit of good times, some crazy hope when they ought to know better. She was lucky enough to have Rob. Was she supposed to wager on that seed and egg game of chance that could leave her weeping or simply laughing at wobbly first steps?

Nancy exhaled sharply, picked up her red drink cup, and gazed into melting ice. She didn't have control over any of it, so shouldn't she just take the ride? In the end, what were her options?

❀

Sara rolled onto her side, hating that she couldn't sleep on her belly as she preferred. Your left side, the books said, something about squashing an artery. The music blared from the open windows into her tent: the Dead now, as if they were all still kids. And

under it the repetitive chirr of crickets. She practiced deep breathing, trying to relax. Sally had gone on about how easy her preg-
nancies had been. Her doctor said she was made for having babies.
Two hours labor and ta da, they slid right out. Sara knew she
wouldn't be so lucky. Nothing came easily to her.

She put one hand on her belly, imagining the small life that
loomed so large under stretched skin. "It's just you and me baby,"
she whispered. She resented Jamie for letting her come to bed
alone, and knew it was stupid. He hardly ever saw Mitchell anymore. Or even Nancy, now that he no longer lived on the road. It
was selfish to feel that giving a big part of himself to them meant
Jamie wouldn't have anything left for her. Did such meager gen-
erosity mean she would be a lousy mother? Sighing, Sara pulled
her knees up, trying to take some of the strain off her lower back,
and wished she'd brought a foam mattress instead of this miserable camping pad.

Through the zipped screen of the tent Sara watched a distant
set of headlights bounce off the spruce at the end of the driveway,
and then the light erasing itself as the car moved toward its own
reflected beams. It vanished down the road. Like her own past life,
erasing itself up to this moment. How had it happened that she
was lying in a tent on an island in Maine, with a little island afloat
within her? This wasn't the family she had been born to, or even
the one she might have chosen, but it was the one that had happened to her.

Sara snuggled into the sleeping bag. The night was growing
chill. She had to get up to pee again but sleep was pulling her
under, a sweet sinking. It was just a matter of surrender, of
giving in.

❖

Mitchell woke to a hangover and the hope that it was ungodly
early, before dawn, and the greyness out there wasn't an overcast
sky. The red printout on the digital clock flashed eight-forty-
seven. No such luck. He pulled back the curtain to see drizzle

wetting the pane and not a stir in the spruce tops. Shit. He wanted to present them with a sail-snapping, ship-heeling, roller coaster of a ride, and instead it was windless and raining.

Downstairs the clank of a cast iron skillet and voices: Carver tormenting Eli, somebody whining about their tent leaking. Jamie's booming laugh. Mitchell wanted to roll over and go back to sleep, but Duke was expecting the whole lot of them at eleven and Mitchell at ten to help ready the boat and bring it around to the marina. All those weeks of overtime for a slow putt on auxiliary in the rain. Some show. What a stupid idea, trying to impress them with how far he'd come. He might as well have invited Dad along to make his failure complete. Mitchell buried his aching head in his pillow and groaned.

❁

Jamie helped Mitchell lift three coolers of lobsters onto the rumbling boat. Inside their styrofoam prisons, the lobsters heaved and scrabbled, pegged and banded claws waving, living sacrifices to a luxury ride.

"Fucking rain," Mitchell muttered.

"Hey, Mitch," Jamie said. "This is the real Maine experience. That's what we came for." It wasn't truly raining, just a drizzle, hardly more than a mist. Jamie liked the way it softened all the edges, smeared distinctions. That could be the island ferry looming across the bay, or the ghost of the Titanic.

Jamie stepped aboard and felt that lovely yielding, the boat rocking gently with his weight. The Windward was an antique double-masted schooner, almost beautiful enough to make Jamie want to leave the hill and live another life. She sported sleek lines, polished brightwork, dizzying tall spars—a showpiece.

Jamie deposited the lobster coolers in the galley, where framed yachting prints hung beside an ornate brass barometer—a galley as elegant as a captain's stateroom. Duke's wife Connie looked up from hoisting stainless steel kettles onto the stove. She smiled: friendly blue eyes above a lantern jaw, sinewy legs in shorts despite the damp weather.

"Need any help?" Jamie offered.

"Nope. Just be a guest," Connie said.

Up on deck, Duke was passing out yellow rain slickers. Sara laughed at her inability to snap her rain jacket closed over her big belly and traded Jamie for his extra large. Eli and Sally's girls glowed brilliant and bulky in life jackets, despite their protestations. All that radiance against the monochrome mist, as if here, every human was a beacon.

When they'd all found some damp perch on bulwarks and teak benches, Mitchell and Duke cast off. Five minutes away from shore, the kids surged over the boat like ants on a campfire log. "Hey Dad?" Eli yelled. "Do we have to eat lobster?"

"Smack that brother of yours for me," Jamie told Emily.

"We brought hot dogs for him," Emily said with a sigh.

Jamie wanted to absorb all of it, take it home with him: the moored boats spinning, bell buoys ringing like a distant school bell, birch lining the coves, colonial houses with their old sheep pastures mowed into lawns. Oak, spruce, and birch scabbed with lichen and all one height, as though the wind had sheared them to streamline the island itself into a bristling, woody ship. And here on the water the quilted diamonds of spume flecks trailing behind.

It was hard to believe they were Mitchell's guests on this rich man's tour. Jamie watched his cousin move quickly about the boat, intent on Duke's orders. It wasn't the same as Mitchell owning his own boat, but not bad. Not bad at all. Jamie felt an odd lifting in his chest, a lifelong worry for his cousin easing, enough to wet his eyes. Maybe men got weird hormones too when their wives were pregnant. He slid closer to Sara, rubbed damp slicker shoulders, bumped gently against her to feel her bump back.

He was losing them all to their own lives. Not losing, but the lines between them were stretched in so many directions, with Gramp's land no longer the hub of some great spinning mandala. What made him think they'd stay together just because Shelby had always been the center for him? It was better this way—Sally with Mel, Mitchell in Maine, Donna prospering with Claude, Nancy married to Rob who, even if he didn't like to share her with the family, took her down to Boston to museums and concerts and Red Sox games. Each of them seeking their own sweet home.

He was the only one left on Gramp's land, clinging to the hill like some old tree fungus, trying to keep the memories alive while the huge rock maples rotted and died. If any upstart saplings grew large enough to replace the enormous trees that had sheltered him all those years, Jamie wouldn't live to see it. All he could do was hold the land together for as long as possible. And hope that it would matter to his child.

❁

Sally gazed into the bottom of the big steel pot. She must've eaten two whole lobsters by herself already. And there were still more claws and tails! She was stuffed, but how could you turn down lobster? She eased a triangle of white and pink-speckled flesh out of a claw tip and popped it in her mouth—briny and sweet. Mmmmm.

She gazed out at the overcast horizon, the distant line of shore, and wished she could paint it. Last year her art class took a trip to Gloucester. She needed to learn a whole new palette for the ocean. Fog color, the shingles weathered to silver instead of the rusty gold of Vermont barns. The beach was rocky, not sugary like Cape Cod or Plum Island.

When you stood on a beach you sensed worlds of distance you knew nothing about. It scared her, just like those times she did acid with Jamie, up in the sugarhouse when they were kids, the way things moved and changed but were still themselves made her think that everyone had the machinery for seeing like that but they learned to filter things out. She guessed that was how Mitchell was unlike the rest of them—he kept trying to see something different, no matter how many times he screwed up. She hoped he'd stick this one out.

In Gloucester she'd gathered driftwood and those little seaweed poppers, like plastic bubble wrap. She brought them home to the girls but they dried and stank. The girls preferred the beach glass she carried back, worn by tides to round pieces you could fit in your palm. It was a mystery, Sally thought, cracking one last claw, how something as common as broken glass could be transformed by abuse to a treasure.

❀

Mel raised borrowed binoculars, squinting through the mist which clung to his hair and wet his narrow face. In every direction he tracked the arcing flights and awkward landings of cormorants, sea gulls, puffins. He nudged Sally and pointed: Seals! Real honest-to-goodness seals flopping around on a rock pile, not in some zoo or kid's book. Mel zeroed in on their bulbous bodies, whiskery dog snouts, and stuffed toy eyes. From watching TV nature shows he knew that underwater all that flab translated to streamlined grace. He wished he could see them performing, flipping like Olympic swimmers doing kick-turns. That old dream resurfaced— exotic animals in his own backyard. But this was better, wasn't it? Even if you only got to see it once in your life. So many people didn't live where they ought to anymore, why steal the creatures from their homes?

❀

Corinne sat on the bulwark with her heels against her haunches, watching Mitchell tip his head back to down a soda. And in that familiar motion, she recalled the first time she met him, when she rode the school bus home with Nancy in eighth grade. She had trudged up a hill, tracing spirals of dust with her toes, then followed Nancy into a brown aluminum-sided ranch house, through the screen door, into an unpainted kitchen.

There he was, leaning back on a tilted kitchen chair, legs spread in cut-off jeans, no shirt, a gallon jug of milk lifted to his lips, a kitten in his lap. Mitchell's adam's apple rolled as he swallowed and swallowed and swallowed, as though he was trying to satisfy the world's biggest thirst. Dumbfounded, Corinne stared at the blond wisps of hair curling from his exposed armpit, the curving biceps, hard quadrants of chest and the honeyed smoothness of it all—shoulders, belly, thighs. Mitchell lowered the jug, wiped his lips with the back of his hand, burped.

Nancy made a face and dropped her books down on the kitchen table. "You are so gross," she chided her brother. Mitchell stroked the kitty, winked at Corinne. He was eighteen and Corinne, a baby-fat thirteen, was immediately, sickeningly in love. And, despite the five years it took to catch him and the nearly twenty more to decide if he was worth it, she still was.

❀

Okay, there was no big wind, Mitchell conceded. It was drizzling. They were running on auxiliary power. But they didn't look miserable. They sprawled around the boat in their rain slickers, gaping and grinning like tourist fools. For about three seconds he tried to see it through their eyes, but that had never been his strong suit. Like he told Jamie, you can't really know what anyone else feels, so why bother?

What *they* would never know was the wet blanket slap of frozen fog in winter, ice crusted on the house shingles and riming the windows. A damp chill that went deep in your bones, not that squeaking snow of Vermont, all the moisture freeze-dried out, the inside of your nostrils pinging, but the pierce of wet cold like a dentist in your bones, and the wind off the sea shrieking like his drill.

Not that Mitchell was complaining. You always had to pay some price. You bore up with winter gale winds so that in the spring you could watch snow geese settle on the bay like dandelion fluff on a pasture. Or so you could inhale the seductive low tide stink every day of the year.

A puff of wind blew up out of nowhere and Duke signaled Mitchell to raise the mainsail. Probably not enough breeze to bother with, Mitchell thought, but Duke had promised the first-class tour and was trying. Mitchell uncleated halyards, hauled line, the boom rising on its brass ring, mainsail flapping like a flag, the sound of banners snapping on a football field.

When Duke trimmed the sails, she caught and cupped the puny breeze like the classy lady she was. Duke cut the engine and all the ocean sounds came back: squawking gulls, small waves lapping against the hull. "Head for that channel marker just off the point, there," Duke said, offering Mitchell the wheel.

Mitchell took it, and as if on cue, the sky dropped a dense blanket of fog that made the Windward's bow, much less the marker, invisible. They slid through shapeless grey like an airplane entering a cloud. Mitchell couldn't see a fucking thing. He glanced over at Duke, sending urgent eye messages: Hey Buddy, you want to help me out here or what? Imagining bow-cracking logs, deadheads, reefs, rocks, islands veering close.

"Just set a compass course, 45 degrees north by northeast," Duke instructed calmly, putting all his faith in that lolling black ball on its standard, a black ball spinning like all the nighttime skies Mitchell had ever feared. "After we hear the bell-buoy, we'll tack west and set another course."

Running on faith.

And nervous as Mitchell was, he felt dopily happy, like the first time he drove that stupid steam train through Santa's Workshop, knowing it was just an amusement park ride but thrilled nonetheless. Duke was right beside him like a Driver's Ed teacher with his own set of brakes, but even so, Mitchell was at the helm. Captain Mitch, legs spread to compensate for the ship's slight tilt. If he let himself, he could imagine he was more than just captain but the boat itself: wooden planks scraped clean of barnacles, caulked solid, refined by salt and wind.

In the fog, without any landmarks for judging speed, it seemed they weren't moving at all. Like in a hot air balloon; he'd heard you had no perception of motion, of traveling through the air. Or when he was a kid, visiting Lenny Garber in New York, riding trains, he could never tell for a second if the train across from him was pulling away or if his train was the one leaving the station.

All motion was relative, he supposed.

Mitchell checked his compass bearing, peered ahead into indistinguishable murk. They were set on some course, but who the hell knew their destination? Muffled by fog, abruptly close, a bell buoy tolled off the starboard bow. Maybe they were sailing, or maybe it was just the world, in all its brutal beauty, gliding up to meet them. But for one still moment, he was the boat, holding them all aloft.

I lived my earliest years in a dying New Hampshire mill town, then was hustled away to suburban Boston for the "better schools" while my father still drove to work in New Hampshire every day and brought home his *Manchester Union Leader*. I'm accustomed to being an outsider—not a bad viewpoint for a writer, although uncomfortable for a kid. As an adult, I chose Vermont as my home and eventually found myself married into an old Vermont family, some of whose members have ended up landless in a time of dying farms and expensive "executive lots." Unease with my new relatives evolved into fascination, followed by admiration, compassion, and love. Although *The Price of Land in Shelby* is a work of fiction, it grew out of my need to understand and honor the people with whom I live.